Is That You, Beth Cherry?

Lucy Dillon grew up by the seaside in Cumbria, and read English at Cambridge University, before working as a fiction editor. She is the bestselling author of eleven novels set in the market town of Longhampton, including Romantic Novelists Association Novels of the Year, *Lost Dogs and Lonely Hearts* and *A Hundred Pieces of Me*. An enthusiastic collector of dog-related junk, Lucy lives in Herefordshire with an English Otterhound, a Welsh Pembroke Corgi and a Scottish Husband.

Also by Lucy Dillon

Lost Dogs and Lonely Hearts
The Ballroom Class
Walking Back to Happiness
The Secret of Happy Ever After
A Hundred Pieces of Me
Irresponsible Adult

Lucy Dillon

Is That You, Beth Cherry?

HODDER &
STOUGHTON

First published in Great Britain in 2025 by Hodder & Stoughton Limited
An Hachette UK company

The authorised representative in the EEA is Hachette Ireland,
8 Castlecourt Centre, Dublin 15, D15 XTP3, Ireland (email: info@hbgi.ie)

1

A CIP catalogue record for this title is available from the British Library

Hardback ISBN 978 1 399 71974 2
ebook ISBN 978 1 399 71976 6

Typeset in Plantin Std by Manipal Typesetters

Printed and bound in Great Britain by Clays Ltd, Elcograf S.p.A.

Hodder & Stoughton policy is to use papers that are natural, renewable and recyclable products and made from wood grown in sustainable forests. The logging and manufacturing processes are expected to conform to the environmental regulations of the country of origin.

Hodder & Stoughton Limited
Carmelite House
50 Victoria Embankment
London EC4Y 0DZ

www.hodder.co.uk

To Hugo, who's right there in so many of the funniest, happiest, most colourful stories of my life, and always will be, until they're polished smooth with remembering.

Tell me about a time you made a snap decision that worked out . . .

Adopting my dog. I didn't intend to get a dog. Like everyone in those surreal days before lockdown, I was spending hours every day doomscrolling through social media to stop my brain from engaging with anything other than the most soothing content – cookie decoration, sand scooping – but once I saw Tomsk I stopped. Instantly.

He looked so scared. Two fearful brown eyes staring out through a matted veil of hair, backed up in the corner of a concrete cell, with the message PLEASE TAKE ME HOME *over the top. Something scratched in my chest. His fear, his submission connected with something in my own heart, and I knew, in that instant, it was* my *home he needed.*

The fact that I was even following Four Oaks Rescue Kennel was a bit masochistic. In my previous, happy, life, Fraser and I had driven over to Longhampton, where his parents lived, to a charity dog show that his mother Martine was judging in her official capacity as the mayor's wife. We only went to support her and Ray, the mayor – Fraser and I weren't in the market for a dog, since we both had demanding office jobs, regular spontaneous weekends away and lived in a no-pets second-floor flat. But we'd talked about it, in that testing-the-water-about-kids-without-mentioning-the-word-kids way you do, after you've been together a few years.

Tomsk was one of ten strays the rescue owners were desperately trying to move into foster homes before they had to close. He was the biggest, and the hairiest, and the caption was very brief, but something about him already felt familiar. He reminded me of the Womble toy my mum had given me, with his long pointed nose and matted grey fur. Without thinking, I was hunting for my outdoor shoes for the first time in days. The poor creature looked bewildered, as if he'd woken up in the wrong life. That, I could absolutely identify with. Right down to the matted hair and confused expression.

My flatmate, Ashley, told me later that when I dashed out of the house with the car keys she was worried I was going to, in her words, 'Do something stupid' – which I kind of was, but not the way she thought. I hadn't left the house for three weeks at this point, and that was *before* lockdown: Ash and I were both in the grip of Post-Relationship-Paralysis, which manifested itself in tea- and tear-stained leisurewear, fear of hearing certain songs on the radio, and heavy reliance on food delivery.

Four Oaks Rescue Kennel was, an hour's drive away, but I was pulling up outside before I knew it. I didn't have a single thought, all the way there, other than: I need to bring that dog home.

I must have looked a bit of a sight when I arrived, because the woman in charge, Rachel, went through the adoption questionnaire very slowly, as if she thought I might change my mind by the time we got to the end.

'Do you have a garden? Can you commit to walking a large-breed dog? Have you owned a dog before?'

I nodded. Ash's house had a garden. And my dad had had a Jack Russell called Ned, a classic publican's dog – patch over one eye, existed largely on crisps – which Dad had taken with him when he moved to London, leaving me and Mum behind, so I'd had a clear lesson about where dogs were supposed to come in your priorities.

But I must have convinced Rachel that I was serious, and eventually she got up and found a spare slip lead.

'We don't know much about Scruffy other than that he's some kind of hound cross and he's been living rough for a while,' she warned me as we headed towards the sound of discordant barking. 'He's a sweet boy, though, and tries to be clean in his run, so someone must have loved him once.'

She paused at the door into the kennel area. 'That's what breaks my heart. When they know what love is, then it's taken away, and they don't know what they've done.'

I bit my lip.

He was hunched in the furthest corner of the concrete run, trying to make himself as small and invisible as possible in the cacophony of barking going on. They'd cleaned him up from his initial photo but there was still the tangy whiff of fear about him. Rachel unlatched the gate and clipped a lead on to his collar, gently leading him out into the main area.

It's still really hard to write about this without crying. Even though I know how it ends.

He allowed Rachel to bring him over, although his wiry tail was tucked right between his legs, and when I stretched my hand out, he cowered. Then I sat down on the floor, cross-legged. I don't know why, I just had an instinct to sit down.

Rachel sat down too. 'Ignore him,' she said. 'Give him space.'

We ignored him.

She asked me what I did for a living – bland talk, the sort you normally do at parties, not on a concrete floor that smells of bleach – and I told her I was an accountant, that I'd recently split up from my boyfriend of five years, that I had plenty of spare time, that my sort-of-mother-in-law, no, my ex-sort-of-mother-in-law, had judged that charity dog show.

'Ah!' she said, raising an eyebrow. 'Martine!'

Which was what everyone said when I mentioned Fraser's mother.

I asked her about the other dogs, since the mention of Martine reminded me of happier, more Henderson times, and I didn't trust myself not to start crying or launching into the Fraser break-up story. Rachel told me about the dogs she'd rehomed that morning – a stray collie, a saggy ex-breeding spaniel. A bonded pair of timid dachshunds whose elderly owner had died, suddenly, with no relatives to take them in. Some had sad stories; some, like my shaggy hound, had none.

'It makes it easier to find new homes if we know their background,' Rachel explained. 'But some . . .' She sighed. 'Some we'll never know what's happened to make them the way they are. What they're living with, what they can't tell us.'

That made my eyes fill up. It still does.

Then I sensed something move behind me. A tentative click of long claws on stone, a rustle. Despite its fear, the dog was inching nearer.

'All we can do is help them start a new story,' said Rachel. 'I've seen some poor things come in, like bags of bones, too traumatised to look at you. But if you're patient, and lucky, and we find them the right people, then . . .'

She paused, because something was *moving behind me again, something coming closer. And closer. She could see what was happening, and from the cautious smile I guessed it wasn't something she'd seen yet from this particular dog.*

I held my breath.

There was a silent slump behind me, the whisper of tired legs folding under a mass of unwashed coat. I felt the point of a long nose almost – but not quite – touching my leg, not yet bold enough to make eye contact, but brave enough to creep closer.

Rachel tilted her head and I got the impression she was sizing me up the same way she assessed the wretched dogs handed in. I knew I looked a wreck. She touched my arm. 'Same goes for humans too,' she said, as if she understood the long nights behind my unwashed hair, the dark shadows under my eyes. 'We can start again.'

I reached behind me, placing my hand flat on the floor, not touching the dog, but offering him my skin to sniff.

After a while, a few long moments, I felt the faintest breath on my arm.

The sigh of a dog who was starting his story again. A good boy. A brave boy.

My eyes filled up. We're going to be OK, I promised him, in my heart. Both of us.

We're both going to be OK.

Chapter one

Lockdown had been over for four years by this point but to be honest, I'd never really returned to what everyone else was calling normal life. I'd secretly enjoyed lockdown. It was such a relief not to have to have opinions, or ironed clothes, or to spend hours sitting in traffic to get to an office where people had genuinely strong feelings about the taxable benefits of solar panels. Plus, I didn't have to explain to anyone about Fraser.

So in my defence, I hadn't been out very much lately.

I mean, other than walking Tomsk, I hadn't been out *at all.* The woman accepting my donation bags at the charity shop was the first human being I'd spoken to in nearly . . . a week? My housemate Ashley, and I communicated mainly in grunts and eyerolls, as you do when you've shared a bathroom for as long as we had, and my professional communication mainly took place via a keyboard, where I had ample time to phrase things neatly, and avoid any awkwardness before it happened.

Not like real life, where I had a microsecond to think of what to say, and no chance to delete *anything*. Even if it was stupid, or rude, or – unintentionally, I swear – both at the same time.

A fresh wave of mortification flashed over me as the woman's face reared up in my mind's eye. Startled, slightly afraid, even. I picked up my pace as if I could outwalk the embarrassment.

Again, in my defence, I was also in the middle of moving house. Moving house is stressful, right? It's basically a personal appraisal, but with bin bags and a running tally of how much money you've wasted on abandoned hobbies. One minute you're stacking paperbacks that you won't read again (if you ever got round to reading them in the first place), next minute you're yanking at what were once your never-fail jeans, which no longer go over your knees, let alone your hips, staring at the stranger in the mirror and thinking, *Who even am I now*?

Maybe that was just me. As I say, I hadn't been out a lot lately.

The worst thing was, I fully *knew* I was going to say something stupid, being so out of practice, so I'd run the conversation through in my head first. I was going to hand over the clothes and books, and say: one, I'd adopted Tomsk from their rescue and two, that I hoped these donations would help other dogs find their forever humans.

I'd even had a follow-up comment ready to go, about how he'd changed my life. Which he had.

The trouble was, the volunteer threw me by pulling out a blue velvet Anthropologie dress which I hadn't meant to put in the bag, even though it no longer fitted. It was perfect – elegant, yet stretchy – and had been Fraser's favourite. I'd worn it on some of our happiest times together: that New Year's Eve in London, his sister Jackie's super-fancy fortieth, an anniversary trip to Paris. It made my blue eyes bluer and had a wonderful swish.

Even now, after so many years, my heart had lurched seeing it – and remembering. A starburst of regret and longing had exploded behind my eyes. Where had that Beth gone?

'Ooh,' she'd said. 'This is *gorgeous*. I might have to bag this for myself!'

And I'd blurted out . . .

I sped up, hot sweat prickling my underarms.

Come on, Beth.

I'd said, 'You're welcome,' while thinking, No problem!, and somehow what had come out of my mouth, very loudly, was, 'You're the problem!'

'I'm . . . what?'

I tried to rearrange the words properly this time, but the pain of letting go of that dress, losing another precious connection to a life I desperately needed to get back to, blurred my brain, and I said, '*You're* a problem! No, I mean, *I'm* the problem!'

'Are you . . . are you all right?'

We'd stared at each other in mutual shock, and I'd spun on my heel and rushed out, because I had no idea how to rescue that particular situation, and I was already too close to bursting into tears.

Thanks to my humiliation-power-walking, I was halfway down Longhampton High Street, where I'd planned to reward myself for my charitable donation/trip to the outside world with a lemon tart at the Wild Dog Café. I could have dropped off my junk somewhere closer to my house – which was, full disclosure, forty miles away, in a different county – but the Wild Dog's lemon tarts were so good they regularly featured in round-ups of the best patisseries in the country. And, if I'm honest, I wanted an excuse to go to Longhampton. Longhampton was my happy place.

It wasn't on any Must Visit list of English landmarks, but Longhampton was the sort of unassuming Midlands market town where yarn bombers covered the postboxes with seasonal displays and everyone turned out for an illuminated tractor parade for charity at Christmas. Sure, it had its low points – the bleak sixties precinct being one – but as I walked along the high street, my still-pounding anxiety was soothed by the Britain in Bloom flower baskets, plump pink fuchsia buds and tumbling heart-shaped ivy trailing prettily down the black streetlights. The rest of the world might be battling graffiti and ugly road furniture, but somehow Longhampton maintained the tidy, cheerful atmosphere of a place where residents arranged town-twinning visits with other tidy, cheerful places in France or Luxembourg. Possibly, I was well aware, down to the iron determination of people like Fraser's parents, Ray and Martine, both long-standing pillars of the community.

I let my eyes drift along the shop signs, checking what was still there, what was new. I kept my gaze high, avoiding the windows themselves – I avoided reflections, generally – and ticked off the familiar landmarks. Boots, Hotel Chocolat, a bookshop, a new bakery, charity shop. Taylor Maid, a housekeeping agency? Blimey, Longhampton must be getting some city relocators if even the cleaners had shopfronts now.

I paused opposite the ornate frontage of Longhampton Cellars, the sign painted in silver on darkened Victorian glass, with 'a family business since 1854' in swirling cursive underneath. Until about ten years ago, Longhampton Cellars had been Fraser's family's business. It wasn't anymore – as Fraser had controversially declined to take up the mantle of Longhampton's premier vintner, in favour of a career in cyber security – but the new owners, a chain whose logo was discreetly set back on the door, had kept the shopfront as it had been for the past hundred or so years, because why wouldn't you? The original golden grapes hanging from a bracket over the double doors were a Longhampton landmark. Also, it had had, for over seventy years, a Royal Warrant for its blackcurrant cordial. That was pretty much the first thing Ray had ever said to me. Did I know Princess Margaret was partial to a hot blackcurrant after a big night out?

The family row had simmered down by then, but I was still instructed *never* to talk about supermarket wine, on pain of death. Or Ribena.

I caught sight of my bulky reflection behind the pyramid of champagne, flinched, and hurried on.

I was having bitter second thoughts about my outfit. I'd thought it was OK at home (loose, flattering, faintly Scandi) but my reflection was giving more Teletubby than Toast. Toast, of course, being one of the reasons I was currently the size I was. Were people staring at me? As I walked on towards the Wild Dog, I tried to keep a neutral but friendly expression on my face, despite a new bubbling of anxiety in the pit of my stomach. My gaze drifted across passers-by; not that I expected to see Fraser – I think he'd moved to London, but I wasn't sure, since he'd blocked me on his social media the day after our break-up. Although maybe he'd deleted it altogether; his job wasn't exactly compatible with a lively social media presence – but there was always that chance that I might bump into Martine.

Martine Henderson was the sort of woman usually described as 'a dame' in films *d'un certain âge.* She had that straight-backed, clear-eyed confidence only doled out to a special few, and whenever Fraser and I attended one of her many fundraisers, she inevitably upsold me in introductions, which only compelled me to explain that, no, actually, I wasn't 'a rising tax specialist', I was just a mid-range standard-issue small-business accountant.

Fraser, her golden boy, was always introduced as doing 'something so terribly important and so top-secret he won't even tell me!' – which he undercut by insisting that he mainly wrote code for credit-card fraud checks. Which wasn't true either, because he *did* have an important security job in a bank, but I think he liked to show some solidarity with me. I wasn't used to people upselling me. I wasn't used to much encouragement, parental or otherwise, but Martine had a way of zhuzhing people up, plumping them like sagging sofa cushions. It induced equal measures of gratitude and anxiety.

Seeing the blue dress again had stirred up memories that now floated mercilessly before my mind's eye; I'd worn it to the James Bond fundraiser at Longhampton's hospice, where we'd won a year's supply of ham in the raffle, and Martine talked us into donating it to the food bank. I tried to distract myself – look! there was the town hall, covered in pastel bunting and posters for an Easter Egg Hunt – but the memory of Fraser, secret agent, refused to shift. He had the perfect shoulders for a dinner jacket, broad and lean. That had been one of the nights I was so sure he was going to propose that I'd had a manicure specially.

'Beth, it's not that I don't love you . . .'

I dragged my attention across the road, towards the Wild Dog Café, and my lemon tart. But there was a crowd on the pavement between it and me, and I was forced to stop my manic walking.

Two paramedics in green overalls were tending to someone hidden by three other people, one in a NatWest blouse, who was shielding the patient from view. Passers-by stepped around the incident with exaggerated care, tilting their heads discreetly to see what was going on while making sure not to catch anyone's eye and get involved.

I stopped, not sure whether to step into the road to get past, or edge by on the pavement. I hoped it wasn't anything serious. One paramedic moved aside and I caught sight of a bare foot, pale and knobbly, and close by, a red low-heeled shoe, lying on its side on the pavement. Like Dorothy in *The Wizard of Oz*. I wondered what it was – an accident? A mugging? No, that was unthinkable.

Then I heard the voice.

'I'm absolutely fine, this is so silly, please, I'm fine . . .'

It was unmistakable: the cut-glass determination, with just a touch of iron under the sweetness. The voice of an old-school newsreader, or a head teacher.

It was Martine.

I hesitated, pretending to make room for passers-by coming from the other direction. Should I go? Was this a sign to turn round and head back to the car? I shouldn't really be stopping, not with a client call at three p.m. and the dog waiting at home.

But it was *Martine.*

'Shall we try to get on our feet then, bab?' inquired a paramedic.

I winced. I could have warned him that tone wasn't going to go down well, and it didn't.

'Please don't call me bab, young man.'

'Seems to be OK cognitively,' muttered his colleague.

I watched as the crowd parted and the first paramedic scooped Martine Henderson up, setting her on the nearby bench as if she weighed nothing.

Which maybe she didn't. Martine had always been slender, but her ankles were startlingly thin, and the hair that had been the colour of the palest champagne the last time I'd seen her was now white in thick streaks. She looked fragile, not an adjective I had ever thought I'd apply to a woman with Martine's very definite presence.

'You're very kind but there's no need to make such a fuss,' she was saying, brushing invisible dust off her summer dress as the paramedic replaced her shoe. She stretched out her foot as if men placed shoes on her feet every day. Like Cinderella. 'I simply lost my balance on the— Oh.'

I took an involuntary step backwards.

She'd spotted me standing in the gap between the paramedics and the bank teller. Martine frowned then blinked like someone seeing a ghost: startled, but unsure whether she'd really seen what she thought she'd seen. And unwilling to draw attention to her mistake, if it was a mistake.

I froze. Needless to say, I had imagined various conversations I'd have with Martine if we met again, most of which were designed to be relayed to Fraser: basic message – my life is amazing but I'm open to a reunion. But now, all I could think of was my outfit. Any doubt vanished, and I knew it was the exact opposite of the blue Anthropologie dress I'd just given away. It was the elasticated loungewear of defeat.

The NatWest lady followed Martine's gaze, saw me standing there, and said, with audible relief, 'Oh, look! Is this a friend?'

Now the paramedics turned too. The weight of responsibility shifted palpably from them on to me.

'Is that . . . Beth?' said Martine.

'Yes,' I said, wincing at the uncertainty in her voice. OK, so I had put on some weight in the past few years but surely not a *transformative* amount.

Before Martine could formulate a response, the bank teller rushed over and patted me on the arm, drawing me into the circle, so she could leave. 'Wonderful, I'll leave you in the capable hands of the paramedics and your friend here. Sorry, we're *so* short-staffed today! I'm glad you're feeling better, Mrs Henderson!' She backed away rapidly, then turned and sprinted up the steps.

The radio inside the ambulance beeped and crackled.

'So, bab, I mean . . .' The paramedic couldn't think of another term of endearment that wouldn't get him into trouble.

'Mrs Henderson,' repeated Martine.

'Do you want to hop into the ambulance and we'll whisk you up to A and E and get you checked over?'

'For heaven's sake. I'm not hopping anywhere and I do not want to be whisked.'

'You've had a nasty fall,' reasoned the other. 'You could have concussion.'

'I wasn't unconscious. I would remember being concussed!'

'You wouldn't,' he said, 'that's the point.'

Martine glared up from the bench. 'I am *fine*.'

'With the best will in the world . . .' The radio on his shoulder crackled; another call, this one urgent. The paramedic pulled his colleague to one side and muttered in his ear. I thought I heard the word 'crash'.

The bab paramedic turned to me. 'Would you be able to run her up to A and E? We'd take her in now, but if she doesn't want to go . . .' He gestured to the radio. 'We were on our way to another job when we got flagged down to take a look at her. To be honest, you're going to get her seen quicker if you just nip up in the car.'

'I don't *need* to go to hospital!' interjected Martine. 'Do stop talking about me as if I'm a million years old, I'm *here* and I can *hear* you.'

The paramedic exhaled. 'We're just trying to make sure you're safe.' He dropped his voice and muttered to me, 'Can you make sure she's not on her own for twenty-four hours? Keep her quiet, any signs of dizziness, loss of balance, deafness, vomiting, bring her up to A and E.'

'But I'm not—' I started.

The radio crackled again, and this time the despatcher sounded stressed.

'Please!' said Martine. 'Get on your way to someone who needs your help. I insist.' She had her handbag open on her lap and was searching inside it. She flapped her other hand dismissively. 'Beth can look after me.'

'If you're sure . . .'

'I'm positive. Now *you* hop it!'

The paramedics exchanged looks, then packed up their equipment at lightning speed and vanished in a flurry of thanks and apologies and walkie-talkie jargon, leaving me standing awkwardly on the pavement by the bench, wondering how this had happened.

'So, Beth!' Martine looked me up and down, and I braced herself for the comment about how much I'd changed since we'd last seen each other. Or something about Fraser. Or something about my outfit. From the expression on her face, she was clearly having trouble deciding on the right thing to say.

I had never actually said goodbye to Martine. One moment I was her son's long-term girlfriend, a fixture at Christmas and birthdays, the next I was . . . gone.

'Would you like me to give you a lift home?' I asked.

'Goodness, no – no need for that. I'm sure I can find a taxi.' Martine straightened her shoulders and attempted to stand up, but in doing so, pain rippled across her face, and I reached out instinctively to steady her.

The cardigan was deceptive; under the cashmere Martine's upper arms were so thin my hands went right round them. She weighed almost nothing.

I couldn't stop myself. 'Are you sure you don't want to go to A and E?'

'No! I do not! I *wish* people would stop behaving as if I'm incapable of making decisions for myself!' Martine snapped.

'Sorry! I'm sorry!!'

She sank down on the bench, closed her eyes and grasped her handbag. The delicate skin on her eyelids flickered as she took two, three deep breaths, gathering herself together. My gaze ran cautiously across her face, checking the familiar against the new in the same way I'd assessed the high street; despite the ugly flush of embarrassment and stress, Martine's complexion was soft and pale, still like double cream. The cheekbones were still smoothly defined, over-plucked brown eyebrows arched over her deep eye sockets. When I'd first met her, she'd already worn her crow's feet proudly, confident that her energy was that of a much younger woman, and they didn't seem much deeper now; her only gesture towards make-up was a slash of deep raspberry lipstick, right now temporarily faded to a faint rosehip. It was a stylistic flourish I'd tried, and failed, to copy over the years. My own round face needed more skilful colouring-in. Unlike Martine, I had no hollows or shadows, just apples.

I felt oddly intrusive, being allowed to observe her like this; it was such a rare moment of vulnerability. I didn't think I'd ever seen Fraser's mother silent for so long, let alone with her eyes closed.

Then Martine's blue eyes snapped open, and in an instant, there was the woman I remembered: the self-possessed matriarch, born wearing a double string of pearls.

'What a ridiculous fuss about nothing,' she said. 'I'm so sorry to put you out, Beth.'

'I was about to go to the Wild Dog Café for a lemon tart,' I said. 'Would you like a cup of tea?'

'I *would*. But I'd like to go home, if you'd be so kind,' she said, with a sweet smile that was half-apology, half-request. 'Can you remember where it is?'

'I think so,' I said.

How could I forget?

Rather than walk Martine back across town, I left her on the bench and hurried back to the car, which was parked in Montague Road, where Fraser and I had once looked at a flat, before he told me he didn't think living in the same town as his parents was a good idea and then refused to discuss it further, and eventually denied ever saying it.

In the time it took to drive back to where Martine was waiting on the high street, I redid my make-up with whatever I could find in my handbag, and dragged out a red scarf from under the seat which I threw on to break up the apologetic beige of my outfit.

As I pulled up – hazards on, ignoring the double yellows – I saw Martine too had taken the opportunity to run a comb through her hair and reapply the raspberry lipstick, but unlike me, she now looked ready to chair a committee meeting.

I got out, unsure of how much help would be acceptable. I opened the passenger-side door for her, then I hesitated. Did she need a hand with the seatbelt? I didn't have much experience with older people. Neither of my parents was around; Mum had died when I was twenty-two, and Dad now lived in France with his new, easier family.

How old *was* Martine? I did some quick maths. Fraser was forty-one now, and he was the youngest, a surprise baby, so Martine had to be . . . nearly eighty?

Martine firmly brushed away my tentative offer of help, in any case.

'I'm quite capable, thank you,' she said, and I retreated to the driver's side and got in.

We set off.

I quickly regretted my lax car-cleaning regime; it smelled strongly of Tomsk. Who also smelled very strongly, albeit significantly less than he did when I first met him. Love had rendered me completely nose-blind to his oily odour of biscuits and old raincoats until Martine got in the car and my nose abruptly returned to factory settings.

I saw her wrinkle her brow, confused and mildly horrified, then an expression of deliberate politeness replaced it, which was somehow worse.

'I've got a dog,' I explained, just in case she thought the smell was down to me, at the same time as she said, 'So, what's happening with you?'

'Oh, the usual.' I concentrated on the road ahead, which was busier than I remembered. My sporadic 'bumping into Martine' daydreams, in which I casually dropped nuggets of information about my new, successful life for her to relay to Fraser, hadn't included wobbly cyclists and speed cameras. 'I'm moving house and of course it's tax return month!'

'Ah! You're still an accountant?'

I nodded. I'd started at Jacobs & Partners as a graduate trainee and assistant to the senior partner, Allen, and now I had my own client list: small businesses mainly – plus some sole traders, a travel writer, a potter, an interior designer. There was some monotony to the work, but, for me, each business was an evolving story, with unique financial puzzles for me to unpick, trading cycles to work around and the owners' personal foibles to negotiate. Some clients communicated solely in brisk emails and flawless spreadsheets, whereas others were happy to open up their messy heads entirely. Allen kept encouraging me to take on more responsibilities – i.e., less hands-on work – but I enjoyed what I did. I liked the stories.

'Same firm?'

I nodded again.

Martine tipped her head, a wordless judgement. 'How long is that now?'

'Coming up for thirteen years.'

'You've never thought about setting up on your own?'

'No, I like working with Allen.' He let me work from home. He signed off my expenses without looking.

'And what about your writing? How's that screenplay of yours going?'

I pressed my lips together. I needed to keep notes on my clients' families, and hobbies; Martine did not.

'Or was it a novel?' Martine added, when I didn't respond.

'No, it's a screenplay. I'm still working on it.'

Martine laughed. '*Beth.* You were saying that when I first met you! *I'm still working on it.* It's the Forth Road Bridge of screenplays.'

I attempted a similarly tinkly laugh in lieu of a reply I might regret. It came out badly. Strangulated.

'The best advice anyone ever gave me,' said Martine, 'was this: you just have to finish it.' She tapped my knee with each word. 'Just. Finish. It.'

Martine had, in the space of a couple of years, written two historical romance novels 'to see if I could'. (She could, naturally.) They'd been published under her pen name, Elizabeth Buckingham. I hadn't read them; Fraser and his sisters had, in a rare moment of unanimous agreement, decided that it would be best if the family remained in happy ignorance of their mother's romantic inner life and nominated Jackie's husband to take one for the team. He reported back with a detailed synopsis and the slightly damning verdict: 'Better than I expected, surprisingly saucy in places' which only cemented the family decision to remain supportively in the dark.

I'd started the first, *The Dancing Heart*, but got distracted and, if I'm honest, resentful at how good it was.

'I'm very busy,' I responded. 'Maybe when *I'm* retired I'll have more time to focus on writing.'

I hadn't meant to put the emphasis on the *I'm* but Martine ignored it. Now she was back in the position of offering help instead of needing it, she was energised.

'You don't need more time, you just need to make better use of *some* time. Ringfence an hour a day. That's what I did, I set my alarm an hour earlier. What was it about? Remind me.'

I gritted my teeth. My screenplay was a historical romance and the subject matter had shifted around over the years. It had started life as a novel, until Martine wrote hers, and broadly Jane Austen-ish, until Martine staked her claim on the early nineteenth century, and I'd had to revise it to a later, darker Victorian period which had never really suited my heroine, whom I'd always pictured in empire-line frocks. Plump arms, plump bosom, skin like a ripe peach, etc. Not forced into crinolines and corsets.

I'd got Act One perfect – Seraphina's (or Camilla's or Josephine's: it varied) shock at her family's unexpected fall on hard times, her hopes of education dashed, the sudden death of her consumptive mother, and her relocation to Highchurch House – but breaking into Act Two was proving a problem. I'd been rewriting the same two scenes for nearly seven years. It was like knitting one sleeve of the same jumper, unravelling it, and reknitting it with a very slightly different pattern only to find it was still too short.

'It's a historical romance,' I said.

'Oh, *yes*, that's right,' said Martine. 'Would it be helpful for me to put you in touch with a mentor? I've met so many romantic novelists since I published *The Dancing Heart*. I know a terrific writer whose just had her novel optioned by—'

'And also a thriller,' I lied. 'There's a thriller element now.'

Martine raised her eyebrows and I inwardly cursed my own defensiveness.

But then again, maybe there *could* be a thriller element? And would it be so bad to let Martine help? No one else had ever taken the slightest interest in my screenplay, not even Fraser. Perhaps *particularly* not even Fraser.

'Right here,' said Martine, pointing towards the turning down into Coleridge Drive.

She hadn't needed to point. I'd driven the entire way across town on autopilot, and now we were almost home.

Not home, I corrected myself. Martine's home. Fraser's home.

A tight, dark sensation spread through me as we passed the postbox, the cherry tree, the mysterious car that was always covered over with a tarpaulin and never moved, until there it was: the pine-green front door and white railings of 13 Coleridge Drive. Home of the Hendersons since 1968.

I realised my hands were gripping the steering wheel.

'Well, thank you so much, Beth,' said Martine smoothly, reaching for the handle. 'I'll see myself out, there's absolutely no need to— Agh!' There was a painful catch of breath as she attempted to open the door and couldn't exert enough pressure.

She sank back, momentarily defeated.

'Let me help you.' I got out and went round to the passenger side to open it for her.

Martine checked up and down the street first to make sure no one could see her accept my help, then reluctantly leaned on me to get out of the car. We made our way up the steps and suddenly, there I was – going back into the house that led straight into my previous life.

Chapter two

The first thing that struck me was that 13 Coleridge Drive smelled exactly as I remembered.

That gave me a bigger jolt than seeing Martine; that familiar smell – house plants and seagrass stair runner and old books in oak bookcases. It took me straight back to a different, brighter-coloured time in my life, when stepping through this door led to interesting conversations and questions and expensive wine and . . . possibilities. Automatically, I wiped my feet on the coir mat, tucked my hair behind my ears, and glanced across to the gilt mirror by the front door to check I hadn't smeared my lipstick or got a coffee moustache.

Mistake number one. While the house hadn't changed, I had. I think I still expected to see my twentysomething face with its centre parting and glasses, but there was the wider, older face that I'd habitually avoided eye contact with for some time now. Mum's apple cheeks, Dad's furtive eyes. I flinched, and dropped my gaze to the bookshelf beneath the mirror. Nothing had moved in the last five years: the same school French and Italian dictionaries, *Wisden Cricketers' Almanacks*, *Guinness Books of Records*. A *Who's Who* (Longhamptonshire edition, for charity) – with Ray in it.

'Do come in,' said Martine, with more politeness than enthusiasm.

I hesitated. I sensed she probably wanted to kick off her shoes and pretend none of the last hour had happened, but this was such a weird and miraculous opportunity, a rare chance to see what Fraser had been doing, that I couldn't pass it up.

And, of course, I had a duty to make sure Martine really was as OK as she claimed.

The sitting room was, again, exactly as I remembered: long sash windows looking out on to whitewashed houses opposite; Victorian plant stands with cascading waterfalls of purple tradescantia. Coffee-table books stacked on the coffee table, invitations tucked behind the pair of Staffordshire dogs and gold clock on the mantelpiece. Not a cup or a crumby plate or a pair of slippers in sight.

Nothing had changed.

Well, apart from the lack of Ray. There was no Ray Henderson sitting in the armchair by the window, reading a Dick Francis novel and sporadically rapping on the window to scare a cat off his borders.

Ray had died just over a year ago. I hadn't been invited to the funeral, but I still followed Fraser's sisters – Jackie, Cara and Heather – on social media so consolations had floated into my news stream like flotsam from friends of friends. There had been an obituary in the Longhampton news group I'd never left ('respected businessman and magistrate . . . stalwart of the sporting community . . . devoted wife Martine and four children . . . blackcurrant cordial . . .'). I'd written to Martine and Fraser, remembering how kind Ray had been to me, how much everyone had always enjoyed his barbecues, and had received the printed card of acknowledgement in return. Martine had written *Thank you so much for your sweet words* on the bottom of the card, but nothing from Fraser.

I have to be honest, I was a little hurt by his silence. I'd thought it was a natural moment for us to pick up our friendship, because when you'd shared as much past as we had, surely that counted for something? And I genuinely felt sorry for Fraser's loss: he'd adored his dad, and I knew what it was like to lose a parent. But grief was a confusing place. I knew that. You had to stumble through the darkness as best you could, until one day you realised you'd stumbled back into lighter air, and while the world wasn't exactly the same, it was familiar enough to keep going.

Ray maintained his patriarchal presence in a shrine on the piano opposite the door. The grand piano was more than just a piano: it was the Henderson family display cabinet, laden in the Balmoral-approved style with framed photos. I'd never seen anyone play it, although Fraser said they'd had lessons as kids – he'd been required to play the boring bits of duets with his more talented sisters. It mainly demonstrated in a subtle way how enormous the sitting room was.

While Martine picked her way carefully to her chair, I furtively gobbled up any clues in the family portraits: centre stage was the black-and-white wedding photograph of Martine and Ray – Ray resplendent in morning coat, and Martine doll-like in a dress like a lace handbell – but the formal portrait of Ray as chairman of the bench had moved up next to it. The photographer had captured Ray's affable worthiness: a red-cheeked, white-haired, blue-eyed man in a tweed jacket, the human embodiment of the Union Jack and British countryside values. Family, business, golf, steak.

Around Ray were his children, and their own satellite children: Jacqueline, the oldest, married to Jerry or Perry (or Larry?); Cara, the financial analyst who'd moved to the US straight after university; Heather, the cellist; and Fraser, the golden boy. There were quite a few children in sports kit, cellos, dogs and skis. Every one radiating cheerful, healthy success. I scanned the smiling faces for the only one I simultaneously wanted and didn't want to see: an official shot of Fraser and the woman who'd replaced me.

I couldn't see one. My heart lifted.

There was the sudden sound of a stack of books crashing to the floor, and I spun round to see Martine struggling to disguise the fact that she'd bumped into the coffee table.

'Don't!' She raised her hands before I could speak. 'It's fine! *I'm* fine!'

I didn't want to argue with her. 'Why don't I make you that cup of tea?' I suggested, picking up the books and restacking them. 'And then I'll ring Jacqueline and—'

'No! There's no need to call Jacqueline!' Martine's face tightened.

'Martine, I have to call *someone*. The paramedics were clear – you need someone looking after you for the next twenty-four hours. Unfortunately I've got a work call at three so I can't stay long.'

She frowned. 'There's absolutely no need to disturb Jacqueline. She's extremely busy.'

I couldn't argue with that: Jacqueline was always busy. As well as bringing up her children to be as accomplished and driven as her own siblings, the evidence of which I regularly saw on Instagram, she was the head of a nationally successful comprehensive, the sort that single-handedly controlled property prices in its catchment area; she'd appeared on the news a few times celebrating her pupils' wide-ranging successes, which she put down to 'community spirit'. And presumably the sort of unflagging commitment to self-improvement that she'd learned from Martine.

'Is there someone else who can sit with you? A neighbour perhaps?'

She winced. 'Next door are away on holiday. And I don't . . . I don't really know the other side very well. New people.'

This was unlike Martine. She knew *everyone.*

'OK. Is there a friend I could call? Or a cleaner? I mean,' I corrected myself, remembering that Martine never had *cleaners*, 'a housekeeper? Does Dawn still come?'

'No. Dawn retired, so we moved on to an agency and they're just not the same. They never send the same girls twice.'

I was running out of options. Obviously Cara was out of the question in NYC and I didn't even know where Heather lived, when she wasn't on holiday. It left only the elephant in the room. The handsome, elusive, cybersecurity elephant.

'Well, shall I call Fraser?' I asked casually.

'Do *not* call Fraser.' Martine fixed me with a gaze that I couldn't quite interpret.

Did she mean he wouldn't want me to? Or that *she* wouldn't want me to? Or that she thought I'd been stalking him?

I swallowed. My heart rate had gone up a gear. But I had to ask. When would I ever get this chance again? 'How . . . Um, how *is* . . . ?'

And then there was a ring at the doorbell.

Martine started to rise from the chair, but her knees failed, she staggered and slumped back, stunned by her own vulnerability.

I blanched. Maybe I should call Allen and postpone our meeting.

'Can you get that?' she asked, reluctantly.

'Of course. Don't move.' I put out a warning hand. 'I'll be right back.'

The doorbell rang again, two impatient trills and a long one. I hurried down the hall, hoping it would be one of Martine's many friends and acquaintances – not, of course, that she'd want them to see her looking less than her usual self, but needs must.

I flung open the door, and the almost-familiar woman on the step opened her mouth, stopped, stared harder, then said, 'Beth?'

I pulled myself up to my full height. If I'd wished I'd worn something a bit less tent-like to bump into Martine, I definitely wished I'd bothered now.

Jacqueline – Jackie – was almost as sheeny as she appeared on social media, but what really struck me was how much like Martine she'd become since we'd last met. She looked like a woman who had answers – and the spare keys, life experience, phone numbers, fail-safe tips. Her face had sharpened into Martine's model bone structure, and she was fiddling with a clover pendant that gave off Significant Birthday Present vibes. She'd always looked younger than me, thanks to her diligent approach to everything extending to skincare and nutrition, but now she'd graduated into a different bracket of ageless womanhood. I did a swift mental calculation: Jackie was nearly ten years older than Fraser – fifty. Ish?

Fifty-ish. Wow. I tried not to notice that this also made me nearer forty than thirty.

'Hi, Jackie!' I said, in case she thought I was a hallucination.

'Beth?' she said again, as if one of us was lying.

'I was just about to call you!' I hurried on, conscious of her bewilderment and also my recent normality-fail at the charity shop. The next few sentences were critical, if a decent report of me was to get back to Fraser. It would be self-centred to start explaining why I was there, wouldn't it? Instead of focusing on her mother's accident? Presumably there was some kind of fall alarm on Martine's phone, one that had summoned Jackie to the rescue. 'No need to panic, the paramedics gave Martine a thorough check-over, and there doesn't seem to be anything broken, but—'

Jackie's confusion abruptly shifted to horror. '*Paramedics*? Jesus.' She took a step back, glancing past me down the hallway. 'Mum? Mum!'

Then she glanced back at me, more sharply. 'What's happened?'

Oh God, I clearly hadn't got this right at all. Did she think *I* was responsible? 'I wasn't involved in the actual accident, she slipped outside the bank,' I gabbled. 'In town! Not here! I was passing, so I brought her home and . . .'

Jackie squeezed her eyes shut. 'Mum was at the bank?'

'Yes, I think she slipped on the steps. I didn't get the whole story, but the paramedics—'

'Beth! Who *is* that?' shouted Martine from the sitting room. 'If it's one of those parcel people, don't let them leave anything here!'

'And you say *you* found her?' She frowned.

I suddenly felt hot, then cold. None of this was going the way it did in my imagination; Jackie wasn't hugging me, delighted to see me again, and confiding she thought Fraser had lost his mind, as she did in the version I'd scripted. My whole body felt fidgety and wrong: this bra – my last good one that still fitted, because I wasn't spending bra money on something I intended to diet out of any time now – was pinching the skin into my ribs, and my knees ached. For some reason, Martine hadn't asked what on earth I was doing in Longhampton, but Jackie was about to, and I was suddenly overwhelmed by the prospect of having to invent swathes of details about my life to disguise the fact that the last five years had been spent vegetating in a duvet-laptop-box set loop.

Shame swarmed up inside me. Jackie had used lockdown to train for a 'virtual marathon', according to her family Instagram. I'd downloaded Duolingo and done one Welsh lesson.

Run, said the anxious voice inside my head. Run, while you still look like a hero for rescuing Fraser's mother. While you're still a mysterious coincidence.

'I'll let you take over from here, shall I?' I gestured towards the door. 'I'm so glad I was there at the right time, but I've got a meeting at three, so I should—'

'Why are you here again? Sorry, I'm still not . . .' Jackie's brow creased in further confusion, and I kicked myself.

Did this look like I was trying to scuttle away from the scene of the crime?

She rubbed her forehead. 'Sorry, sorry, that sounded rude. I was supposed to be taking Mum to a hearing-aid appointment, which she's clearly forgotten about. So why don't you stay for a cup of tea and fill me in? I doubt I'll get the whole story from her.'

I wavered. The voices in my head were having an argument.

If I left now, I might never have another chance to chat with Jackie in real life, and finally get some closure about Fraser. Why he'd blocked me. Whether he'd met someone else. Whether there was any hope of trying again. As Ash said, it was hardly surprising I struggled to move on: one minute we'd been on the brink of serious commitment, the next . . . silence. Didn't I deserve to understand how that had happened?

But if you stay, another voice countered, they'll know you've done nothing with your life since the break-up. No matter how clever you try to be about it. Jackie and Martine were forensic about winkling details out of people. They were like those bra fitters in posh lingerie shops who knew your bra size without taking out a tape measure, regardless of whether you were wearing a padded push-up bra and three layers of clothing.

My uncomfortable bra was dominating my thoughts to an unhealthy degree.

Then Jackie smiled. 'And you haven't even told me why *you're* in Longhampton! Come on, stay for a quick cup of tea.'

Even if this was just Jackie's tactic of disguising a 'did you push my mother down the steps of the bank?' interrogation, when she added, 'It's been too long, what have you been up to?' – *as if she really wanted to know* – I couldn't resist.

It was pretty clear that Martine had forgotten about the hearing-aid appointment but she styled it out.

'Of course I hadn't forgotten, darling,' she insisted, with just a *soupçon* of affront. 'I'm ready to go now!'

Jackie was already texting to cancel. 'Mum, no, you need to stay here for the rest of the day. Beth says you've had a fall.'

'What?' Martine glared at me, then turned back to Jackie with a tinkly laugh. 'Nothing of the sort! I slipped! I *slipped*, Jacqueline. Old people have falls.'

'You're eighty, Mum. That is old.'

'How *rude*.'

How *brave*, more like.

I caught Martine's eye and we exchanged faux outrage while Jackie's attention was still fixed on her phone. It gave me a nice nostalgic feeling: there was always an in-joke flashing around the Henderson gatherings, between Fraser and his dad ('We're outnumbered, son!'), or everyone rolling their eyes at 'I tell it like it is' Cara, who took everything so seriously, or at Jackie for bossing them around.

Jackie looked up. 'Right, that's the hearing-aid appointment cancelled. We'll have a cup of tea then I'll drive you over to the surgery so Dr Robson can give you a quick check, OK?'

'No!'

'Mum, please. It doesn't help to minimise things.'

Martine made a dismissive gesture. 'Don't start this again, Jacqueline. I know what's happened to Perry's parents is very sad, but that is no reason to treat *me* as if I have dementia too.'

Yes! Perry. That was Jackie's husband's name. *Perry Dent.*

I smiled blandly while they continued to argue politely about whether Martine should see a doctor, but my attention had slid back to the piano; where were the Dents? There they were, close to their grandfather in the high-achievement zone. Jackie's children were unmistakable clones of her, beaming gap-toothed smiles in their cherry-red school uniforms and cricket whites, clutching trophies.

Sitting down provided me with a new angle and – at last – I found what I couldn't see before: Fraser. Excitement swept across my skin like a cool breeze, raising the hairs on the back of my arms. It gave me a pang, seeing this new photograph, evidence of a life going on without me; Fraser had a glass of wine in his hand, leaning on a barrel as he smiled that confident smile. Blue shirt open at the neck, light tan, a few silver threads in his blond hair. My brain rattled through possibilities: fortieth birthday wine-tasting? Holiday?

Honeymoon?

I searched for the things that were unchanged in his face; the watch, that was the one I'd given him! He was still wearing it. I couldn't see his ring finger, which was out of shot.

'Beth?'

I swung my attention back to Jackie.

'Sorry?'

'I was just saying, how bizarre that you were the one to find Mum.' She raised her eyebrows. 'What are the chances of that?'

'Yes, I know! I was in town to drop off some donations at a charity shop – I'm moving house at the weekend and . . .' I shrugged, in a 'you know how it is!' way. 'So much junk!'

'Oh, I love a good sort-out! So cathartic!'

'I cannot ever move,' Martine announced. 'It would be easier to burn this house down than attempt to pack up fifty years of my life. Jackie's keen for me to *downsize* to some awful workhouse for geriatrics but I'd rather be carried out of Coleridge Drive than sell it, thank you.'

'Mum . . .' Jackie shot her a long-suffering look, then returned to me. 'Where are you moving to? Are you renting, buying?'

'Renting, with a friend. It took us *ages* to find somewhere,' I went on, glossing over the house-hunting nightmare of the past months. 'But it's a lovely place, with a garden – which we needed, for my dog.'

My and Ashley's new flat had been worth the painful rigmarole of bidding, missing out, bidding again, expanding search parameters, etc., etc.: it was bigger but slightly cheaper than our current place, amazingly enough, and near a wood where Tomsk could snuffle around to his heart's content. As soon as I'd walked in, I'd got happy vibes from it, and I honestly wasn't the sort of person who 'got vibes' about anything. I was more of a 'do these figures add up?' kind of person, as was Ash.

'Sounds like everything's going well,' said Martine. 'Good for you.'

I beamed. 'Thank you.'

Without meaning to, my eyes were drawn again to the photograph of Fraser and I was about to bite the bullet and ask how he was when my phone beeped with the reminder that my meeting with my boss was in exactly one hour.

'Is Fraser . . . well?' I blurted out.

Martine and Jackie exchanged glances. Again, I couldn't quite read their expressions.

'Yes, I think so,' said Jackie smoothly. And smiled, as if that was the end of that line of questioning. 'Did you say you had a meeting at three? Just so you know, the traffic going out of town is really awful. It took me nearly a half an hour to get through the lights . . .'

So I had no choice but to leave, Cinderella-like, in a rush, and without any of the answers I'd hoped to find.

Although I had my own clients, my boss Allen and I had a Wednesday catch-up online, officially to discuss my case-load, but usually for him to warn me about a new scam he'd read about. Occasionally he tested me on pension reforms. Most weeks it was the only time I saw anyone from work in person, as it were.

'We missed you at lunch,' he said, as an opener.

Lunch? What had happened at lunch? 'Oh . . . yeah, I was sorry not to be there.'

'It was Carryn's leaving do – she said to thank you for those lovely cakes.'

I had a momentary twinge of guilt; Carryn was the receptionist and in the days when I was in the office more often, I used to bake birthday cakes for her kids' parties. She was a nice lady, organised a lot of events for the hospice.

Allen read my mind. 'I put a tenner in her leaving envelope on your behalf – you can ping it over to me later.'

'Thanks.' I scribbled a note to send Carryn a card. 'I don't think I knew it was her leaving do today.'

'There's been a notice up in the kitchen for ten days.'

Allen raised an eyebrow. He was bald, but still had incongruously full, dark eyebrows, so any silent eyebrow language felt like shouting.

He didn't need to eyebrow-shout. I knew what he was intimating. He'd been dropping gentle hints for some time but he was too kind to come straight out and ask if there was a reason I'd barely set foot in the office for such a long time. I suspected he knew there were murky 'personal reasons' behind it, and didn't want to wade into troubled waters. Our HR director, Lisa, was very hot on respecting boundaries.

(For the record, I *had* been in. But not on days when anyone else was around.)

On the sofa, Tomsk pricked up his ears. This normally meant Ashley's car was turning down our road, but it was only just gone three, and she was never home before five.

'Anyway,' he went on. 'I was hoping you'd make it this week because there's something I need to have a chat with you about.'

I smiled blandly. I could make a good guess as to what it would be: Christian, our new managing director, who'd recently joined us from a London firm, had sent round a high-priority email making a case for entering every award we were eligible for, 'to raise our profile'. Allen hated things like that – his maxim was that accountants should be as invisible as possible – and I suspected he wanted me to do any submissions on his behalf.

'Can't you tell me now?' I asked.

'I'd rather discuss it face to face.'

'OK.' I pretended to flip through my diary, which was empty. 'When would be good for you?'

'Any time next week. We could meet somewhere for a working lunch if that's more tempting?'

My attention snapped back to Allen on my laptop screen, and my cheeks burned. Why lunch? Was he trying to lure me out with food? Did I come across as someone who needed to be tempted out of her den with a burrito?

'We don't have to have lunch,' I said defensively.

He looked baffled. 'OK. Coffee then. How about Wednesday?

'Yes, Wednesday's fine.' There was time to get out of it, if necessary.

Tomsk's tail thumped against the sofa cushions, alerting me to the click of our metal gate being opened.

'Good. Eleven o'clock at the golf club. You know where that is, don't you?'

I heard a key in the front door, then the door opening. This was unusual. Tomsk slipped off the sofa, his feathery tail now raised in 'welcoming Ashley' mode, so I assumed we weren't being burgled.

'So! All set for your big move this Friday?' said Allen, business over.

'Yup,' I confirmed. 'Mail redirection's on, utilities ready to go, everything packed. And I've specifically started our broadband from Saturday morning, so I'll be up and running for Monday's meetings.'

'Good for you, Beth. Sometimes a change of scene is what you need. New starts, fresh fields. New beginnings.' He raised his eyebrows again.

What was that meant to mean?

The conspiratorial look on Allen's face abruptly faded. 'Oh! Sorry, that's Christian just popped into my office for a . . . What? Now?' He frowned off-camera. 'Beth, I have to go, I'm sorry. '

'OK!'

When I turned back, Ashley was standing in the doorway, one hand absent-mindedly patting Tomsk's head, the other clutching her phone.

'Beth,' she said. 'I need to talk to you about something.'

'If it's about the deposit, I've already calculated how much is owing, if it's in the right account . . .'

'No.' She bit her lip. 'It's bit more serious than that.'

And that's when my day, which had already been like a strange cheese dream, turned into an actual nightmare.

Chapter three

When I first met Ashley Donaldson, she was recovering from a soul-destroying break-up almost as mortifying as mine.

Serendipitously, the same week as Fraser and I parted ways, Ashley's boyfriend up and left her for his friend from the cycling club, Duhan. Our mutual friend, Lydia, introduced us: I urgently needed somewhere to live, Ashley urgently needed someone to help her with Jake's half of the rent. We both urgently needed someone who wouldn't tilt their head in fake concern and ask dumb questions like, 'Wow, didn't you have *any* idea?'

For the next few weeks, we sat in silence eating giant bags of crisps and watching the longest box sets we could find to make the time pass. Occasionally one of us would let out a sudden sob, and the other would open another bag of crisps and pass them over. As soon as we could get out of Ashley and Jake's lease, we moved into a different, bigger place which was when I adopted Tomsk, and we'd been there ever since.

Ash and I didn't have a lot in common other than our broken hearts but we got on well, probably *because* we didn't have a friendship to corrode under the strain of sharing a bathroom. She was a project manager for a construction company, so we were both used to discussing money, which made sharing a flat so much easier – we had a house account for bills, and a cleaner once a week, and we never argued. She was cool about Tomsk sleeping on the sofa, and I was cool about her taking up the harp during lockdown. If our landlord hadn't been selling off his rental portfolio to move abroad, we'd probably have carried on living in the flat indefinitely.

I'd never known Ash shy away from an awkward conversation. So it was rather unsettling to see her biting her lip like this now. I wondered if it was Jake. Maybe he'd got back in touch. Maybe Duhan had cycled off with someone else.

I closed my laptop. 'What's happened?'

Ashley took a deep breath. 'I had a call from Zara at the estate agent's about the new house this morning. There's a problem with the rental agreement. We can't take the dog.'

'What?' I hadn't been expecting that. 'But we signed a waiver specifically saying we could. I got him a reference – from the groomer!'

I'd had to take Tomsk, who didn't enjoy being bathed at the best of times, to a groomer for two months, purely to secure the reference. We'd *all* suffered in the cause of finding a new home.

She nodded. 'I know.'

'So, how?' I spread my hands in disbelief.

'They mixed up the details,' she said flatly. 'The landlord has several properties, but our one is no pets. We should never even have been shown it.'

'What?' My brain initially refused to accept the idea. I could feel it bouncing off, even as I tried to process what she'd said. 'But we've *signed the contract.* It's a legally binding document.'

'Doesn't matter. Zara printed off the wrong contract. She's phoned the landlord, apparently, to see if he could be persuaded to change his mind.' She shook her head. 'He won't even discuss it. We're not moving at the weekend.'

'OK. But if one of his properties *does* accept pets, why can't we have that one instead?'

'Already let to someone else.'

'So what are we meant to do?' My disappointment started to sharpen with panic. 'The movers are coming on Friday to take our stuff! Bryan's buyers are literally arriving on Monday. We *have* to be out of here.'

'Zara's trying to find other places, but she says we need to explore other options ourselves. I mean, we know how little there is out there. For renters with dogs.'

The knot of anxiety tightened in my stomach as Tomsk wandered back in, and lay down by my feet, clearly aware something was up. His trusting sigh only made me feel worse. 'So? What are we meant to do?' I repeated.

Ashley's eyes shifted microscopically to the side, and I had a sudden, cold feeling there was more to come.

'Surely the *lettings agency* is obliged to find us somewhere else?' I protested. 'It's Zara's error. We've incurred costs! I've redirected the post to the new place! And set up broadband!'

She let out a deep sigh. 'Look, this isn't how I wanted to talk about it, but sometimes things happen for a reason, don't they?'

'Meaning?'

'Beth. I'm going to be straight with you.' Ashley took another breath, and looked me right in the face. 'I honestly think Fate brought us together to get us both through the bad times. I'd have never have worked out what I need in a relationship if I'd moved in with Lydia – she'd have talked me into giving Jake another try, whereas you were so honest in a way only a total stranger could be, and that's exactly what I needed.'

Total stranger. I opened my mouth, then closed it again, hurt. We'd been sharing for so long, I'd almost forgotten what a pragmatic arrangement it had been at the start. Those bleak days of wordless misery had faded into an uplifting story about the power of female friendship: two heartbroken losers recovering with the support of each other's empathy, box set-and-curry nights, and, of course, dog-walking. It made up for the fact that I barely heard from Mali, Sophie or Poppy – my actual friends – since the Fraser disaster.

But was that not how Ashley saw it? Were we not proper friends? Just flatmates?

She was still talking. 'Leo and I . . . well, who knows where we'll go, but he is a million times better for me than Jake. And I only know that because you've helped me understand what I—'

'Stop,' I said. 'Leo? Leo the guy you've seen for dinner about twice?'

Ashley raised her chin. 'It's been a bit more than that.'

'Has it?'

'Yes! Quite a lot more. I didn't want to rub your nose in it.'

I stared at her. Rub my nose in what?

'Anyway, forget Leo,' she said, getting back into her speech. 'It's been an important part of my life, like . . .

hibernating. Wintering. I've worked out a lot of things about myself – as I know you have too.' She paused, then ripped off the plaster. 'And I think what I need now, to keep moving forward, is my own space.'

I pressed my lips together, but inside my mind was howling. This *was* about Leo. But also about me.

I felt Tomsk shift his big head on to my feet, the soft heat of his breath warming my socks. He was very subtle about offering his comfort. I wondered if he could sense stress coming off me in waves. It was a small payback for the nights I'd lain on the kitchen floor next to him while he whickered and whimpered in his sleep. We were both bad containers of stress.

'And look,' Ash continued, eager to smooth over the uncomfortable atmosphere that had sprung up, 'you've moved on a lot too. You've *grown*. I mean,' she added, quickly, 'spiritually. Emotionally.'

Her gaze darted around the room in search of examples of my life moving on, so we could both ignore her comment about me growing. There were only packing boxes.

'I mean, you've been promoted, haven't you?' she said, clutching at straws.

'Not really.'

'Well, you've helped so many people build their businesses with your advice! Look, Beth, don't take this the wrong way. I've *loved* living with you, but this,' she gestured around our empty sitting room, stripped of its books and ornaments, no longer the cosy nest it had been, 'came about because of an unexpected disaster, right? Well, the contract thing is another disaster! So maybe this is the universe trying to . . .'

Ash finally ran aground on the stony shore of my silence.

'Trying to what?' I prompted her.

'To make you get *out* there.'

'Get out there, meaning what? Find a new boyfriend?'

'Yes! But also *literally* get out there. How many times have you been into the office this year?'

'I don't need to go into the office. They're fine with me working from home.'

'That's not the point. You need to see people, be around colleagues.' She paused, trying a smile. 'I mean, does your ID even work?'

I flinched. My ID was a sore point long before I'd stopped going in; there'd been many, many attempts until I'd finally got a version of myself that I could bear to have hanging round my neck on a lanyard, and I'd swerved every subsequent request to update it. It was a reminder now of how very different I was to that Beth – the single chin, the confident smile, the blond French pleat – I wanted to be *that* Beth again, not this one.

And I could get her back, I knew that. I'd been on enough diets in my life to know what I had to do. I just didn't want to face the judgemental gaze of Natasha and the others at Jacobs' until old Beth had returned.

'And it's not like I don't leave the house,' I said defiantly. 'I was out today.'

'To avoid something at the office, I bet.'

'No!'

'Beth, you're your own worst enemy.'

She knew me too well. That was the trouble. We'd lived together long enough to have a background feel for each other's schedules, as well as our foibles.

I changed tack. 'So are you moving in with Leo?'

Ash opened her mouth to deny it, then nodded.

'Why didn't you tell me? You could have let me know before we started looking for a new place! We could have saved a stack of money, for one thing.' I hated myself for saying this. I hated, hated, *hated* conflict but I felt as if I were on the edge of a cliff, scrabbling to stop myself being shunted off.

'We'd started talking about maybe finding somewhere eventually, but this kind of sped things up, and— Ugh! Don't look at me like that.' She ran a hand through her hair. 'I'm starting to worry about you. You *need* to move on. I sometimes think you believe that if you stay here, in your room, really quietly, not changing, one day you'll wake up and it'll be the day before you and Fraser broke up, and somehow you can stop it happening.'

'No . . .'

'Yes! And while you're trying to will him to change his mind by liking his sister's Instagram stories, you're just wasting your own time. You could be dating! You could be joining clubs or volunteering, doing things where you'll meet someone better than Fraser Henderson!'

'I *have* done dating!'

'You've talked to people online and then bailed out of meeting them. That's not the same.'

I stared mutinously at the large box marked *BETH BOOKS*. It was all right for Ashley. In the beginning, we'd been comrades in low-maintenance sofawear, but about a year ago her mum and sister had dragged her to a personal shopper for her birthday. She'd left the house in a stained hoodie, and returned with highlights, better eyebrows, and a booklet of 'Clear Winter' fabric swatches. Though we sniggered about it at the time, something had changed. Ashley resembled her security pass again. I wasn't just jealous of the transformation, my entire being ached for the family who loved her enough to boss her into action.

I didn't know where these dark, negative thoughts were coming from. They were flying at me like bats out of a cartoon cave.

'Beth! I'm trying to help you,' Ashley insisted. 'There's a life out there that is literally waiting to get going, and you're hiding from it, pretending that everything's OK when it's not.'

I stayed silent. I knew if I opened my mouth I'd start crying. Yesterday that wouldn't have bothered me – God knows Ash and I had cried rivers and rivers of ugly tears in front of each other, without a single word spoken – but today I was on my own again.

The warm dead weight on my foot shifted, as if to say, *Not quite on your own.*

'I know what you're thinking, and you're so wrong.' Ashley continued. 'You don't need some big transformation, you just need to get out there. You're absolutely fine the way you are.'

'The way I am?' I squeaked, without even wanting to.

She raised her hands, then dropped them in despair. 'Yeah, the way you are.'

I looked up at her, my eyes swimming with tears.

The blurry Ashley sighed.

'Look, I'm not going to apologise for what I've just said. I genuinely want you to be happy. In a year's time – maybe less! – you'll look back at this cock-up with the flat and think, thank God that happened.'

I summoned up my remaining dignity. 'Well, let's hope so.'

Ashley met my gaze. 'Stop being so dramatic. The universe has spoken and it says, Move. On.'

When I sat down at my desk the next morning, not even a second, proper coffee and the comforting presence of Tomsk at my feet could lift the gloomy cloud hanging over me.

I knew, in the logical, accounting side of my brain, that this was hardly a monumental task. I'd dealt with *way* worse than this.

I'd had to organise my mother's funeral, a task so awful I'd already blanked half the details and locked the rest in a box at the back of my head. It wasn't even just that: growing up with two parents who hated each other hadn't been fun, Dad leaving was a whole other psychologist's dream, and then there was the break-up with Fraser.

And I was lucky enough to have savings: I'd squirrelled away a decent deposit for the house I assumed I'd be buying with Fraser. But after our break-up I'd attempted to fill the hole in my heart with shopping (you never had to diet into shoes or table lamps) and I'd horrified myself so badly by how quickly I could blow through months of diligent budgeting that I'd locked the entire lot into a super-high-interest account, which I couldn't touch for another two years. OK, so that wasn't necessarily the greatest idea, but it wasn't as if I could afford somewhere on my own now either.

I could work anywhere, I just had to find a rental for me and my dog.

So why did it feel so overwhelming?

Because it wasn't the house, was it? I stared unhappily at the lukewarm cafetiere. What I hated most was feeling so stupid – *again*. I'd thought I was happily moving on, to a new place with a *friend*. Just like I'd thought that Fraser only needed a sign I'd say yes to a proposal. Was I so bad at reading situations? What else was I missing?

I shook myself. What I needed was a plan, the sort of simple, emotionless plan I encouraged my more hysterical clients to make when the savings account they thought they'd been putting their tax money into turned out to be empty because they'd accidentally set up their household direct debits from it.

'Estate agent,' I said to Tomsk. 'Let's start with her.'

Zara from Foxley's wasn't as embarrassed by her mistake as I felt she ought to be. And, as Ashley had predicted, she didn't have much to offer beyond apologies for what she called 'the little mix-up'.

I acknowledged her unconvincing apologies, then insisted that she look – right now – for a solution to the pressing issue of my homelessness.

There was a lot of clicking and sighing.

'Um, no . . . oh, no pets. You couldn't . . . ?'

Tomsk had quietly slunk away to his favourite chair, and was curled up with his long nose tucked into his shaggy haunches, as if he didn't want to hear. 'Absolutely not,' I said.

'Tsk. Shame.' More clicking. 'Or there's . . . no. Ah!' Finally. 'There's a one-bed flat in Hedley Linton that's coming up, the tenants are waiting on a house sale. We haven't marketed it yet, but I could put you on the waiting list.'

'The *waiting list*?'

'We've had some early inquiries before yourself. It's mad right now. People are bidding for properties.'

I channelled Martine. She was un-fob-off-able. 'I'm well aware of that, Zara. I had to bid for the property I would be moving into – if *you* hadn't made the mistake with the contract.'

Grudgingly, Zara conceded I could go to the top of the list, and I tried not to let the relief show in my voice. The only problem was, it wouldn't be available for another two months.

'And where am I supposed to go until then?' I demanded.

'There are a couple of short-term properties you could have a look at this afternoon.' Zara sounded distracted already. 'We've got a lovely one-bed just outside Ludlow. Cottage garden, secure parking. No pets, but can't you just leave the dog with a friend for a few months? Stick it in kennels?'

I glanced over at Tomsk, curled up so tightly he was just a shaggy mass. I knew he was listening; he could pick up on the tension in the air like a radio.

There was no way I was putting Tomsk in kennels. Something about the fearful hunch of his spine reminded me how submissive he'd been when I'd first met him, how desperate he was to make himself invisible in that concrete run. I couldn't bear to let him think he'd been abandoned again.

'No,' I said, firmly. 'He can't go into kennels.'

Zara was losing patience. 'Friends? Family? Surely there's *someone* you could ask.'

I bristled. Why did everyone assume everyone else had an army of friends and family to turn to?

'No,' I said abruptly.

'In that case all I can do is keep you in the loop about this flat in Hedley Linton.' Zara felt she'd done her bit. 'Who knows? It might be sooner than two months.'

I bit my lip. 'Let's hope so.'

That done, I should have started some tax returns, but my mind refused to focus on the numbers in front of me. Instead, with every breath, the knot in my stomach began to move slowly up my body, until it filled my chest with a dark, frantic panic.

Without thinking, unable to bear it, I pushed myself away from the table and ripped the packing tape off the box of crockery I'd packed the previous day. I pulled out my big cake cup, and tore open the box marked 'store cupboard ingredients', lining up the usual suspects packet by packet on the scrubbed and empty worktop. Pale-blue self-raising flour, custard-yellow caster sugar, earth-brown cocoa: old friends. On autopilot, blanking the pain building in my heart, I added four spoons of sugar, three spoons of flour, two spoons of cocoa to the mug, and stirred it together.

One egg, two spoons of oil. Three spoons of full fat milk. The pale sand slowly vanished into a thick sludge of rich, chocolately mud that clung to the sides of the cup, and the smell of cocoa rose like an aromatic hug. So comforting.

I looked down at the mixture, hesitated for a second, then opened the cupboard box again. I tipped in the last half-packet of chocolate chips, then put the mug in the microwave, set it to ninety seconds and stood, hypnotised and impatient, as the mug went round and round in the light. Working its magic. In thirty seconds, twenty seconds . . .

The thick chocolatey crust of the mug cake, speckled with flecks of cocoa, pushed every sad, scary thought out of my head for a few blissful moments, and with a teaspoon I carved a neat hole in the middle and poured a generous slug of cream straight into the molten heart.

I admired it for a long second. Then I started eating.

Ashley's words kept coming back to me, but kinder now. Chocolate made everything feel kinder. Maybe the universe didn't want me to move into that house because something better was in the offing? It was a comforting theory – that everything happened for a reason – and one that she and I had repeated to ourselves like a mantra in the early days.

Something great is just about to happen. The next step in my life is already unfolding. I'm one day closer to the most amazing development.

When my phone rang, I had the insane thought that the mug cake had worked some proper magic this time, and it might be Zara calling back with a flat.

But it wasn't.

It was Fraser's sister, Jackie.

'Hello, Beth!' she said, in that confident Henderson voice that reminded me of parties and happier times. 'It's Jackie, Jackie Dent. Fraser's sister? Is this a good moment?'

I put down the half-eaten mug cake. Well, half-eaten. There was maybe one spoon left.

'Yes,' I said. 'It is a good moment.'

Chapter four

Jackie launched straight into the reason for her call, which was a good thing because my voice sounded extremely chocolatey.

'So sorry to bother you but did you leave a scarf at Mum's house yesterday? A red one, with tassels?'

I hoped Jackie had noticed the label; it was what my mum used to call 'a good brand'. 'Yes, that's mine.'

'Oh, excellent. Mum was adamant it wasn't hers, but she can be rather forgetful these days. I'll stick it in the post this afternoon. Where would you like me to send it?'

'Can you send it to fourteen—' I stopped. No, this wasn't my address anymore. My life from Monday onwards was a blank. I didn't have an address. I didn't have a bed.

I felt the floor drop away from me. *What was I meant to do with all these boxes*?

'Beth? Beth, are you still there?' A sound like someone clamping a phone to their shoulder to mute it. Then a muffled, 'I'm talking to *Beth*, Mum. She says it's her scarf. Yes! She's sure.'

The phone was moved back. 'Sorry, didn't you say you were moving this weekend? Do you want to give me your new address?'

'I can't – bit of a crisis, actually, the house fell through at the last minute, but I still have to move out of here on Friday. I still haven't found anywhere I can go, so I'm technically homeless!' I gabbled, trying to get it out before my brain caught up with the reality of what I was saying.

'Beth! Oh no! How *awful* for you.'

There was a click, and Martine said, 'Homeless? Who's homeless? Have you taken in a homeless person, Beth?'

'Mum!' snapped Jackie.

'What?'

'Mum, put the phone down.'

Another vivid flashback: I knew exactly where Martine was right now – in the kitchen, on the extension, an old-fashioned, wall-mounted thing with a long cable that had been installed years ago to allow the (female, obviously) user to conduct a phone conversation without breaking off from vital housework.

Martine ignored her. 'What's happened? You said you were moving to a lovely new place. Have you been let down?'

I told her, and she said, 'Oh *dear*.' The audible disapproval of both the estate agent and Ashley in those two syllables was a comfort. 'Can't the lettings agent find you somewhere else?'

'There might be something in a few months but not immediately,' I said. 'I mean, crazy long shot, but if you know anyone with a holiday home . . . or even someone with a spare room who doesn't mind dogs?'

'How big is the dog?'

I looked at Tomsk. There was no point lying. Even curled up, he was the size of a hairy sack of compost. 'Quite large.'

'We'll have a think,' said Jackie.

In the background, I could hear kitchen cupboards and drawers being opened and closed, briskly, as if someone was searching for something.

'Jackie, why have you put these eggs in the bin? They're perfectly good. Sell-by dates are just a *guide*. Oh! And this ham is *fine*. You've been through my fridge again, haven't you?'

'Mum! Stop!' Jackie sounded distracted. 'Look, Beth, fingers crossed you find somewhere soon, and if I hear of anything, I'll give you a call, OK?'

'Thanks. And—'

The phone went dead.

I looked at the phone, then down at Tomsk, who had uncurled himself from the chair and lain down at my feet, his massive head a precisely judged centimetre from my toes. The thick veil of hair hanging over his face hid his eyes.

He thumped his tail apologetically against the floor, as if he knew how much he was complicating matters. Don't leave me, the tail said. Please don't leave me.

I knelt down and threw my arms around him. Keeping my promise to take care of Tomsk was often the only thing I had to feel good about on a bad day. 'You're making my life a million times better, not harder,' I murmured into his bony shoulder. 'Let's go for a walk.'

As usual, my mood began to lift after Tomsk and I rounded the corner: I felt the sun on my face, and saw a grey squirrel steal something shiny from a furious magpie, and watched him sniff a hundred different smells. That was the thing about dog walks. There was always something.

I wondered if I should call Jackie back about my scarf. She'd sounded frazzled. And what would I tell her anyway? My work address was the only one I had but I didn't want her to send my scarf there because then I'd have to go and get it. I could offer to go back to Longhampton to collect it, I supposed, but she hadn't suggested meeting up.

The possibility of maybe bumping into Fraser, this time with a totally legit excuse, gave me a small thrill, and I parked the idea in the corner of my brain reserved for Fraser-based daydreaming, like a bit of cake saved for later.

The rest of the day was taken up with filing VAT returns for clients, although I kept a couple of tabs open to check on inquiries I'd made about holiday cottages. I tried not to notice that Ash didn't come home at her normal time.

Then I tried not to think about the romantic dinner she was doubtless enjoying with Leo. Maybe even discussing me in that safely sympathetic way you can, when your own situation's nice and secure.

By midnight, I was no closer finding somewhere I could move my boxes in less than forty-eight hours, and was about to take myself off to bed for another sleepless night when my mobile rang.

'Hello?' I said, stiffly, assuming it was Ash calling from Leo's to say she wouldn't be back.

'Hello, Beth, Martine Henderson here. Is this a bad time?'

'No, not at all.' I struggled up to a sitting position. Did Martine know how late it was?

She breezed on, as if it was entirely normal to be calling someone at midnight. 'I've been giving some thought to your little problem, and I might have a solution.'

'Really?' I said cautiously. On one hand, Martine knew a lot of people with spare homes, but at the same time, something Jackie had said about her mother getting 'rather forgetful' rang a warning bell.

'It was staring me in the face the entire time! I don't know if you ever knew, but we have a flat over the garage. It's where our au pairs used to live.'

I did know about the garage flat; after Fraser and his siblings outgrew the au pairs, it had been the dream teen hang-out, according to him, anyway. Close enough to the house for fridge access, far enough to be out of earshot. Long before my time, of course, but it loomed large in Fraser's favourite tales from his childhood; the Hendersons were big on family tales, recounting them over and over until you forgot you hadn't actually been there yourself.

'Jackie keeps telling me I should do it up as one of these Airbnbs,' Martine went on, 'but I'm far too busy to get round to sorting it out. And of course, I don't want just anyone in my back garden!'

'Mmm,' I said.

'But it occurred to me – maybe that might be the solution to your predicament? It needs a bit of a clean – we've been using it for storage – but there's a bathroom, kitchenette and so on. You're more than welcome to camp out there until you find somewhere better.'

And just like that, a solution, glowing like a unexpected yellow taxi light on a dark, wet night. I didn't know what to say. It was so easy and generous, a blanket of kindness thrown round my shoulders when I was feeling more alone than I'd ever felt before.

'Really? Martine, are you sure?'

'Of course! You were such an angel when I had my mishap in town, it seems only fair to return the favour.'

'Well, if you're sure, that would be amazing. And I'm happy to give you the same rent that I'd be—'

She cut that off straight away. 'What? Goodness me, no. It's only for a few weeks, isn't it? No, no. We can talk about wine or plants for the garden or something.'

'And you're absolutely *sure* you don't mind me bringing the dog?'

'Not at all. As long as you don't let him disturb my rosebeds. He's not a digger, is he?'

I glanced over at Tomsk, upside down on a chair, pretending to be asleep, his languid paws dangling over the arm. 'No, he's not a digger.'

'Well, then.' Martine sounded pleased. 'It's settled.'

I leaned back on my chair, overwhelmed. 'Thank you, Martine. I can't tell you how grateful I am. I really—'

'When did you say you needed to move?'

'This weekend, ideally.' I'd cancelled the movers, but they'd insisted on keeping my deposit as it was such short notice, so I reckoned I could talk them into re-rearranging.

'Shall we say any time on Saturday afternoon then? After two?'

'That would be incredible. Again, Martine, this is so kind.'

'Don't mention it,' said Martine. 'I'll see you and the hound on Saturday.'

And that was that.

Martine hadn't been exaggerating when she said the garage flat had been used for storage for some time.

A tidal wave had seemingly rushed through the Hendersons' house, and washed the flotsam and jetsam of family life down to the bottom of the garden: suitcases, empty boxes for computers and televisions filled with packets of photographs, discarded printers, an exercise bike, boxes marked *jacq uni stuff* and *jacq clothes*. Everything in random piles, left where they'd been stacked before the stacker had fled down the stairs and away.

The flat itself, underneath/behind the boxes, seemed in decent repair. As she let me in, Martine told me that it had once been the living quarters for the horse, the family carriage, and the grooms (in that order), then when a carriage was no longer required, downstairs had been converted into a garage, with rooms upstairs for a chauffeur to live with his wife, the housekeeper. Now, Martine's powder-blue Saab sat on flat tyres in the garage, while above it was a bedroom, a bathroom with a cast-iron bath, and a kitchen-sitting room with a saggy sofa that had probably once cost about the same as the car, its chintzy covers hidden by banana boxes of VHS tapes. The windows needed a clean. It all needed a clean.

But it was somewhere I could stay. And, more than that – much more than that – it was somewhere I'd been *invited*.

'Good God, it's worse than I remembered. I'll call Jacqueline and ask her to take some of her junk home. It's about time she sorted through it.' Martine gingerly peered into a box. 'Feel free to cart some of this downstairs to make space.'

'Thanks. I'll move it back once I know how much room I need.' Already I knew I'd be telling the man with the van outside that we'd be making another trip to the storage units with everything but my desk chair.

Martine was peering into a shoebox marked *M letters*. 'Hmm? Yes, of course. Do whatever you need to do.' She tucked the box under her arm and handed me the keys. 'I'll leave you to settle in.'

I hesitated, lost for words. I wanted to say something to acknowledge how much it had meant to have been offered this lifeline, by someone who hadn't seen me for years, and didn't really know me all that well in the first place. Fraser loved his mother, but he always said they got on best when they spent a maximum of thirty-six hours together at a time. 'She has an obsession with improving things,' he said, 'and I'm happy with how I am.'

I didn't mind being given advice, though. I still used Martine's trick with a needle for making tulips stand up in a vase.

'I *really* appreciate this,' I started. 'It's so kind of you to help me out. Even though we're not . . . I mean, I'm not . . .'

Martine patted my arm. 'Glad to be able to help, Beth. Now, make yourself at home. I'm sure that dog of yours is dying to get out of the van and have a sniff around the garden. You should get your laptop out and try to write a chapter or two before bed, too! No time like the present!'

I listened to her tapping her way down the stairs, then the double ker-clunk of the door.

Outside, birds were singing in the long garden that separated the Hendersons' house from the garage, and I closed my eyes to listen for a moment, feeling the peace and quiet and *relief* seep into my bones. This wasn't my home, and I wasn't meant to be here, but I had the oddest certainty that the universe had delivered me to exactly the right place.

And yes, I thought, opening my eyes, maybe I *would* get my laptop out.

Several hours later, I closed my eyes again, this time on the sofa with a mug of tea and Tomsk draped over me like a weighted blanket, his nose exhausted from a long inspection of our new neighbourhood.

My back ached and I'd broken three nails. But I was in.

The van man and I had stacked the boxes and general junk in the corner of the room and thrown dustsheets over the rest. Once it was piled up, I'd discovered a red Persian rug framing the seating area, and a gas fire on the far wall, surrounded by yellow tiles that fanned out in sunrays. Along one shelf was a collection of solitary Staffordshire dogs of various sizes and colours, some tiny and black with gold features, some huge and white, covered in spiderweb crazing. Most of my stuff had gone to the storage unit, but I had what I needed for the time being: my work chair, my kitchen essentials, some books and a bag of clothes. It was funny, but not being surrounded by familiar things made it easier: more like being on holiday for a few weeks than rudely ejected from my own life.

Besides, there was enough immediate admin to distract me from darker thoughts – stopping redirections, cancelling utilities, and so on – and when my phone rang at half-five, I was surprised to see how late it had got.

'Beth?' It was Jackie.

I sat up straighter on the sofa. 'Hello!'

'Beth, I've just had a call from Mum – she says you've moved into the coach house? Is that right?'

'Um, yes?' The way she said it made me wonder if there was a right and a wrong answer. 'Just for a few weeks, until this new flat is available. It's incredibly kind of her, I don't know what I'd have done otherwise.'

'Oh! OK.' Jackie sounded wrongfooted. Hadn't Martine discussed it with her first?

'If she called you asking you to move some of your boxes there's absolutely no rush,' I added, in case she was feeling aggrieved about that. 'I've moved them downstairs but I can bring them back up when I move out.'

'No, it's fine, they've been there thirty-odd years, I can't say I've needed whatever's in them. I'll come round soon and get them out of your way. It would be good to have, um . . . a chat with you, in any case.'

I braced. About what? Fraser? Had he got married? Would he mind me being here?

'It's just that . . .' She seemed to be struggling for the right words. 'Look, it's only fair that you know – Mum's amazing for her age, don't get me wrong, but she's not quite as hale and hearty as she makes out. We're all worried that house is getting too much for her. I mean, it *is* too much for her. It's ridiculous, it was too big for her and Dad, but she refuses to discuss any help. And I'm not sure she's always completely aware of—' She stopped herself. 'I'll be honest, Beth, after that fall last week I tried to persuade her *again* to think about somewhere more manageable, but she simply won't accept she's not fifty anymore.'

I murmured sympathetically, but was privately rooting for Martine here; Coleridge Drive was a dream home. You'd have had to drag me out of it too.

'So while it *is* very kind of her to let you camp out there,' she went on, 'I have to warn you that it's probably one of her little schemes. I asked her what would happen if she fell down the stairs, whether she was happy knowing help wasn't exactly at the bottom of the garden.' Jackie let out a frustrated breath. 'And now – conveniently – there *is* help at the bottom of the garden. You! I'm sorry, Beth. You know what Mum can be like. I don't want you to get dragged into one of our ridiculous family mind games.'

Honestly? Quite apart from the fact that it solved my housing problem, it was actually almost heartwarming to be dragged into the Henderson family's goings-on. Admittedly, it took a tiny bit of shine off Martine's generous offer, but part of me was flattered that she trusted me enough to involve me in her plan. After all, hadn't she said she didn't want just anyone renting the garage flat?

'I appreciate you telling me that,' I said, 'but she's doing me a huge favour, and it shouldn't be for too long. I'm happy to keep a discreet eye on her, if it puts your mind at rest?'

'Would you?' Jackie sounded weary. 'I *worry* about Mum, but I can't be in ten different places at once. I suggested we have a look at a lovely assisted living place just up the road and you'd think I'd asked her for her funeral plans.'

'It must be hard, being here without your dad.'

'Yes.' A sigh of remorse. 'Yes, of course it is. They were such a pair of bookends, Mum and Dad. But part of the reason he sold the business was so they wouldn't have any worries about decent care when they needed it, and—' She stopped. 'Sorry, you don't need to know all this. We must have a coffee some time, catch up!'

'I'd love that.' I wasn't sure if Jackie meant it, but it felt nice to be asked.

We said our goodbyes, and I'd nearly put the phone down when Jackie said something I didn't quite catch.

'Sorry?'

'I said, watch out for the servant's bell.'

'The what?'

She laughed. 'Sorry, that's just me being mean. Probably doesn't even work anymore. Take care!'

I'd gone to bed, and was nearly asleep when I heard something ringing, a shrill peal like an old-fashioned telephone. It was coming from the sitting room but I definitely hadn't seen a phone in there.

For a second, I thought I was dreaming but Tomsk was already sitting up in his basket, growling low under his breath. The whites of his eyes gleamed in the dark as he scanned the darkened room.

I sat up, heart hammering. Was this place haunted? Was that what Jackie had meant? Did their au pairs complain of a ghostly bell waking them? Surely that would have been part of the family folklore if so?

The phantom telephone carried on ringing. I swung my legs out of bed, and followed the sound. Where was it coming from?

And then I saw it, hidden at an angle on the wall by the window: an old 1970s handset like the one in the kitchen of the main house. Tentatively, I lifted it, bracing myself for the crackle of static (I listened to a lot of podcasts about ghosts).

'Hello? Hello?' said a very real voice.

'Martine?'

'Beth! Did I wake you?'

'No,' I lied.

There was a clock on the wall: it was quarter to one. I had no idea Martine kept such late hours; she'd always gone to bed at ten whenever Fraser and I visited. I leaned to one side to see out of the window and saw two long windows illuminated upstairs in the main house, elegant rectangles of dull gold against the darkness.

'I just wanted to see if this still worked. I thought it might have been disconnected but obviously not! We found it so handy for the au pairs, so we didn't have to be running up and down the garden to get them.'

I wondered if that had happened a lot.

'Did you need something?' I asked.

'No, no, I just wanted to check you were settled in, had hot water and so on.'

'Yes, everything's fine, thank you.' Did Martine *know* it was nearly one in the morning?

'Wonderful. Do shout if you need anything.'

'I will! And of course, give me a ring if *you* need anything,' I said, without thinking.

'So kind of you,' said Martine. 'Goodnight, Beth!'

And she hung up.

I stood there in the darkness, staring at my bare feet in a pool of moonlight on the parquet floor.

That was weird, I thought. If this was a fairytale, I'd basically spoken the words that made me staff, just like the chauffeur, the housekeeper and all the au pairs.

Don't be so dramatic, I told myself, and went back to bed.

Chapter five

Lewis Levison's initial impressions of Rosemount Court Residential Home were not favourable.

First, he noted the lawns hadn't been mown in some time, and the rose bushes that should have offered an uplifting welcome to residents and visitors alike were underfed and unpruned. It was late March, but even so, Lewis would have had daffodils in the beds, at the very least. Tulips too: red and yellow, for optimum cheeriness.

Second, there were five black wheelie bins visible by the imposing stone porch, two of them overflowing with cardboard, which should have been in the green recycling bin.

And third, an elderly lady in a wheelchair was being forcibly wheeled down the drive by her middle-aged son and his wife, who were engaged in a furious argument with three nurses and a woman of a similar age in a pink suit, while several residents watched on from upstairs windows. And the windows needed a good clean.

Fortunately, none of the residents were filming it on mobile phones, Lewis thought. Small mercies.

He pulled out the small notebook and integrated pen that he carried everywhere with him from the pocket on the back of his Lycra cycling shorts, and wrote down: *rose bushes, spring colour, bins, window cleaner?*

This wasn't how he'd planned to introduce himself to his new staff, but since the confrontation showed signs of boiling over, he propped his bicycle against what had once been a half-barrel of geraniums (but which now contained weeds and discarded vapes), unclipped his cycle helmet and walked towards the scene, ruffling his thick brown hair back up where the helmet had flattened it into a second under-helmet.

The participants were too fiercely engaged to notice Lewis's approach, even with his cleated shoes clicking on the tarmac.

'I'm taking my mother home now, and you can expect to hear from my solicitor regarding the fees by the end of the day,' roared the man. His eyes bulged with indignation. 'It's appalling. Absolutely appalling.'

'Appalling,' agreed his wife.

The old lady in the chair shifted her eyes from her son to the nurse, then on to another nurse, then back down to her lap. Lewis thought she looked embarrassed, not maltreated.

'Mr Stafford, please. I hear what you're saying, but can we not discuss this in a more . . .' stammered the woman in the suit.

Was this the temporary manager? The suit looked as if it had been borrowed from a much bigger person, or picked up in a hurry from a charity shop; the sleeves were too long for the petite woman inside, and the skirt had washed out two shades lighter than the jacket. The name badge on the lapel said PAMELA WOODWARD, jotted in hasty capitals that got smaller as they went on, to fit in all of Woodward. This woman looked more like someone who'd escaped from a conference than the competent captain of a flagship retirement home.

Lewis checked himself. He couldn't be critical of the suit. Pamela Woodward was doing her best to project authority, and it was better than the awful 'team sweatshirts' in the last home he'd had to overhaul for his boss, Eric. Pamela clearly wasn't a suit person, but she was trying and that was half the battle, in Lewis's opinion.

'There's nothing to discuss! I've seen enough with my own eyes,' Mr Stafford went on theatrically. 'This place is a shambles. A shambles! My poor mother has told me things that make me ashamed we ever considered letting her live here.'

'Terrible things!' echoed Mrs Stafford the younger. 'Terrible!'

Pamela Woodward seemed on the verge of tears. Her round face was flushed a painful crimson, which didn't go well with her outfit, and she kept pushing her glasses back up her nose with her forefinger. 'I can assure you that we are aware of the problems, Mr Stafford, well aware, and there is a plan in place to—'

But Mr Stafford wasn't finished. 'My mother tells me that she's seen rats in her room! And that two of her neighbours have been hospitalised with food poisoning in the last week alone! And that another resident was trapped in their own bathroom for nearly twenty-four hours before any of the nurses even noticed!'

There was a sharp intake of breath from all three nurses. 'Eunice!' said one reproachfully. 'You never told—'

Mr Stafford wheeled on the nurse. 'Are you calling my mother a liar?'

Mrs Stafford crouched by her wheelchair, at eye level with her mother-in-law. 'Eunice. You didn't tell me about the rats!'

Eunice Stafford's eyes went from side to side, then she sighed deeply and closed them, as if too exhausted to speak.

Mr Stafford pointed at her, with a sharp 'see?' look towards Pamela Woodward. 'I will be seeking legal redress for the fees we've already paid.'

Lewis had seen quite enough himself. He had a busy day ahead and, besides, more faces were gathering at the windows, goggling at the spectacle below.

The Staffords and the staff been too preoccupied squabbling to acknowledge his approach – probably assuming he was a visitor – but now he stepped forward, projecting the business confidence for which he had won several awards in the care industry.

'Good morning, everyone. Mr Stafford? Mrs Stafford?' He held out his hand and the Staffords were too confused to do anything but shake it. 'My name is Lewis Levison, I'm the performance consultant for Acorn Care Homes. I'm so sorry to hear about these experiences your mother has had. Quite inexcusable. However, as Ms Woodward says, there is indeed an ongoing review in place to address these concerns, and I'd be delighted to set your minds at rest regarding Mrs Stafford's care plan – perhaps in more congenial surrounds?'

He gestured towards the house, and smiled.

The Staffords – and the three nurses and Pamela Woodward – blinked.

Lewis smiled back.

He knew they were taking a moment to reconcile his unexpected appearance (the long legs and the sturdy chest clearly demarcated in his cycling gear, the red ring around his forehead where his cycle helmet had been, the brisk business-like voice coming out of the body of a weekend triathlete) with the confident way he'd taken control of the situation. And his moustache. Lewis's lavish moustache was a multitasker: it drew attention, it conveyed authority, it broke the ice, it gave his boyish face a focus, it hid his natural shyness. It also, he hoped, made him look older than thirty-eight, which is what he was. For some reason, despite his track record and years of experience, no one had taken him seriously until he grew the moustache, as if a man of his tender years couldn't be driven by a lifelong mission to improve elderly care.

It had been his grandfather who'd advised him to grow the moustache. Granda Levison had flown Lancasters over occupied France the summer after he'd sat his Higher School Certificate. A thick moustache, he'd told Lewis, had somehow strengthened his spine.

'Ms Woodward?' He turned his smile towards the woman in the suit, who nodded, stunned. 'We can arrange some tea and biscuits?'

'Of course,' she said, suddenly on more solid ground. 'We also have coffee, and homemade pastries?'

According to Lewis's briefing notes, emailed to him over the weekend by his PA Freda, Pamela Woodward had been the housekeeper before her unexpected promotion to acting manager.

Mrs Stafford appeared swayed by the offer of pastries, but her husband put a hand out to stop her turning back, and fixed Lewis with a beady glare.

'I only have one question. Has this home, or has it not, failed the most recent CQC inspection? And,' he added swiftly, as Lewis opened his mouth to reply, 'was that investigation, or was that investigation not, triggered by a series of shocking reports in the local paper, including some revelations from a whistleblower on the staff?'

There was a muted gasp from one of the nurses.

'Yes,' said Lewis. He didn't believe in fudging big issues. You had to face them. 'Yes, I'm sorry to report that Rosemount failed a recent inspection. And yes, you're also correct that the local paper has taken a keen interest in the matter. However, the reason I'm here is because Acorn Care Homes takes any dip in our care provision very seriously. I've been tasked to ensure that by the time the inspectors return to repeat their assessment, Rosemount will have become the first choice for anyone thinking of moving into supported accommodation within a hundred-mile radius.'

'You're going to do that?' Mr Stafford adopted a semi-sneer which Lewis ignored.

'I have done exactly that several times before.' He was being modest, but accepted that was probably going to be lost on his current audience. 'And I will do it here.'

The Staffords stared at him, as did Pamela Woodward and the nurses. Out of the corner of his eye – Lewis wasn't going to risk losing the moment by turning his head – he was aware of yet more residents gathering at the upstairs windows. It was like an advent calendar of old people.

He made a mental note to get the windows checked for safety catches and bars. It wouldn't do to have someone falling out.

Finally, Eunice Stafford spoke, in a reluctant tone. 'I suppose I could manage a *small* pastry.'

'No, mother, we're going home,' announced Mr Stafford.

'Why don't we have a pastry first,' the younger Mrs Stafford piped up. 'For the journey? It'll save us stopping on the way. You know how much service stations charge for a croissant.'

'They're extortionate,' agreed Lewis. 'Ms Woodward, why don't you go and expedite some tea and pastries, while I assist Mr Stafford with his mother?'

And before Mr Stafford had a chance to argue Lewis had swivelled Eunice Stafford's chair in one dynamic motion towards Rosemount, and was propelling her back towards the house faster than she'd ever been pushed, the nurses following behind at a quick march.

'Wheee,' said Eunice, under her breath, without meaning to, as if the morning had taken an unexpectedly exciting turn.

Lewis's plan had been to use the twenty-mile cycle ride from his rental house to circle the country lanes around Rosemount Court, taking in the locale while processing his plan of action, then shower in the staff quarters in order to assess those facilities, then change into the suit he'd had couriered to his new office the previous day, and begin his overhauling.

He wasn't going to let the small matter of a resident moving out derail that. Not when so many new strategies had occurred to him as his long, powerful legs pumped both blood and good ideas to his brain.

However, now he was here, the scale of the task in front of him was more daunting than he'd realised. Mr Stafford hadn't been wrong, thought Lewis, as he briskly towelled himself down with a threadbare apricot towel that could have been left over from the establishment's boarding school incarnation, circa 1963–81. (PA Freda provided thorough briefing notes.) The place *was* a shambles. As he'd passed unloved rooms and messy nurses' stations en route to the showers, Lewis's business brain had begun its background whir of calculations and causation, yet the overriding impression he got wasn't financial, but emotional: he was struck by a feeling of intense sadness.

Sadness hung in the corridors, as noticeable as the cobwebs in the corners and the dust shading the detail on the skirting boards. It was as physical as the greenish odour of boiling vegetables and bacon fat, or the powdery spots of mould speckling the window frames; this general sense that once this building had been grand and proud, and now it was filled with . . . well, something that wasn't grand or proud any longer. It was falling apart, decaying with hopelessness.

Lewis was thrown by how much this upset him. He normally strode into a premises and began reorganising it from the reception up, in the same way a naturally neat person instinctively tidies a room as they pass, collecting empty coffee mugs and straightening cushions like a brisk wind blowing through. But the sadness in Rosemount tripped him off balance.

This was going to be a much bigger job than it looked on paper, he conceded, staring at his reflection in the staff bathroom mirror as he brushed his thick hair back into its neat half-quiff.

Lewis then made a mental note to make a literal note in his book about the staff showers, which were not completely clean and definitely not hot enough.

Once dried off, he dressed himself in his work uniform: white shirt, pressed; grey suit, freshly dry-cleaned; black shoes, polished, and his lucky tie, which had belonged to his other grandfather. He polished his glasses and neatened his moustache, and with one last adjustment of his tie in the age-spotted mirror over the basin – an ornate gilt mirror that had perhaps once hung in an upstairs room, instead of this echoing basement area – Lewis frowned at his reflection, reminded himself out loud that he was more than up to the task in hand, and headed upstairs to the staff meeting he'd called for nine o'clock.

'I want to be honest with you from the start: we need to make significant changes, if Rosemount is going to deliver at the level I believe it can. Not many of those changes will be easy. But I'm confident that once we've *made* those changes, everyone will feel the benefit, not just the residents who rely on us. I believe that, before you know it, you'll be bouncing into work with a spring in your step because this beautiful home will be the best place to work in the whole county.'

Lewis looked around the dining room where the staff (minus those engaged in essential duties) had assembled to hear the worst. It was obvious from the expressions – which ranged from defensive, to exhausted, to curious – that the rumour mill had been churning 24/7 since the unexpected but inevitable departure of David Rigg, the man even the senior management team were calling something unrepeatable.

'Is anyone going to tell us what happened to David?' The nurse at the back of the room had her arms crossed over her narrow chest, already defiant. 'He was sacked, right?'

'David left for personal reasons, which I'm unable to go into right now.'

The owner of Acorn Care Homes, Eric Alexander, was a fair man, and he had allowed David to invent an unprovable medical reason for his 'resignation'.

But he'd definitely been sacked. Decisions were still ongoing about whether he'd be arrested or not. The financial director had taken four days off to go through the accounts, and wasn't answering his phone.

The nurse turned to her neighbour and muttered something Lewis didn't catch, but her expression told him that she didn't believe that for a moment. He made a mental note of her name badge: Ellie. She was clearly a smart cookie. One to get onside.

He moved on smoothly. 'But what I want to say to you is this: as of today, things *have already changed* for the better. This report was hard reading, but it's a turning point for Rosemount. By taking an honest look at the problems it's raised, we're already on our way back up. What's happened has happened, but there's always something we can learn from it. We can only improve as a team, and that's what I'm here to do – to turn us into a team. From the moment each of us walks in each morning, we need to ask ourselves: is this somewhere I'd be happy for my mum to live? My dad? My grandparents? Is it somewhere *I'd* want to live? And if not, what can I do to make it better?'

He let his gaze drift across the room. The unhappiness of the building had infected the staff; they looked so miserable. Tired and uninspired. Three carers had handed in their notice and walked out before the meeting even started.

'Little changes,' he said. 'Lead to big changes.'

Ellie rolled her eyes. As did four other nurses.

It was the first thing they'd done as a team.

Lewis planned to speak to every member of the staff in turn, one by one, to find out more about who they were, what motivated them, but most importantly, what the real problems were in Rosemount. You found out more that way. Especially if some of the problems involved people right there in the group meeting – and his instincts had already identified a couple of weeds in the flowerbed.

None of his sit-downs would last more than ten minutes – Lewis could gather what he needed to know in under five – and he'd requested the weekly rota ahead of time, so Freda could work out a schedule that was convenient for everyone, and so he could winnow out those making up excuses for not attending.

Pamela Woodward was first on his list, and she was there on the dot of her assigned time.

'I didn't ask to be made interim manager,' she said, before she'd even sat down.

'But thank you for stepping up to the task,' he said. 'That shows oomph.'

'And I never liked David,' she added, biting her lip as she spoke. 'I didn't like the way he talked to the nurses, especially the ones who don't have English as their first language. He used to mutter.'

'He muttered?' echoed Lewis.

'I was always told it was rude to mutter. And of course, our deaf residents didn't appreciate that either. None of us appreciated it, to be honest. You always left the room wondering what he'd said. David always had to have the last word. Even if he muttered it.'

Lewis sat back in his chair and regarded Pamela.

She responded by sitting up in hers, her back straight, her lips folded inward like a child braced for a telling-off. She had a kind face, soft and anxious, and dark mahogany hair tipped with red highlights, cut into a spiky style that didn't seem to fit her personality.

Lewis wondered if the hair was an attempt to project a different Pam to the world. Like his moustache.

'Pamela – is that what you like to be called? Or Ms Woodward?'

'Pam's fine.'

'Pam.' Lewis smiled. 'Let's draw a line under David. He had his strengths but this particular role wasn't the best match for his skillset. Our focus now is Rosemount. I've got a checklist covering every official issue we need to address.' He tapped the file in front of him. 'Those boxes *will* be ticked. Make no mistake about it. That CQC inspector won't recognise this place when he comes back. But what's going to transform Rosemount isn't box-ticking, but understanding our people.'

'People,' repeated Pam cautiously. 'The residents?'

'All of us.' Lewis spread out his hands. 'Cleaners, cooks, nurses, carers, volunteers, managers. I'm interested in making everyone feel like a vital cog in our machine. I mean, there's no point serving a spectacular lunch if there are cobwebs in the dining room, is there?'

Immediately, Pam's gaze flicked up to the corners of the room.

There were no cobwebs in Lewis's office. Not now, anyway. He'd made sure he'd removed them before the meeting. There was no point in making Pam feel even worse than she already did; besides, he knew that *she* would know he'd removed the cobwebs.

'You're a housekeeper, you're the person who knows how this machine runs best,' he said. 'In your opinion, what do you think are the three most important things that need to be fixed first?'

Pam shifted in her seat. 'Mr Levison . . .'

'Lewis, please.'

'Um, Lewis, before we start, I didn't know Eunice Stafford's son was going to do what he did this morning. I would have *done* something. I'm mortified, first impression you got of us was that . . . scene. I'm getting hot flushes thinking about it.'

Lewis sipped his tea. He liked the fact that Pam had brought out the VIP cups and saucers with the company crest, a winged gold acorn. He liked the fact that she wanted to get on the front foot with an apology, not excuses. 'Why do you think Mrs Stafford wanted to leave?'

'I'm not sure she does. I mean, she's threatened to often enough, but that's who Eunice is. She *likes* a grumble. Keeps her mind active. She's always writing to the local paper – not about us, but complaining about litter and taxes and what not.' Pam pursed her lips. 'Her son's the problem, always finding fault – room's too hot, room's not hot enough, food's repetitive, spices upset his mum's digestion. Everything he complains about, we fix, but I think in his case . . .' She glanced downwards. 'I think he's looking for a discount. I think he was going to use the scandal of the inspection to negotiate a better rate. He's not the quickest when it comes to settling up.'

'I see,' said Lewis.

Her small hand flew to her mouth. 'Should that be confidential?'

'You can tell me anything, Pam,' said Lewis.

Because he'd find out anyway. Not that she needed to know that just yet.

He topped up her tea, and decided to reset the conversation. 'Maybe we should start with something positive instead. What's your *favourite* thing about working here?'

Lewis was all about the positives. Negativity worked hard enough without his encouragement.

The other interviews were equally revealing.

In the space of an afternoon, Lewis learned that the agency cleaners were late, inefficient and glued to their phones (from Ellie, the eye-rolling nurse); that there were regular complaints about boring, bland food (Basia, another nurse), the constant staff turnover was 'a nightmare' (Toni, and Roxana, both care staff), and general 'attitude' (too many people to list).

He was relieved to hear there were none of the upsetting issues he'd encountered in other places, harrowing tales of abusive carers, or disturbed residents with inadequate or incorrect diagnoses, but the combination of petty problems and the glee with which the staff laid into each other gave Lewis a headache. Worst of all was that rumour of a whistleblower on the staff.

But he soldiered on, listening, querying, pretending to write things down to give people time to ramble, inevitably letting slip the nugget they weren't going to reveal at first. He knew the staff were wary of him, but that was normal.

Wherever he could, Lewis tried to give out small wins, as with Kemi, one of the care team managers, who asked him, outright, 'Are you here to shut this place down?'

'No, I'm here to raise it up.'

She hoisted an eyebrow, unimpressed. 'You know David put his personal laundry through the main wash house?'

'I did not.'

'The things that would go through that dryer.' She rolled her eyes, then stared at Lewis. 'You not going to write that down?'

If Lewis had been writing down every single one of David's misdemeanours he would have run out of paper in his notebook before lunchtime.

'No,' he said.

'Why not?'

'Because David's gone.' Lewis wished he had a pound for every time he'd said that too. 'Unless you feel it should be a staff perk? Discounted laundry?'

Kemi was about to snort, but changed her mind. 'That would not be a bad idea.'

Lewis wrote down: monthly laundry tokens.

'You've been a carer here for five years, Kemi,' he said. 'What do you feel are the three things we should focus on, to make this a happier place?'

'What? Me? You're asking me?'

'You spend the most time with the residents. You know what they complain about, what they enjoy.'

Kemi considered for a moment. 'They like to talk. Some of them. Some of them don't, and that is fine with me. They like things to be clean. They like bingo, even if there's no prizes.'

Lewis wrote down bingo, cleaning, talking. Talking was high on his own plan.

'And the staff also like to talk.'

He looked up. Kemi was giving him a beady look.

'We like to feel listened to. David never listened to anything we said.'

'I hear you,' said Lewis. 'I want you to feel heard.'

'Nuh-uh. No jargon. Please.' She raised a hand as if stopping invisible traffic. 'Do not come here with your management "I see you" and "I hear you". We need a pay rise, more staff and a better rota. Not a lot of words.'

Lewis liked Kemi. She was straightforward, and upfront. Her uniform was spotless and she wore shoes that suggested she expected to spend a lot of time on her feet. She was here to work, and he respected that.

'Understood. If you think of anything else, please email me or leave a suggestion in the box by my door. Would you send in Helenka, please?'

Only two more today, he told himself, and then he'd let the cycle ride home process the findings.

Chapter six

It's fair to say that my boss Allen was a father figure to me. He was the kind of patient, encouraging, reliable father I'd have liked, instead of the brooding bully Mum had landed me with. Dad being a largely absent parent had once been a source of pain for me, but now, I'm not sorry to say, it was a relief.

Allen was your classic business accountant who'd been 'about fifty-ish' since his early thirties, and he'd been nothing but supportive since I'd started at Jacobs' as his assistant. He had that Good Dad knack of letting me get on with things myself without too much micromanagement, but he intervened on my behalf when necessary. On the rare occasions when he did feel moved to dole out advice, it usually meant I was in danger of seriously messing up, which was why this 'out of office' meeting was giving me major anxiety vibes.

'Thanks for trekking out here to see me,' he said, when I found him in the golf-club lounge, wearing exactly the kind of golfing outfit I expected him to own, i.e., a polyester ensemble that looked cheap but probably cost a small fortune.

'Not at all,' I said. 'This is just up the road from me now.'

Being in the middle of so much green countryside was still a novelty. I'd only been in Longhampton five days, and I'd already downloaded an app that identified birdsong and bought some wellies. Tomsk was snoring in the back of the car, preparing to investigate the nearby Forestry Commission woodland for his lunchtime walk. He'd spent hours decoding the scent messages in Martine's garden, the canal walk and the park, so a forest full of squirrels and foxes would be heaven. He loved his new home. His tail even wagged in his sleep, which made me emotional.

'So, are you settled in yet?' Allen asked, waving at the waiter for more coffee. 'It was this weekend, wasn't it? The big move?'

'Ah no. Slight change of plan.' I explained yet again about the contract catastrophe – abridged version because even I was sick of it – finishing up by saying I was temporarily staying at Fraser's mother's house.

Allen choked on his biscuit.

I wasn't the sort of person who Brought Their Whole Self to Work, far from it. I only brought my Work Self to Work. Now, of course, I didn't even do that. But I'd been at Jacobs' since I graduated, and obviously, in the olden days when office parties were still a thing, Fraser had come to one or two, so I'd introduced him to my colleagues. That was as far as I wanted my private life to mix with office life, thank you. Unfortunately, I'd had to book some annual leave for the Paris ultimatum weekend, and when Harriet, the office manager who'd never seen a date on the calendar that couldn't be improved with helium balloons, had asked me if I was going somewhere nice, I'd stupidly told her that Fraser and I were having a surprise minibreak. She asked, head tilting eagerly, if it was a *special occasion*, and I said, Well, I certainly *hope* so.

(I know. Reckless. But I was so excited, and Mali, Poppy and Sophie had convinced me I'd be coming back an engaged woman.)

When I *did* come back on Monday morning, newly single and wearing sunglasses to hide my alarmingly tear-swollen eyes, it was to a desk covered in confetti and a helium love heart tied to my phone. Harriet was hovering in the kitchen with a Congratulations on Your Engagement cake which Allen had to grab from her, and stuff in his filing cabinet until I'd slunk off home.

I wish it had ended there, but it didn't. The whispers that stop when you enter the kitchen went on for weeks, as did the confetti I kept finding in my desk, and the tilty-head 'how's it going?' sad-faces. The trouble about being the focus of office gossip is that you stay the focus until someone is done for drink-driving or has an affair. And we were a firm of extremely respectable accountants, so as you can imagine, I was 'poor Beth' for so long it almost became my official name.

Anyway, I mention this only to give Allen's reaction some context. Back then, he'd sent me out of the office to do a three-day onsite audit, and spoken firmly to Harriet about 'professional boundaries'; now, he said, in a neutral tone, 'Your ex, Fraser? *His* mother?'

'Yes. Martine.'

He looked pained. 'You should have said, we've got a couple of clients who have short-term lets round here. Want me to give them a ring? I'm sure I could pull in a favour.'

'It's just temporary!' I said breezily. 'I've got somewhere lined up in a few weeks. All under control.'

'Well, you only have to say the word.' Allen sat back on the sofa, and gazed out at the view of the car park and the putting green as if steeling himself for the main event. 'Speaking of fresh starts, that brings us rather neatly on to what I wanted to talk to you about.'

I nodded, and braced. I knew what was coming.

I'd been waiting for Allen to tackle my ongoing absence for months. There was nothing specific in my contract about having to be in the office (I'd checked) but it had been drawn up in the days before hybrid working was a thing.

It wasn't as if I wasn't *ever* going to go back. But at a really basic level, none of my old work wardrobe fitted, and what was the point in spending hundreds of pounds on new clothes when I wasn't going to be this size much longer? If I put my mind to it, I could probably drop a dress size in, what? A month or so? It was just that I felt weirdly nauseous and panicky when I thought about setting foot in the office again, seeing people look me up and down, whispering in the kitchen. You'd think that would be a diet aid, but it was the kind of sick feeling that made me put another round of toast in the toaster.

'Keep this between ourselves for the moment,' said Allen, 'but I'm stepping back in a few months' time.'

What? I hadn't expected it to be about *Allen*. 'Are you taking early retirement?'

'No, I'm launching a business – teaching sign language to parents and grandparents.'

My eyebrows shot up. 'Oh.'

Allen beamed, pleased to have surprised me. 'Yes, our grandson is deaf, and I thought, Why aren't there any classes for grandparents like us to go to? And signing has benefits for hearing children too, of course. The company's already up and running, Devora's done the teaching qualifications, we're all set!'

'Wow,' I said. 'That's . . . what a brilliant thing to do.'

'Well. It's time for a change. I've been telling people the same things about tax thresholds and VAT since I was twenty-one. There's only so long you can do that. And I've registered for a film extras agency,' he added. 'Apparently I've got a very medieval face.'

He did too. Allen helpfully offered me a demonstration gurn, and now I looked closer, you could have put him on the side of a cathedral.

This was the most random conversation we'd had in the thirteen years we'd been working together. Allen seemed almost relaxed, a state I'd rarely seen him in.

'What brought this on? If you don't mind me asking?'

The cheeriness dimmed a notch. 'Sad, really. A couple of my friends have had serious health problems lately. I'm not an old man, but you get to the point where you realise you don't have an infinite number of days left. I've got a decent pension, Devora and I are comfortable – time to let someone else tear their hair out over HMRC.'

Did I mention that Allen was bald? He'd had a tough time with HMRC.

'So, what this means for you,' he went on – back to his tax-advising voice, 'is that there's going to be some changes at Jacobs'. Strictly off the record, you understand,' he added, gesturing at the leather easy chairs and glass tables around us. 'Golf club rules, and all that.'

This was the closest I'd ever got to one of those Boys' Club Conversations On the Golf Course. I supposed I should be honoured.

I gave a quick Brownie Guide salute. 'Understood.'

'I would *strongly advise* you to spend some time in the office between now and then.' Allen fixed me with a meaningful look. 'I'm not going to ask why you've stopped coming in, and I'm not allowed to say that anyone has noticed, but someone asked me last week if you'd left. And you should also know that there will be a new head of HR starting in a few weeks, because Lisa is also leaving – and before you ask, I have no idea why, she's been very clear that she's not answering questions, so it must be juicy – so I don't know what the score will be there. Christian will be taking over my role. He's got big plans for the business, which is why we brought him in, and he's already tabled a senior management discussion about five-year strategies.' He took a deep breath. 'Off the record, Christian's planning to interview everyone and reassess their strengths and weaknesses, and *redeploy accordingly*.'

This sounded less good. 'Is that a fancy way of saying he's going to be sacking people?'

'I don't know that for sure yet. But there's been discussion around streamlining the team.'

Which meant yes. I felt cold.

'More to the point, Christian has particular views about working from home,' Allen warned me. 'He's been vocal about getting everyone back into the office to build a high-performing team ethos.'

'Allen, we're accountants. We're not rowing a boat across the Atlantic. It makes no difference whether I'm filing tax returns at home or five feet away from Christian's desk.'

'I know that. You've been extremely productive from home, and you've always had excellent client feedback.' Allen shrugged helplessly. 'All I'm saying is, don't let yourself get sidelined. *I* know how good you are for us, but Christian doesn't. I'll be making recommendations, obviously, but it's no substitute for letting him realise your capability for himself.'

I stared at the board of club captains, starting back in 1887 (men) and 2001 (ladies). Someone called M.R. O'Shaughnessy had hogged the captaincy for most of the post-war era. I knew I should say something but I could feel the strange, stiff resistance building up in me, like those mythological women who turned themselves into trees to avoid being interfered with by rampaging gods.

I reached out and took a chocolate chip cookie from the plate next to the silver coffee pot. The cookie I'd been successfully ignoring up until now.

'Lisa would go mad if she could hear me saying this, but what the hell,' Allen went on, 'if you're going to move up the ladder, Beth, now's the time. When your pal Natasha was promoted, I did wonder if that might have encouraged you to push for a bigger role yourself, but . . .' He trailed off, conscious that he'd galloped halfway across an HR minefield, but manfully ploughed on. 'I sometimes wonder if I should have done more to help progress your development. I'm sorry we never got our mentoring lunches up and running again properly after lockdown – I felt they were helpful. Weren't they?'

I nodded.

He was framing it in appropriately mentoring terms, but finally the concerned dad in Allen burst through his professional reserve.

'Beth, is there something in the office that's stopping you from coming in? Because if there is, for Pete's sake *tell me*, while I'm still in a position to help.'

I bit my lip.

I wished he hadn't brought Natasha into this. Natasha was definitely not 'my pal'.

Natasha Sinfield had joined the firm a year after me, and for a while we'd been good mates – we were the two youngest members of staff, both young female graduates in a mostly middle-aged male team, and we gravitated together, drinks after work, sandwiches from the deli near the office, that sort of thing. But slowly I'd noticed an edge to her. She was competitive. She hacked into the system and found out how much everyone was getting paid, then leveraged a pay rise. She made jokes that weren't quite jokes when you thought about them later.

Natasha was still really sweet towards me, but something was slightly off, and once I'd noticed, I couldn't un-notice. I'd find her in the kitchen chatting to colleagues, and the conversation would stop when I'd walk in; after Fraser and I split up, she hugged me in front of everyone, and said she'd told Harriet not to give me the collection card for Sophie's baby shower 'in case it upset you'. She'd hand me a big slice of whatever office celebration cake Harriet had left in the kitchen, but then pat her own flat stomach and said, 'Not for me, it's so hard to lose weight once you're over thirty, isn't it?'

It wasn't anything specific I could put my finger on; it just made me feel unsure of my own reactions, a horrible sinking-into-quicksand sensation that I got high up in my chest every time I got in the car to drive to work. Days when I didn't go in felt so much easier. Days when I was just myself over the phone to clients.

But I didn't want to say that to Allen. I'd sound jealous of Natasha who was, undoubtedly, an excellent accountant, ambitious, a natural networker. It wasn't her fault my life had got stuck; that was on me.

'I don't want to intrude, but after all these years . . . If there's something I could offer advice on, I'd like to think you could trust me?' Allen continued. 'I'd like to step back knowing you're set on the right track.'

He risked a hopeful smile and if I could have come out with a coherent explanation as to why the prospect of going into the office, even to save my own job, filled me with horror, I think I might have done. But I couldn't articulate it, even to myself, and then I saw a familiar car pulling up outside which distracted me completely.

Eddie Davidson, head of compliance, drove an old London black cab, the only one in the area. The office opinion was that he only had it because it gave him 'a fun fact about yourself that no one knows!' to use in interviews, in the absence of any other fun facts.

'Are you expecting anyone?' I asked.

'Yes, I'm speaking to a couple of people, off the record.' Allen tapped his nose. He seemed to be relishing behaving in such a cloak-and-dagger fashion. It was most unlike him. This, clearly, was the magic of a midlife career change. I wished he'd tell me how to do it.

'Eddie?'

'At eleven o'clock, yes.'

'Well, he's early.' I started to gather up my stuff. I didn't want to see Eddie, or rather, I didn't want him to see me. Allen was the sort of person who genuinely wouldn't notice I'd gone up three dress sizes since I last saw him, but Eddie wasn't. He'd had a warning about making personal comments to a couple of temps (Natasha had hacked into the HR emails, and told me the full extent of his bitchiness, and also his punishment; she'd pulled a very sad, but not totally convincing, face).

'I'll skedaddle before he sees me,' I said, pretending it was for Allen's benefit, not mine. 'Thanks for the coffee!'

'There'll be an email in the next couple of weeks, but Christian will start informal interviews by the start of next month.' Allen gave me another warning look. 'Get everything up to date, create some projects. He's big on prospecting projects for clients. Getting us into management support. You know the type of stuff people like him get hot and bothered about.'

People like him, eh? If Allen was relaxed enough to be throwing shade at Christian, his leaving date must be sooner than he was letting on.

'Got it,' I said, scanning the room for a different exit. There! By the bar. Brilliant.

'You don't have to dash off,' Allen was saying but I was already dashing, bumping into tables in my haste to get out, unseen, unjudged.

I sank into the driver's seat, feeling overheated and bruised by some sharp table edges.

Right on cue, Tomsk uncurled from the back and laid his big head over my shoulder. His beard was damp with sleep, and he smelled of the blanket he'd been snoring on. I used a lot of fabric conditioner to combat his natural aromas.

Life at home was simple, I thought, willing my banging heart to return to its normal rhythm.

I made a list of work for the day.

I stopped for lunch at one.

I shared a walk with my dog.

I finished the work.

I tinkered with my WIP, deleted almost everything I wrote, got happily lost in a different world where corsets hid a multitude of sins and I was in charge.

I fed myself, and my dog.

I went to bed.

I didn't have to talk to anyone I didn't want to.

If I had to go back to the office, all that would vanish in an instant.

Vertigo hit me, as if I'd just plunged down a rollercoaster, and I gripped the steering wheel until my fingers went numb.

And yet, it hadn't always been like that. Allen was right – there had been a time when I had everything mapped out: I'd be a partner around the same time as Fraser would be promoted to director of his team of internet secret squirrels, then I could have a break for children, come back part-time, then full-time . . . I'd created a spreadsheet of dates and savings and promotions, and whenever I'd felt wobbly, I pulled it up, and looked at it, and everything felt better.

Where had that Beth gone? I stared out at the golf course. Without Fraser, it didn't work. I couldn't imagine having a child with someone that wasn't him. The spreadsheet Beth was already a mother of two, whereas the real Beth hadn't moved at all. My mid-thirties had tipped into late thirties – was there even time to find someone in time to have children?

I felt sick.

My phone was ringing. I dug it out of my bag, thinking it might be Allen again, that I'd left something behind, but it was Martine.

I'd already spoken to Martine today; just after breakfast, she'd called me on the kitchen phone to remind me that it was bin day tomorrow morning 'if I needed to put out any recycling'; I'd made a note to take out her bins. We'd spoken the previous evening too, when she'd called to ask if I'd seen the full moon, which was apparently known as an Apple Blossom moon in country folklore. 'Why don't you use that as a creative writing prompt?' she'd suggested, quite perkily for someone calling at nearly midnight.

I guessed what she was doing: being in contact just enough for me to know she hadn't fallen down the stairs, so if Jackie asked, I could reassure her. But I didn't mind. And the full moon was indeed worth leaning out of the kitchen window to appreciate in its dazzling glory; it lit up the garden like a Hollywood film set.

'Hello, Martine,' I started but she cut straight across me.

'Beth! Finally!'

Finally?

'It's Martine. Did you get my messages?'

'Sorry, I've been in a meeting,' I said. 'When did you ring? Are you OK?'

I could hear her breathing hard. She was hissing too, as if she didn't want to be overheard. Where was she?

'Look, it doesn't matter, I need you to do me a favour. I'm at the old people's home on the Worcester road, and I need you to collect me as soon as you can, please.'

'Which old people's home? Why are you there?

'Rosemount Court. Oh, it's too ridiculous! I was at the hospital for a routine appointment and the transport service dropped me off here instead of taking me home. I only got out to help one of the old dears inside and when I turned round, the silly woman had left! Can you come and get me, please? As soon as possible?'

'Well . . . yes. I'm at the golf club at the moment but—'

'Oh, you angel. As soon as you can, I'd be so grateful, Beth. Thank you.'

And she hung up.

Tomsk exhaled heavily on to my shoulder, a warm biscuity resignation.

'I'm sorry,' I said, stroking his long nose as I searched on my phone for a postcode for Rosemount Court. 'I'll walk you just as soon as I've worked out what on earth's going on with our landlady.'

We weren't too far away, as it turned out, and as I drove, I checked my missed calls and messages; there were several to catch up on, including the regular monthly query from a client about whether some random personal item could be claimed 'as a business expense' (answer: no) and then Martine's first message.

'Beth? Beth?'

Her voice sounded so panicked it took me a moment to recognise her.

'Beth!' A long pause. 'Beth, are you there? Oh *dear*.'

There was a sigh of despair – fear? – that made the skin on the back of my arms creep. Then she hung up.

She'd called again, three minutes later, this time more composed but speaking in an undertone sharp with anxiety. 'Beth! It's Martine. Henderson. I need you to come here. At once.' A long pause with voices in the background. 'At once, please. I'm in . . . oh, for God's sake, where am I?'

A kindly voice, off to one side, said, 'You're in Rosemount Court, my love. Can I take you—'

'No!' Martine snapped. 'No, I don't *live* here. Excuse me!'

There was something else, a short exchange, then the message ended.

No more messages.

What on earth had happened, I wondered? And why hadn't she phoned Jackie? Why had she phoned *me*?

I shook my head. Duh. That was obvious: Jackie would probably see this as evidence that she should be *in* the home, not being rescued from it. (How true this was, I didn't want to think about.)

It was probably a simple misunderstanding, I told myself, turning on to the main road. A funny story that Martine would doubtless tell with relish at a family gathering in the near future. A family story with a small but crucial walk-on part for me.

I don't mind admitting that that gave me a little glow of happiness, a glow which dispelled any lingering gloom about the impending changes at Jacobs'.

Chapter seven

Lewis started the morning with his bike ride into work, skimming along the quiet roads and narrow lanes that circled Rosemount Court. He filled his lungs with the fresh dawn air, sharp with the scent of green leaves, and breathed out the stale thoughts inside his head, letting them go. You had to let things go. Cycling flushed away negativity better than anything else; it was the physical exertion combined with forward motion.

He freewheeled past an orchard that stretched up and over the hillside, endless lines of short trees in rows, each branch tipped with the tiny jade buds of the new crop. Every corner of the landscape was bursting with energy, changing, growing and dying, then growing again. There was something about that turning wheel of life that Lewis found comforting. Lewis's grandparents, with whom he'd spent most of his childhood, had been farmers and their matter-of-fact attitude to life and death had taught him not to be scared of death. It was *not* growing that you should be worried about. Stagnation, rot, that was worse. Dying before the wheel had turned properly, that was the worst of all.

His strong legs pumped hard as he headed up the drive to Rosemount, pushing himself to set the time he'd aim to beat over the coming weeks, and he crested the brow with a gasp of triumph. Lewis wheeled the bike round to the back of the main house, where he dug out the bunch of keys from the pouch at the back of his shorts and unlocked the dilapidated sheds that had once, when Earls of Longhampton had lavishly overstaffed the house, been manned by a squadron of gardeners, under-gardeners, lawnsmen and nurserymen. The previous evening Lewis had conducted an examination of the maintenance files; David Rigg had been paying four professional landscapers to work three afternoons a week, a cost that seemed somewhat sus, given the lawn was full of dandelions and in dire need of a mow.

The accounts could wait, but in Lewis's opinion the lawn could not. Eventually he found the ride-on mower under a pile of empty wineboxes, which bore out his theory of where the money had been going.

Fortunately, there was still petrol in the tank. Lewis had a knack with machinery and after a few attempts, he got it started and chugged out to the front lawn. It pained him that the first thing the residents saw when they got up, and the first thing their families saw when they arrived to visit, was a neglected lawn. Especially one like this, that should be magnificent, mown into stripes and edged with beds full of bright flowers. Lewis would normally have waited until after breakfast to make so much noise, but he had a full day of meetings ahead and it would annoy him, he knew, until it was done; fidgeting away in the back of his brain when he needed to concentrate on the many tasks in hand.

Lewis mowed the first straight stripe across the lawn, then turned, left space for the return journey and set off again. There was a technique to mowing stripes, a pattern you had to follow that didn't make sense until the final pass; it was satisfying. Deep down he felt a connection to the distant agricultural relation who'd spent his summers patiently guiding a heavy-footed Clydesdale up and down a field, carving thick corrugations in the soil. Lewis sometimes felt a sort of guilt that the closest he got to that sort of skilled, productive work was keeping grass short, but he reminded himself that what mattered was the act of improvement, that pride in his surroundings that made life better for everyone.

He was concentrating so hard that he wasn't aware of anything for the first ten minutes or so; the morning's cycling had thrown up plenty of ideas and focusing on the straightness of the lines allowed his brain to shuffle them into order. But when he looked up, rounding the fifth bend, he realised he was being watched from the upstairs windows: an elderly man in pale-blue pyjamas with a bald head. Lewis raised a hand in apology for the noise, but the elderly man nodded in acknowledgement and gave him a thumbs-up.

Another face appeared at the window beneath: a white-haired lady in a green jumper. She seemed curious rather than annoyed, and when Lewis gave her a friendly wave, she waved back, then tapped her watch at him crossly.

By the time he was coming into the final straight, the line that would reveal the perfect back-and-forth stripes, six spectators were observing his lawn-mowing, including Pam Woodward, who had arrived in her red Beetle and parked in the space marked Housekeeper.

She was standing there, arms crossed, watching him with a frown, as if trying to work out what he was up to. He waved at her with a smile, and she waved back uncertainly.

It would do no harm, Lewis knew, for her to return to the staff kitchen and tell them she'd seen the manager mowing the lawn. He noted that she had abandoned her pink suit and returned to a more comfortable uniform of black trousers and a short-sleeved lilac jumper, with a gold cat pendant over the top.

A window opened, and a bald man leaned out to applaud. 'Good job!'

'Thank you!' Lewis raised an acknowledging hand.

'Good job? Have you seen the time? I'm phoning the manager!' shouted the lady in the window below. 'You're meant to start after nine!'

'I'll let him know!' replied Lewis, and chugged back to the sheds.

After a quick shower and breakfast, Lewis spoke to three more carers (Shefali, Becky O and Becky Mac), Marek the chef, and Karen, the specialist matron in charge of the Memory Wing for residents with dementia.

In between noting their feedback and observations about the current state of Rosemount – most of which inevitably concerned David Rigg – he added to his expanding action plan, divided into three different timescales, and jotted down twice as many things in his personal notebook.

At eleven thirty, Lewis headed to the kitchen ostensibly to locate some fresh milk but really to familiarise himself with Rosemount's complex layout. It was a big house, full of corners and corridors, and Lewis wanted to be able to stride around it as if he always knew where he was going.

As he strode, he made notes of windows that needed repairing or carpets that were worn, and was scribbling down 'replace houseplants' when someone barrelled round the corner at some speed, and crashed into him.

'Careful!' he said automatically, and the lady spun back, staggering as if she might fall. Lewis steadied her but when she flinched, he took a polite step backwards to give her space.

He didn't recognise her from his breakfast in the dining hall, but as Pam had explained, not everyone ate in there. The woman was tall, thin and seemed extremely agitated. Panicked, almost. That panic in itself, thought Lewis, seemed to be panicking her. Everything about her appearance – her smart clothes, her silk scarf and her amber brooch, her hair set into smooth waves – was gracious and composed, but she was glancing around her in confusion, if she'd unexpectedly found herself in a strange place. Which, of course, wasn't an unusual experience in a place like Rosemount.

'Hello there! I don't believe we've met,' he said, extending a hand. 'My name's Lewis, Lewis Levison. I'm the new manager.'

'I don't *live* here!' The woman looked outraged, and glanced over his shoulder, then down the corridor opposite, as if half-expecting someone to catch her up.

Lewis didn't contradict her. Many residents had moments when they genuinely believed they were still in the houses they'd first moved to after their marriage.

A nurse – Shefali, from earlier – turned the corner with a tray of medication, and the woman visibly jumped.

'Hello again, Shefali!' said Lewis.

'Hello, Mr Levison.' She corrected herself, '*Lewis*.'

'Everything OK?'

'Everything's fine, thank you!'

They both smiled, relieved to have got each other's names right, and Shefali headed up the stairs to the Memory Wing.

Lewis turned back to the trembling woman in front of him; had she wandered down from there? 'I'm so sorry, I should know exactly who you are but . . .' He held out his hand again.

This time, an automatic response seemed to take over, and she shook his hand. 'Martine Henderson.'

Her handshake was firm, but he could feel a fluttery agitation vibrating from her. The scarf rose and fell rapidly on her chest, her nostrils flaring as if she'd just run a race. *Martine Henderson.* The name wasn't familiar from the residents' list, but again, that didn't mean she didn't live here.

'I was about to have some morning coffee in my office,' he said. 'Would you care to join me?'

'I told you, Mr Levison, I'm not . . .' She hesitated and then said, with a quick glance down the hall, as if she was afraid someone might turn the corridor and find her, 'Oh, why not?'

Lewis led Mrs Henderson back to the manager's office, offered her the deep leather armchair opposite his desk, then buzzed Pam Woodward on the internal phone to request some fresh coffee. He wouldn't normally have disturbed Pam but it was a good reason to invite her to his office to put Mrs Henderson at ease, and also find out – discreetly – if there was anything he should know.

Her composure had returned almost as soon as she'd sat down in the armchair, and now she was assessing the artwork hanging on the red walls with a curious eye. Her knees were pressed together, slanted elegantly to the left, and her back was straight, shoulders down, neck long. Like a dancer. Or the Queen.

'Won't be a moment,' he said, replacing the phone. 'Not too soon after breakfast to tempt you with a pastry, I hope? They're very good.'

'Not for me, no. I don't eat pastry.'

'A cup of coffee then?'

Martine Henderson tilted her head, as if to say, 'There's always time for coffee.' 'Would you mind if I made a quick call?'

'Of course not. Would you like to use my telephone?'

'No, thank you.' She opened the handbag on her knee and took out a mobile phone.

Lewis turned to his computer and pretended to be checking his email – there were already one hundred and fifty-two unread emails in his inbox. He'd cleared it before leaving work the previous evening.

He heard a polite cough and looked up.

Mrs Henderson was staring meaningfully at him, mobile phone in her hand.

'Oh.' Lewis pointed to himself, then to the door. 'You want me to . . . ?'

'If you wouldn't mind?'

'Not at all.' He wasn't fazed; she was probably going to pretend to call someone who would then be unable to collect her – Lewis had seen this before too.

'So kind,' murmured Mrs Henderson.

He pushed back his chair and headed into the hall; he noted that she didn't even lift her mobile phone until he was almost out of the room. Lewis pulled the door to – but not closed – and stood behind it in the corridor until he heard her start to speak.

Mrs Henderson really had called someone.

'Beth,' he heard her hiss in an undertone. 'Finally! It's Martine. Did you get my messages? Look, it doesn't matter, I need you to do me a favour. I'm at the old people's home on the Worcester road, and I need you to collect me as soon as you can, please.'

Pam Woodward was hurrying down the corridor with a tray. She'd unearthed some silverware from somewhere, although it needed a polish, and piled her mini pastries into a wire basket lined with a paper doily.

'Mr Levison, um, Lewis,' she started but Lewis put a finger to his lips.

They stood at the door and listened. Lewis dismissed any guilt at eavesdropping; Mrs Henderson had a very carrying voice, even when she was hissing discreetly.

'Oh, it's too ridiculous! I was at the hospital for a routine appointment and the transport service dropped me off here instead of taking me home. I only got out to help one of the old dears inside and when I turned round, the silly woman had left!'

'Who is that?' Pam mouthed.

'A lady called Mrs Henderson?' He pointed upward. 'Is she from the Memory Wing?'

Pam's eyes rounded. 'Mrs Henderson? Martine Henderson?'

He nodded.

'God, no! She's not one of ours – she's a local . . .' She struggled for the right word. 'A local dignitary? Well, her husband was. Ray Henderson, the mayor, did a lot for charity. He died last year.' Pam rattled off the information, casting quick glances towards the office to reel off all the facts before Martine reappeared. 'Golf-club chairman, lovely man. Round Tabler. Father Christmas at the hospital for years. Family had Longhampton Cellars, the posh wine merchants on the high street. I had a Saturday job at the Cellars when I was at school, plum job it was – Mum was thrilled, thought I'd meet a nice boyfriend there. I didn't, but I learned how to mix a good gin and tonic. And one time—.'

'Ah! Mrs Henderson.' Lewis gave Pam a nudge as the door opened to reveal Mrs Henderson, her phone call completed. Whatever had been discussed had restored her equilibrium, and now she was drawn up to her full height. 'Here's the coffee.'

'Hello, Mrs Henderson,' said Pam politely.

Lewis watched as Pam also stood up straighter, her shoulders drawing back so suddenly the cat pendant bounced on her bosom. She was one reaction away from a curtsey.

'Pamela!' Martine Henderson's voice was warmer now. 'What a nice surprise to see you here.'

'I'm the housekeeper,' said Pam, as Lewis said, 'Pamela is our acting manager. She's been excellent.'

Martine nodded approvingly. 'Well done, Pamela.'

'She was just telling me how you two first met,' said Lewis. 'The more I hear about this community, the more I like it.'

'That's Longhampton!' said Pam. 'Everyone knows everyone. No secrets here!'

What was that tiny ripple passing across Mrs Henderson's face, wondered Lewis? Her smile took a microsecond longer to appear than it should have done.

'Will you excuse me?' said Pam. 'I'm run off my feet this morning settling in a new resident. If I'd known it was you, Mrs Henderson, I'd have put the blackcurrant jam on the tray!'

They both laughed, as if Lewis should know understand the significance of the blackcurrants, and then Pam deposited the tray on Lewis's desk, and hurried off.

Lewis poured the coffee. 'We're very lucky to have a housekeeper like Pam, let alone someone who can step up to acting manager the way she has.'

'Pamela's a very capable girl,' said Mrs Henderson, although Lewis put Pam somewhere north of fifty. She added one lump of sugar to her cup with the tongs Pam had found along with the silverware, deploying them with an elegant deftness. 'How are *you* settling in? Lots to do, I expect. I heard about the inspection.'

Everyone had heard about the inspection.

'It's not the result we wanted for our residents or our staff,' Lewis conceded. 'But I intend to use the report as a launchpad for improvement. I've already started planning strategies to change Rosemount's environment for everyone, staff included. It's important that the whole team feel as if they're part of a bigger picture, too. For instance, have you heard of the Life Story project?'

Mrs Henderson shook her head.

He leaned forward. Pam had intimated that Mrs Henderson was a community-minded woman, and right now Lewis needed volunteers. Plenty of volunteers to make his big plans for Rosemount work. Starting with the plan that he hoped would turn around Rosemount's 'attitude' problem.

'One of the biggest problems we encounter in the care sector is staff turnover. Care assistants come and go, there's constant pressure to get things done with limited resources, everyone's always rushing, people leave, new people start – we do our best but sometimes the checklist takes over from the human beings. What the Life Story project does is to remind us that we're not just names on a rota, we're individuals with a past, a present and a future.'

'That sounds rather idealistic. How does that work in reality?'

'We invite our residents to share their life stories with volunteers – the parts they want to share, of course. And then our volunteers hand their notes over to a creative writer who creates a master document that we can use as a reference point, and which the resident can keep for themselves too. It's the best way for us to really understand them – the child, the young adult, the parent, the sister, not just the person they are now. Plus, it helps us to target care, having a broader understanding of where our resident has been, how they've been shaped by their experiences, what makes them proud or scared. The most important aspect, in my opinion, is that it gets us talking. Talking is always a good thing.'

Lewis made himself stop. He could get carried away with his pet projects, so he'd trained himself to pause in order that the other person could digest. Pauses were polite. And also power.

Mrs Henderson had started off listening half-heartedly, one eye on the window which looked out on to more neglected flowerbeds and a weed-speckled croquet lawn, but her attention had returned to Lewis. 'And you need a creative writer to do that?' she said.

'As the project leader says herself, stories aren't always about hard facts. Sometimes they're about what people leave out. How they choose to recall events. The stories hidden in the gaps, as she put it. Creative writers are good at spotting those.'

She nodded. 'How interesting.'

'Isn't it?' said Lewis.

There was a knock on the door and, without warning, the most beautiful face Lewis had ever seen peered around it.

He was about to tell Mrs Henderson about the introductory session he'd arranged for Friday, and whether she'd like to come along herself, but every thought slid straight out of his head to be replaced with a wordless sense of wonder, like a perfect chord. The chord his laptop made when it started up in the mornings. Randomly, Lewis wondered if this was his heart, starting up.

'Ah, Beth!' said Mrs Henderson. 'At last.'

The clouds had drifted away outside, flooding spring sunshine into the corridor behind the office door, and all Lewis could think was: this is an angel. The woman at the door was pure golden softness, a round face with huge blue eyes and a high, smooth brow, the kind normally adorned with flowers in Victorian paintings. Her hair was blond, scooped up into a messy bun escaping around her face, and judging by the loose, oatmeal-coloured drapery she was wearing, she seemed to have come straight from a potter's studio or a yoga class or something – Lewis wasn't strong on women's fashion. What he did suddenly understand, very clearly, was that all the nonsense talked about Cupid's arrow was real, because he felt a distinct piercing sensation in his chest, as if he'd been hooked by something invisible. It made him feel exposed, yet at the same time, weirdly elated.

'Sorry?' She sounded apologetic. 'Am I interrupting?'

Lewis blinked. His throat had gone dry. He felt light-headed. For once, he didn't know what to say.

Although Lewis had managed nearly every crisis imaginable in his career, from unexpected leaks to unexpected deaths, he hadn't had a lot of practice at managing romantic situations, thanks to an unfortunate combination of bad luck, bad timing and circumstances in his early life. Not that he didn't want to meet the right person – he very much wanted that – but spending most of your working hours surrounded by elderly people and their demanding relatives didn't offer many opportunities to meet suitable candidates.

He struggled to his feet. 'Hello there! Lewis Levison. Lovely to meet you.'

His voice sounded wrong in his head, his tongue too big for his mouth. *Hello there*, too hearty, like a vicar in an Agatha Christie novel, ugh.

'Lewis, this is Beth Cherry, my . . .' Martine frowned, then smiled. 'How would one describe you, Beth?'

'Your lodger?' she suggested.

Martine laughed and Lewis sensed there was another in-joke there he wasn't getting. He really, really wanted to know. He wanted to know everything about Beth Cherry.

'Delighted to meet you, Beth,' he said, and extended a hand. When she took it, and shook it, electricity tingled up his arm at the contact with her warm palm, and out of shock, he dropped her hand, much sooner than he should have done. Or wanted to.

She reacted, startled, and Lewis wanted to grab it back and start again, but that would have looked bizarre, so he smiled too hard instead and, going by the freezing of her expression, that didn't help.

Oh God, he thought, despairing at his awkwardness.

Luckily Martine had taken charge. 'Lewis was telling me about a fascinating project he's planning for the residents,' she explained. 'He needs volunteers to gather life stories from the old people. Wouldn't that be perfect for you?' She turned to Lewis. 'Beth is a writer! She's been working on a screenplay for as long as I've known her, so I'd say she'd be ideal to help out with this project of yours.' Almost as a second thought, she turned back to Beth. 'Wouldn't you?'

'Um, yes?'

Of course she was a writer. She looked creative, Lewis thought. He didn't know any writers or artists or actors, but he imagined this was exactly what they'd look like.

'When are you planning to hold the first session?' Martine inquired.

'Friday,' said Lewis. 'But there will be more than one introduction session, I hope. I want all the staff to attend so we're staggering the sessions around rotas.' That wasn't true – yet – but he didn't want to give her a chance to say no.

Martine turned to the angel. 'Would that work for you, Beth? You're working from home, you said, so you're flexible, aren't you?'

'I'd have to check my diary,' said Beth mildly. 'Working from home doesn't mean I don't have client meetings.'

'Do you write for clients?' Lewis asked. 'What kind of writer are you?'

'I'm not a writer, I'm an *accountant*.' She looked down at the floor, then up again. 'The writing is . . . it's just a hobby. I'm not even . . . I mean, I wouldn't say I was—'

'Good!' Martine clapped her hands together. 'There we go. A positive outcome! Thank you so much for the tea, Lewis – so kind of you. Beth, would you like to try one of these *pains au raisin*?'

Beth eyed up the plate with reluctant interest, and Lewis found himself offering her the whole plate. 'Take them,' he said. 'Please. With our compliments.'

She looked shocked. 'Um, no, honestly, I'm trying not to . . .'

'Oh, you must,' Martine urged her. 'Pamela will be hurt if we don't take some home.'

'Yes. Please do!' Lewis needed no further encouragement to fold up the pyramid of pastries into the paper doily Pam had added to the plate 'to give it a bit of occasion'.

Beth took them, to put an end to the argument. 'Thank you,' she said. 'And . . .'

She met his gaze, then flicked her huge blue eyes momentarily towards Martine, who was fiddling with her handbag, then back to him, as if she was trying to convey something. Lewis didn't know what, and again, he desperately wanted to know. 'Thank you for taking time to chat to us when you must be so busy.'

It was there and it was gone, and he wasn't sure what she intended by it, but the intimacy of that tiny shared moment made him feel dizzy.

'Oh, it was my pleasure,' said Lewis. In the back of his mind, his professional instinct was shuffling the interpretative options: did Martine often turn up in managers' offices? Was she prone to wandering? Or was she just very bossy?

But he didn't get very far, as Martine and Beth were standing up, and Beth was shaking his hand again, and the rest of his mind was flooded with a warm sense of spring, bursting out across his soul like the green shoots on the trees outside.

Chapter eight

When I pulled up outside Rosemount Court three days later – because obviously I hadn't been able to say no to Martine's volunteering – it was clear that changes were already afoot.

Someone had taken secateurs to the rose bushes and chopped back the dead wood, clumps of geraniums had been planted in the empty beds, and there were two men suspended from pulleys, washing the windows. I didn't envy them that job. There were a lot of windows, and at least two critical faces supervising the washing process from inside.

I shouldered my bag, containing notebook, pens, bottle of water – it was a while since I'd been to a workshop – and stared at the imposing front porch.

Anxiety was beginning to climb in my chest.

You can do this, I told myself, taking deep breaths. It was ridiculous to be nervous about something that was, after all, a volunteer event. No one would be filling in a feedback form afterwards. And no one knew what I looked like before, just what I looked like now. Which wasn't exactly a positive, but at least there'd be no 'Beth?' double takes. Hopefully most of them would be old and very short-sighted.

I checked my reflection in the car window, spotted a flash of blue bra, and hunched my shoulders, pulling the material forward so the button didn't gape. I'd been in two minds about this shirt even as I was leaving the house but it was the only one that worked with these trousers. And these trousers were the only ones that worked with my current body.

I glanced back down the drive. Was it too late to . . . yes, I told myself sternly, it was too late. For a moment, I considered bailing on the whole thing: going into town and having a lemon tart and a coffee in the Wild Dog Café. But then I remembered Martine would ask how it had gone, and Martine wasn't the sort of person you could lie to easily. I wasn't *that* good a creative writer.

As I marched up the stone steps of what had probably been an elegant country house in its heyday, I reminded myself that this was good research material. Seraphina's story was set in a mansion just like this. I could absorb useful background detail about fireplaces, servants' bells, and the like.

Inside, there was a noticeable difference too. Instead of the stale smell of boiled vegetables and dust that had hit me earlier in the week, there was now an equally aggressive bouquet of cleaning products: lavender wood polish, pine tile soap and lemon window spray. A cleaner in checked overalls was scrubbing the parquet floor and as I pushed the door open, she shouted, 'Careful! It's wet!'

'I'm here for the storytelling workshop?'

She frowned, wrung out her mop, then pointed at the easel by the reception desk.

ARE YOU READY TO TELL THE STORY OF YOUR LIFE? it yelled cheerfully, in red block capitals, surrounded by cartoon pens and notebooks. MEET GAYLE BURTON, STORYTELLER, IN THE LIBRARY AT 12 P.M. TEA AND BISCUITS!

Underneath was a photograph of Gayle, resting her elbow on an impressive stack of books and smiling at someone off-camera.

'Thanks!' I said, and the cleaner went back to her mopping as I set off towards the library.

I could tell from the gleaming state of the tiles (and the faint tut that I could hear from behind me) that this part of the house had already been 'done'; the dusty flower arrangements gathering more dust on the window ledges had gone, letting light through the leaded windows, which you could now see had small stained-glass diamonds. Pink cardboard arrows directed me at neurotically short intervals down the oak-panelled corridor towards a set of doors at the end, where a final sign read *STORY OF MY LIFE SESSION 12 P.M. COME ON IN!*

I took another deep breath, and went on in.

I knew I'd be the first person there. I'd allowed way too much time for traffic, being out of practice at meetings, and also because I wanted to make sure I could get a seat at the back.

The back of anywhere was my preferred location – it meant you could see everything without being seen, and also guaranteed that no one could talk about you behind your back, if your back was several rows behind them.

Annoyingly, someone had anticipated this strategy by arranging the seats in a single wide horseshoe.

I tiptoed across the library and secured the seat furthest from the door, near a bay window overlooking a patio area with two rotten picnic tables, with a pair of rotten folding chairs propped against them. It was an atmospheric library, or at least it had been once upon a time: it was a long, narrow room, carpeted in that dark tartan pattern beloved of mid-century pubs, with three more windows filled with padded window seats and mahogany bookshelves from floor to ceiling. The top shelves were solid with sombre red and green leatherbound editions, the lower shelves were dog-eared paperbacks and cookbooks.

In the middle of the long wall was a marble fireplace that you could have roasted a pig in, but which now contained an inadequate gas fire and a lot of pinecones.

I felt sorry for the fireplace. You only had to look at its carved swags and flowers to see it had once supported a crop of fancy invitations and fresh garlands from the greenhouses and fine china ornaments and ormolu clocks, but now it just had a card with *In the Event of Fire* instructions on it, and an inhaler.

Shadows began to move in my imagination: this would be the perfect setting for Seraphina's heartbreaking goodbye with her hero. Arthur was going to break into her family house for one final kiss before being banished on a year's enforced travel by his disapproving parents; a break which would not, he swore, diminish his love.

I took out my notebook and a pen, and scribbled some notes.

Fireplace: represents all-consuming nature of their love in formal/domestic confines. Also, S vows to keep the flame burning while Arthur is away. Plus, can show changing seasons with montage of stuff on mantelpiece, flowers, Christmas garlands, etc.

'My heart burns as hot as this . . . No, my love for you is enough to heat . . .' I muttered. One of the how-to books I'd read recommended reading dialogue aloud to see if it sounded real. I spent enough time alone for this to be useful advice. 'Even in the coldest countries, I will think of you, Seraphina, and my heart will burn like the hot coals of—'

'Gosh, you're keen!'

My head bounced up, and I saw Lewis Levison standing by the door with a sheaf of photocopies under his arm. He was juggling a tray with water and glasses while trying to close the door with his foot.

Had he heard me? My skin crawled with embarrassment.

'Um, sorry, I didn't realise . . . followed the signs,' I babbled.

'Don't worry, we're not starting quite yet,' he went on, 'I'm just making sure everything's set up properly. Lewis, Lewis Levison.'

He put down the tray and was approaching me with his hand outstretched, a broad smile on his face. It reached above his moustache and made his eyes twinkle. He had a sweet, reassuring smile, but I guessed that was Lesson One, Day One, if you worked in a residential home.

'Lewis, it's Beth, we met on Wednesday,' I said stiffly. Had he forgotten me already? Bit rude.

But he was shaking my hand anyway. 'Of course! Forgive me. So pleased you're going to be joining us on the project!' He was still shaking my hand. Now he added a second hand on top, trapping me. 'How *is* Mrs Henderson?'

'She's very well, thank you. Very keen to find out how today goes!' I politely extricated my hand, pretending to push my hair behind my ear.

'Tremendous!' He handed me the photocopies. 'I don't suppose you could pop one of these on each chair for me? We've had a great response from our volunteers, and I've encouraged the staff to come along too – I'm hoping for twenty or so today, and with any luck we'll pick up a few more as the project gets going. I don't like making things compulsory – I prefer people to see what a positive impact something like this has, then they *want* to be part of it.'

The front page of the worksheet featured a smiley cloud with the words 'communication', 'context', 'understanding', 'posterity', 'identity' and 'value' radiating out; it didn't fill me with optimism.

'Have you done this before?' I asked.

Lewis was setting up the table between the trainer's chairs in the middle of the horseshoe, moving a plant, adjusting the cushions, frowning with concentration.

'Not personally, but I've introduced it in other situations,' he said. 'It's a wonderful way of getting to know people – the staff get to know the residents, the residents get to know the staff, the staff learn things about each other, families often see their own relatives in a completely new light. I'm not a betting man, but I would bet you a tenner right now that there'll be at least one person here who'll have a story that you wouldn't expect in a million years.'

'Is that a good thing?'

'I think so!'

The door opened and a couple of older ladies peered nervously around.

'Hello, Lewis, are we too early?' asked the taller of the two.

'Janice! No, not at all! Come on in and meet Beth – Beth, this is Janice, one of our volunteers, and Sheila, one of our PALS co-ordinators. Sheila, you can explain to Beth what happened with Mrs Henderson – Beth, I made a point of speaking to the hospital transport to ensure that won't happen again, but Sheila can put your mind at rest.'

I could tell by the look on Sheila's face that the last thing she wanted to do was talk about Mrs Henderson. 'It was fine in the end,' I said quickly, in case she thought I was about to lay into her. 'We laughed about it later!'

(We didn't.)

'Tremendous! Will you ladies excuse me?' He gestured at his watch. 'Our guest speaker will be arriving in a moment and I want to make sure she has everything she needs. Ah! More volunteers! Excellent!'

And Lewis hurried away, holding the door open first for the volunteers, also older ladies in smart jackets, who came in and took the seats at the other end of the horseshoe.

'So, I did *apologise* to Mrs Henderson,' began Sheila, with a deep sigh, and I was stuck, nodding, in a long explanation of how hard it was to organise a minibus route to visit all the various residential homes in the Longhampton catchment area when half the passengers couldn't be relied upon to give an up-to-date address to the driver. By the time Sheila had finished – and I'd heard some hair-raising stories about worse places Martine could have been abandoned, corroborated by Janice – the other seats had filled up with a mix of volunteers and staff in lilac overalls.

And then the doors were flung open again, and Lewis returned with a small lady in a long chiffon cardigan the colour of flames, with close-cropped white hair and silver Doc Marten boots. Immediately, everyone's attention swung in her direction like iron filings to a magnet. Gayle Burton floated across the room, trailing a strong but gorgeous perfume, and a sense of something about to happen.

When the excited whispering died down, Lewis spread his hands wide, encompassing the whole room as if addressing the Royal Albert Hall. 'Hello, everyone, and welcome to Rosemount Court. Thank you so much for giving up your time this morning. We are very lucky to have Gayle Burton here to lead our Story of My Life project, and to explain the basics of what we'll be doing to help our residents tell their story, in their own words. And I won't say any more, other than I know you're going to find this hugely rewarding – over to you, Gayle!'

Lewis turned to go back to his chair, on the end nearest the door, but a nurse had snuck in while he was speaking and taken it. Without missing a beat, he walked over to the chairs stacked up by the window, lifted one from the top and set it down next to mine.

I tried not to show it, but I felt awkward. I'd chosen to be on the end so I could cross my legs without impinging on anyone's space. Lewis was quite close, so I had no choice but to give him a quick, tight smile which I hope conveyed annoyance but also resignation, and in return he beamed his disconcerting bright smile at me, then turned his attention back to Gayle.

I focused on Gayle too, adopting an expression of intense concentration, but in truth, I was hyper-aware of the button on my shirt, the one that was straining over the widest part of my bust. I hunched my shoulders further in.

'What happens when we share our stories with other people?' Gayle held up one finger; she had enviable glossy nails. 'We offer context to our lives – not just about who we are now, but who we have been, who we want to be.' She held up another finger. 'We form a bond with the person listening to us, we build trust and we feel *heard*.' She held up another finger. 'We learn things about ourselves, by looking back and selecting the moments that feel most significant. Maybe we see events differently, through the lens of experience. We can recognise the value in ourselves by seeing our lives through another's eyes.'

Next to me, Lewis nodded sagely.

So far, so Live, Laugh, Love, I thought. Ash and I had read a *lot* of self-help books in the Heartbreak Wilderness Years.

'But most of all,' Gayle went on, 'when we tell stories, we create conversations. And isn't that the most important thing, when you live and work in a community? *Proper* conversations?'

There were murmurs of agreement.

Gayle explained how the project worked: over the course of eight weeks, we would sit with residents for an hour – 'not too long, it can be overwhelming' – and ask them guided questions about their lives that triggered memories, which we would compile into notes to be written up into books by the writing team, with photographs and other media included, if they wanted. The end result would be something residents could keep updating, perhaps with family members, as a future heirloom. 'It's helpful to have something to refer to, as memories blur, or for guests who find it hard to make small talk. It's easy to open the book and prompt more stories.'

From Rosemount's perspective, she said, it helped the care co-ordinators to dive more deeply into likes, dislikes, fears and beliefs, information that could be incorporated into individual plans, 'so we're confident that we're interacting with them not just as the older, more vulnerable person they are now, but as the person they've been throughout their lives.'

Gayle talked us through the pages of the hand-out which outlined how to approach the interview sessions. 'It doesn't have to be linear,' she cautioned us. 'And it doesn't have to be complete. Or strictly accurate. The benefit is in the remembering, not necessarily the documentary accuracy. There may be aspects of someone's life that they don't care to remember. That's fine.'

Around me people were starting to murmur to each other; Gayle's enthusiasm had set a few volunteers off down Memory Lane, even before they'd got to the residents.

'I know it can be awkward asking complete strangers to tell you personal details like this,' she said, raising her voice slightly to be heard over the sound of people whispering '. . . *Juke Box Jury . . . decimalisation . . .*' 'Which is why we're going to practise here first. I'm going to put you into pairs and you're going to get the answers to three of the questions on the worksheet. All right?'

Without warning, she started going round the horseshoe matching people up, until she got to the end, and reached me, the odd one out.

'Sorry,' I said. 'I don't mind not—'

'Not at all!' Gayle smiled and for a moment I hoped she'd say I could interview her. 'Lewis, you'll be Beth's partner, won't you? Just for this exercise?'

Lewis had been scribbling in a ridiculously tiny notebook, like something you might find in a Christmas cracker, but now snapped to attention. 'Of course! I can't wait to get started on this project.'

'Are you going to have time to do it yourself?' Gayle looked doubtful. 'Pam said you were absolutely snowed under.'

'I never ask volunteers to do anything I'm not doing myself. Besides, I can't wait to get to know the residents better.' Lewis swivelled his chair round, straddled it, and faced me with disarming keenness. He had the eager brightness of a Labrador. With a moustache. 'Beth, would you like to go first? Or shall I?'

Gayle raised her eyebrows at me over Lewis's head, and glided off to oversee another couple.

'I'll go first,' I said. Might as well get it out of the way. I glanced down at the worksheet, scanning the questions for something suitable for a total stranger under the age of forty.

A good question: how old was Lewis?

I glanced up again, trying not to make it obvious that I was scrutinising him. The moustache made it tricky, but he was probably about my age; his skin, now I looked closely, was smooth and faintly freckled, and there were no silver threads in his thick brown hair. But he was wearing a tie for work, and his socks had tiny owls on them. He couldn't be more than thirty-five, I decided.

He was staring at me, smiling dopily, so I blurted out the first question my eye fell on, 'Um . . . what makes you happy?'

'Cycling,' he said at once. 'Never happier than when I'm out on my bike, flying down a hill. Any weather, any season, never fails to make me feel alive.'

'Have you ever fallen off?'

'Once or twice.' He beamed. 'But no broken bones. Touch wood! Are you a cyclist?'

'*Me*?' I almost laughed at the idea. 'God, no.'

'Why not? It's the best feeling.'

'I'll have to take your word for that.' I didn't want to picture myself perched on a bike, thanks. 'Um, tell me about a moment that changed your life?'

'A moment that changed my life . . . Wow.' Lewis seemed thrown for a second. He glanced down to his left for a second, then looked back at me. 'Passing my Cycling Proficiency Test!'

'Really?' I said, in disbelief. Surely not even Mark Cavendish would choose 'passing my Cycling Proficiency Test' as a life-changing moment. 'Not meeting your first girlfriend? Or . . .'

My mind went blank. I couldn't say 'getting married' or 'having a child' because I'd hate him to ask *me* those things; there were so many milestones I was nowhere near achieving. Or ever would, at this rate.

Lewis seemed to sense my discomfort. 'Do you want to swap over? Where were you born?'

'Abergavenny,' I said.

Immediately, a photo album opened in my mind: my parents' first pub, the Shepherd's Crook, them standing outside it, me on Mum's hip. We'd lived there until I was seven. Then we'd moved to Bristol, ostensibly because of a better opportunity for Dad in a better location, but actually, as I found out from Mum later, because Dad had fallen out with the brewery over money. And also, as I found out from Dad, because Mum had had an affair with a barman.

'Wales, lovely!' said Lewis. 'Or should I say, *da iawn*? I do like to try to pronounce the names on the signs if I'm ever over the border, but I'm sure I'm doing it wrong. Do you speak Welsh?'

'No.' The barman Mum had an affair with had been Welsh. He was called Dewi. He taught me some swear-words. Dewi. I hadn't thought about him in years. He had a tattoo, before everyone did. And a sort of knowing smirk – which of course he would, wouldn't he?

Lewis was waiting for me to say something, that look of expectation on his face.

'No,' I said. 'I grew up in Bristol.'

The Sailor's Arms, Dad's pub in Bristol, hadn't been much better, but at least Mum and Dad had only stayed together until I was thirteen. Dad spent half his time yelling at Mum, and half his time yelling at me. On my thirteenth birthday, he moved to London with the policewoman he'd been seeing on the side, while Mum and I stayed in Bristol and I did my best to stop her drinking herself into oblivion every weekend.

'What was your favourite childhood memory? Can be anything from a television programme to a favourite toy!'

Lewis waited for me to elaborate but an old tension had gripped my heart, squeezing it tight. As soon as my mind slid back to Bristol, I could smell that stale beer pub smell again. That looming fear of saying the wrong thing, of Dad's silent glare across the table, never having friends back, long nights falling asleep with my iPod, earbuds hurting my ears so I couldn't hear Mum crying.

'Nothing interesting,' I said, as casually as I could. 'Just the usual boring memories – *Toy Story*, Harry Potter, My Little Pony, you know. Can we . . . ?'

'Fair enough! Let's fast-forward.' Lewis consulted the handout. 'What's your greatest achievement?'

My mind went blank.

Why had I agreed to do this? It wasn't meant to be about me. Yes, my childhood had had its share of sad moments but I spent as little time as possible thinking about it; I found it didn't help. My life had started at university, and then *really* started when I met Fraser. That's when I found the life I was supposed to be living, hanging out with interesting people, being taken seriously, going to Latitude and the Hay Festival and . . .

Lewis was looking at me with that 'and?' prompt.

What *was* my greatest achievement? There wasn't really anything. No marriage, no awards, no children, no house, no quirky hobby. What could I tell Lewis that was true and at the same time hid the complete lack of achievement in my adult life?

I heard myself say, 'I've perfected a recipe for making the perfect one-person chocolate cake in a mug.'

'Really?' said Lewis, as if I'd revealed I was the genius who'd invented email. 'How?'

'Three tablespoons flour, three sugar, two cocoa, an egg . . .' I rattled off the ingredients and method. 'Oh, half a teaspoon of espresso, that's the secret ingredient. It brings out the chocolate flavour.'

'How did you discover that?'

'I didn't,' I said. 'My mum did. She was a chef. Sort of.'

Dad liked to think that he could have been Gordon Ramsay, had he only been allowed more time to perfect his cooking instead of running a pub, but it was Mum who had the knack of making something out of nothing.

'You can add a splash of brandy,' I said, thinking of her. 'Just not too much.'

Lewis was scribbling away.

'Are you writing this down?' I asked.

'I want to try it later.'

'Really? You don't . . .'

'How are you getting on?' I felt Gayle's hand touch my shoulder. She smelled lovely, of ripe figs.

'We've got it cracked,' Lewis announced. 'Beth is a creative domestic goddess who was born in Wales, but grew up in Bristol.'

'And Lewis?'

'Lewis likes cycling. And, um . . .' I'd failed to find out anything else about Lewis.

I saw his face fall.

I glanced at his owl socks and quickly added, 'Lewis loves nature, enjoys travelling around Britain and history.'

'Yes!' said Lewis, apparently astonished.

Gayle looked between the two of us and nodded. 'Good start.'

'Shall I ask Pam to bring in the refreshments now?' asked Lewis. 'I think we're ready for a break.'

Gayle made a brief flicking gesture and I glanced down: the button on my shirt had popped open, revealing a flash of blue bra. Mortified, I clasped the material shut over my chest, and half-turned, nearly bumping into Sheila and Janice in my haste to find somewhere to adjust my clothing.

It turned out to be a lovely oak-panelled cloakroom that would have been a perfect setting for one of Seraphina and Arthur's trysts, had I been in the right frame of mind to take notes, but I wasn't. The memories, the contact with strangers, the *chat* . . . suddenly I felt overwhelmed. And so I made my excuses to a passing volunteer, and went home.

Chapter nine

Martine was keen to hear how the Story of My Life introduction had gone.

She called me on the kitchen phone, late on Friday night. Already, I half-expected its old-fashioned peal now somewhere between ten and eleven. She never chatted for longer than a few minutes but always dropped some interesting nugget about the house or the town. She'd asked me twice 'how the writing was going', which had the (no doubt intended) effect of making me more focused on Seraphina and Arthur than I had been in some time. It was one of Fraser's grumbles about his mother, what he called her 'relentless need to chivvy people'.

I didn't mind, though; it was nice that she was interested. In fact, when the phone rang, I was sitting up in bed with my laptop on a pillow, writing – or more accurately, writing and deleting – the pivotal library farewell scene while Rosemount's baronial fireplace was fresh in my mind. It wasn't going well, and I was happy to abandon the weirdly stilted non-conversation Seraphina and Arthur were having.

'So can you choose whom you interview?' Martine asked, after I'd regaled her with the whole thing. 'Or are your interviews allocated at random?'

Since Martine knew virtually everyone in the town, one way or another, I wondered if she'd draw up a priority list for me. To interview, or perhaps to avoid. Maybe that was why she hadn't volunteered herself; the temptation to correct people's inaccurate memories would be too tempting.

'It's random, I think.' I opened Pam's email again to check. 'My first interview is with a couple called Horrobin? Do you know them?'

'Hmm.' Martine pretended to think, but I knew she knew. 'Would that be Bill Horrobin? The greengrocer?'

'Maybe?' I said. 'Pam just sent me names, not any other details.'

'Well, if it is, Bill Horrobin's a lovely chap. You must let me know how it goes! But don't let me distract you – I saw your light was on. Are you writing tonight? Or still working?'

I looked at my laptop, stuck at Arthur's wooden goodbye speech. Were there any new ways to say 'I love you?' I couldn't find any. The fireplace they were embracing in front of currently felt more animated than the lovers.

'Writing,' I said.

'Then I won't disturb you,' she said. 'Strike while the iron's hot! Don't let anything distract you!'

'Good night, Martine,' I said, and we hung up.

Tomsk was lying in his new favourite place, close to the gas fire, squinting through his fringe at the mismatched pack of pottery dogs on the shelf, as if daring them to move. When I ended the call, he looked up at me with his soft brown eyes.

I told Tomsk I loved him several times a day, in ludicrous, if creative ways. But I didn't think Seraphina would appreciate Arthur telling her that she had the warmest, softest ears in the world and her feet smelled of digestive biscuits.

Tomsk laid his head on his paws, as if reminding me it was getting late.

'Ten more minutes,' I said. 'And no, I'm not giving Seraphina a dog.'

Although it would give them something to talk about, I thought, turning back to the fireplace and Arthur's stilted goodbyes.

'. . . and was it 1976 when we moved to Surbiton, Bill? Yes, it was. That was when that programme came out, *The Good Life,* and your sister thought we were going to buy a pig! Of course we didn't, but you did get a Flymo . . .'

Linda Horrobin had not stopped talking since I'd taken up position on the armchair opposite the sofa where she and her husband Bill sat, side by side.

I'd heard about the flat they'd lived in when they got married, off Upper Street in Islington, bought 'when no one wanted to live there, of course now our little place would be worth millions!', and the early mornings Bill had worked, supplying fruit from Covent Garden Market to restaurants and luxury hotels across the city. Linda had started her nursing career at St George's Hospital, 'of course, it's a fancy hotel now, can you believe!' I heard about the red satin pants he'd bought from a shop called Mr Fish that Linda 'couldn't believe were men's trousers', the Mini they'd driven around Nelson's Column 'on two wheels!' the night England won the World Cup, the time they shared a table in a nightclub with Tom Jones. That was just the first half-hour.

Bill smiled, but hadn't said a word.

Linda glanced across at him every other sentence, and included him in the conversation so naturally that it felt as if he was participating – 'we liked dancing, didn't we, Billy, although not so much when it all went a bit hippy-like, we grew up with proper dance floors and bands who could *play*, like those jazz men at the Flamingo, oh, you loved them, didn't you, Georgie Fame and his Blue Flames . . .'

I was scribbling this down as fast as I could but I was barely keeping up. As per Gayle's instructions, I was recording our conversation on my phone, but I wanted to jot down details that my phone couldn't see.

Like when Linda flicked her gaze at Bill, either for confirmation or in the hope the same memory was forming out of the fog in his mind. Every time she checked and he smiled back, I caught flashes of the heartbreaker she'd fallen for: the deep blue eyes, the jutting cheekbones, the tenderness in his expression.

I jotted down the way she took his hand now and again in hers; I made a note of the faint movement as Linda squeezed it, the sigh of a memory escaping.

I wrote down 'Elnett hairspray', and the single fat pearl in Linda's ears like a dot of punctuation under the swirled hair; Bill's ironed blue shirt and striped tie under the lambswool jumper, the pressed trousers, the velvet slippers with the dashing skull and crossbones on the toes.

'Everything had a bit of glamour in the old days,' she said, when I commented on what a stylish pair they were. 'People made an effort.'

'Well, you two still do, clearly.' I waved a hand in the general direction of my own hair, scraped up in a messy bun. 'Your hair looks beautiful, Linda. Like a film star's.'

She patted the back of her roller-set, suddenly self-conscious. 'Oh, I'm not the glamorous one in this marriage. Bill's too modest to say, but people used to tell him he was the spit of Albert Finney.'

'Oh, I can see that.' *Google Albert Finney.* 'What about you? Who did people say you had a look of? You definitely remind me of someone.'

She shook her head, shy but delighted. 'Well, I couldn't . . .'

'Petula Clark,' said Bill unexpectedly.

We both swung our attention back to him. His voice was so quiet I wondered if I'd imagined it, but Linda's reaction confirmed I hadn't.

I held my breath, in case he spoke again, but he didn't.

'Oh, love,' said Linda.

There was a knock-knock on the door and Pam Woodward popped her head round.

'Sorry to interrupt,' she said, 'but just to let you know that there's refreshments for our volunteers in the lounge. Gayle's come back to give some advice about writing up your notes.'

'Are there refreshments for the interviewees?' Linda gave me a cheeky wink. 'Hard work, this reminiscing.'

'Lemon drizzle today,' said Pam. 'Your favourite! I'll pop a slice aside. Same for you, Bill?'

We all glanced at Bill, in the hope he might speak again.

'Bill, do you have a favourite cake?' I asked, and there was another pause while we waited for him to say something.

He gazed towards the window with a blank expression, and after a moment, Pam broke the silence.

'He loves a scone, am I right, Linda?'

Linda was nodding agreement, when Bill's lips parted and he said, in a whisper, 'Bakewell tart.'

I caught Pam's eye and although she indicated not to make a fuss, she seemed pleased.

'We'll have to add that to the list, Bill!' she said. 'Bakewell tart, eh? Was that one of Linda's specialities?'

Another long pause, but the silence didn't feel as empty as before.

'No! I can't bake to save my life! Bill liked the Café Royal in town.' Linda gave her husband's hand a squeeze. 'We used to go there before the pictures, didn't we?'

'My mum *loved* the Café Royal!' said Pam. 'She said the waitresses had special silver cake slices, and white gloves. Do you remember those, Bill? The white gloves?'

There was no reply. Bill's gaze had returned to a point outside the window, but there was an energy in his expression that hadn't been there before, as if his imagination was spooling vivid images across his mind's eye.

'Well, thank you for such an entertaining afternoon,' I said, standing up quickly. I hadn't expected to feel so emotional. That two people could still love each other like that after decades together was simultaneously hopeful and humbling. What were the chances of meeting that one special person? 'I hope you enjoyed it as much as I did!'

'You'll be coming back, won't you?' Linda looked up. 'We barely got started!'

'Of course,' I said. 'I want to hear more about the fruit and veg market! And Georgie Fame!'

'We'll get your photographs out for next week, Linda,' said Pam. 'That often helps,' she added to me, under her breath.

'We've got some terrific albums, haven't we, Bill?' said Linda. 'All those holidays in Spain!'

A faint smile twitched at the edge of Bill's pale lips, and I wondered if he was back in the Mini with a giggling Linda, circling Hyde Park as he tooted the horn for the World Cup winners. And who could blame him, with memories like that to slip back into?

'You'll have to tell Mr Levison about that,' said Pam as she hurried down the corridor. She moved urgently at all times, as if there were an alarm going off somewhere, stopping only to check the big table lamps in the corridor – flicking them on and off, then frowning. She didn't say why.

'Tell him what?'

'That you got Mr Horrobin talking. He'll be chuffed. He's barely said more than a few words since he and Linda moved in.'

'Is Bill . . . ?' I didn't know what the correct term was, and didn't want to seem disrespectful.

'Living with dementia? Yes, he has an Alzheimer's diagnosis, but he's fit as a fiddle, bless him. There'll come a point when we should really move him upstairs to the Memory Wing but . . .' Pam shook her head. 'Linda takes such good care of him. They're like swans, those two. Mates for life. I'd hate to separate them now.'

I felt suddenly very sad at the thought of Bill sitting alone in silence, cut off from Linda's energetic torrent of memories.

Pam pushed open the door to the lounge. Inside, an excited buzz was centred around Gayle Burton, who had returned, majestic in a peacock cardigan, to deliver a pep talk about our conversation-starting skills, as well as advice about writing up our notes.

'Use their actual words, if you can,' she said, once we'd loaded up on tea and cake and sat down to listen. 'Especially if they're using their local dialect. That's a great starting point, if you get stuck – what other words haven't they heard since they were kids? What's their favourite dialect word for something – bread rolls, earwigs, playground games. People love talking about different words for things.'

I scribbled that down, along with 'JFK?' and 'the best advice you've ever had'. I didn't think Linda Horrobin would need prompts, though; the hard part had been finding a gap in her stories to ask a question.

Pam looked round the group. 'Does anyone have a specific query about what they've done today?'

A couple of volunteers raised their hands, with questions about contradictions and what to do if someone became distressed by a sad memory. Or if they didn't want to speak at all.

Gayle answered everything with admirable patience and then redirected us to the tea table.

I was hanging back, trying to resist a second slice of lemon drizzle, when Gayle herself approached me with a big smile.

'Hello, Beth!' she said.

'Um, hello.' I was amazed she'd remembered my name, then remembered I was still wearing the badge we'd been given to reassure the residents that we weren't a relative they'd momentarily blanked.

'I'm going to come clean.' Gayle raised her hands. 'I need to ask a favour. Can I persuade you to join the writing-up team? I haven't been able to persuade anyone to join me, and there's just too much for me to do on my own.' She tilted her head to one side. 'Lewis tells me you're a writer!'

I felt my cheeks burn. Had I told Lewis? I definitely hadn't mentioned it. My never-ending work in progress wasn't something I brought up in public, because it was too embarrassing to admit how long it had taken me to fail to finish it.

Then I remembered that Martine had told him I was a writer when I'd rescued her. Of course. Lewis struck me as someone who noticed *everything*.

'No, no, no. I wouldn't say that!' A woman standing near us was giving me a curious look. 'I mean, I've, um, I've got something I've been working on for a while.'

'How interesting! Are you in a writing group?'

'God, no! It's not anything I'd *show* anyone. It's . . . well, it's terrible.'

'I bet it's not.'

'It is. If it was any good, I'd have finished by now.' That was the most unintentionally truthful thing I'd said about my writing in years.

'Are you stuck?' Gayle managed to sound sympathetic, even though she'd probably heard this a million times. 'Do you need a brainstorm?'

'Well . . .'

'Don't be shy – everyone needs a bit of help now and again.'

'Yes,' I admitted. 'I'm stuck.'

Gayle smiled. 'OK, well, here's the deal: if you don't mind writing up a few of these stories, I'll give you an hour of coaching. Email me what you've got so far, and we can have a chat after one of these sessions? Work out what's blocking you.'

'Would you?' I wasn't sure I wanted to hear all the things that were wrong with it.

'Don't look so scared! In my experience, everything you need to finish is already in there. You just can't see it yet.'

I wasn't so sure about that, but it was nice of her to say so.

I left soon after, citing the dog waiting for me in the back of my car, but had hardly reached the car park when I heard someone shouting my name, and the clatter of footsteps.

'Beth? Beth!'

I turned. Lewis was sprinting towards me, covering the ground with long strides, waving urgently, his tie flapping over his shoulder. 'Beth! Wait!'

Instinctively, I checked in my pocket – yes, I'd got my phone, my bag. Had I left something? Was there a confidentiality thing I was supposed to sign?

He reached me in a matter of seconds, and wasn't even out of breath.

'Thank goodness I caught you before you left,' he said.

'Is everything all right?'

Lewis nodded. 'Yes, of course. I just wanted to ask, how is Mrs Henderson? Martine?'

'Martine? Um, she's very well, thank you.' I wondered if Jackie had made a call to discuss a visit. Or if he was subtly asking if she'd turned up in any more unexpected places lately. 'That was an honest mix-up with the hospital transport the other day – she was just unsure about how she was going to get home. She's perfectly fine now.'

'Ah, I see.' The smile intensified. 'Glad to hear it.'

'In fact,' I went on, feeling rather protective of her, 'she's very keen to hear more about this story project.'

I was about to tell him some of Martine's connections with the town – in the unlikely event he hadn't already heard them – when a long nose shoved its way through the gap I'd left in the car window. It eagerly sniffed the air around Lewis, who jerked backwards.

'Tomsk!' I said. 'Sorry, that's my dog. He's been so patient, waiting for his walk. We're going up to Coneygreen Wood.'

Tentatively, Lewis peered into the back of the car where Tomsk was now sitting up, swishing his tail. He filled the entire space with enthusiasm and hair. 'Big chap, isn't he?'

'Massive. He's a softy, though. Do you want to say hello?'

'Um, no, I . . .' Lewis coughed. 'It's fine, I don't want to, er, delay you. He looks lovely! Lovely chap!'

I wasn't one of those dog owners who thinks everyone should worship their hairy friend, but I'd mentally classified Lewis as a dog person. He had that outdoorsy vibe going on. Maybe he'd been knocked off his bike by a dog. Or run one over.

He certainly seemed uncharacteristically flustered now, and Tomsk was still firmly harnessed in.

Lewis took a step back. 'Beth, I have to confess something.'

'Oh?' The sudden change of tone threw me. Was this about the Horrobins? Had I done something wrong? 'What?'

'I tried your mug cake recipe at the weekend.'

'*Really*?'

'It was . . .' Lewis mimed a chef's kiss with a theatrical flourish. 'Exceptionally good. And so quick! I had it mixed up and baked before my ice bath had finished running. I have an ice bath after cycling,' he added, while I was still struggling to get my brain around 'ice' and 'bath' in the same sentence. 'It's good for preventing cramps. Not that you devised your cake around ice baths, of course. But perfect timing! I just wanted to let you know.'

I shifted awkwardly. I'd never told anyone about my mug cake experiments, apart from Ashley, who'd benefited from some trial runs. There was something slightly shameful about them, that urgent need for sweetness, so urgent you couldn't even wait half an hour for a normal cake to bake. Mug cakes were one of the few uncomplicated childhood memories I had – that cosy, safe feeling of Mum pressing a warm cup into my hands, curling up next to me with her own. Both of us shutting out the world, teaspoons clinking against china as we scraped out every last bit.

Lewis was still talking. 'I wasn't sure about the mug – you didn't specify a size – but I borrowed a range of options from the kitchen and it worked! Well.' He paused. '*Bit* of overspill initially, but that was my fault.'

He grinned, and his sincerity melted something inside me. 'Try it with a spoonful of crème fraîche on top,' I suggested. 'It cuts through the sweetness.'

'I *will* try that!' Lewis made it sound as if I'd just gifted him the formula for liquid gold. 'You know, I've heard a *lot* of "what is your greatest achievements?" over the years, and they're usually tedious and frankly self-aggrandising – but your mug cake is the only one that I can give an actual, personal, thumbs-up to.'

'It's not really my greatest achievement,' I said, unable to let it go. 'What I meant to say was that I got the highest mark in the region for my tax qualification. Second highest in the country. That's my greatest achievement. Not the cake. I don't know why I said the cake. My mind went blank.'

'Really? OK.' He nodded. 'That's also very impressive.'

'I just don't want you to think that . . .' *That I am the kind of uncontrolled, greedy person who only thinks about scoffing cake, ideally as quickly as possible.*

'That what?' said Lewis, baffled.

I looked away, anywhere other than into Lewis's face. My eye fell on the flowerbed nearest my car. It had been dug over and planted up with red and pink busy Lizzies, hopeful microdots of colour in the expanse of brown soil. Lots of room to grow. Maybe slightly *too* much room.

'That, you know, I just think about cake,' I mumbled.

'Why on earth would I think that?'

'Well, because—' I started to make a gesture at my body but managed to stop myself.

Lewis continued to look at me, as if I was talking some strange language, and then shook his head and smiled, holding my gaze for a long second.

The shiver it gave me took me by surprise. I'd seen Lewis beaming before, with that jolly Labrador positivity that he sprayed around the place like an out-of-control hosepipe, but this was different. There was an unexpected vulnerability in his eyes, once you got past that ludicrous moustache, and it made him seem closer to his real age. Which was about the same as mine, except he was running a high-turnover business with responsibility for vulnerable lives, and I was emotionally bullied by my own security pass.

I didn't know what to say. When Lewis smiled like that – as if all he wanted was for me to smile back at him – he looked so different, a whole other person revealed without warning, that I could only nod in response. After so long in my own company, I found his directness unsettling.

To be honest, I found any directness unsettling, but Lewis's even more so.

I would probably have continued nodding if his phone hadn't pinged and Tomsk hadn't barked at it. It was a snippet of Lewis's own voice saying, 'Chop chop!'

'Ah, that's my ten-minute warning for our health and safety meeting.' He gestured at the house, and shook his head, baffled. 'Would you believe we've got a lightbulb thief now? Anyway, please let me know if you have any more recipes to try. I have an appallingly sweet tooth, for my sins.'

'*Really*?' It was hard to believe, given how athletic he was.

'It's why I cycle so much. Got to burn it off somehow!'

I found myself nodding – again – and stood watching him as he strode up the drive, radiating positive energy in every direction.

Lewis was moving forward, but as he went he waved to a resident watching from an upstairs window, then bent to pick up a discarded plastic bottle, diverted to an overflowing recycling bin, repositioned the bin to its rightful place, flipped up the lid and disposed of the bottle, opened the door for a cleaner coming out, and then vanished inside Rosemount.

I stared for a moment, not sure what I was feeling. Normally dynamism like that made me feel squat and defensive, but Lewis didn't provoke that reaction. It wasn't performative, designed to make others feel inadequate, it was just who he was.

Instead I felt . . . I hunted for the right word. Boosted?

But maybe that was the sunshine, I thought, as I set off with Tomsk for our walk. The spring sunshine, and hearing long and happy marriages were a real thing, and the daffodils, and the fact that I'd made Bill speak, and Gayle offering to read my screenplay, and resisting a second slice of cake. Not a bad morning's work.

I found an oldies station on the radio, and sang all the way to Coneygreen Woods.

Chapter ten

Lewis's to-do list was a constantly evolving document which he revised every night before he went to bed, but one name remained at the top of it: Eunice Stafford.

Eunice, Lewis had decided, was his key to success at Rosemount Court.

Eunice's eagle eye for problems would help him target every minor flaw in the operation the second it happened, and, if his suspicions were correct – that someone was behind a dirty tricks campaign – might help lead him to whoever was responsible. Lewis had seen similar tactics before; Rosemount was a well-equipped home in a prime location, and after a report as bad as the one Rosemount had just had, other care home groups would be circling like sharks, ready to snap it up at a knockdown price if Eric Alexander decided to cut his losses.

Besides, in a more general sense, if his planned improvements could crack a smile from Eunice, then the rest of the residents would presumably be in a state of delirious rapture.

'Let me make you a deal,' he'd said to her son Michael, once Michael had finally stopped listing his grievances. 'I will personally oversee Eunice's care plan and if she's not happy in one month's time, and she still wants to find different accommodation, I will not only help you find somewhere that better suits her needs, but we'll refund her fees for that month.'

There'd been a somewhat undermining intake of breath from Pam Woodward as he'd spoken, but Lewis had kept his reassuring smile fixed on Michael. He was confident that it wouldn't come to that, and in his experience you had to raise the stakes to get results, starting with yourself.

Michael had glanced across at his wife – not at Eunice, Lewis noted – and grudgingly said, 'Fine. But I'll be checking in with Mum. She deserves the very best.'

'Of course,' Lewis had reassured him. 'That's what I want for her too.'

Obviously he'd had to record his offer in the weekly management report, and expected some pushback from the senior team, but Lewis wasn't worried. One of his strongest skills was finding the silver lining (a phrase he had earmarked for his future management training manual/autobiography), and Eunice's detailed list of complaints had provided Lewis with a strong set of easily achievable wins, as well as several harder wins that he wasn't sure he could deal with immediately (poor weather, the distance of Rosemount from the hospital, etc.).

Given the energy Eunice seemed to derive from complaining, Lewis thought the Story of My Life project was something she'd actively enjoy, if only for the chance to exercise her grumble range across multiple decades. In addition to that, she'd be sharing valuable insight into her life experiences, which in turn might offer a clue as to how Lewis could make her happy.

Lewis was of the belief that everyone could be made happy somehow. Even Eunice Stafford.

Rosemount's enrichment officer was Pam Woodward, who'd been landed with the job in addition to acting manager and housekeeper, after Jodie Ryelands, the previous incumbent, was sacked by David Rigg for fixing the Easter raffle. (Or not fixing it, depending on who you talked to.) Pam didn't like the title, she explained to Lewis, partly because it sounded agricultural and partly because it made her feel responsible for something she couldn't control – other people's enjoyment of life.

'You can take a horse to bingo, but you can't make it *enjoy* it,' she'd explained, when he'd queried the limited amount of 'enrichment' on offer.

'But, Pam, residents do expect a decent quality of entertainment these days.'

'We have movie nights,' she protested.

'We need to offer much, much more than movie nights,' Lewis reminded her. 'Living here should be like living on a grounded cruise ship. But with gardens. And hospital access. And no seagulls.'

Pam had given him the uncertain smile that Lewis already knew indicated that she wasn't sure if he was joking or not. She extracted a piece of paper from the file that was permanently tucked under her arm, and passed it across the desk. 'So, anyway, here's the volunteer rota I've made for the Story of My Life sessions.'

Lewis read it and frowned. 'Wait. You've missed someone off!'

Her face froze. 'Who?'

'Me!' Lewis pointed to himself for emphasis. 'You've missed me off!'

'What? I didn't think . . . You're too busy for this.'

'First thing you need to know about me, Pam, is that I'll never ask anyone on our team to do anything I'm not prepared to do myself.'

Pam looked shifty. 'Before you say anything, *I'm* not on that list because I was keeping myself as a reserve when people drop out. People always drop out.'

'Good planning,' agreed Lewis. 'But in any case, it's more important for me to do this. It's a chance for me to get to know people. You know everyone already.'

Of course it also opened the opportunity for him to bump into Beth Cherry again, but that wasn't his main reason for wanting to lead the charge. That was merely a bonus, he told himself.

'So put me down for any three residents,' he went on, 'one of whom should be Eunice Stafford.'

'Eunice? Are you sure? She's very . . . negative.'

'That's precisely why I want to get to know her,' said Lewis. 'I want to find out *why* that is.'

'On your head be it,' said Pam darkly, and Lewis respected her for not muttering it under her breath.

Eunice was available for her first session the following day; Lewis fitted her in between meetings with the catering supplier and the owner of a replacement cleaning agency, which could not, in Lewis's opinion, be any worse than the outfit David Rigg had hired.

There had been another outbreak of mouse droppings in the kitchen, despite the visit from pest control the previous week. As soon as Lewis crossed one problem off his list, a fresh one seemed to appear. He made another note, on his secret list, to put some security cameras in the area to see where the mice were coming from.

'You might not need a whole hour with Eunice,' Pam warned him. 'I've seen her own children leave within five minutes.'

'I'm sure she'll have plenty to tell me,' said Lewis, setting off with his notebook and Gayle's question prompts, which he'd laminated.

Eunice's apartment was on the first floor, at the back of the building, overlooking what had once been a kitchen vegetable garden and was now just a mess. Like most of the residents, she'd condensed a family home into two rooms and the effect was a huge amount of teak in a small space, giving Lewis the overwhelming sensation of being inside a coffin.

'Now then, Eunice,' he said, moving three scatter cushions to sit down on the chair opposite hers. 'I've come to talk to you about your life.'

'Hnngh.' Eunice's sniffs went from unimpressed through to judgemental. 'Hnngh' didn't sound completely dismissive, though.

'You've heard about our new project? Have your friends mentioned it?'

'There's been talk at lunch. I hear the Horrobins have been interviewed already – how did they get to the top of the list?'

'You're top of *my* list, Eunice – my very first interviewee! I've been looking forward to hearing more about what you did before you joined us here.'

She rolled her eyes but Lewis was sure he could see a flicker of interest.

He got out his notebook and clicked his pen, placing the prompt sheet on the coffee table in front of him.

'Now then. It says here to start at the very beginning – it's a very good place to start, ha-ha! – so where would that be for you? Are you a native Longhamptonian?'

Eunice sighed and crossed her feet at the ankles. She wore soft leather shoes with Velcro straps but they were red. Lewis thought they looked like a medieval child's.

'Why are we doing this again?' she asked. 'Is this a marketing scam? Pretending to be interested so you can sell me funeral cover?'

'What? *Why*? Why would we do that?' Lewis was bemused. 'No. The better we know who you are, the better we can look after you.' He gestured towards the tray on the table between them. 'Like with your tea. You told Michael your tea was never strong enough, so we made a note for the kitchen to put an extra bag in your pot. And Marek came to ask you if there was a particular brand of tea you'd like, didn't he? And now?'

'It's not as bad as it was,' Eunice acknowledged.

'Tremendous! So that's what this is about – learning more about each other. Your family's had nearly eighty years to get to know you, whereas we've got a bit of catching up to do.'

'Hmmph.'

Eunice had the sort of pale-blue eyes normally found in portraits of closely related aristocrats, the type that looked right through you, and judged hard, toying with the possibility of execution. There were one or two examples of those still hanging around the house, too big to be removed during the house's various incarnations from home to school to hotel to home again. Lewis was no stranger to awkward stares but there was something about Eunice that was particularly challenging.

Still, he liked a challenge.

'Have you always taken your tea strong, Eunice?'

She seemed to be weighing up an answer.

Normally Lewis would have deployed his Pause of Power, but he heard himself say, 'Did you *have* tea bags growing up? When were they invented, tea bags? Did you have tea leaves? Did you know someone down your street who could tell fortunes with tea leaves?'

'Are you calling me a witch?'

'Not at all!'

'Who's doing this interview, you or me?'

'It's a team effort!'

'Nggh.' Eunice's lip curled.

Lewis sat back, momentarily winded.

She weighed him up for a long moment. 'I'll tell you why I like strong tea, Mr Levison. My stepdad was a mean bugger, always made us reuse tea leaves. Soon as I could afford my own, I put an extra bag in the pot and damn the expense.'

'There you go,' said Lewis, making a note. 'And we're off.'

Not the magical memory he'd hoped for, but a chink of light into what might have shaped Eunice's jaundiced world view.

'He used to water down the milk too. And make my mother reuse stamps. We never had the fire on, not unless someone was coming round. I was nine before I realised most people take their coats *off* when they go inside.'

Lewis waggled his pen. This was fascinating social history, but he wasn't sure this was the sort of conversation topic that was going to lead to a more joyful Rosemount experience. For either of them.

'So, on a brighter note . . . What would you say was the most memorable moment of your childhood?'

'My dad dying in an accident at the steelworks when I was five.'

Bloody hell. Lewis blanched. 'Oh dear, Eunice. I'm sorry about that.'

'Mam wasn't. *I* wasn't. He was a mean bastard too.'

'But then she met your stepfather and . . .'

'He were my dad's best mate.'

'Oh.' Lewis hastily cast his eye around the room for more uplifting inspiration.

On her sideboard, amongst the usual crop of china dolls and dogs and pigs, was a group of family photographs: her own black-and-white register office wedding, Michael's brightly coloured nineties wedding, and a couple of baby photos of frowning toddlers with massive foreheads, wrinkled in familiar displeasure.

'What about your wedding? Looks like it was a lovely day!'

Eunice huffed. 'It rained.'

'People say that's good luck.'

'It was for the man in the shop selling umbrellas near the church. He did a roaring trade.' But there was a twinkle in her eye.

'So where did you get married? Was it near here?' he started, but she interrupted him.

'Are *you* married, Mr Levison?'

'Me?' Lewis was caught off guard. 'No, I'm not.'

'Sweetheart?'

'Um, no.'

'Boyfriend then?' And when Lewis spluttered, she said, 'No need to be shy, Mr Levison.'

'I'm not gay,' said Lewis. 'Not that there's anything wrong with that.'

Eunice tipped her head to one side with a sly smile, much more engaged than he'd ever seen her. He was reminded of the cat that hung around the kitchens, staring fixedly at a spot behind the skirting boards, biding its time.

'Broken heart, is it?'

'I . . .' He could hear himself spluttering again, searching for the words. Not a broken heart, but a longing for the *right one*, with its accompanying wariness of the *wrong one* – so many slippery reasons why he'd never quite managed to do what everyone else seemed to do almost by accident. He'd got off to a bad start. Long school holidays spent with grandparents, not hanging out with kids his age, absorbing the unspoken rituals of the opposite sex, the whispers and giggles. No practice as a teenager, despite many female friends at the girls' school twinned with his. In fact, according to more than one of them, that had been the problem. Girls 'liked him too much as a friend' to want to spoil it with romance, but on being pressed, wouldn't explain why, exactly. And somehow, despite a new haircut and contact lenses, that had followed him to university. This time cemented with an unfortunate Freshers' Week misunderstanding that no matter how many times he'd tried to explain only seemed to reinforce the initial assumptions. Once some well-meaning friend had decided you were gay, it seemed, it was actively homophobic of you to try to insist otherwise, let alone anyone else.

But Lewis hadn't given up hope. He'd seen too many very, *very* late-doors romances blossom in care homes just like Rosemount to believe that love had an age limit. The problem was, most of the women he met were over seventy-five and judged any new man by standards he wasn't sure anyone under forty could possibly meet.

'You can tell me,' said Eunice, with an unconvincing show of sympathy. 'Was there someone once? Someone you're not quite over? A sister-in-law, maybe?'

'*What*? No!' Lewis pulled himself together. 'Nothing like that. I'm just too busy for a relationship. It would be very unfair, when my work takes up so much of my time and energy. I'm committed to making Rosemount—'

'Before Rosemount? Were you too busy with another residential home to find a girlfriend?'

Eunice was very forthright.

'Yes,' said Lewis. 'I was, since you ask.' There had been a few promising dates, some set up by the same loyal female friends for whom he was now 'the best godfather ever!'. But his hours were long, and the older he got, his continued bachelordom became its own 'red flag', whatever the hell that meant. What were you supposed to do about it, anyway? Embroider your love life CV, the way some people added degrees and fictitious promotions to their work experience? Lewis didn't like lying.

He gave Eunice a direct look. 'When I make a commitment I stick to it, and the last few years have been challenging, as you know, for the care industry.'

'That's so sad. You spend your whole day with us old folk, and you don't even have a warm body to go home to at the end of the day.'

'Eunice.' His voice sounded strangulated, even to his own ears. 'Please. Tell me about your—'

'Because it's not like you're getting any younger. How old are you, Mr Levison? And don't pretend it's a state secret – there's no room for coyness in here. I've got to put up with strangers asking me about my bowel movements twice a day, as you well know.'

'I'm thirty-eight.' Lewis drew a line in his head under that fact. He wasn't going to let Eunice turn this into a session about him, not her. But as he said it, he noted that thirty-eight suddenly sounded a lot older than thirty-four. Lewis had always rather looked forward to turning forty – it felt like a good age, experienced, but still energetic – but his imagination had always supplied a happy, supportive wife and three inquisitive primary-school children, which he realised he couldn't now deliver within that deadline.

'Thirty-eight?' She raised her eyebrows enigmatically. 'Mmm.'

Don't rise to it, Lewis told himself.

'What was the most exciting thing you did as a child?' he asked swiftly.

'I didn't do exciting things as a child. I had three brothers.'

'Was that not fun? Didn't you get to climb trees and ride bikes with them?'

'Hnngh.' The snort again. 'I wasn't even allowed to *learn* to ride a bicycle.'

'Why not?'

There was a momentary hesitation. 'Because that's how my dad was killed, on his way to work one morning. Got knocked off it by a lorry turning into the yard without looking. Mam said no way would we ever get on a bike.' Eunice pursed her thin lips. 'My brothers had bikes, course they did, bought them with their paper-round money, hid them in their mates' sheds. But I wasn't allowed one. A job, or a bike. Not allowed anything, me.'

She glanced out of the window, and Lewis caught a lifetime's resentment flickering across her face, escaping from a hairline crack in her memory like a wisp of smoke.

'Didn't you ask?'

'Didn't want to upset Mam. She hated the damn things. Wouldn't let my kids have one either, I had to promise her.' Eunice looked up. '*And* I kept my promise. Before you ask.'

'So you've never been on a bicycle?' Lewis felt sorry for her. He felt sorry for anyone who'd never felt so close to flying.

'Are you deaf? No.'

'Would you like to?'

Eunice turned back to him and the familiar tartness had returned. 'Would I like to go to New York? Would I like to water-ski? Would I like to have a night of wild passion with Tom Selleck? There's a time and a place, and at my age, you have to admit the time for bicycles and the like has passed.'

'We'll see about that,' said Lewis, then quickly added, 'Not about Tom Selleck. No can do, on that front.'

Eunice sat back on her sofa with a huffy snort, and crossed her legs, but Lewis noted her left red shoe was now wagging. With amusement, he hoped.

Afterwards, striding back to his office for his meeting with Marek about the mouse droppings, Lewis debated with himself about whether he'd responded properly to Eunice's memories of her stepfather – or her father.

The only downside of this project, in his opinion, was its potential for stirring up long-suppressed pain. Was Eunice now stewing on those unhappy memories? It would be wrong to assume people would only select happy memories, and Lewis's own view was, why would you want to dwell on sadness – sadness that you couldn't change, at a time in your life when the present day held enough unavoidable pains already? But that might not be true for everyone.

Lewis stopped opposite the portrait of the Earl of Longhampton, whose pale and bulbous eyes reminded him of Eunice's, and made a note in his book to ask Gayle for advice on keeping stories upbeat. She'd warned him of potential points of friction – allowing each spouse to tell their own version of a story, not being afraid of tears or silence, and so on. She seemed almost excited by the potential for drama.

'You often find,' she'd added, 'that the stories the families know and the stories the volunteers are told don't always match up exactly!'

Lewis wondered what Michael Stafford's version of the bicycle ban would be, whether he too had kept a secret bike in his mate's shed.

As if by serendipity, as he was making his note an email from Gayle pinged on to his phone. It was a reply to his request for a volunteer update, and when he saw Beth Cherry's name as a lead writer, along with her email address and phone number, Lewis's heart lifted unexpectedly.

He stared at her contact details for a moment, amazed that something as mundane as an email address could feel so exciting. Lewis knew other men would probably find an excuse to get in touch without a second thought. Before he left that evening, he'd make dozens of calls, to his boss, to families, to the oil supplier, to contractors, not always with good news or easy questions, but he'd launch into those conversations without a second's hesitation. And yet when it came to Beth . . .

Why was it so different?

It was an invasion of privacy, he reminded himself. Highly unprofessional.

And what would he say? Lewis had been on an Equity, Diversity and Inclusion course only last month; the minefield of potential offence had grown exponentially since he'd last been on a date and even then he hadn't been totally sure if he was supposed to say his friend Helen's cousin looked nice or if that was objectifying her.

He looked up and the withering gaze of the Earl of Longhampton reminded him of his grandfather, when he'd made excuses for not ironing the bits of his shirt hidden by jumpers.

Before he could think, Lewis found himself dialling Beth's number, but the moment it started ringing out, his brain howled in protest.

What are you doing? Hang up now, Lewis!

'Beth Cherry?'

Too late. 'Hello there, Beth! It's Lewis Levison. From Rosemount Court.'

Lewis! This is an egregrious breech of data protection regulation!

'Oh, *hello*, Lewis.' Beth's voice was warm and soft. She could have done voiceovers for Marks and Spencer. 'You don't have to say all that, I know who you are by now.'

'Ha-ha!' Lewis's heart swooped around his chest in an embarrassingly teenage way. 'I was . . . I was ringing to, um, thank you for stepping up to join Gayle's writing team. I've just had an email from her – I really appreciate the extra time you're giving us. It'll make a huge difference to the project.'

He was congratulating himself on coming up with a legitimate reason for the call when she said, solemnly, 'Ah, well, I've got a bone to pick with you about that.'

'What?'

'*Someone* told Gayle I was a writer. You know I'm not, right? I really hope you're good at managing expectations!'

'But I thought . . .' Was her voice really stern, or was she joking? He couldn't tell. He stared up at the Earl, who was no help. 'I'm so sorry if I've—'

'Stop it! I'm only joking. Well, sort of. I guess it'll be a learning experience for us all!'

'Is there anything I can— *we* can do to help?' he asked quickly. 'Do you need, um . . .' He racked his brains again. What did writers need? 'Pens? Or paper? Extra notebooks? Just say!'

Lewis would have happily delivered an entire stationery cupboard to Beth, personally, in a wheelbarrow, had she asked.

'Hmm, now you're asking.' She sounded amused. 'I always need new notebooks. And if you think a special pen would be a good idea . . .'

'No problem,' said Lewis, wriggling his small notebook back out and leaning against the wall to scribble down *notebook* and *pen*.

'I've got a couple of journalists on my client list who claim the most ridiculous stationery,' Beth went on. 'So I can reassure you that it is tax deductible.'

'Ha-ha!' Lewis's nerves began to rise. This was the point in the conversation when, legitimate reason for call concluded, someone more experienced would pivot smoothly to flirting, maybe even an offer of a thank-you drink? But Lewis didn't have anything like that in his armoury; his mind had gone blank and the pause was extending and the conversation was hanging by a thread.

Beth was waiting for him to say something, and when he didn't – although he desperately wanted to – she said, 'OK, then, I'll see you next week, will I?'

'Yes!' said Lewis. 'I'm looking forward to it.'

'Me too!'

He heard the big dog bark in the background and remembered he could have asked her how Tomsk was, but she was saying goodbye, in that sweet friendly way, and the call was over.

Lewis pocketed his phone with mixed feelings. That had been fifty per cent successful. Much better than not calling at all, surely.

The Earl of Longhampton, he felt, would have rolled his eyes, if he could.

Chapter eleven

Hey, Harriet! So sorry not to be able to make it tomorrow for your baby shower. Wishing you a smooth and safe delivery! All the best, Beth x

For good measure, I'd sent Allen twenty quid for her collection, and arranged for a special stork-shaped balloon to be delivered to the office first thing.

I sat back on the sofa and pressed send, already luxuriating in the relief of not being at Harriet's nappy-themed party. I'd been to enough showers to know the drill: Natasha circling the room with a Colin the Caterpillar, pressing everyone to have a piece, particularly those on diets, cooing about 'magical memories' with Harriet and any other mothers, then shooting me an 'aw, this must be hard for you' sad face, which I'd have to acknowledge in a way that made me look appreciative of her concern yet not crushed by my own spinsterdom.

No one could object to a prior volunteering commitment, right?

I'd heeded Allen's warning about the gathering storm, but this wasn't the best day to go back in. I'd done some research on Christian and the initiatives he'd led in his previous workplace, but also on my hybrid working options. Obviously I'd have to return at some point, if only for the meeting where I persuaded them to let me work from home full time. Allen would support me; we both knew I was more efficient at home than I'd ever been in the office, with all the politics and moods and kitchen dramas.

But, for my own confidence, if nothing else, I needed to get myself back to my old self first.

Motivated by my proactive message to Harriet, I pushed myself off the sofa and went to try on the one office outfit not currently in storage: a slouchy grey trouser suit that had hung off me in a flattering way when I bought it in a fit of extravagance, encouraged by Fraser. I used to style it with a tight black T-shirt, or – in what he'd called, 'my Parisian literary agent look' – with a green silk shirt. It had made me feel understated but very cool, and somehow it always, always fitted.

Not anymore.

Now the waistband was at least seven centimetres off doing up, and the jacket strained around my upper arms, as if I might burst out of it like a caterpillar, or the Incredible Hulk. That was a whole new humiliating sensation, tight jacket sleeves. I had to force myself to look in the mirror, and could only hold my own gaze for a nanosecond before looking away again.

Disgusted, I peeled it off, and pulled my jersey harems back on as quickly as I could. I hated feeling exposed, even when there was only me to see.

That honestly wasn't what I looked like, surely? How had I not noticed how bad it had got? I'd kidded myself that I hadn't put on *that* much weight recently but every single item in my (very limited) current wardrobe was either stretchy, elasticated or had the word 'lounge' somewhere in its description. I was slowly expanding to fill my harem pants, avoiding mirrors like a vampire. A fat vampire.

I sat gripping my head in my hands for several minutes, sinking deeper and deeper in a toxic puddle of my own contempt and panic, then sat up.

No. I could still fix this. There was time. Generous, kind, guardian angel Allen had given me a tip-off, and I had to take full advantage of it.

I downloaded yet another fitness app, guesstimated my weight, then calculated that if I increased my steps target by seven thousand per day, and did intermittent fasting between noon and seven, I could lose five kilos in about four weeks. That should get the trousers to zip up. I could get my hair cut, that always helped, and some highlights. Enough armour to get me through one meeting, and after that . . .

I wasn't thinking beyond that.

But I had a plan, so at least I was doing something. Things could look very different in a month's time. If I started *now*.

Tomsk was more than happy to support me with some extra lunchtime steps. We went for a long loop around the canal, up through the park (avoiding the coffee cart, which I couldn't help noticing now did sugared doughnuts), and back home, where I found a pile of books on my doorstep.

I guessed, from the subject matter alone, where they'd come from: there were several creative writing guides, and on the bottom, two novels, *The Dancing Heart* and *The Soul of Discretion* by one Elizabeth Buckingham. *Having a clear-out – thought these might aid your inspiration!* said the Post-it note on top. Martine had beautiful handwriting.

I took them as the hint they clearly were and, once I'd despatched my remaining work for the day, settled down to an afternoon's grappling with Seraphina and Arthur.

Seraphina – I wasn't even sure that was the right name now – was more a vague collection of descriptions than a real person. Reading back through what I'd written, I realised that in the course of seven scenes her hair changed colour from chestnut to wheat-blond back to chestnut, and was sometimes bouncy ringlets, sometimes smooth like draped silk, and she sighed too much. Like, constantly, as if she had breathing difficulties. Arthur, her beloved, was much more consistently defined with his characterful face, straight, dark eyebrows and thatch of blond hair; usually he was dressed in riding boots and tight breeches. I could have described Arthur Hammond all day long, but sadly my mental block was preventing me from making him *do* something. I'd eventually finished the tearful farewell at the fireplace (which was quite well described, if I said so myself; *I'd* cried, anyway) but after that I had a yawning blank until the big reunion.

I flipped listlessly through Martine's books, in search of the magic spell that might help my plot come to life. The books were helpful in the sense of telling me *how* to write something, but not – as Seraphina continued to just kind of stand there in the library while the seasons changed behind her on the mantelpiece – *what* to write. I knew there was a painful parting; I knew there was an emotional reunion. But I couldn't work out what came in between.

I stared at my screen. *Seraphina felt as if* . . . What? *What* did Seraphina feel?

Nothing came to me.

I dangled my hand over the edge of the sofa, where Tomsk was snoring throatily, worn out by squirrels and smells. I scratched his head. Maybe I *should* give Seraphina a dog? What sort of dog would she own? Inspired, I made a short-list of four possible breeds, then got stuck – as usual – on the thorny question of names.

I reached for the pile of books, and picked up Martine's novel. Reading often stoked my brain into action, and *The Dancing Heart* promised to be a real page-turner, going by the glowing reviews on the back (albeit from people I'd never heard of).

> *Love is a luxury for a young woman like Bernadette Machin, who dreams of a world far away from the hard graft of farming life . . .*

Or maybe not. I turned to the author biography in the front. There was a soft-focus photo of Martine – or Elizabeth Buckingham – looking pleased with herself in a red polo neck, her chin propped coquettishly on one hand. The accompanying personal details were so deliberately vague it made her seem as if she was in a witness protection programme.

I wondered why she'd chosen to call herself Elizabeth Buckingham, when Martine Henderson was a perfectly good name for a romantic author. Privacy, I supposed.

Opening the book at a random page – it felt as if I was the first person to open it at all – I found myself in the middle of a torrid love scene between Bernadette and someone called Lord Heatherington; despite their close embrace they were managing to have quite a wordy conversation, mainly about estate management. Knowing how much of my own experiences I poured into my writing, I could understand why Fraser and his siblings had delegated Perry to read it for them, and it was almost a relief when Tomsk sprang to his feet, barked, and then two seconds later there was a knock at the front door.

Was it so unreasonable that I'd assume the bouquet of spring flowers was for me? Especially given that the delivery man knocked on *my* door, shoved them into *my* hands and rushed off without speaking.

Fraser was the only person who'd ever given me flowers, and though I barely acknowledged it to myself, whenever I saw a florist's van nearby I secretly crossed my fingers, even now. So when I opened the card and saw the words *love from fraser* printed by the florist, my heart did a massive cartoon *ba-doom* in my chest, and a big stupid smile spread across my face. Had Jackie told him I was staying – and why? Had Martine? Maybe this was his way of saying, Sorry you're having a bad time, glad we're able to help?

'Oh my God, Tomsk!' I said, because I needed to tell someone. 'Look at these!'

He swept his tail from side to side, and I turned over the card, smiling so hard my cheeks hurt. 'Look, it says—'

> *MARTINE HENDERSON, 13 COLERIDGE DRIVE, LONGHAMPTON*

'Oh.' The excitement drained out of me, leaving behind a chilly dampness, tinged with self-loathing. What was I thinking? Ugh. This was what happened when you spent too much time imagining romantic situations.

I went round to the front door, so as not to startle Martine with a knock at the back, and rang the doorbell.

When there was no answer after a couple of minutes, then several minutes, I crouched and peered through the brass letterbox. I could see four black bin bags in the hall, and some crates of books.

'Martine?' I called. No response.

I tried the door, and it was open; she hadn't gone out. I hesitated, unsure as to whether I should let myself in. I hadn't been inside since I'd arrived – and I felt that if Martine wanted my company, she'd have asked – but on the other hand, what if she'd fallen? She'd obviously embarked on some kind of spring-cleaning mission, and if she'd dragged those bin bags down the stairs herself, she could have hurt herself.

'Martine!' I called, louder this time, and rattled the letterbox.

Silence.

I sat back on my heels, debating the polite vs responsible options, then, just as I was about to let myself in, I heard a door open inside the house. Faint music drifted out. I didn't recognise the song but it had a Motown-ish beat, not what I'd have expected – Ray and Martine were Classic FM to the core. I peered through the letterbox in time to see Martine sashaying down the hall with a box, strutting along in a pair of gold slippers, exactly the kind that Jackie worried she'd fall down the stairs wearing. She was singing the song I didn't recognise but, unlike me, she knew all the words.

Relieved, I rattled the letterbox to get her attention. 'Martine? It's me, Beth!'

She stopped, looking round, and nearly dropped the box. 'Beth!'

'Sorry,' I said, through the flap, 'I didn't mean to startle you, I've got a delivery.'

She crouched down to my level, much more easily than I had. 'Goodness, are you all right down there?'

Not really. My knees were killing me, and I struggled awkwardly to my feet, just as she opened the door.

'For you!' I presented her with the bouquet. 'They're not from me, sorry. The courier left them.'

'How *lovely*! I wonder who they're from?' Her eyes were bright, but when she opened the card, I thought her delight dimmed a little. 'Oh. They're from Fraser.'

I feigned surprise. 'How thoughtful of him!'

'Mmm. He sends a bunch every month, instead of coming to see me. I'd rather have no flowers and an hour of his time, but . . .' Martine sighed. 'I suppose it's thoughtful, yes. Would you like to come in for a cup of tea?'

'If I'm not interrupting?' I looked around the hall.

'Not at all! In fact, I was going to ask a favour – if you could take some of these things to the charity shop, next time you're in town, I'd be terribly grateful.'

Now I was inside, I could see there were more bags stacked behind the others; Martine must have been having a real sort-out. 'Any particular charity shop?'

'St Michael's Hospice, please,' she said decisively. 'They have discerning shoppers.' She waved away my offer of help and waltzed off to the kitchen to make the tea.

Immediately I slid into the sitting room like a secret agent, eyes peeled for clues to Fraser's new life. I'd been longing for a chance to snoop, starting with a closer look at those photos on the piano, but the piano lid was bare, the photographs stacked unceremoniously into boxes. Three boxes, all full.

I glanced towards the kitchen, then flipped through the pile. Graduations, holidays, Jackie, the Dents, Heather and her cello, more Heather, more Dents. Where *was* Fraser?

There. I stopped, and so did my heart. It was his graduation photo, closer to the Fraser I'd first met: sun-streaked blond hair flopping into his eyes, the 'yeah, yeah, whatever, graduation photo' half-smile, the gangling almost-a-man. It sent memories blurring across the back of my mind, a fast-forward rush of parties and dates and sex and IKEA trips where we'd bought our first bookshelves and put them together badly, and laughed about it.

Something inside me reached, yearning, for the past. Why had I derailed something so perfect? By being impatient?

'Beth, would you mind taking this for me?'

I stood up, quickly, before Martine entered the room and caught me snooping. She hadn't noticed me crouching down, being too busy concentrating on not dropping the tray or losing a slipper. The slippers were stylish but probably not ideal from a health and safety point of view.

I took the tray from her, setting it down on the coffee table. She'd put out the kitchen mugs, not visitor's china, which was, I supposed, a compliment of sorts. 'Are you having the piano tuned?'

'No, I've decided to donate it to the school. It's ridiculous, having a baby grand sitting here doing nothing. Someone should be benefitting.'

'Are you sure?' Fraser had told me Martine was an accomplished pianist, though I'd never heard her play. 'You don't want to play it yourself?'

Martine shook her head. 'I don't think I could anymore. Anyway, someone's coming to have a look this week.'

'But where will you put the family photographs?' I was only half joking.

She waved a hand, a gesture I recognised from Fraser as much as her. It was funny how many of Martine's mannerisms she'd passed on to her children. 'I'll find somewhere. Anyway, I know what they all look like by now.'

'She's doing *what* with the baby grand?'

Jackie's reaction was reassuring, given how much I'd agonised over whether or not to grass Martine up. It was only when I took the charity shop bags and spotted the lovingly handmade 'Grandma' mugs in there that I'd decided that maybe she needed to know the extent of Martine's spring-cleaning.

'She's donating it to the school.'

'But it's a family heirloom! Grandpa gave her that piano – it was a wedding present! Oh my God. Did she say when this was happening?'

'No, just that someone was coming round this week to have a look.'

'Right. I'll find a reason to drop by asap. If she doesn't want the piano for whatever reason, *I'll* take it.' She sighed. 'Thanks for letting me know, Beth. I owe you a big favour.'

Although I wouldn't say I'd been particularly close to Fraser's big sister in the past, Jackie had done me quite a few favours over the years. She was the sort to spot the shy know-no-ones at a party (i.e., me) and drag them over to another awkward guest, matching them up like odd socks. Three of my longest-standing clients were friends of friends that Jackie had sent my way, not long after I started my own list. I'd never managed to return any of the kindnesses Jackie had done me, but she *had* asked me to keep an eye on Martine, so . . . I was.

'Maybe she's rethinking downsizing?' I told her about the charity bags, safely in the boot of my car. 'Maybe visiting Rosemount has made her realise it's not as bad as she'd heard? The new manager, Lewis, is going through the place like a dose of salts, from what I can see.'

'Nope!' Jackie let out a mirthless laugh. 'Quite the opposite. I suggested another visit, now she'd met the manager, and Mum shut that right down. She's very happy you're volunteering with the old folk, as she calls them, but there's no way *she's* going back, thank you very much.'

'Oh.'

She sighed heavily. 'No, there's a picture starting to build up here. First the funny business with the party, then the bench, now this. Look, Beth, do you mind me sharing this with you? It's just that you *know* Mum, and you're seeing her every day at the moment.'

'No, not at all.' Did it make me a terrible person that I was actually quite excited to be included in Henderson family chat? Probably. Oh well.

'So. Mum's really not been herself lately. After Dad died, we decided – I mean, the four of us siblings and Mum – that we'd donate a memorial bench in the park in his name, and a prize at the sixth-form college. I knew it was what he'd have wanted, he hinted at it a few times.'

Yes, I could absolutely see that. The Raymond Henderson Prize for Business Studies and/or Golf.

'Obviously,' Jackie continued, 'we didn't want to do anything while emotions were still raw, but I felt now we're ready to get the ball rolling. So last weekend I suggested Mum and I had a look at some benches, and she flatly refused to talk about it. Not now, not ever. Denied she'd ever agreed to such a thing.'

'Well, grief doesn't follow a timetable, does it?' I said carefully. 'You can think you're fine one day, then you hear a song, or smell something and . . .'

Even now, I thought of my own mum every time my teaspoon clinked in the brown sugar jar I'd taken when I cleared her bedsit; I thought of Dad on the rare occasions I smelled that stale-beer-and-carpets pub smell. (Pubs had changed a lot since I was a child, thankfully.) I didn't cry anymore, but I couldn't stop my brain flipping up the memories. The months Ray had been gone were nothing, compared to the fifty-something years he and Martine had lived together.

'Absolutely, but I don't think that's it, though. I've watched her like a hawk since Dad died. I was there *a lot* in the early days, I was so worried about how she'd cope. Not just physically, with the house, but mentally. I mean, they were each other's first and only love. Can you imagine literally living your whole life with one person?'

'It's so rare. They were incredibly lucky to have that.'

'Right? So I was super-careful about her feelings, and we'd got to the point where she was still sad, but she was happy to talk about him, about happier times. But then last week, when I brought up the memorial, she sounded almost angry, not sad. I almost wondered if she'd forgotten what we'd discussed, but that would point to . . .' She trailed off. 'Well, it's extremely out of character, put it like that.'

I knew what she was reluctant to say aloud. 'Are you worried she's showing signs of dementia?'

There was a pause. 'Yes. Perry's dad had Alzheimer's, and out-of-character behaviour was one of the first clues. I don't want to be the one pointing the finger, making out Mum's heading that way. And I don't want her to be heading that way! But if she's started forgetting entire conversations, finding herself in strange places, getting rid of things she loves, then maybe we need to help. Have you noticed anything unusual in her behaviour?'

'Nothing that would ring alarm bells,' I said. 'I speak to her on the phone every night, and she sounds as sharp as ever.'

'At night?' Jackie leaped on that. 'What time?'

'Usually between ten and eleven.' Up to midnight. Although I didn't say that.

'Hmm. That's late for her. She's normally in bed by ten. What sort of things does she say, when she calls?'

It wasn't so much the conversation, as the call itself, but I didn't quite know how to explain to Jackie. I'd had similar brief – but heartfelt – 'You all right? I'm all right' midnight check-ins with Ash, meeting by the yellow light of the fridge door in the darker days of the heartbreak wilderness months. Martine was more eloquent but I think the intention, from her end anyway, was the same.

'Anything and everything. She's volunteered my services up at Rosemount, so she wants updates about that, and she's chivvying me about my writing. She's just left me a stack of fiction guides,' I added. 'I'm pretty sure there's going to be a test.'

Jackie sounded relieved. 'OK, that sounds more like Mum.'

'What did you mean, the funny business about the party?' I asked. 'Earlier?'

'Oh! Long story short, it would have been their emerald wedding anniversary next month. Fifty-five years. Dad was planning a surprise party, with as many old friends as were still kicking around. Obviously, he didn't go further than save the dates, but we – the four of us – decided we'd go ahead and have a small family do, so Mum wouldn't have to face the day on her own. Just afternoon tea in the garden, champagne, cakes, very low-key.'

'Sounds lovely,' I said.

'I know, she loves an afternoon tea. Anyway, I thought I'd tell Mum ahead of time, give her something to look forward to, and she said . . .' Jackie paused, as if she still couldn't believe it. 'She said, "Oh, you don't need to make a fuss."'

'*Really*?' Even I knew Martine lived for family parties – parties of any kind. They were the sort of family who owned wine coolers, cake stands, a huge glass punch bowl with matching cups, and a fish kettle. I guessed it came with having access to an actual wine cellar.

'I said, Mum, it's hardly making a fuss, we want to be there! Cara's already booked tickets, even Fraser's requested annual leave.' She let out an emphatic breath. 'He's staying with us, just the one night, obviously.'

'Mm-hmm.' So Fraser was coming – on his own? A delicious detail tucked away to examine later. 'Do you think, maybe, it's still too soon? Is she worried about breaking down in front of the grandchildren?'

'Perhaps. That's what Perry said. Maybe I'm finding symptoms, now I'm looking for them. But then Mum's always going on about how Cara's little boy's going to grow up with an American accent and why doesn't she come home more often? It doesn't make sense.'

'When is it, the anniversary?'

'June 14th. You'll pop in, won't you? For a bit of cake?' She paused. 'You and Fraser . . . you're not . . . I mean, not being nosy, oh dear!' An awkward laugh. 'Maybe I should have asked before now. Sorry.'

'No, we're fine, honestly. It was pretty amicable.' My pulse was already racing at the promise of a legitimate reason to see Fraser. 'I can't say we've been in touch much since, but there was no unpleasantness, no one else involved. We just wanted different things.'

'Oh, good.' Jackie sounded relieved. 'Good.'

'Will he be bringing someone?' I held my breath, my heart balancing on the edge of a cliff.

'I don't know. I'll be honest with you, we barely hear from Fraser either. Bothers Mum more than me, but she always makes some excuse for him. Work or whatnot. I sometimes think Fraser's working for MI5. Except they'd probably give him a better cover story!'

I think we were both glad to end a tricky conversation on a genuine laugh, and I promised Jackie I'd keep an eye on any other furniture making its way out of the house. In return, she said she'd deal with the bags of charity donations in my car boot.

I hung up, feeling sunnier. Not just because I'd finally repaid some of Jackie's kindness, but I had more motivation than ever to get back into my grey trouser suit. The party was in a month's time.

I found my fitness app, and upped my additional daily steps to ten thousand.

Chapter twelve

'After four weeks of focused spot improvement and a root-and-branch review of operations, I'm happy to report that Rosemount Court has met its revised monthly targets.' Lewis flashed his most confidence-inspiring smile. 'I'm happy to take more specific questions?'

Normally he didn't do weekly updates to the senior team, but as Eric Alexander, Acorn Care's owner, had made crystal clear, Rosemount's performance reflected so much on the group as a whole that it required performative oversight.

He'd also made crystal clear that it was by no means a foregone conclusion that Rosemount would be staying open. Even with Lewis in charge.

Donald Partridge, lead nutritionist, jumped straight in. 'Talk to me about those atrocious kitchens that are still giving me nightmares. What's happening there?'

'Ah! Amazing things! Marek has completely overhauled the menus – we're introducing a Round The World in Fifty Meals month, starting today.'

'Nothing too spicy, right?' Cheryl (care director) looked wary. 'The last thing we need is a gastric incident like the one at Darlington Hall.'

'You wouldn't believe how many of our residents don't feel our food is spicy *enough*.' Just that week Lewis had heard about married life in Bangkok and RAF postings in Singapore and community outreach projects in Bangladesh. Judy Vance was sharing her memories in the form of family recipes, as were some of the nursing staff. Lewis had fed it all straight back into the Nutrition Plan. 'Of course there'll still be a choice to suit everyone – in accordance with the CQC guidelines.'

'Rosemount scored very poorly on staff satisfaction and retention,' Greta (director of compliance) observed from the top left of Lewis's laptop. 'Have you got to the bottom of why that is?'

'A pattern is emerging,' said Lewis. Eric and the team were aware of David Rigg's shortcomings; Lewis had noted that Nuala from Legal was now cc'd into any email involving David. 'Historically, communication has been disappointing. Worries turn into problems because staff didn't feel able to raise concerns. I'm reminding staff that I'm available for any queries, no matter how small, and offering on-going training to demonstrate our commitment to supporting their development.'

'And how is team cohesion going?' asked Eric. 'I know that's one of your priorities.'

Cheryl muttered something under her breath about 'paintballing'.

'Good,' said Lewis. 'As expected, there were some resignations to begin with, but I feel that's strengthened the team rather than diminished it.'

Pam had warned him about the handful of 'bad apples' David Rigg had failed to pluck from the Rosemount tree – the slopers-off, the tick-boxers, the half-arsers, the rogue cleaner who stole entire pallets of fabric conditioner and flogged them on eBay. It hadn't taken Lewis long to remove them: he had a system, starting with a friendly chat, moving on to performance plans, and then a less friendly chat. One team-building afternoon (a fiendish escape room he'd personally devised in the library) had flushed out the worst offenders in one easy go, albeit with an unscheduled 'panic attack workshop' from Anita, the first-aid lead.

'Does that include the alleged whistleblower?' Greta arched an eyebrow.

'I'm confident that the whistleblower is no longer part of our team,' Lewis assured her. Despite his ongoing detective efforts and several calls to the editor of the local newspaper, he still hadn't pinned down exactly who it was who'd been leaking damning photos of mould and soggy medications to the *Gazette*'s investigative journalist. *Someone* was. But there had been nothing more in the last week or so, which suggested that they'd been one of the ejected cohort. Or maybe now he was tackling the issues, they felt their job was done. Still, he didn't know exactly who it had been and that bothered Lewis. He didn't like loose ends.

And yet those lightbulbs had gone missing. Why? He frowned. *Don't get distracted.*

'We do need to discuss enrichment!' Frances the HR director insisted. Frances was a keen exponent of theatre across the group's care homes. 'I was sad to read that Rosemount didn't even have a choir.'

'I'm so glad you asked about enrichment, Frances!' Lewis said. 'We've just begun a fascinating project to explore the life stories of—'

'That's tremendous, Lewis – sorry, Frances, I'm going to have to park that for next week, as we're running out of time,' said Eric; Frances had already launched into her usual spiel about the community glue of music. 'But, in conclusion, Lewis, we still need to form a realistic picture of Rosemount's viability. The CQC reinspection could be much sooner than the statutory six months. We're struggling to make the numbers add up, even without the investment it clearly needs. Devin sent you the financial year projections, didn't he? On top of fixing compliance issues, we need at least four new residents by the end of this quarter – I see you're running at eight empty units.'

Lewis nodded. He'd pored over Devin's spreadsheets night after night until it made sense. Figures weren't really his strong point – he tended to see rooms and people, rather than units – but he was confident that if he could get the people right, the rest would follow.

'We're on the way, Eric,' he said confidently. 'Leave it with me.'

Pam knocked on Lewis's open office door while he was writing up his summary of the meeting, and he could tell from the way she was knotting her lanyard around her fingers that there was an awkward question incoming.

It was one of the many qualities Lewis admired in Pam: it was obvious how much she hated asking awkward questions, yet she forced herself to ask them.

'Hello, Lewis.' She had just about dropped the Mr Levison. 'Am I interrupting?'

'It's always a good time!' Lewis gestured at the chair opposite his desk. 'Have your ears been burning? I've just been singing your praises to the senior team.'

She sat down gingerly. 'What about?'

Lewis inclined his head towards his laptop. 'Updating on the great progress we're making, thanks to our dedicated staff. How can I help?'

'Oh, it's silly, really.' She wiped her nose with her hand, another tell. Pam would be a terrible poker player. 'You know Ellie, one of our nurses?'

Lewis nodded. Ellie had scored five out of five on his key staff assessments, and had been a key player in the escape room teambuilding game. Literally, when they couldn't get the door open, and she saved the day with a hair grip.

'Ellie's been recording Ken McConnell's life story, you know, for the project. And he's told her he was in the secret service during the seventies. Went into lots of detail about it, where he served, the mission he went on to East Germany, what have you.' Pam frowned. 'But as long as I've known Ken, he's been a postman.'

'And how long have you known him?'

'Well, he was our postman when I was a kid. I checked with my mum, who used to work at Grainger's jam factory with his sister, and she said she's got no recollection of Ken McConnell being in the secret service. In fact, if anything . . .' She blushed. 'She remembers a story about him having another family in Bradford, but she can't swear to it.'

'But presumably if he *was* in the secret service, then he'd want everyone to think he was a postman?'

'That's what he said to Ellie. That he had to build up a cover story.' Pam looked askance. 'But who was he spying on? And when? I mean, we often have residents telling us some odd tales, especially if they're upstairs.' She indicated in the direction of the Memory Wing. 'And that's fine – the doctors say to agree with them, join them in their reality, as it were. But we don't generally say oh yes, so you used to play bridge with Omar Sharif, then put it on a storyboard in the lounge, do we?'

'We are absolutely sure Ken didn't have a career in intelligence?'

Pam arched her eyebrow. 'You've not been here long, have you? If Ken used to work for MI5, half the staff would be able to tell you his codename. It's not a big place, Longhampton.'

Lewis nodded. He'd already familiarised himself with the care plans and basic notes of each resident, and Ken had no markers for dementia, compulsive lying, or espionage work.

'Ellie doesn't want to upset Ken by accusing him of taking the mick,' Pam went on. 'But as she said to me, she doesn't want him to waste time messing about winding her up when there are folk who want to share real memories and might not – excuse me for saying this – have long to tell us about them. But then . . .' Her face clouded. 'What if he's not making it up? I mean, I feel terrible checking up on him with my mum, but if Ken *was* James Bond and he was protecting national security as well as delivering our parcels . . .'

She threw her hands in the air, defeated by the possibilities.

'It's a good question.' Lewis got up to pour himself a cup of coffee from the filter machine; tea had an important social function, but strong coffee kept his brain in the overtaking lane. 'What's the most important thing here, recording the truth or *listening* to someone?' He waved the filter jug at Pam, who shook her head. 'I'll ask Gayle later

– we're hosting a visit from a journalist this week. Carrie Clark from the *Longhampton Gazette*, do you know her? She's going to come in and do a feature about the Story project. I thought it would be a good bit of publicity.'

And also a chance for him to grill Carrie subtly about the whistleblower.

'This week?' Pam's gaze shot around the room, automatically hunting for cobwebs. 'Are we ready?'

'I think so! Besides, we need more volunteers for the story project, and I need to fill up those four empty rooms. Don't look so worried, I'll show Carrie around, introduce her to one or two of the residents.'

'Not Ken. Or Nigel Callaghan,' said Pam at once. 'Or Eunice Stafford.'

'Noted. She's asked if she can sit in on a session to see how it works. Do we have a volunteer who wouldn't mind letting the journalist observe?' Lewis tapped a spoon thoughtfully against his chin, and waited for Pam to suggest Beth.

'Beth Cherry?' suggested Pam. 'She's rota'd in for Friday.'

Even the sound of Beth's name coming from Pam's mouth made Lewis feel glowy, as if she'd appeared in the chair next to them. He frowned as if trying to remember who Beth was – unconvincingly – then said, 'Oh, yes, Beth!'

'She emailed me yesterday,' Pam went on, 'asking if we'd mind if she brought her dog in with her. One of the residents had talked a lot aobut his dogs – she wondered if he'd like to meet her. We've had therapy dogs visit before, but they need to have an assessment to make sure they're safe.'

'Do we know anyone who could do that?'

'Yes, my vet George assesses the local therapy dogs.'

'Great! Can you arrange it for when she next visits? I'll drop Beth a line,' said Lewis. 'Let her know that Tomsk is very welcome. I've met him, he seems delightful. Huge, but delightful.'

'I'll call the surgery,' said Pam, making a note.

'Killing several birds with one stone there, Pam. Not literally of course!' said Lewis, and topped up his coffee to prove his hand wasn't shaking.

Delightful, he told himself, breathing deeply as the aversion therapy app instructed. Tomsk was delightful. And huge. But mainly *delightful.*

Carrie Clark arrived on the dot of two o'clock on Friday afternoon, punctuality which impressed Lewis.

He welcomed her at the front door, having personally double-checked every area she'd be passing through for pine-freshness, escorted her to his office where he handed her over to Gayle Burton, who'd arrived three minutes previously (being somewhat less punctual than Carrie) to run through Lewis's checklist of topics.

It wasn't that he was a control freak, he assured Gayle, it was just that this was the first time since the inspection that Rosemount had been featured in the newspaper and he wanted everything to be perfect. Gayle said she quite understood.

Lewis hovered in the corridor outside, keeping it free of potential disruptors like Ken or Eunice while Carrie interviewed Gayle; he could hear soft responses to questions about her own writing and what she'd learned from the life story project. She had a very soothing voice. A scruffy young man arrived ten minutes later; before Lewis could shoo him away, he identified himself as the *Gazette's* photographer, Blake, sent to take some 'atmosphere photos'. Lewis summoned Pam, and instructed her to keep Blake in her sights, and ensure he had minimal access to anywhere with too much atmosphere.

Eventually, Gayle put her head round the door and said she and Carrie were ready to join a session in progress. Lewis quickly shoved his little notebook back into his pocket and led the way to the library, where he knew he'd find Beth sitting with Hugh and Kay Lloyd in the library, talking, as planned, in a photogenic arrangement by the bay window that looked out on to a less derelict area of the gardens.

Lewis was pleased to see that Pam had pulled out all the stops, with the proper porcelain, along with small cakes on a stand, a silver coffee pot and an arrangement of white roses in a rosebowl. Good. This was *exactly* The New Rosemount he wanted to project. And Hugh and Kay were the perfect couple to illustrate it.

The Lloyds were already one of Lewis's favourite residents, two octogenarians who barely looked seventy, largely thanks to their refreshingly youthful outlook. They'd 'taken a step back from the rat race' after successful careers in advertising (Hugh) and public relations (Kay), and spent their retirement travelling the world. They'd only moved into Rosemount at the beginning of the year, selling their house in London and moving back to an area they'd always loved; as Hugh had told him, 'Our families are both from the area, although funnily enough, we had no idea about that when we first met!'

'None of them still around now sadly,' Kay added, 'in case you're wondering about our lack of visitors.' A flash of that mischievous smile. 'We're not *that* bad.'

Lewis could see that Hugh was in full flow, his craggy face animated with the ups and downs of one of his stories of outrageous ad campaigns and erratic celebrities. Next to him, Kay sipped her coffee, and now and again leaned forward with a dry aside that Hugh acknowledged with a pretend-annoyed gasp. They had the smooth chemistry of a long-established double act, something Lewis thought was quietly marvellous.

'What a beautiful room,' whispered Carrie, so as not to disturb the conversation, and Lewis nodded without speaking; his attention had swung like a magnet to Beth, engrossed in her conversation with the Lloyds.

She was curled into the winged armchair, one long leg tucked underneath her, leaning on her elbow; the sun was glowing on a hank of wheat-coloured hair that had fallen from her bun. Though Beth's face was hidden, Lewis could see her encouragement reflected in Hugh and Kay's animated expressions; Beth, he thought, was the kind of person it was easy to confide in.

'Shall we?' Carrie whispered.

'Let's wait till they get to a natural pause,' Gayle whispered back, and then Hugh said, in a louder punchline tone, 'And then it turned out we'd boarded completely the wrong boat!'

'Lulu was terribly nice about it,' said Kay. 'And of course we replaced the whisky.'

Lewis was about to cough and announce himself but suddenly Beth leaned forward. 'So what would *you* say the secret to a happy marriage is, Kay?'

'Gosh, is there one? Apart from patience and selective deafness?'

'What was that, darling?' Hugh put a hand up to his ear.

'Oh, and a sense of humour.' Kay nudged her husband, then looked back at Beth. 'I think marrying your best friend is a good start.'

Hugh squeezed Kay's hand, suddenly serious. 'Hear hear.'

Lewis seized the moment. 'Beth! Can I interrupt?'

She turned and saw it was him, then smiled *because* it was him; in that second, Lewis felt physically lighter, as if the invisible hook in his heart was lifting him off the ground.

'Hello there, Lewis,' said Hugh. 'Just in time, too – we've been horrifying poor Beth with tales from the unreconstructed seventies and eighties.'

'*You* have, darling,' Kay pointed out. 'I've been trying to balance that with some stories of great feminist achievements *despite* all that. Right, Beth?'

'Sounds fascinating!' said Lewis. 'I wonder if you'd like to share some more with Carrie? She's from the *Longhampton Gazette* and she's writing a feature about our Story sessions.'

Carrie introduced herself, and Hugh patted the seat next to him. 'Pop yourself down here, Carrie. I was just about to tell Beth about the time I flew Concorde to New York and had an argument with Tim Rice about cricket before we'd even got our seatbelts on.'

'Start by explaining who Tim Rice is, darling,' said Kay.

Carrie indicated Blake, who was standing back behind the chairs, lining up a shot, with Pam hovering anxiously a few steps away. 'Do you mind if Blake takes some photographs while we chat? Just casual ones, with that big window in the background.'

Lewis was already moving an unphotogenic Zimmer frame out of shot, so missed what happened next, but he heard a cup clatter on its saucer, some gasps and a flurry of apologies. When he turned around, the white roses were streaked with coffee, Beth was mopping at her skirt with a napkin, looking flustered, while Blake helped himself to a large slice of Battenburg.

'Would you excuse me a moment?' Beth scrambled to her feet, grabbing her bag from beside the sofa, and hurried out of the room.

Carrie looked between Hugh and Kay, Gayle and Lewis, confused. 'Was it something I said? It is OK to take photographs, isn't it?'

'Hugh? Kay? Do you mind?' Lewis turned to the Lloyds, but Hugh was already adjusting his tie and smoothing down his silver hair.

'It's fine,' said Kay. 'But is Beth all right? That coffee was hot!'

'I'll see if she needs a cloth,' said Lewis, signalling Pam to take over.

Beth was already at the end of the corridor by the time Lewis pushed open the double doors of the library.

He followed her – not too closely, not wanting to chase her – but she didn't stop at the ladies' lavatories, as he'd expected she would; instead, Beth turned that corner and headed even further away, down towards his office and the reception area.

'Beth?' he called out, concerned, and she stopped, just outside his office.

He quickened his step, and caught up with her. If she'd gone to his office, he reasoned, she must want to talk to him. If she just wanted to sponge her skirt, she'd have gone into the ladies'.

'Is everything all right?' he asked, and when she didn't reply, he pushed open his office door, gesturing for her go in first, and she slid inside.

Lewis hovered for a moment, then followed.

She was standing by the window, her back to him, and he could see her shoulders were shaking with each deep 'calm down' breath. Before he could worry about whether to take a step nearer, she turned, and said, 'Sorry about that. Lewis, I . . . I don't want to be in any photographs.'

'OK.' The emphatic way she said it made his mind scrabble for reasons. Was she hiding from someone? A stalker? An abusive partner? 'That's no problem. But is there something we should know? For your security?'

Beth's gaze darted up and down, and her cheeks turned a self-conscious crimson. She gave a nervous laugh. 'This is going to sound ridiculous, but I'm trying to make a case for flexible working, and I probably shouldn't be volunteering during office hours. My new boss is trying to herd everyone back into the office.'

'I see,' said Lewis, with some relief.

'I mean, it's not a problem, my being here, I've done everything I'm supposed to today but he's a bit tricky. Been brought in to take the business to "another level".' Her fingers hooked in the air, and he noticed her hands were trembling.

'I've had a tip off from my outgoing boss that everyone's unofficially under assessment, and I need to demonstrate how I'm "adding value to my role",' she went on, and Lewis suspected nerves were making her gabble more than she meant to. 'So, if you know of any businesses that need accountancy support, tax advice, that sort of thing . . .'

'But you can't have anything to worry about, surely,' he said. 'What with you having the highest score in your accountancy exams?'

'What? Oh, sorry, that. Ha. No, that doesn't count with Christian, I don't think. He's more of an "only as good as your last review" type of guy.'

Lewis wondered if he could pretend he needed some accountancy support; the idea of Beth going through Devin's year-end projections might make them more interesting. 'You have my sympathies,' he said, wanting to make her feel better, somehow. 'That's pretty much my working life too – only as good as my last inspection. And since I only work with care homes that have failed their last one badly enough for me to be there in the first place . . .' He shrugged. 'Then it's on to the next!'

'So you're basically a Mary Poppins for care homes?' Beth seemed temporarily distracted. 'Parachute in, fix it, then move on?'

Lewis nodded. 'Basically. I'm hoping that I might be allowed to stay put for a while in one place. See the project through a bit further.'

Eric had been dangling it for a while; a permanent regional role for Lewis, instead of dropping him in to fight fires across the portfolio. When you didn't have a family, it was assumed you could be deployed anywhere, at any moment, and Lewis was tired of rented houses with neglected gardens and inadequate curtains. And also dealing with frazzled staff, furious families, dysfunctional businesses that he had to unscramble like Rubik's cubes, with ruthless niceness.

'I hope you stay here a while,' she said. 'You're already making a difference. I'd love to know what else you have planned. Oh!' Beth put a hand to her mouth; she had lovely pale-pink nails. 'I never thanked you for the box of stationery! Where on earth did you find such perfect notebooks?'

'Oh, just online.' Not strictly true; Lewis had scoured the internet until he'd found stationery worthy of Beth's attention, creamy white paper, linen-bound in sugared-almond covers. And pens, in lots of colours. 'They're OK?'

She grinned. 'They're almost too nice to write in. Thank you – you obviously understand how important stationery is to the creative process!'

When Beth smiled, a shy smile that reached her blue eyes, everything else in the room shrank and blurred apart from her. Lewis had forgotten this feeling, if he'd ever known it, this floaty sensation, exciting and comforting and precarious, at the same time. He'd seen how losing love could dismantle the sturdiest character, and he'd packed his life full of commitments and responsibilities to stop that happening, but now he didn't have a choice: Beth's smile surrounded him, and disorientated him completely.

Beth's smile abruptly vanished. 'Gosh, I should go back and apologise for running out on Kay and Hugh like that.' She bit her lip. 'I don't want Hugh to think his story was offensive in some way. He's very anxious not to be cancelled. Well, he *says* he is.'

Lewis jumped up. 'Let me deal with the photographer. I'll take him out to the garden, distract him until you've said your goodbyes. I'm sure he's got everything he needs by now.'

'Thanks,' said Beth. 'I'm so sorry for the dramatics.' She reached out and touched his arm. 'I'm honestly not normally like this.'

'Me neither,' said Lewis without thinking, but she was already shouldering her bag, and fortunately didn't hear.

Chapter thirteen

On Wednesday morning, I loaded Tomsk into the car with his towels, his lead, his special teddy – and a present for him to give to an old friend.

Pam Woodward had phoned a few days earlier, to tell me that her own vet, George Fenwick, would be available to assess Tomsk for suitability as a visiting therapy dog if I brought him with me to my next story session. When I told her I knew George – because he was the co-owner of the kennels that had rescued Tomsk – she was delighted by the coincidence. 'It's a sign!' she said. Pam, I realised, loved a sign. She'd have got on well with Ashley.

I hadn't bargained for me *and* Tomsk becoming care-home volunteers, but if George gave Tomsk the all-clear, it would solve the problem of leaving him in the car. Tomsk didn't mind, not if there was a walk afterwards, but my car was starting to smell like a mobile kennel and two air fresheners weren't even touching the sides.

At Rosemount, I parked up next to a mud-splattered Land Rover with the Four Oaks Vets sign on the side. A Border collie was staring at us from the passenger-seat window, silent but curious.

Tomsk swept his tail from side to side and I wondered if he remembered the dog from the brief time he was at the rescue. There was so much I didn't know about Tomsk's past (to my utter misery, he still cowered if he saw a man in a particular kind of hat) but as soon as he saw George chatting with Lewis on the front steps, the wagging suddenly turbocharged, and I was towed across the gravel by the happiest canine steam engine ever.

Lewis broke off the conversation immediately. 'Beth!' He beamed and spread his hands out in welcome. 'You've brought the sunshine! Hello, Tomsk!'

'Tomsk, eh?' George looked amused.

'After the Womble. I had one as a kid.' It had been Mum's; once I'd cleaned Tomsk up, the shaggy grey hair and the pointy nose that wrinkled in confusion were almost identical.

'He's looking magnificent.' George reached down to welcome his old pal, who shoved his nose straight into his hands. Even after five years, the gratitude was still as warm as ever.

Lewis evidently wasn't expecting such a huge dog to move so quickly, and he jerked backwards into a plant pot, which wobbled on its plinth with an ominous grinding noise.

Automatically, George stuck his own leg out to stop it crashing on to the stone steps.

'Whoops!' said Lewis.

At the word 'whoops' Tomsk immediately sat down and looked at me. He heard it a lot. Such was his size that he often accidentally wagged mugs off coffee tables, and only knew about it when there was an unexpected crash in his vicinity.

'Sorry, sorry, Lewis!' I pulled Tomsk back to my side, and looked at George. 'Is that an automatic fail before we've left the car park?'

'Not at all. Good calm reaction,' said George. 'To the plant and the nervous visitor.'

'Yes! That was my fault.' Lewis was busily shifting the pot back into place. 'Health and safety fail, should have checked these pots before now!'

'Not a dog person, Lewis?' asked George mildly.

'I'm not *not* a dog person,' he gabbled. 'Just not used to dogs this size. I didn't have a dog growing up. Parents in the forces. Boarding school . . .' I'd never seen Lewis like this. He'd gone red, and was struggling to project his usual calm competence. It was quite endearing to see him flapping. 'Sorry, I'm . . . Ha-ha! Hello there!'

He reached out to pat Tomsk's head but when Tomsk, encouraged, lifted his nose to show he hadn't taken it personally, Lewis jerked his hand back. Then with an effort, he stretched it out again and tapped Tomsk's head twice, as if his head was a gameshow answer button.

Tomsk looked up at me, bewildered.

George decided enough was enough. 'OK, so Tomsk and I will go for a walk, meet some people, have a chat, and we'll see you a bit later. Rachel says I've to take a lot of photos.'

I gave him the lead, and George ruffled Tomsk's floppy ear with that 'good boy' affection that said more than words. And without a backward glance, my one-woman hound trotted off in the direction of the walled gardens.

'Wow,' I said. 'I had no idea he was so easy to steal.'

Lewis indicated that he, too, was heading back towards the house, but I should go first. 'Ha! He's absolutely lovely. The dog, of course, not George. I mean, George is also tremendous. But Tomsk, yes. What a sweetheart. So . . . big!'

I eyed Lewis as we walked up the path; he still wasn't quite himself. He seemed to be concentrating on his breathing. 'It took me a while to get used to having a small horse around, too.' I touched his arm. 'Don't worry, I'm not one of those owners who expects everyone to worship their dog.'

'No, it's so kind of you to volunteer him. It comes up, over and again, when I'm talking to people about how we can make this feel more like their own home – our residents miss their dogs.'

As he spoke, back on the familiar ground of Improving Rosemount, I could see his natural control returning.

It had been an effort though. That jumpy reaction made me wonder if he'd had a bad experience at some point. A bite, or a scare as a child? Yet he was prepared to suffer some personal discomfort so the residents who missed canine company could enjoy a visit. It wasn't just box-ticking; Lewis genuinely cared about making life better for other people.

We'd stopped, so he could hold the front door open for me, but I felt a sudden impulse to let him know I'd seen that momentary discomfort. 'It's so important, what you're doing.'

'What I'm doing?' Lewis raised a quizzical eyebrow.

'Caring about the little things, as well as the big ones.' I hugged my beautiful new notebook close to my chest. 'I'll make sure Tomsk never goes anywhere he isn't welcome and hopefully . . .' I smiled. 'He might show you just what great company dogs can be.'

Lewis held my gaze. The lustrous moustache distracted from the fact that he had kind eyes; they weren't unlike Tomsk's. Brown and gentle. Trusting. 'I hope so,' he said, after a microscopic pause that made me wonder what he'd been thinking.

I felt myself smile, and he smiled back.

'We're all rowing the same boat,' he said. 'I'm just barking the orders.'

'Barking!' I pointed at him. 'I see what you did there.'

He looked bemused for a second, then laughed, way too generously for the crapness of my pun.

We walked into the house together; Lewis insisted he was heading in the same direction, even though I hadn't told him where I was going. 'Pam showed me the story notes you've already written up – you must be working overtime!'

'I don't have a lot on right now.' A white lie. I didn't have a lot of *social life* on right now, which freed up my evenings for writing up rambling stories of cinema matinees and National Service, three-day weeks and miners' strikes. Some volunteers, it had to be said, were better at winnowing details from the residents than others; the 1970s, in particular, were a notably arid era for fun in Longhampton's recent history. Still, Martine's ten p.m. check-ins added some more colour to prosaic accounts of the old railway routes and milk rounds: with a little encouragement, she'd painted vivid pictures of the town's ancient traditions, the May week parades, and the Blossom Queens on their flower-covered floats, and the candlelit wassailing, and the noisy St George's Day dragon run.

I asked her if she'd been a carnival queen and Martine made a noise that I'm sure was accompanied by an even more outraged expression.

'Absolutely not! I was far too busy studying for my O levels.' Then she'd paused, and said, 'And I don't think my father would have liked it,' in a more ambiguous manner.

'Carrie emailed me to say her feature about the story sessions will be in the paper this week,' Lewis added, as we reached his office. 'Hopefully it'll drum up some volunteers to lighten your load.'

That brought my attention back to the moment, with a deep cringe. I wasn't looking forward to that feature running. Lewis had swallowed my hastily invented excuse about working from home, but in truth it wasn't that. The very idea of appearing in the paper filled me with such a toxic mixture of shame, guilt, self-loathing, horror and embarrassment, with a whole sprinkling of different shame – shame that I was shallow enough to care. I'd seen one photograph of myself sitting in a pub with Ashley two years ago and it had stuck in my head like a splinter. Squashed thighs, a lifesaver ring of belly fat, tiny little head like a diplodocus. Since then, I'd avoided all lenses and, to a lesser extent, mirrors. There were three big mirrors in Martine's flat, and I'd turned them to face the wall.

'Good! Great! Anyway,' I said, changing the subject, 'I'm here to talk to Nigel Callaghan this morning. Anything I should know?'

'Nigel? Oh, he's great fun. He'll keep you on your toes!'

'Really?' What did that mean?

We'd rounded the corner to his office, where Pam was standing outside with one of the nurses.

'Hello, Pam, hello, Kemi!' Lewis beamed at them both. 'Beth's here to talk to Nigel Callaghan about his fascinating life.'

'Dear Lord in heaven,' said Kemi.

'Sorry?'

'Nigel's not the easiest of our residents,' Pam explained.

'In what way?' This wasn't sounding good.

She contorted her face in an effort to find a positive spin. 'We try our best, but I don't think he's suited to communal living—'

'He is a tricky old man,' Kemi interrupted. 'He is rude for no good reason. No,' she corrected herself, 'he is rude because it *entertains* him.'

Pam's eyes swivelled involuntarily towards Kemi.

'Is he local?' If local, a good half-hour could be spent having the Longhampton cinema hierarchy explained to me.

'Originally, yes,' said Pam. 'His goddaughter dropped him off here about a year ago. He'd been living independently for a long time, but there was an accident . . .' Pam's expression indicated that there'd been more than one accident before he'd agreed to move. 'Nigel's got no immediate family, sadly, so she's his next of kin. His cousin's daughter, I think. It was decided that he'd be best moving closer to her.'

'They don't sound particularly close.'

Kemi snorted again. 'I would not like to be close to Nigel.'

'Oh. Why?'

'Because he has not been improved by a solitary life. A man like Nigel needs companionship, like some meats need a lot of spice. Or salt. And a *bold cook*.'

'Kemi . . .' Pam attempted to sound disapproving, but couldn't.

'Don't let him tell you he used to be a spy, like Ken.' She made a clicking noise with her tongue. 'A spy! Ken!'

'Ladies, I'm afraid I must push on,' said Lewis ruefully. 'Kemi, did you want to see me about something?'

'Yes,' said Kemi. 'But inside the office, please.'

Lewis raised a hand of farewell in my direction. 'I look forward to shaking Tomsk's paw when he's passed his test with flying colours.'

Lewis was trying so hard, I thought. As he mentioned Tomsk, I detected a ripple underneath his habitual sunniness, despite his efforts to conceal it. A stiffening of resolve. I was touched that he was making that effort for Tomsk. And, I guessed, for me.

'Let me take you down to Nigel's room,' said Pam. 'I'll get you some refreshments to take with you first, though. You'll need them, even if he doesn't.'

Nigel had a suite on the second floor, in what Pam told me had once been the snooker room. As we went up through the house, she did the same auto-tidying as Lewis: straightening curtains, pocketing loose cutlery, switching off lights, knocking on doors, and so on. I felt exhausted just walking next to her with the tray.

She knocked at Nigel's door, with her brisk housekeeper's triplet, and muttered, 'Wait for it.'

'Sod off,' came a voice from inside the room. 'Unless you're Helen Mirren.'

Pam rolled her eyes, and knocked again. 'Nigel, it's Pam, can I have a word?'

'Is the building alight?'

'No.'

'Have we been invaded?'

'Not as far as I know.'

'Is it absolutely necessary?'

'I have a tray of tea and some French fancies?'

There was a pause. 'If you must.'

Pam turned back to me and muttered, as she shouldered the door open, 'If we didn't have the French fancies we'd never get in.'

I followed her at a short distance.

It was the emptiest room I'd seen so far.

A bed, made neatly with a blanket and sheets. A mahogany sideboard with a single Chinese vase on it. The main feature of the room was a full-height bookshelf filled with books, battered and well read. In one deep wing armchair sat an old man, doing a crossword, a cup of tea by his side.

He did not look up from the crossword when we walked in.

'Nigel, this is Beth, she's one of our Life Story volunteers,' said Pam.

'I've done the Life Story project.'

'No, you haven't.'

'Yes, I have. I filled in that questionnaire when I moved in. Intrusive bloody thing.'

'This is different,' she said patiently. 'That was about basic care. This is about getting to know you properly.'

'Well, I don't want to tell you anything.' He filled in a clue. 'Much more interesting for you to guess.'

'Nigel, you've told me several times that we don't do enough to stimulate our residents mentally. This is your chance to tell us how we can. I'll leave you to it.' Pam took the tray off me, and placed it on the side table, pulled a 'do your best' face, and closed the door behind her.

Thanks, I thought, but Nigel didn't tell me to leave, and instead sighed heavily, folded his newspaper and indicated the chair in the corner, which I brought over and set opposite his.

'So,' I said brightly. 'Where shall we start? What did you do before you retired?'

'Documentary film-making,' he said. 'Talked myself on to a training scheme after dithering about for a few years, ended up working across the world.' He put a whole French fancy in his mouth and chewed slowly, his intelligent eyes fixed on me.

'What an incredible job. What would you say was the most memorable moment you experienced?'

The response took a while, on account of the cake. 'Memorable in what way?'

'Well . . . memorable.' There'd been literally no memorable moments in my working life. Not even the time I managed to get someone's Botox passed as an office expense.

Nigel shrugged. 'Have you seen documentaries about the Munich Olympics? The IRA in London? That sort of memorable? I could tell you about that but I'd just be telling you what was already in the film.'

'But I'd love to hear how you *felt* when that was happening. What it was like to *be* there when history was unfolding?'

'It wasn't my job to feel anything, I was there to record the facts. Most of the time I was scared, if you want to know the truth. Scared of the bombs, scared of not getting the report for my editor in time. Scared of not doing it justice.'

Something about the way Nigel said that made me wonder if I'd hit a nerve. I parked it for later.

'Personally memorable moments then. Not work ones.'

As soon as I said it, I wished I hadn't. Scanning the room for the usual gallery of wedding photographs, portraits, baby pictures, and the like, I realised that there was nothing, not a shred of anyone else. If he'd been less spiky, and I'd had more time to think, I probably wouldn't have asked that, but the unusual speed – for Rosemount – of his responses was throwing me off.

Nigel sat back in his chair. 'The whole point of having a portfolio of stories about the Berlin Wall is that you don't have to maintain an amusing set of anecdotes about your own life.'

'But you're not telling me those either,' I pointed out.

Nigel acknowledged this.

'I suppose my problem, Beth, is that the really special memories, the ones you treasure . . . Sometimes the *reasons* you remember them are too subtle for this sort of Memory Lane cheesiness. If you pin them down,' he made a fluttering gesture, 'they're gone. They're not the same as they were when they were in your head. And then you can never get them back the same way, when they were lovely and loose, floating around in the back of your mind. Like pinning down a butterfly. You must know what I mean?'

I flinched.

In her coaching, Gayle had suggested that we practise what we were asking the residents to do, so we'd be able to offer better help. The previous night, I'd sat down with the pages of questions, shut my eyes, and chosen one at random.

'Tell me about a turning point in your life.'

That was easy, I thought: the night I met Fraser.

The second of June, 2014. I was on a hen night, and he was on a stag; our groups collided in a cocktail bar called Cinderella's, at a point in the long, *long*, plastic-penis-themed evening when I'd already seriously considered going home twice. But then Fraser crashed into our booth, dressed as Baby Spice (literally, he fell off his platform trainers) and before the Long Island Iced Tea had dried on my jeans, my life had changed. Two became one.

I'd told the story so many times, and it always got a laugh and an *ahhhhh*. But writing it down was different. In the space of the first sentence, in black and white, on the screen, I could see the minor tweaks, the small omissions. My fingers hesitated over details that spooled out easily when I told people: details that I glossed over, or buffed up into bigger significance.

For instance, I liked to say how random it had been, 'of all the bars in all the world . . .' but it wasn't random. The maid of honour, Sadie, lived with one of Fraser's friends and she'd deliberately picked the same bar as the one they were going to, so she could make sure Andy wasn't up to anything. (He was, unfortunately, and several drinks were thrown while the bride was singing 'You're The One That I Want' with the best man, with whom Sadie later went home. I missed that out of my anecdote. It was both focus-pulling and inauspicious.)

My fingers also hesitated when I started to type, 'It was love at first sight for me and Fraser . . .' because if I was being honest, it took him three days to call, and when he did, he called me Meg, not Beth.

I'd always had the faint suspicion that he thought I was Mali – now I wrote it down, that leaped out at me again.

And he hadn't been dressed as Baby Spice, specifically; he just had Sharpie freckles and a bra padded with gym socks. Something that now felt quite problematic but had been fine at the time.

But apart from that . . .

'You've gone very quiet,' Nigel observed.

'Sorry,' I said. 'I was just thinking about what you said. How memories change when you write them down. But sometimes factual inaccuracy in the telling is just capturing the spirit of the memory.'

'And that's as important as the facts?'

'I think so.'

'Interesting,' said Nigel, and indicated for me to pass the plate of cakes. 'You might want to dig into why that is.'

I offered him a French fancy, then took one too, to give myself a moment. Wasn't I supposed to be the one asking the questions here?

If I was being honest, I knew why my How We Met story had evolved into a more romcom-friendly version over the years. The Hendersons were natural storytellers with an endless supply of anecdotes – even Fraser, who was hardly Michael McIntyre, could reduce an audience to hysterics with tales of the time a bored Cara had floated baby Fraser's sunhat across a pond and told their babysitting grandparents he'd drowned. (I was aghast.) Or the time Fraser and his siblings attended Heather's first cello recital wearing T-shirts with her face on. (Ditto.)

I had family anecdotes, but they were much darker: like, the Christmas Mum and I found out Dad had remarried because his new wife sent us an M&S hamper. I just wanted one fun story to tell at parties, one with a happy ending. And, for the record, Fraser hadn't ever corrected me. He sometimes joined in. In fact, he was the one who added he'd been wearing platform trainers, even though – now I thought about it – I wasn't totally sure he was.

'I suppose the main benefit of this project is preserving memories for other interested parties,' conceded Nigel, which brought my attention back to the room.

'Yes!' I grabbed that with both hands. 'Like the Horrobins! Bill isn't able to communicate much himself, but it's obvious how much he enjoys hearing Linda talk about their early life together.'

'If, of course, she's remembering the same things as he is.' Nigel gave me a wolfish half-smile. 'Which one do you take as the truth, mister or missus?'

I stared. Was he a mind-reader?

The previous evening I'd opened one set of notes taken from Duncan Chalmers, detailing his colourful life in sales, circling the globe with his overseas postings, and another set from a different volunteer talking to Deidre Chalmers about how miserable it was making new friends every two years, and how she'd spent a fortune importing digestive biscuits into Estonia. I wasn't sure how I could make the two into one version without triggering a divorce.

'And what if the memories that make a person come alive inside aren't ones they'd necessarily want their other half to know about?' Nigel went on remorselessly. 'What if poor Bill is trapped listening to Linda get their stories wrong? What if he has a whole selection of memories she has no idea about?' He twinkled even more. 'What if she's never going to tell you her best memories because *Bill isn't in them*?'

I stared at him. I was out of my depth.

There was a knock on the door and Pam put her head round. 'Sorry to butt in,' she said, 'but George needs to get back to work, and he wants to discuss Tomsk's assessment.'

'You've given me a lot to think about,' I said to Nigel. 'If you remember something you'd like to discuss next time, there's a secure box at reception for any notes that residents want to drop off for us to write up.'

He inclined his head. 'I saw that, yes. Ah-ah!'

Pam was about to take the tray away, but stopped at his brisk command.

'You can leave those, thank you, Mrs Woodward,' he said. 'Brain fuel.'

The Horrobins, my favourite couple, were delighted to be Tomsk's test visit, supervised by George. He let Linda stroke his ears, and he sat stock-still next to Bill, who laid his frail hand on Tomsk's head.

'Reminds him of our Caesar,' Linda told me. 'German shepherd, beautiful soul. You two were great pals, weren't you, Bill?'

'Well, I'd say he's passed with flying colours,' said George. 'Rachel will be so pleased when I tell her.'

I couldn't really take much credit for Tomsk. Whoever had abandoned him hadn't known what they were giving up.

George walked me and Tomsk to the car, and I presented him with the tin of bone-shaped biscuits I'd baked 'from Tomsk' for Rachel. He laughed when I told him about my embarrassing moment at the donation centre, a genuine hearty laugh that made me feel a bit better.

'That'd be Naomi – don't worry, she's heard worse. I'll tell her you're not crazy.'

'Would you?' Telling it had removed some of the cringe. In time, I could see it becoming an anecdote. In lots of time.

'Rachel says why don't you come over and say hi, if you're here for a while?' he suggested. 'She'd love to see Tomsk again.' And that made me feel better too.

Just as we were about to set off, Pam dashed out with some notes from the memory drop box for me to type up later, and then Tomsk and I went home, with a feeling of a job well done.

All in all, I thought, as I pulled up outside Martine's house, it was shaping up to be one of my best days so far in Longhampton: the sun was shining, my dog had got a gold star, I had an invitation and maybe a new friend.

Maybe things were going to be OK, I thought. Maybe.

If you could relive one day in your life, which one would you choose?

I met Nessy in the summer of 1964, picking blackcurrants on a top fruit farm near Hartley Grange. She stood out from the other pickers – literally, a whole head taller than most of the girls, with a straight dancer's back and red hair in a ponytail. I knew most of the pickers – farm kids like me, some mums from the new estates with prams that they'd stash a few bags of fruit in later, travellers that came for the hops – but I'd never seen her before.

There's a knack to blackcurrants – you've got to separate the branches out, picking from top to bottom, not worrying too much about the leaves or the stalks, just get your rhythm going. Strip and drop. Strip and drop. No need to be precise; the little kids – leafers, we called them - went through the wooden trays and picked out any extra bits later before the farmer weighed up for the day.

I could tell she'd never done it before. I was in charge of the section, and the women next to her were taking the mickey, nudging each other. She was picking each berry individually, trying to drop them perfect into her basket. She'd already got sunburned, and I could see her skin getting pinker and pinker while the others whispered, making fun. *Posh girl. Useless. Slow.* Sneaky hissing noises, you couldn't make out what they were saying, but you couldn't ignore it.

I remember stepping into the space next to her, and feeling the hot air on my face, heavy with sweat and fruit and the smell of that greasy sun cream that didn't really do much back then. I guessed it was her smelling of sun cream; I wouldn't even know where you'd buy it round here. The regulars knew where to stand, so as not to get too hot, but she didn't, and they hadn't warned her. I said something like, Did no one give you a demonstration? As if it wasn't her fault, more for the benefit of the pickers next to her, really, so they'd know I was on to them. Brenda Prosser was chopsy, but my dad was a farm manager, so they didn't dare get on my wrong side, not if they wanted more work.

And I showed her, stripping several branches fast as possible while I pretended to teach her the technique, so she'd at least have something to weigh in her basket at the end of the day. I'd done it a million times before, but my hands didn't feel like mine; it was such an odd feeling, knowing her green eyes were watching my hands, trying to commit my movements to her memory. Me, to her memory.

I picked quickly – strip and drop, strip and drop - until I heard the whispers starting again, then I stopped.

Bring a hat tomorrow, I said to her, all brisk. Or a scarf? Gets hot, standing in one place for ages.

I didn't tell her it was partly for the sun, and partly to stop Brenda pointing her out to everyone – she was so easy to spot, 'that lanky girl with the ginger hair'. Those women could be brutal, the way they gossiped.

She found me later, when we'd stopped for the mid-afternoon break. She thanked me for taking pity on her, as she put it. My mother has fruit trees in the garden, she said, I thought I knew what I was doing. What an idiot.

I liked the way she could laugh at herself, didn't mind being given instruction. I introduced myself, and she said, I'm Nessy, it's a nickname. We chatted a little, about the crop that year, about the farm, and I watched her after we went back to work; she was quick as anyone by the end of that day. She'd got her own technique going, a little sway to her arms, precise, sweeping movements, no energy wasted, like a dance. When she carried her basket up to the top of the row to be weighed, it was nearly full. She handed it to me with a straight face, then gave me a quick, secret smile, and my heart did a loop around my chest, like a house martin circling.

I didn't know how to react, so I turned away, pretending to weigh someone's basket. It was a responsibility, being put in charge of the weighing, and this was the first summer I'd been allowed to do it. When I turned back, she was down by the gate on her bicycle, one foot on the pedal, one foot pushing to get the speed up. It looked like her brother's bike, or her dad's, too big really, but it didn't seem to bother her. She did one, two, three little boosts, then gave one final push and threw her bare leg over the crossbar – a flash of pale thigh and green skirt that got a few whistles from the lads down the tractors and trailers, waiting to take the workers back to the housing estate.

At home, that night, I had no appetite. My sisters and my mum were making jam – we all smuggled a bit of fruit home, perks of the job – and my little sister, Mary, asked if I'd got sunstroke I was that quiet. I was just staring at the copper jam pan on the stove, thinking that it was the exact colour of Nessy's hair.

I couldn't drop off to sleep that night, wondering if she'd be back for a second day, or if her mother would see her sunburn and keep her home. But she was there the next morning, this time in yellow shorts, her face lobster-red under a straw hat. When she saw me, she pointed at her hat and smiled.

That was because of me. Something I'd suggested. I felt as if I was falling into a cool dark pit when she smiled through the rows of green blackcurrant leaves. She was other-worldly, glowing pale like the painting over the fireplace in the town library, a copy of a Rossetti, I learned later: pearly, full-moon skin and copper-pan hair surrounded by leaves.

She'd brought a transistor radio with her, and she asked Brenda Prosser if she'd like to choose what station they listened to. I kept half an ear on her chat all day: *Did Brenda like Elvis? Was Brenda watching* Coronation Street? *Oh, how interesting, really? Would you give me the recipe?* I could tell she was smart. If you got Brenda, the rest would follow like sheep. We chatted again while we ate our sandwiches at lunch; one of those circling conversations where you try to find connections, and if she was doing the same to me as she'd been doing to Brenda, I didn't care.

She came to find me at the end of the week, and asked if she could buy me a drink, as thanks for helping her stick it out, as she put it. I said yes. We went to the Feathers – the kind of place the grammar-school set went to, not somewhere me and my mates would go – and we sat in the beer garden with a lemonade. I knew Fred Pugh wouldn't serve us, so I didn't try. Nessy told me she was in the sixth form: Eng. Lit, French, Latin. Proper brainbox topics. She said she was saving up to go to university the following year, and needed some pocket money because her parents were a bit tight like that. They wouldn't let her work in a shop, so she'd found her own holiday job. 'And there was nothing they could say then!' She sounded triumphant. I didn't tell her I'd been working since I was old enough to deliver a paper.

It only seemed fair to buy her a drink in return, and I was glad we were on the lemonade. We spun that lemonade out for ages, talking and talking. Talking, about anything really, so the conversation wouldn't stop and the other could say, 'Well, I'd better be going'. I remember the house martins wheeling over the beer garden; I pointed them out to her, and said I envied them, that they could fly across the world yet still find their way back home, and she said she'd never thought of it like that.

I moved on to raspberries when the blackcurrants were over. So did Nessy.

It's not one day I'd like to go back to. I'd go back to that whole summer. Seven weeks of sticky berry juice under my fingernails, and hot sun on my head, and the mossy scent of green leaves crushed by rubber plimsolls, and the Beatles and Cliff crackling in the packing-up shed, and her beautiful voice, talking and talking, and my heart drinking up every word like cold lemonade.

Chapter fourteen

It was half past ten on a Thursday morning, but I was completely back in Longhampton in 1964. They were only words typed on a page, but the longing in every line of the blackcurrant picker's memory made my own heart yearn in sympathy for such a perfect summer. I would have sat reading it over and over again, lost in that magical falling-in-love moment, had the bubble of hot sun and cool green leaves not been burst by the unwelcome sound of my very real phone ringing.

When I saw the Jacobs' number on the screen, my whole body clenched. Even more so when I answered, and heard Christian's judgy monotone.

'Ah, Beth, at last,' he said. 'We were beginning to think you'd left the country. Sophie's chased a couple of times, voice notes *and* email. Didn't you get them?'

'Sorry, I was just about to call her.' I stuffed the pages back into the envelope and opened my laptop to the spreadsheets I'd been working on before I'd allowed myself to get distracted. The envelopes of memories had come from the drop box at Rosemount, and though I'd tried to keep them until after I'd finished my own day's work, I'd been unable to resist having a quick peek – and then been completely swept away into a more romantic world than the one I currently occupied.

Christian cleared his throat. A bad sign. 'It's not good news, I'm afraid. It's about Allen.'

'Allen?' *You don't know about the plans to step back,* I reminded myself.

'Yes, I'm sorry to say Allen's wife called me this morning to say that he was taken into hospital over the weekend.'

'What?' My eyes widened. 'Hospital?'

'Yes, he fell off a ladder at home. He's broken his wrist and his leg, but he's undergoing assessments for a possible mini stroke too.'

'No! Poor Allen!' I sank back in my chair, winded. All I could see in my mind's eye was Allen in his jazzy Pringle golf jumper, quietly exhilarated to be doing shady meetings at the golf club, full of energy about his Sign Language for Grandparents project. 'Is he going to be all right?'

'Too early to say, but obviously our thoughts and prayers are with Allen's wife and family at this difficult time.'

I hadn't exactly warmed to Christian in the short time he'd been working for Jacobs', but *ugh.* He was exactly the sort of person who'd say *thoughts and prayers,* while not actually bothering to find out what Allen's wife was called.

'Oh, poor Devora, what a time for this to—' I bit my tongue before I accidentally revealed that I knew about the plans this would be ruining.

But it didn't matter: Christian had moved on to the real point of his call. 'From a business perspective, certain plans that were in the pipeline will now be actioned sooner than scheduled. I can share with you now that Allen was intending to move to a non-exec role at Jacobs', triggering a team reset . . .'

I was doing my best to stay tuned in to Christian but he really did talk like a press release, and my mind was still on

Allen. What was he doing up a ladder? I couldn't picture him doing DIY. Devora was the handy one in that relationship, always sanding down something or other, according to Allen's occasional weekend updates.

I opened the NHS website, typed in 'mini stroke' and scrolled silently. How easy was it to recover from orthopedic surgery? Would he be able to sign with a broken wrist? The answers didn't fill me with much optimism.

Tomsk had been stationed on his chair by the window, his favourite place after the warm patch under the shelf full of orphaned Staffordshire dogs, where he'd been eyeballing the squirrels in Martine's mountain ash. Now he turned and gazed at me through his wispy fringe, as if sensing a sudden change in the room's atmosphere.

'. . . for the time being you'll be reporting directly to me, as I'll be overseeing Allen's day-to-day as well as my current role,' Christian press-released. 'I'd like to set up a review as soon as possible. Beth? Are you still there?'

'Yes, sorry.' I swallowed and closed the NHS page. 'I'm just shocked. About Allen.'

'Naturally. We're all shocked. So re your current role – Sophie has taken over administration for my diary and she's sent you some dates for an in-person review.'

In-person? No, thanks. I was still only a week into my four-week-old Beth Recovery plan, and though the trousers went over my hips without threatening the seams, the zip was no closer to zipping.

'Why don't we schedule a Teams call for the end of this week?' I suggested, more confidently than I felt. 'I can do Friday morning?'

'No, all meetings have to be in-person going forward. Hybrid working will continue on a case-by-case basis but the company reset will focus on building a high-performing team, and in my experience, the best way to do that is to connect *in* the office, *around* the table, committing to collective goals.'

What? My heart rate spiked with anxiety just picturing what that would look like. Natasha, Christian himself, Dan, Steve and Mike (the Tax Bros, as Natasha called them), the super-keen graduate apprentices whom everyone was terrified of, all round a table staring at me and wondering whether I was the same Beth who'd been there before, or some new Beth. Who'd eaten the old Beth.

Don't be ridiculous, I told myself. There had been a time when I'd been in the office all day, every day. And I'd been fine. Fine.

But that was *before*, said a little voice. When I had other things going on in my life, better things.

'We're looking at Monday the nineteenth,' he continued.

My head pounded. I dragged my laptop closer. 'I've got client meetings booked for most of Monday,' I said, fumbling to open the shared system, so I could quickly block out the rest of my diary for the month. 'How about . . .'

No! *No no no no no.*

I stared at the screen in horror. There was already a window stretched across all of Monday, marked 'Christian Re-boarding Meeting?'

'Sophie's taken a look at your schedule and Monday seems to be fine our end?' he went on.

'I can't do the nineteenth,' I insisted. 'I've got scheduled meetings. I must have forgotten to put them in the system.'

I felt Christian's wordless judgement whistling down the line. Or maybe he was just breathing out in a particularly judgemental manner. 'And this is exactly why I want to get everyone back into the office.'

The room's atmosphere must have plunged even further, because Tomsk, unable to bear the fraught expression on my face, slid down from the chair by the window and padded across the room to lay his shaggy head on my foot.

I looked down at his gesture of support. I didn't want to go back to the office, and he certainly didn't. Tomsk had never known a world where I even *went* to the office – now nearly an hour's commute each way. How could I leave him for the entire day? He couldn't cope with that.

Anxiety crawled across the pit of my stomach but so did a sudden fierce resistance. I wasn't going to take this lying down.

'I'll revert to Sophie with alternative dates,' I said briskly. 'I'm currently living some way from the office so I'll need to revisit my travel arrangements.'

How long could I put this off? If I couldn't get into the grey trouser suit, I could always buy a new one, but the mere thought of trying on clothes in a shop made me feel stubbornly resistant, that toddler-on-the-verge-of-a-tantrum agitation. The unflattering mirrors. The sizes that wouldn't fit. The styles that I'd once loved that were now my enemies.

I was conscious of my bra digging into my flesh, as if my body was expanding in panic. I'd have to move my haircut appointment forward too.

'Beth? Sophie's made a suggestion. We're having an all-team meeting the following Tuesday, so she can schedule our meeting either before or after that. Which suits you better?'

How many days away was that? Fourteen. How many steps could I do in that time? How much weight could I lose? I felt sick.

'Before or after the meeting?' repeated Christian.

Neither, I wanted to yell, but I heard myself say, 'After.' There was always a chance it would overrun and get cancelled. Although, with Christian, I doubted it.

'Great.' He didn't add, 'Now that was easy, wasn't it?' but the implication was clear. 'If you don't mind, I've got a few people to speak to so . . .'

'Is it OK to send a card to Devora?' I asked quickly. 'Allen's wife?'

'Um, yes, why not? Sophie's organising something, speak to her.'

I finished the call, closed my laptop, and without thinking, I stood up and robotically flicked on the kettle, robotically placed four slices of bread in the toaster, then robotically ate all four slices of toast.

It didn't make me feel any better.

When the phone rang an hour later, I half-expected it to be Christian calling back to move the meeting again, and panic fizzed instantly inside me like an Alka-Seltzer dropped into water (more like three Alka-Seltzers, into acid). It took me a second to realise that it was the house phone ringing, not my mobile.

'Darling, it's Martine,' said Martine. 'Could you do me a favour and drop some donations off at the charity shop? I've been having another sort-out – there are more creative writing books you're very welcome to have.' But it had to be in the next day or two, she added, because otherwise Jackie might come home and start unpacking the bags.

'She seems to think this house is either a storage facility or a museum to her childhood,' she went on. 'If you're not too busy, this afternoon would be ideal.'

Since Christian had pretty much ruined the day for me, I offered to take her into Longhampton after lunch. There were four more bags of clothes and two boxes of books waiting by the front door; three of the bags were filled with jumpers, cord trousers, checked shirts, all top quality. Ray's, I presumed (although, yes, I did have a quick look while I was loading them into the car, and no, there was nothing of Fraser's that I recognised, beyond a couple of football albums).

'Is there any particular reason for this spring-cleaning?' I asked, when we were heading towards the town centre.

'It's spring!' Martine seemed in a good mood. 'And I've been meaning to have a good clear-out for ages. Before you say anything, I am very sure about what's in the bags. There's no point keeping wardrobes full of unworn clothes, especially when Ray spent most of his time in the same three pairs of trousers. As I told Jacqueline, her father would much prefer someone else to have the benefit of those good jumpers, instead of letting the moths get to them.'

I shot a quick glance across the car. 'Sorry, I wasn't being nosy.'

'No, no, I know you're not, Beth. But as I tried to explain to Jacqueline, there's no point being sentimental about things that he never even *wore*. He didn't care for pink. Never did. But Jacqueline did some course or other and decided that that was *his colour*, so she insisted on giving him the same pink jumper year after year.' She sighed. 'I tried to hint that he'd prefer a cologne, or some shaving soap. But no. Once she gets something into her head . . .'

'Are they in the bag?' I asked, trying to lighten the mood. 'I wouldn't say no to a cashmere jumper.'

'There are at least three, and you're very welcome.' Martine gazed out of the side window. 'I highly recommend a declutter, Beth. It helps you see the important things. It doesn't mean you're throwing *memories* or *people* away, just stuff.'

The bitter aftertaste of her conversation with Jackie was almost tangible, and I wondered if Jackie had chalked up the purging of Ray's wardrobe as more 'irrational behaviour'. It seemed pretty reasonable to me; generous, even. But then I supposed it wasn't my dad's dinner jackets being thrown out like last week's Sunday papers.

'What's happening with the piano?' I asked. I'd been out with Tomsk when Jackie had called by to rescue it, but she'd sent the cryptic message CRISIS AVERTED! and three thumbs-up.

'The school doesn't want it! Can you believe that?' Martine widened her blue eyes, outraged. 'Apparently it's "surplus to requirements".'

'Oh.'

'But,' Martine went on, 'I was sorting through some old photographs to show you, you remember you asked me about where the diaries used to be in the town? And I suddenly thought: Rosemount! I got in touch with your friend Mr Levison, and he couldn't have been more delighted. Talked about having recitals and singsongs and all sorts. He's arranged to have it collected later this week – the removal men have already been in touch.'

'That's incredibly kind of you,' I said.

She flapped her hand as if most people had a baby grand they needed to get shot of. 'I think it'll be rather at home in that library, don't you think? I'm sure there's someone up there who'll enjoy playing it.'

I wondered, from the satisfied expression on her face, whether she had someone particular in mind.

If Naomi at the charity shop recognised me as the 'You're the problem!' lady, she was gracious enough not to show it, and she accepted Martine's treasure trove of tweed, lambswool and John Grishams with open arms and a Gift Aid form.

Before I'd hauled her donations inside, I'd opened the boot of the car, and let Martine tell me which of Ray's unworn Christmas jumpers suited me best. All of them, it turned out.

'See? Much nicer on you than on Ray,' she said, once we'd established that baby pink suited my colouring perfectly, and also that Ray and I took the same size in knitwear.

'Are you absolutely sure?' I asked. They were all Brora or Johnston's of Elgin; it had to amount to hundreds of pounds' worth of cashmere. 'Won't Jackie mind?'

'I doubt she'll notice, darling.' Martine raised an eyebrow. 'She never seemed to notice her father *not* wearing them.'

'Well, thank you, Martine and Jacqueline – and Ray,' I said.

'There, everyone's happy.' Martine tapped me on the arm. 'Now, let's get these inside, before Jacqueline pops up from behind a hedge and impounds Ray's sports jackets. You wouldn't . . .?'

'No, thank you,' I said, firmly.

Martine had requested 'a little pottering time' in town, so I took myself off to the Wild Dog Café, where we arranged to meet in an hour.

I'd brought my laptop to type up the new notes from the drop box, and one of the notebooks Lewis had sent for the project work. So far I'd only written one conversation in it – Nigel Callaghan – and since he'd more or less interviewed *me*, that barely filled half a page. It was literally the most exquisite notebook I'd ever seen, and it made me want to write something meaningful in proper ink on its creamy pages, intriguing stories and moving insights that would live up to the splendour of it. I wondered if that had been Lewis's intention in sending me something so gorgeous; it would fit with his general 'inspire to aspire' ethos.

Or maybe he just understood the magic of stationery, I thought, smoothing a clean page flat. I hoped so, anyway. It would be something he and I had in common. Either way, I liked the way Lewis approached things: efficiency with a human touch. Lewis was basically the anti-Christian.

(You know what I mean.)

In an effort to bolster my sparse notes, I did a search for Nigel online and was amazed at how much came up.

Nigel Callaghan was a bona fide BBC correspondent who'd filed reports from Vietnamese battlefields and collapsing regimes in Nairobi; some of his reports had been so historic that clips were on YouTube, Nigel shouting urgently over the sound of helicopter blades and distant gunfire. He'd been a good-looking man in his younger days, rangy and dynamic in a safari suit, with long swept-back hair and intense eyes. Courageous, too – he was often stained with sweat, or smoke, or, in one startling clip, blood. It wasn't clear whose.

I jotted down some questions to ask him next time, although I wasn't sure he'd offer any answers. Nigel was the expert in getting people to talk, and clearly knew every trick to avoid doing it himself. But there were so many things I wanted to ask: what had it cost to live through moments like that, how had he managed to stay calm and analytical while narrowly avoiding having his head blown off? How it felt to come home afterwards? Whether . . . I paused. Whether being so close to danger had affected his personal life, and the choices he'd made. Had he decided not to marry, or had work got in the way?

I couldn't possibly ask him that. It was too intrusive. But if he offered the information?

'Beth! Beth!'

I looked up. Martine had returned, and was draping her coat on a chair by the window, at a prime-spot table with a view of the high street.

'What on earth are you doing, hiding away in that dark corner?' she demanded. 'You can't see a thing from back there! Now, what can I get you?'

I tried to say I wasn't hungry – not wanting to be the fat girl sitting in the window eating cake – but she flapped her hand. 'I'm getting myself a lemon tart. Would you like one?'

After a moment's hesitation, I admitted I would.

'Good,' said Martine, and went up to order. She made things very easy.

'Did you buy anything?' I asked when she returned. 'I see you've got some bags.'

'Just some essentials,' said Martine, then, with a half-frown, reached into her shopping bag and pulled out a large black Staffordshire pottery dog, his soft eyes and nose and ears picked out in dull gold. 'And this. I couldn't resist.'

'He's adorable!'

'Isn't he?' She positioned him between the sugar bowl and the tiny cactus, facing out on to the high street. 'He's a Jackfield spaniel. Made in Shropshire, probably Victorian.'

'Is he valuable?'

'Not really.' Martine angled the dog so the sun glinted off his faded chain. 'They were working people's ornaments, so not the highest quality, but they were precious to their owners. Worth more in a pair, but so many get broken or lost. You can snap up singletons like this for a few pounds. I must admit, they're my secret weakness. I hate to see them on their own.'

That explained the shelf full of odd dogs in the flat. 'Are you trying to match them up?'

'Sometimes I do, yes! But I rather like seeing them in little gangs. Ray absolutely hated my wally dogs – tat, he called them. I was allowed two pairs in the house, and they had to be matching. Most of my collection ended up above the garage. I promised him I'd stopped collecting a few years ago.' Martine paused, gave me a sneaky smile and said, 'Although, just between us . . .' then reached into her bag again and produced another tiny spaniel, no bigger than a nail varnish, white with red ears and shiny yellow glass eyes.

'There's a match for that one in the flat!' I said, delighted. 'I've seen it!'

'I know!' Her eyes twinkled, then she pretended to look serious. 'Don't tell Jackie, after the lecture I gave her about decluttering.'

I promised I wouldn't, even though there was something unexpectedly touching about Martine, remorseless champion of perfection, collecting stray dogs and arranging them in convivial packs, out of sight of her family.

'Would you like me to bring its friend over?' I asked. 'Now it's a pair, it can go in the house.'

Martine thought for a moment, then pushed the little dog across the table towards me. 'No, why don't you take this and put it with its partner?'

I was touched.

'Now,' she said, more briskly. 'What's happening up at Rosemount? What fact-checking would you like me to do this week?'

I told her about Nigel Callaghan, and she visibly perked up at the idea that someone who'd been on television was living in Rosemount.

'Why don't you come with me next time?' I suggested. 'Pam says he's always complaining about a lack of intelligent conversation – I bet you two would get on like a house on fire!'

I thought she'd appreciate the compliment, but no. 'I'd rather not, if you don't mind.'

Too late, it dawned on me that maybe she thought I was trying to lure her up there on Jackie's instructions, showing her how nice it really was.

'But do tell me about your other stories,' she went on, before I could splutter an explanation. 'How many times have you been told about the year Longhampton Town beat Leeds United in the FA Cup? You'd think Town played at Wembley, not Stanton Road, the number of people who claimed they were there!'

I flipped through the notes I'd been writing up. 'Well, someone's very keen to share memories of the railway lines that were closed in the sixties.' I turned over the page of spidery handwriting to find a name. 'Mr Trevor Lowden is still taking the Beeching cuts very personally.'

'Trevor Lowden.' Martine raised her eyebrows and took a sip of tea. 'He would. Poor Sheila.'

'And lots of stories about the asylum, the scout camps, Miss Hicks at the primary school who had a poodle who could count up to thirty . . .' I came to the fruit-picking story and stopped.

Should I share it with Martine? It felt very personal. But the writer had shared it with me, and obviously wanted this memory to go on the record. And she might know the people involved; there couldn't be many red-headed beauties in a small town.

'What is it?' asked Martine, seeing me hesitate.

'It's a love story,' I said. 'But I don't know who wrote it, because they didn't put their name on it.'

'Can I see?'

I passed the pages over and while she was reading, I tried to catch the waitress's eye to order another coffee. Now I'd overcome my self-consciousness about being on display in the window, I was rather enjoying watching the passers-by on the high street, and the flower baskets, and the cheerful energy that was a Longhampton spring afternoon.

The waitress came over with a smile. 'What can I get you?'

'Another latte for me, please.' I glanced at Martine. 'Martine? Another coffee?'

She was so engrossed she didn't hear me. I wasn't surprised.

'Martine?' I repeated, more gently. Maybe she knew these people. Maybe they were no longer around.

'What? Oh!' She looked up, and blinked. 'Sorry, I was miles away. Yes, another coffee, please. Black with hot milk. Thank you.'

When the waitress had gone, I said, 'So, bit of a mystery – whoever wrote that didn't put a name on it. Have you any idea who it might be? It's obviously someone who grew up round here.'

Martine pushed the paper back towards me, and shook her head. 'No, sorry. I don't.'

'Oh.' I was disappointed: I'd assumed she'd be able to identify all parties involved, with full family tree. 'Well, whoever he is, there's a romantic heart still beating up in Rosemount. That was over sixty years ago and it sounds as if he remembers it like it was yesterday.'

'Sometimes those are the last things you forget,' said Martine, and then the coffee arrived and she turned the conversation back to the shops that used to line the high street.

Chapter fifteen

'It's not that I don't believe Gordon Watson is a brave man,' said Ellie. 'It's just that World War Two had been over for two years before he was born, which makes it unlikely that he flew a Spitfire in the Battle of Britain.'

'I see,' said Lewis.

He, Pam and Ellie were in his office with a list of questions collated by Ellie in relation to conversations she'd had with staff and volunteers over the past week. It wasn't just Ken's alleged stint with MI5 that had raised eyebrows. Now Gordon Watson was claiming to be a flying ace and Brian O'Hare had been involved in the original test kitchen team for Nutella.

'I don't know whether Gordon's delusional, or if he's winding me up,' said Ellie. 'Either way, I'm kind of insulted that he thinks I can't do simple maths.'

'And I'm pretty sure Nutella was invented in Italy,' added Pam. 'If Nutella was British, I'm sure we'd have called it something like Spready Chocolate.'

'I see,' said Lewis again and steepled his fingers. He was struggling to concentrate, thanks to two difficult phone calls he'd taken shortly before this delegation pitched up in his office. The first had been from Carrie Clark of the *Longhampton Gazette*, 'reassuring him' that she had nothing to do with the 'other story' running in this week's edition, and the second had been from Sharon McDowall, daughter of Mary McDowall, demanding an explanation for the 'haunted old people's home' story that she'd just read about on the *Gazette's* Facebook page.

Hauntings, for God's sake. The only thing haunting Rosemount was David bloody Rigg.

First things first, Lewis told himself, and refocused on Ellie and Pam.

'So what you're asking,' he said, 'is how do we know if they're making up stories? And what do we say if they are?'

'In a nutshell,' said Pam. 'Yes.'

It was undeniable that the Story of My Life project had turned up some startling facts about the residents. Like Iris Johnson's moment in the sun as a background dancer in the Cliff Richard film *Summer Holiday*, a revelation shared with volunteer, Janice Dolan, and then shared with the rest of the community in a special screening in the television room.

'Why didn't you *tell* us your mum was a movie star, Angie?' Pam had asked Iris's daughter, as she and her stunned family stared at the projector screen Ellie had rigged up in the lounge, watching Iris's lissom eighteen-year-old self frug with barefoot abandon on the studio sand.

'First thing we knew about it was last week. Right, Mum?' Angie shot a narrow look at her mother, who was tilting her white head side to side to the beat and smiling nostalgically at the Shadow pretending to flirt with her.

'I'd almost forgotten about it, hadn't I?' Iris had said equably. 'My boyfriend at the time wasn't too happy about me dancing, so I turned down the chance to do the next film when they asked, and then I married him, and that was that.'

'She's not talking about Dad, by the way,' her son Jason interrupted. 'She married some other bloke *before* Dad.'

'And we only just heard about the first husband last week! After the story volunteer lady mentioned it to us.' Angie turned to her mother. 'Mum, why didn't you tell *us*?'

'Well, it didn't last. We were young and daft. Gretna Green, spur of the moment. Best put behind us.' Iris smiled at herself on the big screen, as if she was watching a different film playing in the back of her mind.

'We've really learned a lot about Mum in the last week or so,' said Jason drily.

Lewis, sitting at the back with a box of popcorn handed out by carers dressed as usherettes, noted the tension in Jason's face, and the bewilderment in Angie's. Personally he admired Iris for putting a false start behind her and moving on – not easy back then, as Gayle had noted in her write-up – but did Iris' children see it like that? Was the omission worse than any scandal? It gave him a moment's pause.

'I don't think we should be too quick to assume an extraordinary story can't also be true,' said Lewis carefully. 'The whole point of this project is to find out who our residents *are*.'

'Maybe they're just embellishing?' suggested Pam. 'I mean, Helen Kelly was a parliamentary speechwriter, Jack Drabble played water polo for Wales – how are you meant to follow that? You can't blame people for wanting to sound a bit more exciting.'

Lewis nodded. Gayle had said something similar in her induction meeting, and it had stuck in his head: 'People don't always see the value in a quiet life lived kindly and honestly; I always hope the story project puts that into a different perspective.'

'No, I reckon it's a game,' said Ellie. 'There's one thing that all these stories have in common. And that's who they're coming from. The question is: why?'

'No need to be cryptic, Ellie,' said Pam. 'You're not Hercule Poirot and I've got a laundry delivery to sign off. Who?'

'Maybe you should go and have a chat with Nigel Callaghan.' Ellie folded her arms. 'He's in the library, doing the crossword.'

Nigel was in his usual chair, filling in the squares of the quick crossword with a red pen. He didn't stop when Lewis approached, but grunted an acknowledgement when Lewis asked if he could sit down.

Eventually, Nigel tossed the completed crossword down on the side table, and said, 'Good day to you, Mr Levison. Are you here to ask me for my memories of the Suez Crisis? Or would you prefer me to talk about how moved I was when Abba won the Eurovision Song Contest?'

Lewis didn't take Nigel's prickliness personally; he'd seen an active mind rattling the bars of a care home plenty of times. 'I'd love to hear your memories of both,' he said. 'I realise our project must feel a bit coals to Newcastle to you, though. If there are any news-gathering techniques you could share, I know Gayle and her team would really appreciate your help.'

'I wouldn't dream of it,' said Nigel, but Lewis wasn't deterred.

'Would you consider talking to the residents about some of your experiences? Personally, I'd be fascinated to hear how news events unfold, from the viewpoint of a real insider.'

Beth had emailed the story team, highly excited, with the revelations about Nigel's previous life, and even as he was enjoying Beth's chatty communication Lewis was kicking himself for not doing better research himself.

'Flattering, but no,' he said. 'As I told that nice blond girl, memory is a funny thing. It's a lens. You don't always see things as they were, in the rear-view mirror. You don't always see them as they really are when you're right there, let alone sixty years later. I don't want to be that boring old fart, telling everyone how much better things used to be. I'm not sure they were.'

Lewis shuffled the cards in his head. He didn't need Ellie to tell him who Nigel ate his lunch with: Ken, and Gordon, and Brian. The spy and the fighter pilot and the inventor of chocolate spread. He could imagine the game they were playing: what was the most outrageous story they could persuade Janice or Beth to write down. Fun for them, but would the other residents feel mocked? Would the volunteers see the joke? A bored resident was never good for morale. A bored resident with a brain like Nigel's was a disaster waiting to happen. A small voice even wondered if it was Nigel planting stories of ghosts and encouraging mice into the kitchen, just for something to do.

'Then I wonder if I can engage your investigative powers on something else,' he said, and reached under his jacket for a copy of the *Longhampton Gazette*. 'Did you see the feature about the story sessions in here this week? It's a great feature – nearly a whole page! I believe you're in one of the photographs.'

Nigel grunted.

'What is less good, however,' Lewis went on, under his breath, 'is the feature on page twenty. Which seems to suggest that Rosemount Court isn't merely failing inspections, it's haunted.'

'What?' He showed a glimmer of interest as Lewis offered him the paper.

'Yes, apparently. Look.' The article was illustrated with an unambitious stock photograph of a Gothic mansion that wasn't Rosemount, but for the purposes of negative publicity was close enough.

> *A distressed resident, speaking off the record to our reporter, told us of nightly temperature drops, strange noises behind blocked-off doors, and other unexplained disturbances.*

'How original,' Nigel scoffed. 'They could at least have been specific. Headless parlourmaids or something. What nonsense. Utterly unprovable, of course. If you're asking me for libel advice, I'm afraid it's not my department.'

'I've sent it to our legal team – but there's not much they can do now. Any damage is already done. What I was hoping you might be able to help me with is . . .' Lewis took a deep breath, and hoped he wasn't making a tactical error. 'Can you help me find out who's doing this? It has to be someone on the staff, or one of the residents. I have my theories, but no proof.'

Lewis liked to believe the best in everyone, which made it hard to think badly of any of the staff, whom he wanted to trust, or the residents, whom he also wanted to trust but additionally didn't dare offend, for fear of losing vital revenue. But he needed to get to the bottom of this, and Nigel, he suspected, was not burdened by either of these disadvantages.

Nigel tipped his head, amused. 'Is this another of your bespoke enrichment projects, Mr Levison?'

'If you like. But joking aside, if someone is trying to sabotage Rosemount's future, I need to know.' He met Nigel's gaze. 'It might be amusing for them, but believe me, this isn't the time for playing games. Much is at stake.'

Nigel, to his credit, registered the understatement. 'Understood.'

Lewis slapped his thighs, the quintessential British end to a tricky conversation. 'And on that note, I am off to provide some bespoke enrichment for another of our residents. You might want to have a look out of the window in about fifteen minutes.'

As he got up to leave, Lewis glanced down at the coffee table and saw that Nigel had filled in every square of the quick crossword with the words *bugger off*.

Eunice Stafford's bespoke enrichment apparatus had been delivered the previous day, while Lewis was conducting a coaching session on conflict resolution for the kitchen team.

The courier had left it in the shed, and he'd only had time to conduct two secret test runs, once before going home, and once very early in the morning, but Lewis was confident that he'd mastered the techniques. It was, literally, like riding a bike. Just a bigger one than normal.

Technically, he should have completed a health and safety form but had run out of time – and, in truth, was too excited to wait. He made a mental note to do it first thing and set off to find Eunice.

She was waiting with Pam in the reception area, swaddled in a pair of jogging bottoms and a sweatshirt borrowed from lost property, along with her soft red shoes. The outfit made her seem even smaller than normal but she looked like an excited child, waiting for a school trip.

Lewis could tell when Eunice was excited because she folded her arms, wagged her foot and pretended to look disapproving.

'What in the name of heavens is that?' she demanded.

Lewis wheeled it up to the front steps. 'It's a tandem.'

'A tandem? I didn't know they even still made those!'

'This is a brand-new model.'

'Is it yours?' She gave him a suspicious squint. 'Have you been splashing the home's cash on bikes for yourself? Because that's embezzling.'

Lewis informed her he'd hired it with his own money.

'Why on earth have you done that?'

'For you,' said Lewis simply. 'You said you always wanted to ride a bicycle but you weren't allowed one. Well, today you're going on a bicycle.'

'No!' said Eunice, but her eyes were darting between the tandem and him, as if she was daring herself to say yes.

'I'm not going to let you steer, if that's what you're thinking,' Lewis went on. 'I'll go on the front, if you don't mind.'

'You've gone funny in the head.' She looked at it again, and licked her lips. 'I should call the police.'

'It's not compulsory,' Lewis pointed out. 'I'm just offering you first go. I imagine there might be a queue, so if you're not fussed—'

'I didn't say that,' Eunice snapped.

'Please don't do this if you don't want to.' Pam was hovering a few steps behind, with Ellie and Kemi as backup.

'Are you trying to stop me?'

Pam stepped back, hands up. 'No, not at all.'

'I see I've got an audience,' observed Eunice. 'Your girlfriend's arrived, Mr Levison.'

'My who?'

He looked across to where Beth was standing, shielding her eyes from the sun. She was wearing a drapey sort of dress, which made her look like a Grecian statue, but her arms were bare – and his heart paused for a second, distracted from beating by the sight of her skin. It was pale as a daisy petal, white but edged with the faintest pink.

He straightened his back, and felt taller.

Eunice was looking at him, smirking and pleased with herself.

'She's not my—' he started to say, but Pam cut in, with a reproachful, 'Eunice!'

'Right, let's get you up here,' he said half to Eunice, half to the nurses standing by to help, but to their communal surprise Eunice startled them by scrambling up on her own.

'Careful, Mrs Stafford!' Pam steadied her, and shot an anxious look in the direction of Ellie as Lewis bent down to adjust the pedals.

Not that Eunice would be pedalling, thought Lewis. She just had to hang on, with those little hands already gripping the bars as if she was in the front car of a Blackpool rollercoaster.

Eunice perched on the seat behind him, and he barely felt any difference in the tandem's balance when he swung his own leg over the frame. The helmet on her head looked as if it weighed as much as she did, and Pam had strapped on some bizarre kneepads too.

Lewis turned.

'Ready?' he asked, with a wink.

'Are *you*?' Eunice's blue eyes glittered.

'Mr Levison, are you absolutely certain we're legally covered to—?' Pam began but he didn't want her to spook Eunice.

'We'll be fine, won't we, Mrs Stafford?' he said, firmly, and pushed off.

A cheer went up from the crowd at the door and he allowed himself a glance across to Beth, to see whether she was smiling.

She was. But there was something else in her face, a conflict in her brow that gave him a moment's distraction.

No, thought Lewis, and focused hard: balancing the tandem with his pedal strokes and his forward momentum, straining his muscles to keep the machine aligned and moving, until they were skimming down the drive.

He heard something behind him, in his ear. A gasping, mewing noise that started out as, 'Ohhhhoooooooo!' and slowly built up into a loud, 'Wooooooaaahhhh!'

Eunice Stafford was squealing and laughing at the same time. 'Faster!' she yelled. 'Faster!'

Lewis increased his speed, pedalling as hard as he could. A bigger joy rose inside him at the sound of Eunice's unbridled delight; this was what made the hours of admin, the spreadsheets, the squabbles and the red tape worthwhile. Listening to Eunice Stafford's inner eight-year-old having the time of her life, screeching as if she really was on a Blackpool rollercoaster.

He did a full lap of the drive that went around the house – down the tree-lined approach where carriages had once clattered towards afternoon tea, around the tarmacked area where the modern extension had been tacked on for the old school – then did it again, urged on by Eunice's small fist beating his back.

When he finally circled back to the front steps, there were multiple faces at the windows, watching. Pam, Kemi and Ellie rushed up to the tandem like a Tour de France support team to unload Eunice and carry her to safety. Pam had to persuade her to get off; Eunice was up for another lap.

Beth approached, smiling, clapping her hands with approval. 'That looked like so much fun. You're going to have a queue!'

Lewis had recovered from the exercise but now his heart rate rose again. 'Good cardio! For Eunice too – I bet that got her heart going faster than the armchair fitness lady.'

'Pam was saying she's never seen Eunice laugh like that. They didn't even know she could smile until about an hour ago.'

'Eunice is all right,' said Lewis. 'Between you and me, she's not had a lot to smile about in her life.'

Beth nodded, understanding. Lewis had uploaded notes from his conversations with Eunice and even he, with his limited imagination, could see the story emerging between the lines: a youth spent caring for others, an adulthood scrimping and saving to make a better life for her children, then slowly being left behind by them in her old age as they ascended the social ladder. 'Her Michael' featured a lot; her daughters didn't.

'And I have to tell you,' he added, peeling off his cycling gloves, 'I enjoyed it too.'

'I bet it goes even faster with two people pedalling,' she said.

Impulsively, Lewis held out his hand. 'Come on, have a go.'

'What?' Beth's energy changed instantly. She took a step back, her hand flying up to her throat. 'Me? No.'

'Yes!' Lewis held his hand out again. 'Come on. Quick spin around the block before tea.'

'No.' She shook her head.

'Why not? Go on, it'll be fun.'

He tried to keep his voice casual, but inside Lewis felt alarmingly light, as if he'd been filled with helium and might float away. The thought of Beth, as close to him as Eunice had been, but with the smell of her perfume where Eunice had emitted a waft of lavender and the industrial washing powder that the laundry used. In his mind's eye Lewis could see Beth's wheat-blond hair falling out of its pins and streaming behind her, her pale chest rising and falling as she leaned in closer. The pair of them pedalling, driving the bike on together.

He'd never wanted anything more, even though he wouldn't be able to see her.

'Please?' he added, unable to stop himself.

Beth's face crumpled. She mumbled something that he couldn't catch – something about herself? – then struggled to regain her composure.

'Sorry,' he said, sticking a finger in his ear and wiggling it. 'I didn't catch what you said. Sorry, I think I'm going a bit deaf.'

'I said, it might . . . tip over or something. I'm too heavy.'

It was so far from the truth that Lewis laughed. 'Beth, *men* ride tandems together. You don't weigh the same as a man.'

She turned her head and, again, muttered something he couldn't catch.

Her whole demeanour had changed and Lewis panicked that the moment was slipping out of his reach.

Forget it, forget it. Change the subject, keep her talking.

'If I'd known you were coming in today, I'd have . . .' Have what? His mind raced. 'Told you about the tandem. Who are you dropping in on?'

'No one, actually.' She tucked a hank of hair behind her ear; there was a tiny silver hoop in her lobe, and seeing the curl of her ear made something twist in Lewis's chest. 'I was passing, so I thought I'd pop in to check the box for any stories. I found a really interesting one in there a few days ago.'

'Really?'

Beth looked up at the house. 'A vignette about meeting a beautiful red-headed girl, in the hot summer of 1964, fruit-picking.'

'Round here?'

'I think so. But no names.'

Lewis started to wheel the tandem back; he wanted to prolong the conversation as far as possible but he did have to talk to the finance team at five. 'Was it handwritten? Pam might recognise the writing.'

'No, it was printed out.'

'Does anyone spring to mind?'

'I haven't talked to everyone, but of the residents I've spoken to so far . . .' She bit her lip. 'It's someone who's good with words, definitely. I just wonder if they didn't put a name on for a reason. Maybe it's someone who wants to preserve a special, important memory but doesn't . . .' Beth searched for the right word. 'How to put this? Maybe it's a memory that they don't share with the person they're with now?'

'But why share it with us?'

'I don't know! Anyway, there was nothing in there today. I thought I'd mention it though. In case you had any ideas.'

They were at the old garden sheds, solid constructions with charmingly unnecessary, and now flaking, wrought-iron decorations running along the roofline; Lewis made a note to get a ladder up there and repaint them. Gold, maybe. He felt celebratory.

'Is this where the tandem lives?' she asked.

Lewis realised Beth had been wheeling the tandem along with her hand on the crossbar, while he'd been steering it. Her gaze was lingering on the red saddle, as if she was trying to imagine herself on it.

'For the time being,' he said. 'I hope I'll be able to get you on it before the summer's out.'

'Ha! Good luck with that!' she said, but there was something in her voice that made him hope she wasn't completely ruling it out.

Chapter sixteen

In my and Ashley's Heartbreak Cave of Gloom, weeks had slumped into months had slumped into years. I completely grew out a set of highlights and Ashley's passport expired, both without us noticing.

In Longhampton, though, time passed differently. The days had the same number of hours, but they seemed to fit a lot more *in*. It came as a shock when my phone reminded me to give Tomsk his wormer, and I realised that I'd only been living above Martine's garage for one month. It felt like I'd been here forever.

Maybe it was a side effect of transcribing Rosemount's collected life stories – galloping through the decades, bombarded with hundreds of names and dates, marriages, dramas and weird coincidences. Then there were the real-life people, all with names and faces, dogs and grandchildren to remember: with every visit, I got to know Pam a little better, and Lewis, and the nurses and carers, and the other volunteers. I still worried that I'd say something stupid, after all those months stewing in my own company, but the atmosphere at Rosemount was so gentle I found myself asking questions that would have made me sweat with anxiety before.

Obviously there were times when I came home overloaded, drowning in other people's memories. The best way to process these deluges of information was a long walk, in silence, along the canal with Tomsk, where – again, to my surprise – I started to have some ideas for my screenplay. In the space of one startlingly productive week, and twenty-one thousand steps, I managed to get Arthur embarked on a steamer to the Yukon Territory's gold rush (thanks for the inspiration, Bob Garfield's great-grandfather) while Seraphina joined a Women's Suffrage movement (just as Wendy Baker's grandmother had apparently tried to do, but been 'talked out of it by her nan'.)

Martine was delighted when I told her I'd finally broken through my writer's block. 'I *knew* you'd get there eventually,' she said, as if it had been her twilight nagging that had done the trick. Which, if I'm honest, it kind of had. 'All those family stories must be giving you plenty of material!'

I laughed, but to be honest, I wouldn't have minded a few more stories from Martine's own family. My attempts to winkle out some fresh details about Fraser had come to nothing. Despite living right in the heart of the Hendersons' universe, I hadn't learned one new thing about Fraser beyond that solitary photograph on the piano. Where was he working? Was he single? What was he *doing*?

Even old facts would have done. I'd never got the full story, for instance, of why there'd been such a drama about Fraser choosing cybersecurity over the family business. Why hadn't Heather taken it on? Or Cara? Martine generally adored being asked questions, but if I nudged the conversation towards Fraser, she always managed to steer it back to something else – Longhampton's plague pits, ice cream parlours, my screenplay – and there were only so many innocent questions I could ask Jackie, in between reassuring her on our Whatsapp chat that Martine wasn't throwing out the family silver or behaving oddly. There were no clues in the boxes above the garage, or in the bags I dropped off at the charity shop.

And so one busy day followed another, ticking off the squares on my calendar until the one with the big red ring around it: Martine's anniversary. But I wasn't wishing the time away because before I could see Fraser again, I had to see Christian, and the rest of the Jacobs' team.

And that meant going back to the office.

The suffocating dread mounted with every twenty-four hours that brought my return to the office closer. I couldn't sleep the night before. My brain was churning, working out what time I'd have to leave, what Christian might ask me, what stupid things I might say by accident, etc., etc., and eventually at four a.m. I got up to make myself a mug cake. Which, for once, didn't help.

Tomsk, at least, had a great day ahead of him. After investigating the various options – I couldn't leave him at home, and he wasn't the sort of dog you could smuggle into the office – I'd phoned George the vet for advice, and he'd told me to bring Tomsk over to the kennels where Rachel ran a doggy daycare facility.

Any guilty doubts I had about triggering Tomsk's abandonment issues were blown away when he gave Rachel the same adoring steam-train-of-love welcome that he'd given George.

'Oh, he is the same boy I remember but so *happy*!' she exclaimed. Tomsk shoved his big head joyfully into her legs. I'd interrupted her dishing out breakfast for the rescue dogs, but she still looked unfairly stylish in jeans and one of George's checked shirts, tousled hair wrapped in a silk scarf, winged eyeliner in place despite the early hour.

All this made my straining grey trouser suit feel even more meh. But I'd squeezed into it, I reminded myself. It was *on*. Just. And I would definitely do up the button on the waistband before I got into the office. I clung to this tiny win. Being too stressed to eat had a silver lining.

'He won't think I'm leaving him here for ever?'

'No! He knows you love him too much to leave him.' Rachel slipped Tomsk something from her pocket. I think it was kibble. If it had been tranquillisers I don't think I'd have cared, as long as he was happy. 'We'll see you at five, is that right?'

I nodded. 'If I can get away sooner, I will. It's my first day back at the office for a while, not looking forward to it.'

She pulled a sympathetic face. 'Best of luck. Do you, um . . . do you want a safety pin for your trousers?'

I glanced down.

There was a long, pale snake of flesh starting on my hip just below my waistband and continuing almost to the knee, where the seam of my trouser suit had split, forced apart under the pressure my thighs had been exerting on it during the short drive over.

I closed my eyes and let out a silent howl of pain in my head.

There was no point going home to change, as this was the only office wear I had. Shopping opportunities before nine a.m. being limited, I eventually screeched into the

Jacobs' car park at twenty-three minutes past nine, wearing a badly fitting skirt and cardigan combo, courtesy of the superstore in the business park. The meeting started at half past, and I knew Christian would probably have a stopwatch. I had seven minutes. *Seven minutes.*

I found a parking space, but then my pass didn't work on the front door. I swiped the pad over and over, but it must have expired, so I had to attract the receptionist's attention from outside, which took a precious, excruciating minute, in which my heart rate peaked, then peaked again until I felt two breaths away from a panic attack.

Was this the universe telling me to go home? I waved my arms, which didn't help my heart rate. Was this another of Ashley's 'signs'?

I was about to spin on my heel, and run away when someone behind me opened the door and I dashed in with them.

'Beth Cherry.' Breathless, I pushed my pass across the desk. 'Might need resetting.'

She took it, looked up at me, looked down at the pass photo again and knitted her laminated eyebrows together in confusion, as if she couldn't connect the two Beth Cherrys. 'Mmm-kay. This is old? We issued new cards two years ago, so . . .'

She clicked away at her keyboard with her butterfly nails and then pushed a temporary card back across the desk. 'HR will make a new pass, but this is only valid for twenty-four hours, so you'll need to do a new photo.'

'Can't HR just upload the old one?' I tried to control my panting. I couldn't.

'No, it has to be a new ID photo. Security reasons. But they'll take it in their office, no worries.' While she spoke, she dropped my old pass in a bin before I could say, 'Give that back.'

I stared at her, and she smiled back sweetly. 'Have a good day!'

So *that* was a good start.

The next challenge to my nerves was that the office layout had been remodelled in my absence, so radically that I wasn't sure if I'd come to the right place.

Every partition had been dismantled; no one had their own door to shut, apart from Christian, whom I could see behind a glass wall, talking to Sophie, Allen's assistant. She was writing things down performatively on an iPad. The desks were now arranged in lines, and seemed much smaller than I remembered, with none of the usual friendly desk clutter of photos and mugs; just a monitor, and a scarily ergonomic chair. Something about the visibility of everything set me on edge, and from the tense, whispered conversations going on, I didn't think I was alone in feeling that.

'Breakout pods' had been set up in the middle of the floor: clumps of green chairs with glass tables with fake cacti on them. How was that going to work with pages of notes and files and all the other paraphernalia accountants usually carted around?

And more to the point, where was my desk?

I looked around, desperately hoping to see a familiar face who might be able to guide me in like a lost plane.

Then, out of nowhere, two hands descended on my shoulders from behind, and someone cooed in my ear, 'There you are! I thought it was a mirage!'

I spun round.

Natasha. She, at least, hadn't changed. If anything, she looked a few years younger and brighter and her nose seemed pointier. Although that could have been the lighting.

'How are *you*?' she cooed, mwahing an air kiss each side of my face, glancing over my shoulder to check if anyone was looking at us. 'You look . . . well!'

I cringed. Every woman knows what that means.

'I'm fine, thank you,' I said. 'And you?'

'Oh, you know.' She rolled her eyes. Natasha had round eyes, like a doll's, which she accentuated with lash extensions. 'Run off my feet, as per, but *soooo* excited for the new changes!'

'Yes, poor Allen,' I said.

Natasha's expression instantly switched to 'sympathetic'. 'God, it's so tragic.'

Tragic? He wasn't dead. 'Yes, it is. He—'

'I used to *beg* him to educate himself about blood pressure.' She widened her eyes even further. 'We had a conversation about it – several conversations, truth be told – but you can't tell men of his generation anything, bless them. They think it's millennial nonsense, healthy eating and exercise, and not letting your weight get dangerously out of . . .' Natasha trailed off.

An uncomfortable silence filled the gap between us, like a fart.

'Shall we head?' Natasha recovered her composure. 'Christian's rearranged the meeting room and if you don't get in quick smart, you have to stand.' She pulled another concerned face which didn't *quite* suggest that she wasn't sure if I could stand for more than ten minutes, but came close.

Oh God, I hadn't missed this. The final dregs of confidence were draining out of me by the second.

I followed her into the meeting room which, as she'd said, had been rearranged. The old artwork had gone, replaced with new artwork which was, incredibly, even blander than what had been there before. Extra chairs had been brought in. How many people were going to be present? How many people worked here now?

I made myself breathe mindfully. Although I'd got used to being around more people at Rosemount, the energy here was different: tension and judgement and watchful eyes everywhere. Conversations at Rosemount were slower – to be honest, *everything* was slower – and I struggled to respond quickly enough to Natasha's questions before she fired another one at me.

How had I found the new bypass?

Oh? So where was I living now?

How was Fraser? Are you two in touch or . . . Oh sorry!

And so on.

She sat down in the middle of the front row, my least favourite seating choice, and started telling me about the house that she and her husband Sam had bought on a new executive development, which had already increased in value by eleven per cent, and had shaved twenty minutes off their commute. Her words washed over me as I watched the Jacobs' team drift in, smiling briefly at the faces I recognised and trying not catch anyone else's eye.

Was I the only one wearing a cardigan? Ugh, I was. Had my colleagues always been this smart? I thought people were meant to be more relaxed with office wear these days? Occasionally someone waved, or mouthed 'hello' and I smiled back awkwardly. Since Natasha and I were on the front row, I was impossible to miss, and I felt hot and self-conscious and itchy.

And then just as Natasha said, 'But enough about me, I thought we'd never see you again, is everything—?' Christian strode in, with the sort of swagger that made me wonder if he was listening to entrance music on his AirPods.

I won't bore you with the details of Christian's presentation.

It was basically an extended press release, with slides. He talked, barely pausing for breath, but actually said very little. Even in the few weeks I'd been doing the Life Story work at Rosemount, I'd got so used to people modestly shrugging off major life events in a few words ('*. . . and then we moved to Uist because I was lead engineer on a project bringing electricity to the island . . .*') that I found myself frowning, trying to work out what specific facts Christian was sharing.

The gist of it was that under his glorious leadership, Jacobs' was going to expand to the next level, providing more services, streamlined client management and aiming, overall, to be the leading accountancy firm in the West Midlands within three years. Negotiations were already underway to acquire the biggest local mortgage brokerage, and a similar pensions specialist 'to bolster our own offer', and to reinvent a wealth creation team for high-net-worth individuals.

'Good luck finding them round here,' Eddie, he of the black cab, behind me, muttered.

I was so grateful for a flash of cynicism that I nearly turned round and hugged him.

The final takeaway was that Christian would be restructuring the departments for maximum efficiency, with immediate effect. Although Allen had warned me, and presumably others too, this drew a low but audible murmur from the room.

'. . . and on that note, I think we can look forward to a fresh and exciting new chapter here at Jacobs',' Christian finished presidentially.

There was a pause, then Sophie coughed and passed him a note.

'Oh! Yes! And an update from Allen. He's out of hospital but will be taking early retirement as of today,' he added. 'Get well soon, Allen. And best wishes for your retirement. He will be hugely missed.'

Everyone murmured, 'Hear, hear,' and next to me, Natasha made a sincere yoga-prayer-hands gesture and inclined her head slightly.

I think I heard someone grumbling something under their breath, so it wasn't just me who thought this was a bit much.

My anxiety levels began to drop once the meeting was over, and everyone trailed out to pick over the lunch buffet.

I escaped from Natasha, and said hi to a few old faces, who in turn said how nice it was to see me.

I had a good chat with Eddie, head of compliance. He'd visited Allen in hospital, since he lived close by, and reported that he was 'over the worst of it' but 'had a long road ahead' and 'it was touch and go for a while'. Which sounded like blokeish minimisation to me, but it was reassuring to hear Allen was on the mend.

I was almost starting to feel normal when Christian loomed up behind us, tapping his watch. 'Five minutes,' he said. 'My office?'

My stomach sank, but I made an excuse about getting a glass of water and headed towards the kitchen to give myself a moment to gather my thoughts.

There were a couple of young accountants I didn't recognise in there, engaging in animated conversation. Eddie had informed me, under his breath, that Christian had brought in several people from his previous company and they were a bit cliquey, but I gritted my teeth and went in anyway.

They were standing by the noticeboard where Harriet used to post a Positive Thought for the Day, and everyone else would post their passive-aggressive reminders about not using their soya milk. Both were looking at something and sniggering.

I made myself smile, even though the smile felt painfully fake on my face. 'Hi! Do you mind if I squeeze past to get a glass from the cupboard?'

They stopped talking, stared at me, and then one of them suppressed a giggle of shock. Then they left in a flurry of mumbled excuses.

What were they looking at?

I took a step closer and saw a newspaper cutting on the board, mounted on a neon-yellow backdrop, with some neon arrows pointing at the photographs. The headline was THAT'S THE STORY OF MY LIFE! and I realised it was the feature Carrie Clark had written about Rosemount.

My mouth went dry.

The neon arrows were pointing at *me*. It took me a moment to recognise myself; I just saw a shapeless, bulging mass in a draped top, like a wardrobe that someone had thrown a dustsheet over.

A scalding wave of embarrassment rolled across me. I looked *enormous*. The photographer had caught me talking to Kay Lloyd, and next to Kay's neat frame my bulk loomed even larger, rolls of fat bulging under my bra strap, my double chin, the worst possible angle for my thick upper arms.

Natasha had made the poster: I recognised her handwriting on the note – *A massive round of applause for our own Beth Cherry!* – written on one of the arrows, just in case anyone hadn't spotted it was me.

I reached out to take it down, then realised I couldn't, not without drawing even more attention to myself. I compromised by pulling off the arrows with shaking hands.

Masochistically, my gaze returned to the cutting, to make sure I wasn't in the background of any more photos. The photographer had done his best to make Rosemount seem like a fun place; in a different shot, Eunice Stafford was nagging Lewis about something while Pam Woodward held a pen and notepad like a secretary in a screwball comedy, and Nigel Callaghan was doing his crossword with a long-suffering expression, one leg crossed to expose a skinny ankle and a raffish red sock. His very pose seemed to say, 'Beirut was preferable to this carry-on'.

But again my eyes slid back to my own shapeless, lumpy form. Was that really me? Was that what everyone saw? I felt a hot, stinging shame that bordered on panic. How could I have changed so much from the woman who went to jive classes with Fraser? He used to be able to swing me round his hips. *Gone.* That Beth had *gone.*

'Good effort with the volunteering, by the way,' said Susannah, one of the mortgage team, swilling out her coffee mug at the sink. I hadn't even heard her come in. She nodded towards the noticeboard. 'My niece is a nurse up at Rosemount, says it's like a different place with that new bloke in charge. *Loves* doing the story sessions with the residents. She's started asking our family about stories too, the things we're learning about my dad . . .'

'That's great! Tell her thanks. Sorry, got a meeting with Christian,' I mumbled, and dashed off to wipe away my tears in the privacy of the loos.

Christian didn't make me wait, as I thought he might have done, but ushered me into his office, and launched straight into a precis of my career at Jacobs': my client list, my involvement in business development, my five-year-career vision. Then he fired off a series of questions that I hoped I answered, as the photograph floated across the back of my mind like a distracting, grossly overweight ghost, and my pulse yoyo-ed accordingly.

'And so, to wrap up – how do you plan to add value to your role?' he finished. 'I'm asking the whole team the same question.'

I guessed this would be coming, and had spent some time constructing a strong answer, something that no one else would come up with.

'What about a community campaign to improve financial education?' I explained that I'd picked up on a lot of confusion up at Rosemount, not just from the residents. 'We could offer mentoring for people who want to get to grips with budgeting, especially if their living situations have changed. Widows who historically let their husbands deal with the finances, say. And drop-in sessions to coach young people starting out. It would surprise you,' I added, thinking of a conversation I'd had in the kitchen about loan sharks, 'what people are embarrassed to ask for help with. Not just the financially vulnerable, either.'

Christian didn't seem keen. 'I was hoping more for ideas on increasing market share and visibility.'

'But this would be great community visibility,' I pointed out. 'And far more organic and useful than just being a shirt sponsor for the football team. Most of all, we'd be giving people genuinely life-changing skills.'

I'll be honest, I'd asked myself: 'What would Lewis Levison do?' and that's what had come out. People first.

'Hmm.' Christian jotted something on his notes. 'OK. I'll think about it. Now, do you have any questions for me?'

While I'd been explaining my idea, my heart rate seemed to have calmed down, so I took a deep breath and went for it. 'Have you considered the points I raised, supporting my request for continued work from home?'

'I have.'

I waited.

Christian lifted his eyebrows, as if there was nothing more to say.

'And?' I asked.

'Well. I'm somewhat unclear about how you can give social anxiety as a reason not to come to the office when you're volunteering at a residential home? Which seems like a terrific initiative, incidentally. It must take up most of your weekends.' He paused. 'I am assuming you're not there during your contracted working hours?'

I started to reply, then flushed red, and stopped. I had struggled with whether to use my anxiety as a reason; I wasn't particularly proud about doing so, but it was what it was. 'But that's . . .'

'Not the same? I don't see how. OK, so, Beth, that was a useful chat. I wish we could speak longer but I have to see quite a few people today. The business is at an exciting crossroads and I appreciate the part you've played in bringing it to this point.' He smiled, but it wasn't a smile you could trust. 'Thanks for coming in today – not so bad, was it? – and we'll be in touch about next steps.'

I'd started to get up, but the words 'next steps' halted me in my tracks. 'Next steps' was what you said at a job interview. Not a casual catch-up with a valued employee.

In what place were you happiest?

23, Grenfell Terrace, Manchester (don't look for it, it's been demolished).

Nessy got her grades for university, of course. One A and two Bs. By then, we were spending every free moment together, although in secret; her parents were strict. They'd have hit the roof if they'd had the first idea she was wandering the lanes when she was supposed to be in the library. Luckily my parents weren't bothered; Mum was too busy dealing with my sister's baby, and Dad with his darts team, to take much interest in my whereabouts. As long as I wasn't in the pub or getting into trouble, they didn't care.

I'd tried not to think about what would happen when Nessy left, but she had a plan. She had a plan for everything.

Dad was pushing for me to get a job at the glass factory; they were looking for bright teenagers to train up in book-keeping and I'd always been OK at maths. Not my favourite subject, but in those days you didn't choose jobs based on what you enjoyed doing. But wouldn't it be better, Ness suggested, if I got myself on to a proper course, with a proper qualification? Marketing, or management, something with prospects? She'd read something in the newspaper about further-education colleges, and before you could blink, there I was, enrolled on a business marketing course in Manchester with a full grant and money from a trust set up in 1865 by some local businessman made good, to 'support the higher education of deserving farm workers'.

My mother wasn't keen on that part. She thought it sounded like charity, as if we were illiterate peasants who needed help. What was wrong with the glass factory? My dad couldn't get his head around me wanting to up and go to Manchester. That said, he told everyone that I was off to university, let his boss buy him a drink to celebrate.

I've forgotten what that last day at home was like; maybe I decided not to remember. We left Longhampton station at different ends of the train, but arrived in Manchester together, and that was that. We were starting again from scratch.

I realise now what a luxury that was, for someone like me. Not just the education and the grant, but the chance to become someone new, not get trapped in the character you'd been assigned at school, then had to wear like an outgrown blazer for ever – the cheeky one, the thick one, the clown. I could already see my classmates turning into their parents, only growing as much as was allowed. The idea of that terrified me. But without Nessy to encourage me, to make everything feel possible, I'd have stayed, I know. I don't want to think about what I'd be like now.

Manchester scared the bejeezus out of me at first – I'd never been out of the county before. But I got used to it; when you're young, you don't know what you should be worried about, do you? It was as if we'd been dumped into a sea of young people, where tides swept you off in new directions, and you swam alongside the people who liked the music you listened to, or the film you'd just seen. Without even trying, we found our shoal of fish to swim with.

It was me who heard about Grenfell Terrace through a friend of a friend who was moving out. The landlady, Geraldine Maltbeck, was a tremendous old soak who'd lived a long and dramatic life, details of which you could prise out of her with Harvey's Bristol Cream. Nothing shocked her, darling: she'd lived in Berlin. That was her motto. Geraldine was happy to let anyone she took a fancy to move into the falling-down house she owned. She liked to collect star-crossed lovers. Below us were a beautiful Jamaican tailor living with a bishop's daughter, and above us were a couple of actors both called Paul who made us rehearse lines with them – Ness was a tremendous mimic. Geraldine taught me to play the ukulele, and I planted up a vegetable bed for her in the yard, using my grandad's soil recipe. We got the horse manure from the rag and bone man down the road – the Pauls were aghast.

There was only one visit from Nessy's parents, who were disappointed she'd moved out of halls. I wasn't there, fortunately – they came while I was at my bar job – but she told me her mother made a big deal about 'the area' and said she wished she'd come home more often. Geraldine put on all her best Kensington airs and graces, however – that went down well. A five-pound note was discreetly left with instructions to call *at once* if any young men were brought home. Geraldine assured her that no such liberties had been taken under her roof, and spent it on gin and another kitten for the house. Juniper.

This was without doubt the most glorious, adventurous time of my whole life, and yet I wouldn't – can't? – separate any memories out of this time as being happier than others. We didn't have a clue these were the golden days: we took it for granted that life would only get better. The happiest moments were probably the ones I've already forgotten: the beans on toast eaten on our laps watching Geraldine's tiny television, or the Sunday afternoons lying in bed watching Nessy flip through one book after another, speedreading for essays that should have been written while we were at parties or in the pub. She got her degree, but only because she was too scared of her parents to fail.

If I try to pull out individual moments now, so long after, I fear I'm reaching for those clichés of the 1960s that you see so often on television documentaries that you forget they're not your own memories. Not the real, fleeting emotions that even then went in a blink of an eye: that racing sensation when you're almost too happy for your body to contain it, or the weightless moment when you look into someone's eyes without speaking, knowing your hearts are exactly, equally balanced like astronauts holding hands, floating in space. Soap bubbles. Dandelions.

All I can say for sure is that I know now my happiness peaked while I was living at 23 Grenfell Terrace. I've been happy since, of course, but not like that. Everything was possible there, every day I learned something, ate something, or talked to someone I'd never have known if I hadn't met Nessy in the blackcurrant fields. I wasn't becoming a different person, but she was helping me find the person I knew I could be, the same way you'd strip the casing from ears of corn to reveal the perfect beads inside. It was what I'd dreamed love would be. It's hard to look back at that now, though, knowing as I do that the sand in our hourglass was already almost gone.

Would I go back? In a heartbeat.

Chapter seventeen

'You seem very upbeat this morning!' Martine observed, as I hummed along to The Monkees on the radio, now permanently set to the golden oldies stations. 'Any particular reason?'

I was dropping her off in town on my way up to Rosemount for a story session with Dodie Lochmead, who was halfway through her thrilling saga of four husbands and seven race cars, in which she had won several club championships and over a hundred trophies. She was going into a lot more detail about the cars than the husbands, two of whom (maybe three) were called Tim.

'Because it's spring!' I said, which was true. But only partly.

I'd expected to be wiped out after the emotional and mental assault course of that meeting at Jacobs'. But even though my entire body still clenched just thinking about that mortifying photo in the kitchen, it was *done*. I was in no great rush to see Natasha again, and I wasn't sure how I'd feel once the reality of Christian's new regime became clearer, but, for now, I didn't have to think about it for a while.

And of course, with the office hurdle cleared, it was a straight run to the weekend, and the Henderson family party – and Fraser.

I beamed vacantly at the cars ahead. I'd trialled various imaginary versions of our first meeting in five years, the same way I'd brainstormed different permutations of Arthur and Seraphina's goodbyes until one felt 'right'. All my versions ended with Fraser apologising for being such an idiot, me graciously demurring, and us agreeing that it was good to see one another again.

And then . . .

I made myself stop there. I didn't want to tempt Fate. The main thing was, we'd get over that initial awkwardness, and find our old connection was still there underneath. That much was reasonable, surely? Who knew what might happen after that?

'You mentioned that you were going back in to your office for a meeting this week,' Martine went on. 'How did it go?'

Blimey. Martine remembered everything. 'It wasn't as bad as I thought it'd be.'

I realised that was true. I hadn't had a panic attack; I hadn't been sacked.

'It rarely is, Beth,' she said, serenely. 'What did you think would happen?'

I shot her a side-glance. For someone who had, in her own son's words, 'Never set foot in a place of regular employment', Martine was very confident about my indispensability. 'Still time to find out,' I said, darkly, then changed the subject. 'Where would you like me to drop you off?'

'At the hairdresser's, I'll give you directions.' Martine touched her hair, which was swept into its usual French pleat. 'Heather made the appointment – said she's booked me in for what she called a "glow-up". Is a "glow-up" what I think it is?'

I assured her that it was.

'It's for this do at the weekend.' She sighed.

'Are you looking forward to it?' I asked. 'Seeing everyone?'

'Well, I'm looking forward to seeing everyone.' Martine paused. 'I wouldn't say I was looking forward to the party, as such.'

Bad choice of words, Beth. How could she enjoy a party that was all about the love she'd lost? 'I'm so sorry, that was insensitive. I didn't mean . . .'

'Goodness, don't apologise! You're not the one who insisted on *throwing* a party! Between us, while I'm always happy to see the children, I'd really rather the whole thing wasn't about me and Ray. I don't want us to be sad. Or even worse, to feel we *ought* to feel sad.' She gazed out of the window. 'Jacqueline has rather fixed ideas about grief. She keeps talking about a *process*, but the human heart doesn't cleave to the schedules of self-help guides.'

I nodded. For a while I'd felt nothing after my mother died. Just guilt, and relief. Relief that the worst had now happened, that I didn't need to fear the phone in the middle of the night. And then, one month after the funeral, the tidal wave crashed over me – in Greggs, of all places. Pure sorrow, that I'd never see Mum laugh, or smell her skin, or be able to tell her anything, or ask her anything, ever again.

I sensed Martine was looking at me. 'I'm sure you know that all too well, Beth.'

Haltingly, I told her things I'd never told anyone else. Not even Fraser. She listened, then patted my knee again, more gently, and we didn't say anything else until I pulled up outside her salon.

Martine's regular hair salon was a discreet establishment called Berenice's (est. 1956). It was down a side street in the nice old Georgian area of Longhampton, next to an antiques dealer and a gun shop. I told her I should be finished by four, and could pick her up from the Wild Dog Café, but she insisted that she'd make her own way home.

'Don't worry about me,' she said, leaning into the car. 'I'll get a taxi back.'

'Are you sure?' I frowned. 'Jackie would never forgive me if anything happened to you.'

'You're my lodger,' said Martine, 'not Jacqueline's granny nanny. Now go and talk to the old dears, and I'll see you later. Once I've been glowed up.'

The sound of someone singing 'The Bare Necessities' was drifting through the entrance hall when I arrived at Rosemount, and I followed it to the library, where I found Hugh Lloyd standing by Martine's baby grand piano, holding forth to an appreciative gaggle of residents; most of them were singing along, every one of them was tapping a foot.

Lewis – also singing in a strong and melodic tenor – spotted me as soon as I walked in. His face lit up instantly; not just his brown eyes, but somehow his whole face. I smiled back. It was impossible not to, really.

He beckoned me over, patting the chair next to his. 'Hugh's taking requests,' he whispered. 'We're down a Disney musical rabbit hole!'

'I'm supposed to be chatting with Dodie Lochmead,' I whispered back.

Lewis nodded towards the front row where Dodie was lustily bellowing about fancy ants. 'Maybe stay for a song or two? She's having a whale of a time.'

I agreed, and when Hugh asked for requests 'from any musicals, Disney or otherwise!' Lewis and I both called out, 'My Favourite Things!' at the same time.

'Good choice!' Hugh turned to his accompanist, Kay. 'I think we know this one, don't we?'

She responded by playing the introduction and the front row cooed and clapped and turned up their hearing aids. It was, as the man in front of me loudly remarked, just like being on a cruise ship, 'but without the pong of diesel'.

I leaned over to whisper in Lewis's ear. 'I didn't have Hugh Lloyd down as an all-round entertainer?'

'Rosemount is a magician's hat, full of surprises.' He turned his head towards me before I could lean back; our faces ended up quite close together and I drew in a deep noseful of an attractive aftershave. I think I'd expected Lewis to smell of something wholesome, like Imperial Leather or Head & Shoulders, but he didn't. Quite the opposite. He smelled *gorgeous*. For a long moment we sort of stared, half-smiling, and blinked at each other – like Lady and the Tramp, mid-spaghetti, ironically enough – then sat back. I felt a little flustered, but Lewis carried on singing, a bit louder than before.

Dodie didn't get to finish her story of how she met Tim III during a pitstop; instead the library filled with residents as we sang our way through selections from *My Fair Lady*, *Mary Poppins*, a few hymns, a 'Beatles magical mystery medley' (which everyone kept up with, despite Kay refusing to give clues about which song was coming next) and for the big finish, 'Bohemian Rhapsody'.

At the end, a hoarse but glowing Hugh took a standing ovation. On the piano stool, Kay acknowledged the applause with a modest wave, and Pam served tea early 'before everyone collapses'.

I genuinely couldn't remember when I'd last had so much fun, and when I told Lewis, he looked so delighted, I thought he was going to hug me.

If he had, I don't think I'd have minded, it had been that nice an afternoon. Martine would have *loved* it, I thought.

When Saturday, and Martine's party, finally rolled around, I didn't want to look as if I was waiting to be invited to join them, so I took Tomsk for a long walk in the morning and then went into town to get my own hair done.

I always felt more confident when I had a glossy curtain of hair to hide behind, and between that and a new dress which actually fitted (thank you, stress; thank you, Tomsk and your insatiable capacity for exercise), I was feeling pretty good about myself when I went back up to the flat, which I proceeded to tidy to an inch of its life, just in case Fraser decided to drop by. I even cleaned Martine's pottery dogs until they looked Crufts-worthy on their shelf.

Every so often, I glanced out of the window overlooking the garden to see what was going on. During the week, Jackie had arranged for someone to tidy up the lawn and flowerbeds, and as I'd left for the hairdresser's, caterers had arrived to set up afternoon tea. 'I'm not beating myself up for not making a cake,' she'd told me, as if I expected someone with her crazy work schedule to find time for baking. 'I just want us to enjoy ourselves.'

To her credit, it looked like something from a magazine down there: a long table covered with snowy-white tablecloths, vases of lilacs and eucalyptus, sparkling glasses, tiered cake stands, and so on. In pride of place was a porcelain tea service which I'd hunted out at her instruction from the storage boxes in the flat: 'A wedding present,' she explained. 'Thought it was the perfect occasion to bring it out!'

It gave my conscience a momentary twinge when I found the tea service, thinking about Martine's wish that the day not be about sad memories, but Jackie had been very specific, so I'd left it on the back step, carefully washed and dried.

I peered cautiously out of the window, not wanting to be seen. Three teenage boys were now slouching by the elm tree, with a fourth, smaller boy dangling on the ancient swing suspended from the lowest branch. I could tell they were related by their studious ignoring of each other, as well as their identical mops of blond hair. All four were engrossed with their phones, until the peace was broken by a shriek from inside.

'Cooper! Cooper, get off!' A woman came running out of the house, jabbing her finger at the tree. 'It's not safe! Get off now!'

Cara! I thought, with a flutter of excitement. She hadn't changed. Same shoulder-length executive hair, same statement black glasses, but now with a noticeable mid-Atlantic accent.

She glared back towards the house, and yelled, 'Do you guys want to stop arguing about a bloody piano and come out here and supervise the kids?' She swung round and tugged at the swing. 'This thing's fifty years old! Has anyone checked it?'

'It's fine, stop being *that* parent.' Jackie appeared with a teapot on a tray. 'The boys are looking after Cooper, aren't you? Oh, honestly, you're not *all* on your phones – can't you play a game in *real life* with each other? Perry? Perry, will you bring Mum's chair out?'

And then they trooped out: Martine, Jackie's husband Perry struggling with a huge wicker peacock chair/throne, Heather (alone, no boyfriend), a man I assumed was the father of Cara's son, Cooper, and finally . . . Fraser.

Time stopped. Even though I'd run this moment through in my imagination over and over, my heart suddenly felt too big for my chest.

He was the same: same blue shirt, same broad shoulders, same intelligent face, hair still thick and pushed back off his face. The man I'd woken up next to for four years, the man I'd assumed I'd spend the rest of my life waking up with.

If I hadn't started that stupid conversation, I thought, I'd be part of this scene, leading my own wobbling toddler, cute and dumpy in her cousins' hand-me-down dungarees, helping Jackie de-clingfilm the sandwiches: I'd be down there, not up here. In a parallel universe, a ghost Beth, a Beth that had ignored Mali's advice and just *waited*, was living this life. If only I could turn back the clock and just keep my mouth shut, I'd materialise in my rightful place:

not a ghost looking down from a garage full of unwanted junk, but a happy, laughing part of Fraser's family.

It was so unfair it made me forget to breathe for a second.

Fraser took Martine's chair from Perry, who was struggling, and hoisted it easily on to the paved area to place it at the head of the party table. I leaned forward to get a better view and must have leaned nearer the window than I meant to, because there was another shriek, this time from Heather.

'Shit! Shit! There's someone in the garage! Look, up there! Someone's broken into the garage! Mum!'

Everyone's gaze swung up and towards me, and I froze at the window, a rabbit in the spotlight of their combined curiosity.

Only Martine didn't bother to look up. 'Oh, that's Beth.'

'Beth? Beth who?' Cara glanced at Jackie, with a subtle 'is this what you mean about Mum losing the plot?' gesture at her temple.

I cringed. *Beth who?* She followed me on Instagram. I'd liked *all* her boring posts about 'Central Park springtime!'.

Jackie beetled her brows at Cara, then looked up and pretended to spot me for the first time. 'Beth! Come down and join us for a cup of tea!'

Her headteacher voice was loud enough to be heard through the window, but she mimed 'come down' and 'tea', just in case. I had no choice, but descended the stairs as slowly as was polite, to give Jackie enough time to fill in the details for anyone who hadn't been told about their mother's lodger.

Even so, when I stepped into the garden through the side gate, I could hear indistinct muttering, spiked with *whys* and *whats*, and caught the tail end of Martine snapping, '. . . still my house, and I still have the final say in what happens here, so really, Cara, it's not relevant what you feel.'

When I appeared, it stopped abruptly.

'Hi!' I raised an awkward hand.

Jackie seemed embarrassed; Cara, impatient; Heather and Fraser, confused; the teenagers were still glued to their phones. Cooper had taken the opportunity to slither back on to the 'potentially lethal' swing.

'Beth.' Martine gestured towards the table. 'We're just about to have some tea. Will you have a cup? Your hair looks *marvellous*, by the way.'

I touched it, and tried not to look at Fraser. It was like not looking at your Christmas presents. Or a solar eclipse. 'Thank you! And . . .' I blinked, taking in Martine's new 'do. 'You look so chic.'

We'd only spoken on the phone for the last few nights so I hadn't seen the results of the 'glow-up' in person: and it was dramatic. Martine's hairdresser had cut her long silver hair into a sculpted bob, curling elegantly around her cheekbones. It took years off her without diminishing her regal aura in the slightest. If anything, she looked more glamorous.

'Oh, it's years since someone called me chic.' She beamed with the compliment. 'Thank you, Heather – what a treat.'

Not everyone seemed in favour of the transformation. 'You knew about this?' Cara turned to Heather. 'Did nobody think to go *with* Mum, in case something like this happened? This weekend, of all weekends?'

'I keep telling you, I booked a *glow-up*,' Heather insisted. 'I didn't ask them to chop her hair off.'

'No, *I* told them to,' said Martine calmly. 'I wanted a change and it's much easier to keep on top of. Now, tea? It's going cold.'

Cara and Heather carried on muttering while herding the boys to the table. Jackie poured tea and handed out the delicate china. 'This was a wedding present from Dad's Auntie Martha and Uncle Ted, wasn't it, Mum?' Martine, I noticed, was smiling, but her expression was a little tight. She gave me an imperceptible blink when Jackie handed me my tea, and I wasn't sure how best to respond.

There was definitely a 'family row' atmosphere. I could tell by the way conversation focused on me with a super-courteous laser beam: first Perry's neutral opener about the rental market (yes, that bad), followed by Jackie's jolly follow-up about it being a 'good incentive to clear out our junk!' from the garage.

Then Fraser, with whom I'd been trying not to make eye contact, in case my heart exploded, coughed, and said, 'If you don't mind me asking, Beth, why are you staying here? I mean . . .' He searched for politer words, then gave up. 'No, there's no other way of putting it. Why here?'

Jackie spluttered. 'Fraser!'

'Well, come on,' he said. 'You're all thinking it.'

'No, fair enough, it's a bit random,' I said quickly. 'It was just one of those serendipitous things! I happened to bump into Martine the day before my move fell through. She was kind enough to offer me a temporary solution until another property became available.'

Cara and Jackie exchanged another 'see? Mum's being odd' look, which again only I caught.

'Good for you, Martine,' said Perry, raising his teacup. 'Very generous.'

But Fraser hadn't finished. 'So, when you say your tenancy came to an end, is that you, or you *and* . . . ?'

'Me and my dog,' I said. 'Tomsk. That's what made it tricky, finding somewhere I could bring Tomsk too.'

'Tomsk is Beth's *dog*,' said Jackie, as if reminding him of something he'd been told.

'Right.' He seemed unclear. 'OK. You're not . . . married?'

What? Was he checking to see if I was single? I mean, there wasn't any other way to interpret that, was there? I felt a powerful *ba-doom* of excitement in my veins.

Heather rolled her eyes. 'I get that you work in IT but that is a deeply inappropriate question.'

'I'm only asking!' He raised his hands and I noted there was no ring in sight on either hand. *Yes.*

'No, it's fine,' I said again quickly. 'It's just me, yes.'

I tried to read Fraser's expression; that was a flirty question, surely, but he didn't exactly look flirty, more confused. Maybe when Jackie had told him about Tomsk, he'd misheard, assuming 'Tom' was my boyfriend?

Still. My heart was racing; the *very first thing* he'd wanted to know was whether I was still single. That had to mean something.

'And you're here for how long?' he asked.

'Fraser!' Jackie's forehead was a monobrow of admonishment.

'A couple more weeks? I should hear from the estate agent any day now about the new place.'

'Although Beth's welcome to stay as long as she likes!' Martine had clearly tired of this conversation being conducted over her head. 'It's rather nice having someone to chat to in the evenings – you should ask her about the fascinating oral history project she's co-ordinating up at that old people's home you're all so desperate for me to move into.'

'Good for you!' said Perry again, as I said, 'Oh, I wouldn't say I'm co-ordinating it.'

'Yes, *do* tell us about that,' said Jackie with slightly too much enthusiasm, and I found myself recounting a couple of the better stories from the project, while the teenagers hoovered up the cakes and the adults picked at the sandwiches.

I ate nothing. Not because I didn't want to eat in front of Fraser but because my stomach was occupied doing pleasant loop-the-loops with every glance I drank in of him.

It was starting to feel wonderfully normal and relaxed, when Martine abruptly shaded her eyes with her forearm. 'Would anyone mind if I went back inside for five minutes? This sun's so bright.'

Jackie and Cara exchanged glances. 'Of course not, Mum. Do you need a nap?'

'No, I . . . Well, maybe yes.'

'Charlie? Charlie, stop that!' Jackie waved at the oldest boy, who was eating two cakes at once to save time. 'Can you help Grandma inside?'

Martine frowned. 'How on earth do you think I get in and out of this house when you're not here?'

Jackie sighed. 'Mum . . . Please.' There was a lot of previous conversation between those two words, I thought, but Martine deigned to let Charlie pull her chair back from the table and escort her away.

Once Martine and Charlie were safely out of earshot, Jackie gestured at her siblings, and muttered, 'I think this is a good time to have a pre-chat chat, OK? Get our ducks in a row.' She turned to me. 'Beth, just so you know, we're going to talk to Mum about her options – staying here, moving to assisted living, getting more help, and so on.'

So this was an ambush, not a party?

Cara opened her mouth to say something, but Jackie cut her off. 'Beth's been keeping a discreet eye on Mum, making sure she's not, you know, putting herself in danger.'

'We speak every evening,' I added. 'On the phone. She rings me. I don't intrude!'

'She must be so lonely in the house on her own.' Heather gazed at the wedding-present teacup, then, tearful, looked up at the house. 'Without Dad.'

'Beth's been a godsend,' said Jackie. 'It's worked out well both ways.'

I squirmed. It was nice of her to say that, but I was feeling increasingly torn between wanting to help Jackie and thinking that maybe Martine wasn't anywhere near as 'erratic' as she seemed to think. She just wasn't behaving in the way Jackie expected her to.

'I'll leave you to it,' I said, before there was any question of me staying or going. 'Tomsk needs his walk about now.'

There was a chorus of 'lovely to see yous', and I paused for a moment, holding Fraser's gaze as we looked at each other, for the first time in so long.

The air crackled between us, and he nodded, with a slight smile touching his lips.

My heart looped in my chest. I nodded back. *Keep calm.*

'Fraser!' snapped Heather.

I felt shivery, I felt normal, I felt as if I'd seen him yesterday, I felt as if I'd see him tomorrow.

This was the start of a new chapter, I told myself. A clean page, a new Act.

I just had to listen to my intuition this time, not other people's bad advice.

When Tomsk and I came home from our walk, an hour or so later, Fraser suddenly appeared by the door – as if he'd been watching out for my return.

'Hey! Look, I just wanted to say sorry if I came across as rude before.' He ran a hand through his hair. 'It's been a weird day.'

I nodded sympathetically. 'I can imagine.'

'Jackie did tell me you were staying, but . . .' He hesitated. 'I'll be honest, seeing you – it really threw me. You haven't changed at all.'

'Neither have you.'

He grinned, and I was spun back on an invisible bungee to the time when he smiled at me like that all the time; in the car, in the supermarket, every morning when I woke up.

I hadn't changed. (I totally had.) Did he say that because he wanted to pick things up where we'd left them?

'So, what I wanted to say was, I'm here next weekend to sort out Mum's internet. Jackie's drawn up a rota.' He nodded towards the house. 'If you're still here too, it would be good to have a coffee, maybe? Catch up?'

'I'd love that.' I told myself to look cool but not quickly enough for my face, which broke out a broad smile.

Fraser looked pleased too. 'Good. Good.'

This was the awkward bit: how did we part? A kiss on the cheek? A hug? Nothing?

Tomsk decided it for me by nudging at the door with his head, as if I needed a clue.

'Someone's ready for his supper! Hello, mate.' Fraser bent down and ruffled Tomsk's long ears. He'd always been good with dogs; he had that inner calmness that they responded to. 'Lovely eyes. What breed is he?'

'Not sure, he's a rescue. Part sofahound, part snufflador?'

'Part hair metaller?' He lifted Tomsk's wispy fringe. 'Love the highlights. Very early eighties.'

The ice had been broken. This was OK. Inane small talk about my dog I could do. But Tomsk, unusually for him, whined and nudged the door with his nose.

'Don't keep him waiting!' Fraser straightened up. 'I'll text you about next week – same number?'

I nodded. Imaginary fireworks were going off around us.

'Great! See you then.'

And just like that, Fraser and I had a date.

Chapter eighteen

I woke up the next day with a euphoric Christmas Eve feeling bubbling in my stomach, and it took me a moment to remember why.

Fraser. I had a date with Fraser.

I wasn't imagining it, was I? He'd seemed happy enough to see me, he'd specifically wanted to know if I was single, and we were meeting up the following weekend. I hugged these facts to myself. No, it was incontrovertibly great news. The universe's reward for facing up to the office this week? Maybe.

I would have lain there hugging my happiness longer, had Jackie not phoned to ask if I could give her a hand moving some stuff back to the garage. 'Sorry to bother you so early on a Sunday,' she said, 'but I need to leave in an hour. And I wouldn't mind a quick word, if that's OK?'

I said it was fine. I hoped the quick word would involve Fraser.

'Mum's having a lie-in,' Jackie explained when she opened the back door to let me in. 'Yesterday took a lot out of her.'

I followed her into the house, trying not to look too obviously over her shoulder to see if he was about. 'The food looked amazing. Did she enjoy herself?'

'I think she did, yes. Perry's taken the boys into town to give her some peace and quiet. Fraser's gone with them, of course. Cara and Heather have gone for a run. First sign of any tidying-up, and everyone disappears, don't they?'

The kitchen table was stacked with the caterers' dishes, crates of glasses, flower arrangements, everything washed and dried, ready to be collected. I felt disappointed by the mass desertion; I'd imagined they'd be having a post-party brunch in the garden, scrambled eggs and bloody Marys, Nigella-style. 'Is Fraser staying here?'

'He stayed last night but he's getting the noon train. Says he's got things to prepare for a new role on Monday. He's being typically mysterious about what it involves, but then I suppose that's the whole point about cybersecurity.'

'To be honest,' I confessed, 'I never really knew whether I didn't understand his explanations or if being super-discreet was part of the job description.'

Jackie laughed. 'Well, he found his vocation. I don't know anyone who's as hard to get information out of as Fraser. Not just about work, about *anything*. We only ever knew what he was doing when you two were together because we could check *your* social media.' She stopped, and grimaced. 'Sorry, I didn't mean it to sound like that's the only reason we'd . . . You know what I mean. Can you imagine if he *had* taken over The Cellars, though? No prices on the shelves, customers having to text their orders several times before Fraser told them how much it was . . .'

'Were you and Perry not interested in carrying on the business? Or Heather? Did it have to be Fraser or no one?'

Jackie flicked on the kettle. 'It's interesting that you ask that, Beth. I don't think we ever considered it. It was always just assumed Fraser would take over, and to be fair, Fraser never said he wouldn't, until the moment came, and he announced that he didn't want to. Dad took it very personally, to be honest – family businesses, you know. I'm guessing Mum encouraged him to sell up, though she'd never admit it. He'd already had one lot of bypass surgery.'

'Did he see it as a snub? Fraser not seeing his future here?'

'I suspect he did.' She spooned coffee into the cafetiere. 'Mum was furious, but in her very silent, controlled way. She took herself away on holiday for a week – Dad went to the Algarve to play golf with his friend Brian, but she didn't even tell us where she'd gone. She probably saw it as Fraser putting himself above Dad's health, because Dad had to struggle on for another year or two before the sale happened. It took Mum and Fraser a while to make it up.'

I noticed a hardback book on the table next to a big box of chocolates. *The Love Story of Martine and Ray* in gold swirling embossing on a blue velvet background. It was the same swirling font as the lettering above Longhampton Cellars.

Jackie saw me looking. 'That's the present we gave Mum last night. Heather designed it. It's got some funny photos in, have a look.'

I turned the pages. It began with black-and-white baby pictures of a chubby Ray on a crocheted blanket, and an even chubbier Martine wrapped in a lace christening shawl, and progressed through their post-war school days, through bare knees, school caps, ponies, quiffs, petticoats, and Christmas trees, to their engagement photograph, taken at a party where everyone already looked fifty, including the teens and the happy couple.

As announced on the formal invitation reproduced next to it, Martine and Ray had celebrated their engagement at the Green Dragon Hotel, on the fifteenth of September, 1967. Elsewhere in the world, students were gearing up to revolt and LSD was turning the world into an acid-drop kaleidoscope but in Longhampton's hotel ballroom, the sixties were not swinging. Ray looked comfortable in a sports jacket and cravat, while Martine sported a three-strand pearl necklace, flat buckled shoes and a piled-high bouffant with a tiny bow in it like a Yorkshire terrier. Even without the invitation to their engagement drinks, hosted by Martine's mother, Mrs Martin O'Shaughnessy, I'd have put it at about 1967. Regular exposure to the photograph albums of Rosemount had made me something of an expert on provincial mid-sixties fashion.

Ray's dimpled smile was identical to the mayoral portrait taken fifty years later, give or take a couple of extra chins. He'd barely changed – the jacket, the beefy arm around Martine, the confident planting of himself at the centre of his own world. Martine, though, looked different; her face was rounder, her expression less straightforward than Ray's. She wasn't quite looking at the photographer, and her mouth was twisted as if she was already regretting her choice of shoes.

Interspersed with the photographs were other invitations, a thank-you list for wedding presents, receipts, postcards, and so on, to reflect the Hendersons' honeymoon, their early travels and first purchases. Monochrome images of the sixties abruptly gave way to orangey technicolour in the seventies, just in time for the birth announcements in *The Times*, the *Telegraph* and *The Longhampton Gazette* of Jacqueline Rae Henderson in 1971, and a fresh flood of baby photos in the same christening gowns.

I turned the pages quickly, trying to get to the arrival of Fraser Raymond Martin Henderson – and there he was, the round-faced Cabbage Patch baby I recognised from the few baby photos I'd seen, truly his father's son. My heart swelled.

And there he was again, smiling in red hand-me-down dungarees and yellow wellies, holding a spade, helping Dad with the gardening.

And again, on the mahogany counter of Longhampton Cellars with a Nebuchadnezzar of wine that was almost as tall as him.

And again, a spotty face peering out from between classic nineties 'curtains', at school prize day with his proud parents.

And again, at a wedding. I frowned. Hadn't I been at that wedding with him?

'You can see where Fraser gets his Desperate Dan jaw from, can't you?' Jackie leaned over and pointed out one I'd missed. 'There, there he is with Grandpa Henderson – see? Two peas in a pod.'

'I don't know about Desperate Dan.' Fraser had a strong jaw, like a Regency hero. 'I always thought he was more Mr Incredible.'

'Ha! Did he tell you to think that?' She paused, her finger lingering over a candid shot of Martine, caught unawares on a sunlounger in big sunglasses, mid catlike stretch. 'I wish I'd inherited a few more of Mum's genes, instead of Dad's. She's got that bone structure that just looks more and more elegant as the years go by.'

I turned the pages, and in a sequence of passport photos, school photos, the soft-focus 'hand under the chin' author headshot I'd seen before, Martine slowly morphed from the willowy teen into a capable mother of four, and then into the distinguished older lady. Always immaculately dressed, always smiling. The mayor's wife, president of the Mothers' Union, all-round pillar of the community.

Something wriggled at the back of my mind: not a question, more an observation, but I couldn't put my finger on what it was.

Jackie was flipping through the book, looking for something.

'Ah. Here it is,' she said. 'This is my favourite photograph of Mum and Dad. Can you believe Mum didn't have a copy? I had to get it from my godmother.'

She turned the book round and showed it to me: it was a very similar photograph of Ray and Martine at their engagement party, but this one was in colour, so you could see the bold tangerines and browns of Ray's sports jacket, and the egg-yolk yellow of Martine's minidress, and the cheerful pink and green streamers trailing down the wall behind them. But what really popped in the photograph was Martine's glorious, piled-high beehive.

I stared at it, as the unspecific thought swam into sharp focus: Martine's hair was a burnished copper-red, a fabulous warm orange like a sleek fox.

Or the same vibrant copper as a polished jam pan.

Wait. Was it *her*? I stared as words and images swam together in my head.

Was Martine the teenage fruit picker with the transistor radio?

I stared at the ambiguous half-smile on the young Martine's face, trying to fit the lovelorn words of the anonymous memory to this person. Was it? Was *she* the confident young woman who'd skipped out of Longhampton to live in Manchester with the lover no one knew about at home?

Nessy. I turned back discreetly to the engagement invitation. Martine *O'Shaughnessy*. Of course!

More to the point, who was the completely head-over-heels man who'd fallen so hard for her? Because it couldn't be Ray.

I racked my brains, trying to work out the dates.

Was it possible that someone was writing these reminiscences *as Ray*? Could Martine be doing an odd creative writing project? But why would she be leaving them at Rosemount? Surely she'd have said something when I showed her the first pages. And she was never at Rosemount.

It could be a coincidence. Lots of people dyed their hair copper in the sixties – it was fashionable – Cilla Black, Jane Asher. Ann-Margret.

'Heather wanted colour photos from the sixties but when I went through the albums,' Jackie was saying, 'I couldn't find a single colour photograph before I was born. I don't know where they've gone. There are gaps, as if they've been taken out at some point, so I guess Mum must have put them in frames and forgotten.'

Wordlessly, I turned back a few pages in the book; in the colour pictures that began in the seventies, Martine's hair was covered up with a Pucci print scarf, or a hat. As the seventies wore on, her signature blow-dry made its first appearance, the palest champagne-grey, effortlessly swept into face-framing waves.

Martine had had that look when I met Fraser, ten years ago. I'd never thought about what colour her hair had been when she was my age; with the solipsism of youth, I think I'd more or less skimmed over the idea of her ever being anything other than exactly as she was then.

'Dad loved Mum's hair long,' Jackie explained. 'It's why Cara was being so touchy yesterday about Mum's haircut – she felt it was the wrong thing to do for their anniversary.'

'When did Martine go grey?' I asked. 'If that's not a rude question.'

'Early thirties?' Jackie's phone pinged, and she checked it. 'Quite young, anyway. She always says it was having Cara and Heather so close together but I think it's just something that happens to redheads. Probably why she took the colour photos out of the albums, now I think of it. So as not to be reminded. Mum can be so vain, bless her.'

I pretended to flip casually but I was looking for something specific, something solid to back up my suspicions, and there it was: a family shot of Martine's graduation, with her parents . . . at Manchester University.

It *was* her! My heart quickened, and then the mathematical part of my brain kicked in. Martine had gone to university in 1964, studied for a three-year degree, then done a teacher-training qualification, then she'd got engaged to Ray in 1967. But she'd still have been in Manchester at that point. *With whoever was writing the memories.*

Who up at Rosemount had danced all night, eaten baked beans in bed, then tripped the light fandango with Martine in Manchester? Who was the lovestruck teenager, now an greying soul with a heart that clearly still beat faster when it remembered her? Was it someone I'd met?

'Jackie, can I ask you—' I started.

'Wait a second, I want to show you something. Here!' Jackie had finished checking her phone, and was turning pages in the book again.

She opened it at a studio portrait of Martine and Ray, and Jackie and her three boys, and Cara and baby Cooper: three generations of Hendersons. All were barefoot, in white shirts and jeans, as per the trend, although thankfully, Ray's bare feet were concealed behind a child. He had one arm around Martine, who looked carelessly stylish, with the very same pearls that she'd worn for her engagement gleaming beneath the open neck of her white shirt; Ray was gazing at her with frank adoration.

'This photo session was our Christmas present to Dad one year.' Jackie touched the photo gently. 'He loved it. Said he'd made a lot of good decisions in his life, but marrying Mum was the best. Everything in his life came from that.'

'They look so happy,' I said.

Jackie put a hand on her upper chest, overcome. 'When I think about how lucky they were to have met their *one* straight away, and how lucky *we* were to have grown up in the middle of that . . .' She managed a watery smile. 'I need to be kinder to Mum. I know she's still grieving. When you've lost the only man you ever loved, the one person who knows you better than anyone, anyone's going to behave oddly . . . Sorry.' Jackie wiped her nose. 'What were you going to ask me?'

'Nothing,' I said.

Martine hadn't emerged from her room when I left.

'I'm going to have another chat with Dr Robson,' Jackie said confidentially, as we said goodbye. 'She was quite snappish with me when I asked her again about Dad's memorial. I might ask about anti-depressants.'

She went on to tell me what I'd already heard from Fraser: that following a family conference, it had been decided that Martine would need a more organised system of support from the siblings, if she was to stay in Coleridge Drive, and they'd all do their bit.

'Fraser's going to set up her grocery delivery and a Ring doorbell and a fall alarm, and whatever electronic stuff will make her life easier,' she went on. 'Cara's in charge of anything that can be done remotely, and Heather's going to . . .' She trailed off, with a frown. 'You know, we didn't pin down what Heather's going to do.'

'Will Fraser be staying overnight when he comes back?'

'I assume so.' Jackie was distracted with her phone. 'Sorry, Perry's texting, forgotten his banking login *again*. Fraser's going to put in a few discreet cameras so we can keep an eye on Mum. Is that terrible?'

'Worse if Fraser actually knows how to install secret cameras?'

Jackie looked up from her phone, amused. 'Fair point. To be honest, I prefer the system you and I've set up, actually talking to her. I know it's a bit of an imposition.'

'It's not at all,' I said. 'I learn something new every day from her.'

'We do appreciate this, Beth. And Dad, wherever he is, definitely does.'

I smiled to acknowledge the sweet compliment Jackie intended, but to be honest, I wasn't so sure Ray *would* appreciate my involvement, if he had the first idea.

Safely back in the flat, I read the two Nessy memories through again, this time with the photographs of Martine and Ray at the front of my mind.

I didn't know what I was supposed to think about this, let alone what I was supposed to do with a secret that could undermine a family's understanding of each other.

Fair enough, we'd asked the residents to write down their memories, and that's what this person had done. But why give it to someone else to read? Why not, as Nigel Callaghan would have it, just let it stay in your own head? Why make sure it ended up out in the open?

I had to ask someone for advice, but that was another dilemma. Who?

Lewis was responsible for the story project, and might have an idea, from the confidential information held about each resident, who the writer was. He was discreet, and I knew he was kind, but his remit extended to neatly cut lawns and customer satisfaction. Would he be sympathetic to whoever needed to share this story of lost love, or would he consider it something he'd have to address, a form of harassment, even?

I shied away from that: I didn't want to get anyone into trouble.

I could tell Jackie . . . I dismissed that immediately. Jackie wouldn't want to deal with the idea of her mother two-timing her father.

And why upset Martine even further? Martine knew that I knew, from the memory she'd already read – that was awkward enough. And just because her real childhood sweetheart still held a torch for her didn't mean it was reciprocated. Jackie was right, she was grieving. It sounded as if a whole afternoon with the family but no Ray had been too much, if she'd taken herself off to bed afterwards. And – another thing Nigel had said floated into my mind – what if the writer wasn't single himself? What if the reason he was writing this down was because he couldn't speak it aloud in front of his wife?

It was complicated.

I made myself some toast while I thought about it, but ended up giving half to Tomsk, without reaching a conclusion, and went back to thinking about Fraser, and what we'd talk about over coffee the following weekend.

Later that evening, I got a call from someone I hadn't heard from in weeks: my former flatmate and co-resident in the village of Little Misery, Population 2, Ashley.

'Hey!' The forced brightness in Ash's voice told me that she was nervous. 'Long time no speak!'

If she'd called me forty-eight hours earlier I might have been less friendly, but right now my life was being soundtracked with romcom strings, and I was willing to extend an olive branch.

'Hello! How are things? Is Leo stacking the dishwasher to your liking?'

'He's learning,' said Ashley. 'Listen, I've got good news. Zara from the estate agent's – remember her? She left me a message to say that there's progress on your flat. The tenants have completed and should be out imminently. Which means you can move in.'

'She phoned *you* to tell you that?'

'She thought she was phoning *you*. Can you believe she had the wrong phone number attached to the file? Anyway, ring her tomorrow and get on her case.'

'Yup. OK. Will do.' I could hear the lukewarm enthusiasm in my voice, but the new flat, perfect as it was, was on the other side of the county, miles away from Fraser and the Hendersons, and much nearer the office. In the space of a few weeks, *this* had become my home.

Tomsk could tell from the tone of my voice that something wasn't right. He laid his head on my feet.

'You don't sound very excited,' observed Ashley. 'I thought you'd be packing your bags before you put the phone down. I still don't understand why your ex's family let you move in after what you did.'

After what I did? I frowned, then I remembered that was the version I'd told Ashley: I'd dumped Fraser, not the other way around. 'Water under the bridge.'

'OK.' Ash sounded unconvinced.

'Actually, I saw Fraser at the weekend,' I went on breezily. 'They had a family party and I popped in to say hello.'

'Oh, Beth . . .'

'No, it was fine! We talked, and he kept asking if I was single, ha-ha, and we're meeting for coffee next weekend. So we can talk.'

There was a long silence at the other end. Ashley had never been a big fan of Fraser, despite not having met him.

'Obviously, I'm not reading too much into it,' I lied, 'but I suspect Fraser's dad dying made him re-evaluate where he is in his life, and what he wants, and maybe he's realised that he's ready now to take that next step.'

With me.

'He's over forty, Beth. If he doesn't know what he wants now, is he ever going to?'

Ashley didn't sound as pleased for me as I'd thought she might. Had I told this right? Fraser had checked on my single status, told me I hadn't aged in five years, asked me out on a date.

'You're sure he's not married?' she asked.

'If he was married or in a serious relationship, he'd have found a way to work it into the conversation, wouldn't he?'

'Absolutely,' said Ashley, deadpan. 'Men *never* forget to tell their exes that they're with someone new when they bump into them at parties.'

'They do, though, if they think you're hitting on them, and they're not interested.'

'Yes and no.'

'So, anyway, obviously I'm not reading anything into this . . .'

'You already said that.'

'. . . but who knows? I keep thinking about what you said, about how the universe sends you signs. I think this is one.'

There was a groan on the other end.

'What?' I demanded. 'You were *always* going on about the universe sending signs.'

'Look, Beth, as your friend, I have to tell you this is a bad idea. You've moved on from this, someone better is out there. Don't go back to someone who didn't appreciate you first time round!'

She had no idea, I thought furiously. She'd never met Fraser, she didn't understand our relationship. Ashley thought like a project manager, not a romantic novelist.

'You're wrong,' I started to say, but she talked over me.

'Tell me one amazing thing about him that you don't believe you'll ever find in another man. Just one.'

'That's not . . . there's loads of things.'

'Apart from comfort and familiarity,' she went on. 'Apart from the fact that you invested all that time with him, and you're the only accountant in the world who refuses to recognise Sunk Cost Fallacy.'

Ashley sighed impatiently. 'Look, I'm not going to argue. Good luck. But if you don't call Zara and get that flat locked down tomorrow, I will do it for you. OK? And that's not a sign, that's a promise.'

And she hung up.

Chapter nineteen

For the last week or so, Lewis had been having his recurring cycling dreams, which was not good.

In his dream, he was coasting along a perfect stretch of road, with the wind at his back and the sweeping downhill stretches unwinding like a ribbon in a golden landscape of ripening wheat. Although he was on his old racing bike, he had the sense of someone behind him in the same way Eunice had been behind him on the tandem, and, without looking, he knew it was Beth. Joy rushed around his body like the blood pumping from his heart, as his wheels hummed and the wind blew through his hair.

And then, without warning, a sleek and healthy fox appeared on the road ahead – not running, just sitting on the white line, staring straight at him with yellow eyes. He yelled, but it didn't move. In his efforts to avoid hitting it, Lewis swerved, the front wheel skidded sideways from underneath him, he was hurled on to the tarmac and across the road, and the fox laughed, an eerie human giggle.

Lewis sat bolt upright in bed, sweating. He reached for the water on his bedside table, next to his glasses, and tried to slow down his hammering pulse with controlled breaths.

He'd had these dreams in the past, always before something bad happened at work. It was his subconscious telling him there was a detail he'd missed, or an unhappy employee nursing a problem, and as soon as he redoubled his efforts to meet targets and encourage communication, the dreams went away.

Try as he might – and he was trying with superhuman determination – Lewis was no closer to controlling Rosemount's chaos. There was now a substantial, and growing, thread on the *Gazette*'s Facebook page about 'unexplained phenomena' people had experienced while visiting relatives. One of the cleaners had slipped on ripped lino in the cellar, and Lewis had found loose wiring that he was sure hadn't been loose before. More mouse droppings. Fewer calls from Eric Alexander, more from the finance team. Another two residents leaving at the end of the month. Nigel Callaghan had 'a shortlist of culprits', but he wanted to be sure before pointing a finger.

It hadn't escaped Lewis's logic that the culprit might be Nigel himself.

No wonder he was having the cycling anxiety dream night after night.

This time, though, Lewis had the uneasy feeling his subconscious was trying to tell him something different, not a target or a grievance he was missing: this was something he didn't have a strategy for.

It was nearly three, and bright moonlight cut through the thin curtains on to the wall opposite his bed; the rental house had unsatisfactory curtains, no blackout lining. Not up to his usual requirements. A moth battered its wings against the window, drawn to the meagre light coming from Lewis's phone on the bedside table, and he flipped the phone over, for the moth's sake.

Lewis stared up at the ceiling. The moonlight picked out pockmarks; it needed skimming and repainting too. He hated not having a plan. Doing nothing felt like failure in itself; his whole ethos was built around never wasting a moment, never letting an opportunity pass. Yet when it came to Beth Cherry – because he knew that was what the dream was about, his all-consuming, tongue-tied crush on Beth – every tentative attempt at romance came to nothing. He wasn't giving it his all, because he couldn't bear the thought of failing, and that was a side of himself Lewis didn't recognise. And didn't much like.

He threw back the covers, got up and made himself a perfect chocolate mug cake which he left on his neighbour's doorstep, before he embarked on an extra-long bike ride to clear his head.

Lewis's official work day began at eight with a pot of coffee, ploughing through the emails that had built up overnight, before his regular nine o'clock with Pam. His to-do list already ran into two sides, but he was determined to block out a story hour somewhere, as he'd spotted that Beth was due in, with Tomsk.

He was much keener to see Beth than Tomsk. He'd listened to his hypnosis seventeen times now, and wasn't sure how many repetitions it would take before he'd be able to deliver wholehearted confident dog-fussing; however, there was no Beth without Tomsk, and no Beth was unthinkable.

Pam knocked on his door at nine on the dot, bearing a tray with two mugs and a plate of Viennese swirls.

'Morning!' Lewis's coffee was in a new mug, bright yellow with the word Sunshine in gold capitals. When he raised an eyebrow of query, she explained, 'I had to order new mugs for the staff room, and I thought why not follow your lead and get some inspirational ones.'

After their first review meeting, in which he'd identified her fundamental lack of confidence, Lewis had presented Pam with her own mug; it was red, the most motivational colour, and had A Cup of Ambition on the front.

'They weren't more expensive than the old ones,' she added quickly. 'And I thought it would set positive intentions, if we're drinking a cup of happiness, rather than a cup of Sanitex Hygiene Supplies.'

'Great idea,' said Lewis. 'Managerial thinking.'

She blushed, pleased, and opened her notebook. 'So, today's agenda.'

Lewis ate a Viennese swirl as his brain shuffled ideas around like a pack of cards. Pam's confidence as a leader was developing, but not as quickly as he'd hoped. Although he wasn't sharing it with the team, that morning Lewis had had another, unsettling, email from Eric headed 'LL exit strategy'. Lewis knew what that meant – Eric wasn't convinced he could save Rosemount, and if he couldn't, Lewis would be redeployed, possibly before he'd had a chance to help the Rosemount staff find new jobs. Consequently, Lewis was determined that Pam should get the experience she deserved to aim her CV at bigger and better jobs if Rosemount should – much as he hated thinking about it – not survive the finance team's axe.

'So, run me through today's highlights,' he said, and sat back as Pam reeled off the varied daily events of a residential home: the new hairdresser, hospital visits, weekly menus, electrician checking faulty call bells and alarms, and the one Lewis had been waiting for, volunteers.

'And Beth's coming in with Tomsk,' she finished. 'She's got three story sessions, he's got a general appearance in the lounge.'

'Tomsk's more popular than the hairdresser,' Lewis observed.

'Not more popular than Beth, though – she's got a waiting list now, you know! She's the only volunteer people specifically ask for.'

'She's a good listener.' Lewis had tucked away the memory of the way Beth had listened to him while he'd babbled on at that practice day. He wished he'd been able to relax enough to answer her questions honestly. He'd never shared much about his personal life, because it wasn't a short conversation – not just his mum who'd died when he was ten (how did that feel?), his grandparents (did you mind being brought up by them?), boarding school (a whole can of worms), lack of girlfriends (do you think you might be gay?), on and on, and, as Nigel Callaghan had astutely observed, it was easier to turn the questions back on the other person than to come up with answers that satisfied their curiosity but didn't expose you to even more questions.

Lewis didn't have the answers, in any case. He didn't enjoy thinking about those things in his own leisure time, let alone in social settings. Life moved on, and you had to move on with it, or be swept underneath the waves. Experiences like his tended to be the headline people remembered about you, and he didn't want his losses to be a badge.

Yet Beth, he sensed, was someone who understood pockets of sadness in otherwise happy people. She'd hesitated over some of her own answers. But then Beth was the one person he wanted to hide his complicated, melancholy childhood, his lack of experience *from*. He wanted to be as easy as possible for her to love. Not a project.

Pam was unaware of Lewis's inner turmoil. 'I see you're down to talk to Stan Walkingshaw this morning. He's one of Nigel's lunch gang so don't be surprised if he tells you he was in the original line-up of the Bee Gees.'

Lewis snapped back to attention.

'Great!' he said. 'Looking forward to it.'

'So, Stan, if you had one piece of advice to offer the thirty-year-old you, what would it be?'

Stan Walkingshaw heaved a dramatic sigh. 'Blimey, Lewis. Where would I start? Don't marry Lorraine, would be one. Don't marry Cherise would be another.' He paused. 'And definitely don't get into anything with Cherise's mother.'

'Maybe not so—'

'Don't invest in Betamax. Don't take up golf, it's a fool's errand. Do get travel insurance.' He stared over his tinted glasses at Lewis. '*Always* get travel insurance, Lewis. You don't know pain until you've been medivaced. And I mean financial pain, as well as physical pain.'

'I'm a firm believer in insurance,' said Lewis, even though it had been years since he'd been on holiday.

Stan sank back in his easy chair. 'It was Cherise who wanted to swim with sharks. Not me.' He pointed at Lewis. 'Oh, and there's another. Don't trust men who wear bracelets. *Never* trust a man who wears a bracelet and calls you "mate". No one who calls you "mate" is *ever* your mate. Ditto people who call you "pal", "bud" or "my friend".'

'Noted,' said Lewis.

Over the last forty minutes, in answer to the question, '*Where were you happiest*?' Stan Walkingshaw, longtime expat and retired casino owner, had covered happy moments in nightclubs, Concorde, a shark tank, the Isle of Wight, and the birth of two children. 'I've been a lucky fella, Lewis.'

'But take it from me,' Stan added, leaning forward to tap the table for emphasis, 'I could have given the thirty-year-old me some crackin' advice, but would I have listened? Would I heck as like.' He sat back with his arms crossed, and smiled the smile of a man with few regrets. His tan, still deep golden twenty years after returning from the Costa del Sol, gave the lounge a welcome air of glitz.

Lewis felt an ungrudging admiration for Stan, even if he had just told him a few things Lewis thought he'd better forget, for the sake of Stan's families, both of whom visited twice a month.

'So, what about general advice?' he said.

Stan gave him a long look, and when he spoke, his voice had lost its previous joking tone. 'I'd say to you that you only regret the things you don't do, not the things you do.'

'What? After everything you've just told me about Lorraine? And Cherise? And the boot full of duty free—'

'Ah-ah!' Stan tapped his nose. 'What happens in Story time, stays in Story time.'

'That's the exact opposite of what Life Story work's about, Stan.'

'You know what I mean.' He winked. 'In my experience, you know in your gut when you should have taken a chance. Then when you look back on it, you're not just thinking about what could've been, you're kicking yourself for not being braver. Double bubble.'

Lewis nodded. 'If you could go back in time, and say something to anyone, what would it be?'

Stan's expression suddenly crumpled. 'I would tell . . .' His voice cracked. 'Sorry, got a bit emotional there. I would tell a special someone that . . .'

'That what?' Lewis leaned forward. Was this going to be the advice he needed?

There was a knock on the door, and Pam put her head round.

'Sorry to interrupt,' she said, 'but the electrician's here? To do the call bell testing?'

'Terrific. Could you show him where he needs to go, please?'

She looked uneasy. 'I don't really know what . . .'

Lewis checked his watch. The electrician was ten minutes early but this felt like a good moment to give Pam some additional responsibility. Plus he was enjoying this chat with Stan. Any minute now, he felt, Stan would deliver the key advice, like a Brummie Dalai Lama. 'There's a file on my desk. The checklist, his quote, my notes, house policy and so on. You take the lead, and I'll catch up with him before he goes?'

'Am I authorised to do that?'

'I trust your judgement, Pam.'

'OK,' she said, and retreated.

'Thank you, Pam!' Lewis turned back to Stan. 'Now, where were we? If you could tell anyone anything?'

Stan sat back in his chair, more himself again. 'I would tell anyone I ever loved, that I loved them. Because you just don't know if there's a double-decker bus coming round the corner, know what I'm saying? And,' he added, just in case Lewis hadn't got his point, 'by double-decker bus, I mean another bloke, or cancer, or . . . an actual double-decker bus.'

Lewis nodded. 'That's good advice, Stan. Very wise advice.'

'But will you take it?' Stan laughed. 'Will you heck as like.'

Lewis rushed back from Stan's rooms in time to see Beth and Tomsk in the reception, signing the visitors' book. Beth was getting a pass for herself, and an official pet visitor rosette (Pam's idea) to clip on to Tomsk's harness.

As she chatted with Wendy, the receptionist, Lewis allowed himself a moment inside the contentment that settled over him whenever he saw Beth. No longer than that; he didn't want to feel like a weirdo. But long enough to note the way her cheeks dimpled, like little hallmarks of authenticity, when she smiled; the unconscious way she pushed escaping strands of blond hair behind her ear, revealing the marble curve of her lovely neck. Every time he saw her there was something new to notice and tuck away.

Just ask her out for a drink, urged Stan's gruff voice in his head. What's the worst thing she can say? No? It's not like you haven't heard that before.

Lewis hadn't heard it that often before, not often enough to know how to brush it off so neither of them were embarrassed, the way men like Stan could. But he had to *try*.

He took a half-step backwards, then set off briskly, as if he'd just marched down the nearby corridor.

'Beth!' he said, 'what a nice surprise! And Tomsk! Hello there!'

'Hello, Lewis!' She'd been bending down to fix the rosette properly, and stood up with a smile, unfolding herself. Today, instead of her usual soft draped clothes, she was wearing leggings and a sweatshirt, despite the sunshine outside.

'Off to the gym?' It was, Lewis thought, a stupid thing to say but it was the first thing that had come into his head, and he was trying to keep his dog anxiety at bay with deep breaths, in and out, while trying not to look at the dog, although the dog was looking at him, waiting for the customary fuss.

'Yes, I'm on a bit of a health kick.' Beth looked as if she didn't want to talk about it. 'Are you all right?'

'Yes, I'm fine.'

'You're breathing quite oddly.'

'Hay fever,' said Lewis.

She gave him a funny look. 'Wendy, can I get the key for the memory box, please?'

'Of course.' Wendy beetled her brows at Lewis – what for, he didn't know.

'So, any more mystery deposits in there?' Lewis asked, as Beth opened the box and sorted through the contents.

Wendy had turned her attention to the dog – 'Oooh, who's a good boy? Is it Tomsk? Is it my friend Tomsk? I think it is!' and so on – although the dog's attention remained fixed unsettlingly on Lewis, through its flopping veil of fringe.

He knows, thought Lewis. He knows we're in competition for Beth's attention.

Beth was examining a brown A4 envelope. 'Just this. Wendy, can I give you these, please?' She handed over the parish magazine, two hospital appointment letters and a crisp packet.

'Sorry, some residents do like to post things,' sighed Wendy. 'I try to stop them but I'm not here all the time.'

'So there's no way of knowing who's dropping things off? No cameras?'

'Not there. We've got one on reception but it misses that spot.'

Beth looked thoughtful, and Lewis seized his moment.

'Have you got time for a cup of tea before your session or are you in a rush? I think Pam's made biscuits?'

She turned, with a rueful shake of the head that went straight to Lewis's heart. 'I wish! But I'm trying to be good at the moment.'

'Viennese whirls,' confirmed Wendy. 'Melt in the mouth.'

'Don't tempt me!' Beth held up her hand in self-protection. 'But you can walk me down to the Horrobins,' she added.

'I think I have time for that,' said Lewis.

Did Wendy just roll her eyes?

'Hay fever,' she said, before he asked.

The minute walk to the Horrobins' apartment was another conversational challenge, and Lewis's mind went blank again.

'Good weekend?' he asked, a bland opener, he knew. *So* bland. But what *did* Beth do when she wasn't here?

'Lovely, thank you. Martine – Mrs Henderson, remember? – had a party in her garden. She has a perfect garden for summer parties, lots of nooks with honeysuckle and lilacs, and a swing.'

'I've been meaning to ask,' said Lewis, 'when we met, she said you were her lodger, but it sounded as if there was more to it than that?'

'Yes, it's a bit more than that.' Beth smiled, and it was a different kind of smile to the ones Lewis had seen so far; it had a soft, secretive feel, as if she was thinking of something else. It set off a frisson at the back of his mind. A fox on the road, locking eyes with his. 'I was in a relationship with her son Fraser for a long time.'

No.

'Ah.' Heart plunging, Lewis clung to the word *was*. *Was* in a relationship.

The contented smile was still playing on Beth's lips. 'But I've stayed in touch with the family. The party was for Martine and Ray's anniversary – he died last year, sadly. Such a nice man.'

'Had they been married a long time, Martine and Ray?' said Lewis, who didn't particularly want to know much about Ray but definitely didn't want to know more about Fraser.

'Over fifty years.'

'Childhood sweethearts?'

'Yes. I suppose so.' The smile faded from Beth's face, and her eyes flicked to one side, then she said brightly, 'Yes, so it was great to catch up with Fraser again. It's funny, isn't it, how some people you don't see for ages, then when you do, it's as if you only saw them yesterday? But then I always thought that when the time was right we'd come back into each other's lives.'

This time, a darker cloud went across Lewis's stricken heart. A bigger fox on the road.

'It's like Minnie Little said to me last week,' Beth went on, unaware of the freezing effect her words were having on Lewis's soul. 'What's meant for you won't go past you.'

Minnie had a saying for every occasion, in Lewis's experience. All of them trite, and most of them in direct contradiction of another.

They were nearly at the Horrobins' door, and Lewis was running out of time to ask Beth out in the casual, non-face-to-face way he'd decided would be best.

Management training had drilled into Lewis the importance of only asking questions that you already knew the answer to; ten minutes ago he'd just been unsure of the best way to frame it, but now every instinct was telling him not to ask the question at all, when the answer was staring him in the face.

'Beth . . .'

She was bending down to adjust Tomsk's harness. Tomsk himself seemed to be giving him a pitying look.

Come on, Lewis, don't be pitied by a dog.

'I was wondering if . . .'

Beth looked up, her face still dreamy in that way he hadn't seen before, and Lewis's courage failed him at the last minute. Suddenly he knew exactly what Stan had meant by the double bubble of regret. It was his lack of nerve standing between him and a date with Beth, not just this Fraser, and he regretted that as much as the lost opportunity.

And it was so stupid, because Beth was kind, and she wouldn't say no in a hurtful way, but once he'd asked, he couldn't ask again. It would embarrass them both.

'What?' she said brightly.

'I was wondering how you were getting on with the write-ups,' he finished lamely. 'If there was anything interesting – anything you think we should discuss?'

She looked at him, thoughtful, and bit her beautiful pink lip. Lewis was filled with a hopeless desire.

'Actually, yes,' she said. 'There's something I wanted to discuss.'

'Beth!' The door was flung open and the tiny figure of Linda Horrobin appeared. 'And Tomsk! We've been looking forward to this all day, haven't we, Bill? Bill's put his dog socks on specially! Are you two going to come in? We have B.I.S.C.U.I.T.S,' she added, in a conspiratorial undertone.

The dog looked up at Beth hopefully.

Lewis felt an irrational double rejection.

'Not for me, I hope,' said Beth, with a regretful pat of her hips.

'You're perfect,' he blurted out, to the surprise of both of them.

'Isn't she just?' said Linda Horrobin happily. 'Bill says Beth reminds him of Diana Dors. Now, come in.'

'If only I got a reception like this everywhere!' Beth put a hand on Lewis's arm. It felt like the same gentle 'hand on arm' the nurses gave the residents, a reassuring contact, nothing more. Yesterday it would have set sparks scorching across his skin; now it felt different. Sisterly. He'd felt enough of those to know what they meant, that kind 'don't make me say the words' gesture his female friends at college had made, forestalling any awkwardness. 'I'll catch up with you another time.'

Just beyond the door, he could see Bill Horrobin, sitting upright in his chair, white hair freshly brushed, eagerly waiting for the arrival of Tomsk and Beth. There were no words, but his eyes darted between Linda, and the dog. Always back to Linda.

'I'll just . . .' Lewis indicated over his shoulder. 'Lots to do.'

Beth smiled.

Lewis smiled back, but inside the cloud had gone over his heart, and it had started to rain.

If you could go back in time and say anything to someone, what would it be?

The clearest memories I have of Nessy are the first time I saw her, and the last time.

The last time was almost five years to the day from the first. That was the only significant thing about that week; everything else was just as normal, or as normal as Geraldine's house ever was.

I'd finished my course, and started working full time, selling ad space for a pirate radio station. My job involved lots of parties, and meeting people, and talking. I was great at talking, and even better at not getting hangovers – those were the only two useful things I'd got from my dad. I had a reputation for being good with celebrities, but it was because I was too embarrassed to wear my glasses to parties, so I never recognised anyone – Nessy often had to take me to one side to tell me who I'd been chatting to.

I'd been offered a couple of jobs in London off the back of these chance encounters – that was how things happened in those days: you'd have a stoned conversation with a hippie about electronic brain interference, and the next day a Rolls Royce would appear outside your office with a single apple inside, and an invitation to have tea with John Lennon. One guy wanted me to help set up an advertising agency aimed at teenagers, but I said no. Nessy was only halfway through her teacher-training course at that point, and our plan was to move to London together. That had been the plan for so long we used to look at *A-Zs* and choose the streets we'd buy our house in, when we won the Pools. Geraldine would tell us stories about some areas that'd make your hair curl – so they were top of our lists.

That week I'd had a telephone call about a real, serious job with a media agency in Soho. Ness was almost qualified, so I'd said to her: why not look for teaching positions in London? We knew her parents would say no, but she said she'd talk to them, maybe if the school was posh enough, they'd come round to the idea. She didn't moan about them as much as she had done in the beginning, so I assumed they'd finally accepted that she was going to do something different with her life. Not be the dutiful daughter they expected her to be. In her own way, she had as much to escape from as I had – neither of us were doing what our families thought we should.

It was a normal Friday night for us. I'd gone out to get our usual curry order from the New Delhi tandoori house. Same dishes every week, for the two of us, plus Geraldine, and the Pauls, and whoever else was around.

When I left, they were all sitting at the kitchen table, shrieking their way through *The Sound of Music* soundtrack album, which Geraldine used to put on the record player most Friday nights. We loved a singalong. Nessy was playing the spoons, and one of the Pauls was wearing a nun's habit, miming the Mother Superior parts. I could hear the singing through the open windows all the way down the street.

When I walked back down the street half an hour later, with two bags of the finest curry in Manchester, there was no singing. That was unusual. Once Geraldine had finished *The Sound of Music*, she often put on *The Jungle Book* or *West Side Story*. The singing only stopped when the sherry ran out.

I couldn't hear anyone talking when I opened the front door. The house was deathly silent, like the

Marie Celeste, but I assumed they were playing a trick on me. We used to do that to Geraldine – hide under tables and make humming noises, or pretend to move in slow motion to make her think she'd dropped acid. Stupid stuff, really, but we thought we were hilarious, as kids always do.

And then I heard the voice. In the kitchen. At first I thought it was the radio, the World Service, or maybe one of the Pauls doing an impression of Peter Sellers.

I can't remember now exactly what he was saying, but I can remember tiptoeing down the hall and looking through the open door to see Geraldine, and the Pauls, and Geraldine's friend Mavis, frozen at the table like waxworks.

A bloke with a big red face was sitting in my seat, chatting away as if it was completely normal to talk for sentence after sentence without any interruption from anyone else. He seemed perfectly at ease sitting there in a tweed jacket and a hat, despite the fact that everyone else was in tie-dye and crocheted waistcoats. He looked more like an actor than either of the two Pauls ever would, except he was playing the part of a public-school idiot, and not very well either.

Nessy wasn't at the table. She was standing at the sink, her back to everyone. She was washing up – she *never* washed up – and she was wearing an apron over her miniskirt. She never wore an apron either. Her shoulders were shaking, and I couldn't tell if that was because she was washing up so furiously, or there was something else going on.

I don't know how, but suddenly I knew.

'Ah!' The man saw me, and stood up. 'Curry. Tremendous. Do they deliver in the city? How modern.'

Geraldine stood up quickly too. 'Darling, this is Raymond. Raymond, this is—'

I remember the bone-crunch of the handshake, the disinterest in hearing who I was in his haste to impose himself. 'Hello there, don't worry, I won't be joining for supper, I'm here on a rescue mission. I need to whisk this one away.' He nodded towards Nessy as if she was a child he was collecting from a minder.

'Nessy's father has been taken ill.' I remember Geraldine signalling with her plucked eyebrows. 'Unfortunately she seems to have missed the messages for her to call home, so Raymond's come to collect her.'

'It's very good of you to drive all this way, at this time of the night,' observed Mavis. Who had remained seated, three cats on her lap, port and lemon in front of her.

'That's what fiancés are for! Coming to the rescue of the damsel in distress!' boomed this total stranger. 'Chop chop, poppet. I told your mother I'd have you back before midnight. Your poor dad's asking for you.'

Poppet. Chop chop, poppet.

Nessy turned round at the sink, but she didn't look at him. She gazed in my direction with a face that still haunts me now.

The life had drained from her face, leaving her eyes blank. She was like a ghost. A ghost of herself. I felt sick.

'Ooh, fiancé,' marvelled Mavis. 'You kept that quiet, Nessy.'

It was so obvious. She hadn't renegotiated her life with her parents. She'd just built a fence so I couldn't see it. And I hadn't wanted to see it. I never went home to Longhampton, because *this* was my home now, but she did, and she never talked about what happened when she went back, because I didn't want to know.

Slowly Nessy took off Geraldine's silly frilly apron, without breaking my gaze.

I didn't need to turn my head to know the Pauls were staring between us, back and forth, as if they were at a tennis match.

My eyes couldn't move from hers. Her unhappiness was loud in my own chest, as real as the unhappiness I felt myself. Did she feel that too, I wondered? Was she going to say something?

'You do look drained,' said Mavis. 'Has it come as a shock, your dad being unwell?'

I knew as well as Nessy did that her dad was probably hale and hearty and sinking pints in the Feathers. He'd done this before, inventing these family crises when she hadn't been home as often as they'd like. But he'd never sent her *fiancé* to get her.

This was a statement. The party's over, it said. Your real life wants you back.

She said nothing.

I put the bags of curry down on the table, and left the room. The house. The street. I don't know where I went, but my feet kept moving.

When I came back, Nessy had gone, and so had he.

When I went into our room, her clothes had gone, but what broke my heart was that she'd taken one of the china dogs we'd bought together at a flea market. They were like us, she said; a matching pair of spaniels, with chains round our necks that we'd snapped. Now only mine sat there on the shelf by the bed. A half. Worth nothing.

The following week, I packed my bags and moved to London.

If I could go back to that moment now, with the few scraps of wisdom I've gained over the years, would I say something? To her, or to him?

It's certainly the only time in my life when I *saw*, right then, that the world as I knew it was shifting, and in a moment it would have changed forever. You don't often get those moments, when you actually see the background of your life moving like the scenery on a stage.

Even now I know there was nothing I could say. I could have fought and demanded but it would have made no difference. Some moments in life turn on a sixpence; some are like tectonic plates, starting years before and moving so slowly you can't even see.

But if I could go back, I would open my arms and hug Nessy even as she was leaving, hug her really tightly, and hope that she'd somehow understand that these arms would never stop wanting to hold her, that this heart would never stop loving her, and that no matter where we drifted on these tides of life, what we'd shared together would be like a lighthouse. A lighthouse of love, a light we could always navigate back to. If we wanted. If the tides ever came right again.

Chapter twenty

There was another memory waiting in the box when I next called into Rosemount, and suspecting what I now suspected, I couldn't even wait to get home before reading it. And when I did, it made me ache with sadness.

The story this time was about the sudden, unhappy end of the relationship, and although I'd been expecting something along those lines, I sat for a moment, utterly hollowed out. I'd known there couldn't be a *happy* ending, but I hadn't expected to feel so bereft by the abrupt stop to such an adventure. It had finished too soon. I needed to know what happened next, for the writer, at least.

I looked up at the big house in front of me. Behind one of those windows was someone who'd been young and full of fizz and dazzle, a sixties teen who'd kicked off the limitations of their rural life in the noise and lights of the city, someone who'd fallen completely, utterly, hopelessly in love with a woman who'd felt the same way, sharing that exhilaration of being young and free – yet she'd ended it with clear eyes, stepped back into her old life, and never told a soul.

Who *was* it? And why? Did he know Martine was widowed and lonely? Was he hoping I'd tell her and engineer some sort of reunion? Was I the only person who could do that – or was I the last person who should get involved? And did she know he was there?

My curiosity was tinged with real unease. I'd had similar qualms when I spotted suspicious hotel bills in clients' accounts, or cash payments that set off alarm bells. I always adhered to strict professional codes, but I couldn't *not* notice. Or stop my imagination whirring. Another reason I wasn't sorry not to have face-to-face meetings anymore.

I'd nearly asked Lewis when I'd bumped into him that afternoon – I had to hand it to him, he managed to be here, there and everywhere, despite the size of the place. But something he said reminded me that he didn't really know Martine, and the Henderson family, not the way I did. And even if I'd wanted to share it with Martine, I couldn't: I'd come in from walking Tomsk on Monday to find a stack of local history books, a vintage brooch and a bottle of wine on my step, with a note saying, *Cara and family have taken me to Bath for a 'minibreak'. Back Thursday night. Fondest, Martine.*

So I was left to stew for the week. At least I had my Sunday-morning coffee date with Fraser to obsess about instead.

Fraser texted on Friday to ask if I was still OK for Sunday, and did I have anywhere in particular I'd like to meet?

I'd thought carefully about this. It was always easier to discuss personal things while moving with both parties facing forward (on a walk, in a car, though not necessarily on a plane), so I suggested Fraser joined me and Tomsk for our Sunday walk *before* coffee. In a painstakingly casual text, I mentioned the town trail that I'd found: along the heritage canal walk, through the colourful flowerbeds of the park, and down the high street, ending up at the Wild Dog Café where I'd pretend to enjoy a black coffee.

Fraser agreed that that would be a plan, and on Sunday morning I was waiting by the front gate at the bottom of Martine's steps, butterflies cycloning in my chest, having already taken Tomsk on a quick pre-walk to minimise excited pulling.

Tomsk and I, despite the pre-walk, were both unrecognisably groomed. I'd got up early to run through the beauty routine that I hadn't bothered with in months (years), while Tomsk also had a thorough bath and comb-out the night before. He kept tilting his big head in confusion, as if he couldn't work out where the pleasant smell was coming from, and more worryingly, where his own oily-biscuit whiff had gone.

I was two minutes early; Fraser was on time but still apologised for being late. Maybe he was, by a cyber-critical nanosecond. 'Sorry to keep you waiting!' he said, closing the front door behind him. 'Had to convince Mum that the internet still works if I leave the house. I think she thinks I've got a key to it, or something.'

I smiled, but knowing Martine a bit better now, I wasn't sure that was entirely true. It sounded like she might even be winding Fraser up.

He paused when he reached me, as if he wasn't sure where we were in terms of greeting. After a moment's hesitation, we did an awkward cheek kiss and a half. ('Hi . . . mwah . . . oh, OK, ha-ha, we're doing two? OK, mwah . . .')

It was a bit cringe, but our mutual embarrassment broke the ice, and we set off easily enough. Tomsk gave us plenty of questions and answers to get conversation started – the rescue that he'd come from, did it bother me that I knew nothing about his past, why did I choose him, etc. I loved talking about Tomsk, although I edited out the part where I drove there to collect him in a zombie state after our break-up, and instead reminded Fraser about the dog show Martine had judged for Four Oaks Rescue, the reason I was following it in the first place.

'The dog show! God, I'd forgotten all about that,' he said. 'That was the one where Mum got huffy and refused to award the Prettiest Bitch prize because she said it was demeaning?'

Martine had insisted they scrap it in favour of a Cleverest Trick prize instead. Which I had forgotten too, but now thought was quite cool.

I smiled at nothing, out of sheer happiness. It was a perfect Longhampton Sunday: the sky was as blue as a Wedgwood plate, the park was in full bloom, there were no squirrels on the footpath to show up my inadequate training skills, and as the conversation meandered from dogs to Longhampton to the party last weekend, we naturally ended up talking about Rosemount.

'So I hear Mum's got you volunteering up at the retirement home?' Fraser shook his head. 'You can say no to her. She's not *your* mum.'

'Ah, it's OK, I've enjoyed it.' The universe was doing me a favour for once, and an outside table at the Wild Dog Café came free as we strolled up; Fraser grabbed it for us. 'Some of the stories I've heard have really put things in perspective – I can hardly make a fuss about having to wait a few weeks to move when I'm talking to someone whose family home was flattened in the war. Or who didn't have an inside loo until they got married.'

That came out a bit mealy-mouthed, but it was true. More than once, my interviewees had asked about my work, and I'd been too embarrassed to say I was too anxious about my weight to go back to the office full-time. I mean, it sounded *mad.*

Fraser nodded. 'So what is the situation with your new place? Have you got a date yet?'

'Yup, I spoke to the agent yesterday, and she confirmed I can move in a month from now. This is the agent who mis-let the original flat,' I added, because if I was honest, I didn't mind if a month became two months, not if Fraser was going to be dropping into his mother's, 'so I'm not taking it as gospel, ha-ha! I might be around for a while yet.'

'Good!' He studied the menu, but my heart skipped. 'Good, good.'

Good!

'So what's the best story you've heard so far?' he asked, signalling to a passing waitress.

I told him about Nigel Callaghan standing on the Berlin Wall next to David Hasselhoff and refusing to recognise him, much to the Hoff's irritation, and then ordered myself a black coffee. I couldn't eat; my stomach was full of lightness.

'There isn't a single person who doesn't have at least one good story,' I told him. 'Even the ones who think they've done nothing, there's always something. They just don't see it for what it is.'

'Are you allowed to contradict them?' Fraser asked. 'Like, if they tell you they met JFK and you're pretty sure

JFK never came to Much Didley, are you allowed to say, "Seriously, Betty"?'

I laughed. 'No. We just write it down. But it's funny how couples rarely remember things exactly the same way. I sometimes think we should interview them separately and see if anything matches up.' I gave him a flirty look over the rim of my coffee cup. 'Do you remember how we first met?'

'Ah, now you're testing me! Of course I remember. It was that stag night. And you were on a hen night.'

Yes!

'And you were dressed as?' I prompted.

His avocado toast arrived and Fraser played for time. 'Um . . . Oh God, I should know this. I remember there were knee socks involved. Britney Spears?'

'Try again.'

Fraser furrowed his brow, then said, 'The Spice Girls. A Spice Girl.'

'Yes!'

'And you spent the whole night arguing about the bill with the barman, because they'd added it up wrong!'

I frowned. 'Did I?'

He nodded, amused. 'You got a calculator out of your bag. I remember thinking, Who carries a calculator in their bag? And you said, "Accountants are never off duty". Which I thought was very funny, if a bit tragic.'

Wow. He remembered *that*? 'And yet you still called me!' My voice sounded mildly strangled. 'I honestly have no recollection of that whatsoever.'

'Ah, well. Long time ago. Ten years. A decade ago, Beth! Different life.' He cut his toast in half. 'The last few years, well . . . Dad dying was a real reminder that *we're* the parent generation now, not "the young people" anymore. Time to grow up.'

I bit my lip; the insensitivity of that was a bit of a scratch on the lovely mood, for a couple of reasons. One, OK, so Mum had died before we'd met, but had Fraser forgotten I'd had that revelation while I was barely out of higher education? And two, don't talk to me about being the parent generation, when we broke up because you weren't ready to be one.

But maybe Fraser was keen to talk about how he'd changed since we last saw each other *for a reason*, so I took a deep breath and launched into it. 'And are you any nearer that yourself?'

'Nearer what, sorry?'

'Parenthood.' I made myself look him in the eye. 'One thing I remember very clearly – when we broke up – was you saying that you weren't ready to take that step.'

'Did I say that?'

'You did. I wanted us to make a commitment to each other, and you said you weren't ready.'

I tried to sound casual but I could recite the whole conversation. It was burned on my brain.

I'm just not ready for the life you want. Not yet.

Fraser shook his head, as if he didn't *want* to contradict me, but couldn't let it pass. 'That's not how I remember that conversation, Beth.'

I faltered. I'd just congratulated myself on making a reference to our break-up without flinching, but now he'd drawn attention to it, he'd thrown me off my stride, and like a gymnast who'd fallen off the beam and now had to clamber back on and carry on as if the slip-up hadn't happened, I had to find a way back into that key sentence. But my balance had gone.

'Well, um . . .' I gazed across the table at Fraser, willing him to help me out by saying something like, '*It was a terrible mistake but I've reflected since we've been apart, and I'm ready now, so let's move in together and get on with it.*'

Fraser didn't do that. He raised his eyebrows, encouraging me, so I pushed on.

'Um, the last few years have been pretty weird, but they've taught me a lot about myself,' I floundered.

'I know exactly what you mean,' he agreed. 'Sometimes you need to have that shock to really examine what you need, not what you *think* you need.'

'Great!' OK. *Back on track.*

Tomsk shifted by my feet. He'd been good so far, if still somewhat wary of Fraser – which was unusual, given how relaxed he was with the Rosemounters. Maybe he sensed the competition for my affections.

'You have to rebuild for who you are now,' he went on, 'not who you were ten years ago.'

'Absolutely.' I nodded, too hard. But what should I say next?

All week I'd lain awake planning how I'd manoeuvre the conversation around to 'us', nipping and nudging topics of conversations like a sheepdog to get it going in the direction I wanted, but now it was happening, it was going too quickly. I didn't feel in control.

'It's funny how we've come back into each other's orbits now, isn't it?' I said, as if it had just occurred to me. It hadn't;

it was a metaphor Seraphina liked to use about her and Arthur, and their star-crossed love. 'Almost as if we were meant to be apart for that exact amount of time, and now . . .'

'What?'

'Here we are!'

His brow furrowed.

'Like planets.' I faltered. This had sounded much better in my head when Fraser was murmuring agreement, instead of narrowing his eyes. Arthur got it straight away, but then he did have a Victorian gentleman's education. 'Coming back into each other's orbits.'

There was an agonising silence, and then Fraser squeezed his forehead with his thumb and forefinger. 'Oh. OK. No. Beth, whatever I say, you're going to take the wrong way, so . . .'

'No, I won't!'

Fraser looked uncomfortable. 'Clearly we have different memories of this, and that's fine, but when we broke up, it was a *break-up*. I wasn't putting us on some kind of hiatus. I'm not a total bastard.'

'But—'

'You gave *me* an ultimatum.' His expression was indignant but firm. 'You said you wanted commitment, and a family, and that, as a woman, you didn't have an infinite amount of time. And that if that wasn't what I wanted, we needed to go our separate ways so you could make that happen.'

That was, word for word, what Mali had told me to say. But when he said it, that wasn't what I remembered saying. Or at least, it wasn't what I'd *meant*.

'You didn't explicitly accuse me of stringing you along, but that was the general impression I got.' He shook his head, as if the memory still stung. 'If we're being honest, I felt you were dumping *me*. I was pretty happy as we were, but you were clear that marriage and kids were now top of your agenda, rather than the life we had. So . . .' He shrugged, as if I'd have been happy with *any* wedding ring, and *any* kids. 'You'd clearly spent a lot of time reaching that decision for yourself, and it couldn't have been easy, so I thought the right thing to do was to let you get on with it. I mean, I assumed you'd be settled down by now.'

'What? No!' He was making me sound so cold, so fixated. 'Fraser, I didn't want imaginary kids more than I wanted you.'

'No?'

'I wanted *your* kids,' I blurted out. 'And *you*. I wanted *our* kids. I just thought you needed me to tell you I was ready for that. I thought it was what you wanted too.'

He didn't answer. He dropped his gaze awkwardly. And that sliced into me deeper than any words could. I felt my heart plunge in my chest.

Silence fell across the table.

I forced myself not to speak. This would be the moment when Fraser would reach his hand just that tiny bit further and take mine, and say, with a crooked smile, how stupid we'd both been, and that it would be even more stupid to waste another second.

He didn't. He put his fork down on his plate, toast half-eaten. It clattered off the plate, and on to the table.

I knew I should just stop at this point, but I heard my own voice, and it sounded accusatory when my brain was aiming more for 'reasonable'.

'You said you weren't *ready*,' the whiny voice insisted. 'Which to me, suggested that you weren't ready *now* but you would be, at some point.'

'Well, I wasn't going to say, No, you're right, I don't want to have kids with you.' He sounded offended. 'Give me some credit.'

'But telling me you weren't *ready* . . .'

Whereas I sounded like a stuck record.

'Beth, does it matter? Why are we arguing about this? We broke up, end of.' Fraser's face was full of sympathy. Not love. Sympathy, and growing concern.

'But . . .'

'Beth.' He put his hand over mine. 'Don't do this. Please.'

I stumbled to a horrified halt, as the full extent of my self-delusion peeled back and revealed the cruel reality beneath.

I'd told Ashley and anyone else who'd listen that it had been me who instigated the break-up – go, me! High five, girl power! – but the truth was that beneath the crying and devastation was a secret conviction that one day there'd be a knock on the door and it'd be Fraser with a bunch of flowers, and a grovelling apology. Underneath the blinding pain of the break-up, my deluded brain reassured me that we hadn't really broken up, because in the future yet to come, we were already safely back together. I'd been so sure of it, it had become a reality.

I suddenly saw it. I'd subconsciously put my life on hold for *five years* waiting for something that was never going to happen.

I took a little gulp of air that sounded like a sob.

'Look, in the end, does it really matter what we said or didn't say?' asked Fraser. 'We'd come to the end of the road – it happens. At least we didn't spoil the memories with a nasty break-up. I've got too many friends who've done that – they end up losing years of their life, pretending they didn't exist between the ages of twenty-four and thirty because they can't bear to talk about their exes. We're not like that, right?'

I stared at him, unable to form words. Had he forgotten this was only the second conversation we'd had in the last five years? Because he'd put a solid screen around his life, cutting me out of his?

'I mean, you're more like part of the family,' he went on, oblivious to my inner agony. 'As Jackie says, you're doing *us* a much bigger favour keeping an eye on Mum, than Mum letting you squat in her junk room.'

He smiled, that old smile that had always turned my insides to water. It was no longer lovely. It was some bloke, smiling at someone he felt a bit sorry for. The Fraser I'd kept in my head was retreating with every second, like a vivid dream fading with each bleary morning blink, turning him into this stranger in front of me.

'Right?'

I could only nod. I couldn't speak because there was a sob backed right up against my lips that I was only just holding in.

'Some of this is on me,' Fraser conceded, more confidently now he'd established he wasn't in the wrong. 'I shouldn't have blocked you, that was just stupid male pride. I didn't want to see you getting married to the next bloke you met. Having those babies you were so keen to get started on.'

I felt like laughing, bitterly, because if Fraser hadn't blocked me so comprehensively, he would have seen that I'd barely appeared in my own Instagram feed for years.

'In fact, Iwona was impressed by how chill you were, staying friends with my sisters on social media. She saw it as evidence of my maturity, so . . . thanks!'

'Iwona?' I said robotically.

Fraser's eyes moved from side to side.

'Jackie didn't mention Iwona.'

He wiped his face with his hand. 'OK. So, Jackie doesn't know about Iwona. None of them know.' Fraser seemed to be weighing up whether to tell me or not. Then in the spirit of our rekindled friendship, he said, 'Iwona and I decided not to share with the family just yet because it's complicated. She's got two little girls from her previous relationship and her ex is a prick, to be honest. Lots of legal stuff to get through.'

I tried to breathe slowly, in and out, in and out, but my heart was beating too fast.

'How long?' I managed. 'Have you been together?'

Fraser calculated in his head. 'About four and a half years?'

Four and a half years? So, just weeks after we broke up? He wasn't ready for a family, then suddenly he was – as long as it wasn't with *me*? My nerves were zinging with pain.

'Whatever you're thinking – I know.' Fraser raised his hands, and said in an infuriatingly smug way, 'But what you've got to remember is that my family are all control freaks. And when kids are involved you have to put their feelings first, and I didn't want them exposed to the drama we've been dealing with since Dad died. Mum's been struggling, so's Jackie – it wasn't the right time to introduce them to everyone.'

Wow. No. That wasn't what I was thinking. It wasn't even my third thought.

Fraser misinterpreted my horrified silence. 'You won't tell Mum, will you?'

I don't know where it came from, but I heard my voice snap, disbelievingly, 'Aren't you a bit too old to be worrying what your mum thinks?'

We stared at each other, both stunned at how far off the predicted piste the conversation was going, and then Fraser's phone rang on the table, and a photograph came up on the screen: Iwona.

Or rather, Fraser and Iwona, their heads squashed together in a loved-up selfie on a ski slope, two happy little baby heads squashed below. A family.

My throat closed up with a sudden, powerful rush of tears, the kind you can't stop once they start, and I felt my chair move.

Tomsk had stood up and was trying to walk away. Since his lead was wrapped around the leg of my chair, he was taking me with him.

'Are you all right? Is he all right?' Fraser frowned. 'Beth? We're good, right? I've honestly only ever wanted the best for you, that's why I wanted to see you, to find out . . . Beth, don't walk away. Don't leave like this.'

I stared at him. This might be the last time I saw Fraser – I certainly didn't want to *ever* have this conversation again – so I might as well burn down the house. 'You can dress it up to yourself however you want, Fraser, but if you knew you wanted a family, just not with me, you should have had the guts to tell me. You shouldn't have waited for me to make that decision for you.'

'But . . .' Did he look guilty? Had I hit a nerve?

'I've got to go.' I fumbled in the pocket of my cardigan, pulling out the change I kept for the coffee cart and the homeless man with the collie by the park. 'Here, sorry.' I tipped all of it on to the table.

'Beth? Oh, for God's sake, Beth, don't be like this.'

Fraser reached out, but I ignored his hand. I knew people were probably looking, but I didn't care; nothing felt real, apart from the hot, tearing sensation in my chest. In any case, Tomsk had decided it was time to go, and since he was the only one in my life who had my best interests at heart, I was willing to let him.

Chapter twenty-one

I won't lie, the next few days were not good.

I got through a lot of mug cakes – or rather, I made them compulsively, ate a single spoonful, then felt too sick to eat any more. I wanted to sleep, to stop the unwanted looping of Sunday's humiliation in my head, but I couldn't: my brain kept jabbing me awake with fresh takes. I alternated between lying on the sofa feeling so suffocated with unhappiness that my muscles were like lead, then feeling a furious need to *move*, to not be anywhere that might remind me of Fraser, and the ridiculous assumptions I'd made.

Which meant dog walks, obviously. Tomsk was fine with that.

The misery swamping me was hard to deal with because it wasn't just one emotion. I pinballed between several, each more unpleasant than the last. There was the agony of Fraser's rejection all over again, but this time it was edged with a masochistic fury, knowing that I'd inflicted this entirely on myself, plus a new shame, of knowing that my worst imaginings had been true – it *was* me that he didn't want. He'd found someone else almost immediately, and not only that, he was happy enough with her, and their future, to start parenting instantly.

That meant there had to be something wrong with me. What other explanation was there?

How had I done this to myself? I felt as if I'd woken up in the wrong life, the goalposts now somewhere totally different. Fraser was not my future. There would be no happy ending for us, no journey of discovery ending in a magical reunion. I didn't even know what my ending looked like now. I didn't know what I wanted anymore. And I was nearly forty, which didn't leave me much time to work it out.

I cancelled my Rosemount sessions for the week; I texted Pam to say I had a bug I didn't want to pass on. Her reply was so kind, wishing me better soon 'because we all miss you!'. I burst into tears. And I told Martine I had laryngitis (I had to come up with a reason not to talk on the phone) and she actually came round with a hot toddy in a Thermos, knocking on the door while I pretended to be asleep.

I turned off my phone. I didn't want to deal with anything. I didn't want to be me.

Eventually, though, I had to turn my phone back on, and almost as if my subconscious brain was still operating on a professional level, it rang while it was still in my hand.

I sat up in bed, startled. It was Friday morning. No one rang me on a Friday morning. No one rang me this early, full stop.

'Hello?'

'Hi, Beth, it's Sophie from Christian's office. Just wanted to check in before this morning's meeting – do you need a parking space and a desk?'

I struggled upright, trying to process this sudden and unwanted information.

'I'm sorry?'

'Our new desk policy? It started on Monday, and I noticed you hadn't reserved a desk space or a parking space.' She paused. 'I did send a whole staff reminder last Wednesday but maybe you missed it.'

'Ah, I have my catch-up meetings on Teams.' I tried to make my voice confident. Sophie was about thirteen. I had no reason to be intimidated by Sophie, I told myself. I'd debated Brexit with Nigel Callaghan, an actual BBC reporter. 'I don't have anything specific I need to discuss, in any case. It's just a check in, I can't see it taking more than five minutes, tops.'

'Did you get Christian's agenda?'

'No?'

'OK. Well, I'm sending it to you – now. Can you make sure my emails are going into your priority folder, please? There are some proposed evolutions to your role that he wants to discuss with you.' She left a pause exactly long enough for me to open my email, had I been at my desk, then said, 'You've got it?'

'Yes, I can see it,' I lied.

'Good. So would you like me to book you a desk and a parking space?'

Why did I have to go in? Did Christian need to see me to sack me? A high-speed montage of the last meeting flashed across my mind's eye – the receptionist who didn't recognise me, the whispering when I walked in, Natasha, the photo in the kitchen, the sniggering new people – and the anxiety turned into a solid lump at the pit of my stomach.

But interestingly, it was edged with something new. Fury.

Why should I have to go into the office? Why was I suddenly not trusted to work unsupervised? Why should I have to dance to Christian's stupid new tunes?

I was taken aback by how furious I was.

'Beth? Are you still there?'

'I can't come in,' I said. 'It's too short notice.'

There was a long pause. 'I can reschedule your meeting for two this afternoon? Would that give you time to make arrangements? Otherwise we're looking at the end of the week and I know Christian wants to see everyone before he goes to Manchester.'

'Why's he going to Manchester?'

'Accountex International,' said Sophie, as if I should have known.

Was that a conference? Allen never went to conferences. He hated other accountants.

I bit my lip. I felt like one of those cartoons where someone's hanging on to a doorframe with their fingertips as an unseen force drags them by the feet, then scoring deep grooves in the lino with their nails as they resist with every ounce of their being.

'Beth? I'm allocating you car parking space nine and desk four,' said Sophie, losing patience. 'I don't want to tell Christian you're not coming in. You didn't hear this from me, but two people are already on warnings and he's got a new HR consultant looking over everyone's contracts. So just be here for five to two.'

'OK,' I said, but I didn't add the final, '*Fine*!' until I was sure she'd hung up.

I don't honestly remember how I got into work.

I necked eight herbal calm tablets with two double espressos, begged Rachel to make room for Tomsk in her daycare, and squeezed the grey suit jacket over my least pyjama-like lounge trousers. I found, once I opened my wardrobe to put together a work outfit, that my fury didn't care what I looked like, so long as my body was covered up. Meanwhile my brain was struggling to focus on anything other than snippets of conversation with Fraser, repeating over and over in a masochistic punishment loop.

Iwona.

We're like planets.

Iwona's adorable children.

You had a calculator in your handbag. A bit tragic.

Iwona and Fraser, family skiing.

I looked at Christian's agenda once; it was in business jargon so oblique it might as well have been encrypted. It only added to the distracting cacophony in my head. To block it all out, I put on a playlist of songs I'd curated for Bill Horrobin, at Linda's request – songs they'd danced to in their youth, which she thought he might enjoy when she was having a nap.

Then I turned it up, really loud, and made myself sing all the way to Jacobs'. 'Yeh Yeh'. 'Ruby Tuesday'. 'The Last Time'.

Thirty minutes later, when I pulled on the handbrake in parking space nine, I was fully immersed in a toxic blend of calming herbs coagulating with caffeine, shame, regret, Mick Jagger, and lack of sleep. I was simultaneously hyper-focused and trippily detached from myself.

The building receptionist tried to stop me as I nipped through the barriers behind a workman – obviously I hadn't been to HR to get my new photo ID – but I pretended I hadn't heard her and went into the office to find desk number four, which turned out to be my old desk, but with a large plastic *four* on the corner.

'It's like working in the café at Morrisons,' muttered the stranger on desk number five, and I laughed so hard he edged away.

Three minutes later I was in Christian's office.

(It was a bit like being hungover: one moment I was here, the next I was there. How many calming tablets had I taken?)

Christian immediately took charge of the meeting, which was perhaps just as well, and I tried to keep up with what he was saying. He spoke quickly, scattering acronyms I didn't recognise, in a slick business-school dialect that Allen had done his best to knock out of us. It reminded me of my French GCSE listening comprehension exercise where I understood most of the words but they were passing too quickly for me to grab any sense of what they might mean together. I found I could not be bothered with any of it.

The gist emerged, however. In the great Jacobs' reboot, Christian was offering me a choice: work from home on what he called 'essential support system projects' (i.e., data entry) or return to the office and, effectively, do the job I was doing before, with additional targets for business creation. But reporting to Natasha and someone called Xavier who he'd brought with him from his previous team.

'. . . it's up to you,' Christian concluded.

I looked across the desk at him. How could I phrase this?

I didn't want to work there anymore. I just didn't. It was as simple as that. A tremendous weight lifted off my shoulders. Although that might have been the herbal calm tablets kicking in again.

'Just to clarify, is this a demotion?' I asked. 'Or am I being moved sideways?'

'We've thrown out the previous structure,' he said. 'No one's being moved anywhere. It's a whole new chessboard. You don't have to make a decision immediately,' he went on smoothly, checking his screen for his next meeting. 'But we'd like to start implementing change within the next week.'

The next week? I couldn't remember what my notice period was. Could you force someone out of their job in a week?

'So I'll leave it with you,' Christian repeated, and nodded at the door.

Numbly, because I genuinely couldn't force the wheels of my brain round fast enough, I got up and left.

Instantly, I bumped into Natasha who was standing suspiciously close to the door.

The out-of-body me observed that this probably wasn't a coincidence.

'Are you OK?' Natasha tipped her head.

'Yes?' I wasn't sure what she was asking.

'No, really. You can tell me.' She made that sympathetic squinchy face.

'Why wouldn't I be OK?'

'You just seem like you might not be feeling well?' Head-tilt of concern. 'You weren't at the meeting this morning?'

'I'm fine,' I said defensively. Had she somehow intuited my Fraser humiliation? 'I slept in a little bit.'

'Aw. Did you? It's just that . . .' Natasha touched my arm as if to steer me away from the searching eyes of the office and into the safety of the kitchen. She dropped her voice to a concerned, but still audible to the nearest desk, murmur. 'Beth. Did you know you've come into work in your pyjamas?'

'These aren't pyjamas,' I informed her. 'They're harem pants.'

The sympathetic face squinched even further. 'Are you sure?'

'*Yes*.' My cheeks burned.

'OK. Well, look, I say this with love, Beth, but, as your friend, they're not doing anything for you. They make you look a bit . . . Nelly the Elephant. And they're not really appropriate for a professional workplace.'

'Fuck off, Natasha,' I said.

My voice sounded so crisp. And how enjoyable it was to say those words after only thinking them for so long.

She started back, as if I'd shoved her.

'I beg your pardon?'

'These are perfectly good Hush harems from last season, I'm not holding a client meeting today, which is why I am not dressed for a client meeting, and, in any case, it's never appropriate to body-shame your colleagues.'

'I wasn't body-shaming you!' She glanced around to make sure there were witnesses. 'I wasn't body-shaming her!'

Susannah, who'd been my graduate mentee before Covid, was taking a call at desk seven but now looked up from her keyboard. She didn't speak, but she gave Natasha a quizzical head-tilt, and that was enough.

'Susannah!' she protested dramatically. 'Oh my God! No!'

And Natasha was going to be my new boss, I realised. I'd have to deal with her passive-aggressive drama every single day, undermining what little confidence I had.

No. No. No.

I let my gaze travel around the office I'd once enjoyed working in, now full of strangers sitting at uncomfortable desks. It wasn't just the décor that had changed. The atmosphere had changed. The direction had changed. Would I apply for a job here now? No, I would not.

The fog swirled in my head, but began to lift, blown away by the rising wind of this strange rage.

What right did Natasha have to be so rude about me? She was hardly Grace Kelly herself. There was a line along her jaw where she hadn't blended her foundation in properly.

'This isn't like you, Beth. You don't look well,' said Natasha, with faux concern, again making sure everyone could see she was being gracious.

'You're right,' I said. '*I* should probably fuck off.'

So I did.

I picked up Tomsk from Rachel's – she actually *complimented* me on my bold pairing of harem trousers and a suit jacket, so that helped – and drove over to Rosemount.

It wasn't my day to go in, even if I hadn't cancelled my appointments, but it was on my way home, and I was curious to see if there was anything from Martine's mystery ex in the memory box. I also wanted to tell Pam how much her text had meant to me. In the depths of my misery, I'd thought to myself: I have no friends, no family, no one, but that wasn't completely true. Not really.

As I drove up towards the house, I saw a crowd of people standing outside in the car park: nurses in their lilac overalls, some residents, a couple of contract cleaners in red jumpsuits. There was some cheering and clapping, and when I got nearer I could see Lewis was cycling round the car park on the tandem, this time with Kay Lloyd in the rear seat.

Despite the helmet, knee pads and elbow pads swaddling her like a Teenage Mutant Ninja Turtle, Kay was having a whale of a time. Unlike Eunice Stafford, she was pedalling like a demon, and together she and Lewis were getting up quite a head of steam. I could hear her shouting, 'Faster, faster!'

I scanned the crowd to see if Hugh was there, but there was no sign of him.

While Kay and Lewis were coming in to land, to the sound of applause and cheers from the crowd, I parked and watched Kay dismount with the help of Pam and Ellie. Then Lewis cycled over to me before I'd even got out of the car.

'Beth!' he said. 'Can I tempt you this time?'

He was out of breath, and grinning with that relaxed energy that comes after hands-in-the-air dancing or an uninhibited laugh. It made his face look boyish, guileless and unguarded, and I smiled back. Lewis had a tremendous smile. It carried up through his ridiculous moustache, all the way into his brown eyes. It felt churlish to resist.

'Go on,' I said, and saw the smile change, intensifying into something warmer.

'Excellent!' he said. 'Let's get you padded up. Pam?' He turned and waved at Pam Woodward. 'Pam, have we got some spare knee pads?'

'No, just give me a helmet.' I didn't want to think about it too much, and trying to make kneepads fasten around my chunky knees would kill the moment. I had a weird urge to do something that might blow some fresh air through me. The fog had been lifting slowly ever since I'd left the office, and my head was now much clearer than it had been. I felt strange but in a different way; a funny giddiness had come over me, displacing the rage somewhat.

Maybe it was telling Natasha to fuck off.

Maybe it was the unexpected thought that if I got sacked for telling a co-worker to fuck off, it would take a decision out of my hands.

'So, you get on there,' Lewis was saying, and without further encouragement I swung my leg over the bar and hoisted myself on to the saddle. Pam handed me a helmet and I fastened it under my chin, trying not to think what I looked like.

'Come on then,' I said, gripping the handlebars.

'Have you done this before?'

'Nope.'

'You've ridden a bike?'

'Years ago.' I'd had a pink Raleigh for Christmas one year, until Mum drunkenly reversed over it and it wasn't replaced. I suddenly wondered what her version of that fun family story was, what had caused her to be so drunk on Boxing Day. I never could ask her now. I pushed away the gulp of sadness. 'I'm guessing that riding a bike is kind of like . . . riding a bike?'

'Then you'll be fine.' He was balancing the tandem, squeezing the brakes to stop it moving, and I could tell from the stability how strong Lewis must be. It gave me an unexpected thrill. 'I'm the captain, I do the steering, and the brakes and whatnot. You're the stoker, so all you have to do is pedal – and trust me. OK? When I say go, you start pedalling. Right foot down first. Like you mean it. You can do this, Beth.'

I stared at Lewis's back. He'd changed into a cycling top (of course he was the kind of man who'd have the specific, professional-grade kit) and I could see the broad curves of his shoulders under the Lycra, and solid triceps bulging under the tight sleeves. I hadn't imagined those were lurking under his suit. He was close enough for me to smell that unexpected aftershave he wore, plus a top note of honest sweat. It was the smell of someone who'd been working hard while pretending to enjoy themselves for the benefit of other people.

No wonder Pam and Eunice and Kay and Iris adored Lewis, I thought. He *did* stuff. He *finished* things. He'd probably make the kind of old-fashioned husband the widows of Rosemount were always sighing over. The sort they regularly told me didn't exist anymore.

'Did you tell Kay Lloyd and Eunice to pedal like they meant it?' I asked Lewis's back.

'You're not like Kay and Eunice,' he said without turning round.

'No, I—' I started, and before I could say, 'I weigh twice as much as them put together,' Lewis said, 'One, two, three, go!' and I put my right foot down as hard as I could and somehow – no idea how – we were moving.

I couldn't stop myself squealing as we wobbled forward, to the general applause of the crowd. Adrenalin surged through me like nothing I'd felt since – well, since I was a kid going down a slide, probably.

'You've got it!' shouted Lewis, and, encouraged, I pedalled harder.

Without even trying, our legs were working in unison and soon the tandem was going faster than I'd expected. A feeling of elation started to build inside me as the wind rushed across my skin and my heart started pumping. With Lewis on the front, controlling our direction and speed, there was nothing I could do apart from pedal, so I lifted my face up to feel the sun on it, and let the sheer joy of movement blow through me like the wind.

'This is amazing!' I yelled, and I couldn't make out what Lewis said in response. It sounded like 'You are amazing,' but the tyres were loud on the tarmac and there was a lot of cheering going on. Residents had come to their windows to watch, and I waved at faces I recognised – Nigel, and Eunice, and Linda Horrobin.

The uncomfortable saddle apart, I felt euphoric, fizzy with energy, bursting and blossoming inside with lemon-yellow and tangerine-orange like Minnie Little's lava lamp. We were skimming around the path at some speed, round the car park, down the drive, taking a right hand along the path that circled what had once been Rosemount's walled gardens. Lewis was cycling like he had a point to prove and I was matching him with power that was coming from a place inside me I didn't know about.

I'd forgotten the physical sensations of riding a bike. The hiss of the tyres and the rush of air in my nose made me feel hyperaware of every raw breath, every blink, every lungful of fresh leafy air. I was here, right now, breathing and living and after months – years! – of sitting at my desk, digesting tax periods that had been and gone, yearning for times in the past when I'd been happy, wishing I could go backwards, instead of forwards, the shock of the adrenalin sent me into a strange high. I didn't feel weightless exactly, but I sensed that my weight, and the force of my pedalling, was driving the tandem along faster once we'd got going, a positive momentum rather than a dragging anchor.

It wasn't just the tandem. There was another well of suppressed energy inside that had been cracked open, and the two were blending to create powerful forward motion. I was still devastated and ashamed and furious about Fraser, but it felt like hot lava pouring out of me, not pushing me down.

You can do this. Lewis was right. I could do this, I could do anything. If I couldn't go back, I'd have to go forward – and was that so bad?

I felt a rush of gratitude towards him. With every shove of the pedals I was pushing Natasha down, pushing Christian and Fraser down, pushing myself forward, towards the next stage in my life.

Impulsively I leaned forward and let my forehead touch Lewis's Lycra-clad back, in a silent thank-you, just for a second or two. We went over a bump and my nose and my lips brushed the bumps of his spine, and I jerked back before I broke my nose by accident.

His muscles flexed in response and he sat up suddenly. 'Are you OK?' he shouted over his shoulder.

He must have thought I'd collapsed.

'I'm fine!' I yelled. But I was better than fine. I was *alive.*

When we get off this bike, I'm giving this man a hug, I decided. And as the thought went through my head, I thought what Lewis's body would feel like pressed against mine, only the fine skintight Lycra separating my hands from those muscles of his toned back, his strong arms. I flinched. Inappropriate, Beth.

'Sure you're OK?' he shouted, and I was about to say yes when something caught my eye.

We were rounding the side of the house now, coming back to the front. There were more people at the windows and I raised a hand again to wave.

Nigel gave me a cheery two-fingered salute but I barely had time to acknowledge it when my eye was caught by a different sort of gesture, in a window one storey up.

Eunice Stafford was leaning out, waving and shouting, but not at us – she was trying to get the attention of the crowd below.

'Help! Help!' she shrieked, her thin voice carried away on the wind. 'Help!'

'Lewis,' I yelled, alarmed. 'Lewis, look up there! Eunice is going to fall out if she's not careful.'

He looked up and saw what I'd seen.

'Bloody hell,' he said and if I thought we'd been going fast round the paths, it was nothing to the acceleration that followed.

Chapter twenty-two

For a weightless second, Lewis had felt himself catapulted forwards by a wave of joy, joy beyond anything he'd ever experienced: Beth behind him, the tandem skimming the tarmac like a perfect machine in motion, the air filled with the sound of laughter and applause.

He was generating so much happiness that he thought his body would burst from it. It was the same warm feeling of 'rightness' as his dream, that sense of Beth's heart beating close to his, their legs moving in synchronicity, that wink from the gods that this was approved, that the cogs in his world had finally lined up in the sequence they'd been made for, and the energy they created was pure light.

They couldn't speak, and he couldn't see Beth's face, but Lewis felt the power surging from her pedals; she was matching his rhythm, and he was pedalling hard and fast. Every so often he heard an inarticulate noise – exhilaration? Frustration? – and the power would surge again behind him. He had a sudden mental picture of his grandfather's soft-eyed dairy herd when they were let back out on to pasture for the spring, flicking up their delicate heels and galloping with a mad kind of pleasure that was touched with wildness, kicking away the winter's confinement as much as revelling in the fresh air in their nostrils.

And then, without warning, that pressure of Beth's forehead against his back, then the magical change of pressure as she lifted her head and he felt her lips brush his spine . . .

And then it had been snatched away.

Eunice rapping at the window, drawn with panic, frantically waving her little hands to get his attention.

Lewis recognised the specific panic in Eunice's expression as soon as Beth had shouted and pointed up at the window; he'd seen it before. It was shock, and a special, personal, fear: one of the elderly residents had had an accident that might just as easily have befallen her. The grim reaper's cloak had brushed her as it passed.

Instantly, Lewis's brain clicked into emergency mode.

One: *get to the door, fast.*

(One a: *make sure Beth safely off bike.*)

Two: *assess situation.*

Three: *emergency services.*

He slowed down before they reached the group of watchers, dismounted in one movement, and helped a confused Beth do the same.

'Don't react,' he said in a low voice, as she adjusted her clothes, breathless and jumbled, 'I don't want anyone panicking. Wheel this to the sheds as if everything's fine, and tell Pam to come inside as fast as she can.'

Would he remember later what it felt like to steady Beth's hot back with his hand as she dismounted, how gracefully she swung her long leg over the saddle? Lewis hoped so, even if his brain didn't have the luxury of noting it now.

'Where shall I say you've gone?' She looked scared.

'Phone call? Loo? Doesn't matter.' His brain was clicking over checkpoints; every second made a difference.

'Of course. Lewis?'

He'd set off but turned back, to see her smiling uncertainly.

'Thank you. That was everything you'd said it would be,' she said. 'Now run!'

Lewis didn't run – that would draw too much attention – but he set off at the rapid stride that he deployed normally, and when he got into the house, he sprinted up the stairs, three at a time.

Eunice was on the landing outside Hugh Lloyd's room; she looked as if she'd seen a ghost.

'Hugh's had a heart attack,' she said, succinct with fear. 'Linda slipped trying to get him up. Looks like her hip's gone. She was talking before, but she's out cold now.'

Lewis pushed open the door to see for himself, even as he was dialling 999 on his phone.

Hugh was slumped face down over the foot of his single bed, as if he'd been saying his prayers and had fallen asleep. Linda was lying on her side just inside the door. Quickly, Lewis turned Hugh over. His face was the same colour as his maroon jumper, and Lewis struggled to find a pulse.

A flicker of an old, old panic rippled through his subconscious as it always did, a distant child's wail of fear, but Lewis blocked it out with training. He lifted Hugh's floppy body on to the floor, moved him in the right position for chest compressions, and braced himself to start resuscitation.

'Let me,' said Kemi, pushing him aside. 'I am good at this. You phone the ambulance.'

Next Pam appeared in the doorway, flushed and out of breath. 'Oh no! Oh no . . .'

'Hello, ambulance, please.' Lewis stepped aside so Ellie, following Pam with the first-aid bags, could start administering help. He was relieved to see how calm and confident she and Kemi were with Eunice; that would go in the report he'd already mentally begun compiling.

'Is the patient breathing?' asked the call handler.

'Is he breathing, Kemi?'

Kemi had started chest compressions on Hugh, quick and strong, with muttered words of encouragement on each shove. Now she put her ear to Hugh's mouth. 'I do not think so.'

'Yes!' said Ellie, who was leaning over Linda. 'Yes, we've got a pulse, but I'm worried about moving her.'

Linda let out a groan. 'Don't move me. Hip. Warm.'

'She's a nurse,' said Kemi. 'She knows best.'

'One breathing, one not breathing,' said Lewis. He gave the address, listened to the instructions, then stood up. 'Pam, stop anyone coming up here for the time being, and take charge downstairs, please? We don't want everyone getting into a flap. Usual drill.'

Lewis routinely constructed protocols to roll out in the event of accident or other distressing events that inevitably happened now and again in residential homes. Not quite ordering the band to play 'Nearer my God to Thee' while lifeboats were loaded, but in his experience a sense of business of usual helped keep things from spiralling.

'Stay with us, Linda,' said Ellie, with a wobble in her voice. She'd found a blanket and draped it over Linda's small body.

'Good job, Ellie. Now could you find Kay? Before the ambulance gets here.'

Ellie's breathing was quick and too fast; he could tell she was struggling, and he squeezed her shoulder. 'Stay calm. The ambulance is on its way.'

'I just wish I'd been . . .' Her face crumpled.

'Stop that,' said Lewis. 'I take full responsibility for this afternoon's events.'

'But I didn't hear a call bell!' she almost wept. 'Why didn't we hear the call bells? My bleep didn't go off! No one's bleep went off!'

Lewis didn't want to think about sabotage, not right now. 'Ellie, please go and find Kay. One thing at a time.'

She wiped her eyes with the back of her hand and hurried down the stairs.

Kemi was still doggedly performing compressions on Hugh, and when Lewis approached she indicated that she did not need to be relieved.

Instead he crouched down next to Linda and touched her hand, to let her know he was there. 'Hang on, Linda. Help's on the way.'

She was trying to say something, even as she was struggling for breath.

'What is it, Linda?'

'Bill.' It was little more than a rustle. 'Look after Bill.'

Lewis flinched against the sudden punch of emotion: another memory from his grandparents' house, but one that came long after he'd first seen the cows joyfully kicking down the spring air in the meadow. *Henry. Henry.*

Whenever this happened, and it had happened many times in his career, it was never just the resident in front of him that he was fighting to keep with him. If Lewis closed his eyes, he could smell his grandmother's White Linen eau de toilette, his other grandfather's darned woollen jumper, his gran's papery skin.

'Help's on the way, Linda,' he said with all the authority he could muster. 'Hang on there, for Bill.'

And for me.

Once Lewis had sprinted up the stairs and I'd passed on the discreet message to Pam, I wasn't sure what to do.

Lewis snapped into action so efficiently I didn't think he needed anyone's help, let alone someone with office first-aid skills as rudimentary as mine. But I wanted to help somehow; I was dithering in the reception area when Pam Woodward came trotting down the stairs, now in a full panic; I could tell she was in a panic, because when she saw me her expression changed from terror to fake happy, as if someone had swiped across it with a finger.

'Hello!' she said. 'Everything's fine!'

That told me it wasn't.

'Is the ambulance coming?' I asked, and with some relief she nodded and gabbled, 'Linda's broken her hip and I don't know what's happened to Hugh, he's out like a light. Lewis wants me to carry on as if everything's normal so we're going to have tea early, I think,' she went on, her voice getting higher. 'I need to let the kitchens know. And the carers.'

'Are you all right, Pam?' I asked, and she nodded again, more violently.

'I'm fine! I'm just . . .' She shook her head. 'I don't know why the call bells didn't sound! We should have heard.' Her eyes widened, as if a thought had suddenly struck her, then she looked devastated. 'Oh God. That electrician.'

I squeezed her shoulder. 'Tell me what I can do. Do you want me to help get people inside? Shall I speak to the kitchen staff? Can I get *you* a cup of tea?'

Pam looked as if I'd offered her a stiff brandy. 'Oh, Beth, I would. I'd love that.'

I helped usher the residents inside for tea, and waited until the ambulances had left and an anxious calm had settled over Rosemount. Then, when I was sure there was nothing else I could do, I went home.

I collected Tomsk from Rachel's, and drove to the nearby Forestry Commission wood where we walked in silence around the whispering trees. I couldn't bear to go on our usual route around town, when I thought of how I'd snuck glances at me and Fraser in the windows. It ended up being a longer walk than I'd planned as my feet just kept going and going, and after supper, Tomsk fell asleep on the sofa, his body draped over my lap like the most comforting weighted blanket in the world.

Dusk had started to fall, but I didn't feel like supper.

Instead I gently removed myself from beneath Tomsk, and started to type up some of the stories for Gayle, but the notes at the top of my pile were about Hugh and Kay; they'd been telling Ellie about how they'd met (in the lift, at an awards ceremony at the Dorchester), and I couldn't bear to think about that, knowing that Hugh would be in hospital by now, and poor Kay would be sick with worry.

I spun on my office chair and looked at the kitchen.

My brain was telling me to make a mug cake to cheer myself up, but I didn't feel like eating.

Instead, I spun back and picked up my phone. Before I could think too hard, I called the number I had for Rosemount.

It rang a few times, and then I heard Pam's recorded message

'Hello!' It was her telephone voice, more self-conscious than her normal one. 'You've reached Rosemount Court residential care home. Our office hours are nine a.m. to six p.m. If you'd like to speak to Lewis Levison, please press one. If you'd like to speak to Pamela Woodward, Housekeeper, press two.'

I pressed two, and the line reconnected and rang out again, different ring tone.

I waited for Pam to pick up, and thought about Hugh and Linda.

I wondered, with a pang, how poor Bill would manage without Linda's comforting chatter. Would the nurses be able to interpret his silences the way Linda did? Would it help if I offered to take Tomsk in to see him? My heart hurt for how little anything would probably help.

'Lewis Levison?'

I spun all the way round in my chair at the sound of his voice in my ear. 'Lewis? Sorry, I was expecting Pam.'

'Did you call Rosemount? I diverted all the numbers to mine, just in case there were any more press calls.'

'Press calls?'

'I don't know why but apparently it's been on some neighbourhood website that there's been nothing short of a massacre up at Rosemount this afternoon. Old people collapsing like skittles, it said. Air ambulance in attendance, multiple ambulances.' He sounded despairing. 'Where do people get these stories from? And why do people want them to be true?'

'Why would anyone want to make up something like that?'

'Who knows? But they are. Carrie Clark called me for a quote. I mean,' he added, 'she knows the place isn't a death trap, she was only here a few weeks ago!'

This probably wasn't the moment to mention Pam's concern about the call bells.

'How are Hugh and Linda?' I asked. 'Any news?'

'Linda's stable. She's going into surgery first thing in the morning, but Hugh's still in intensive care. I'm waiting for an update from the ward sister any moment now.'

'You're still at the hospital?'

'Yes. It took a while to get them checked in.'

I looked at the clock on the wall. It was nearly ten o'clock.

'Have you eaten?'

'Um, no. I'm reluctant to start wandering around the hospital in search of food in case I miss the update.'

'Do you want me to bring you something?' Longhampton Hospital was only five minutes in the car, and it wasn't as if I was doing anything. 'You need to eat.'

I was already opening the cupboards, getting out the cocoa, the sugar, the eggs. The special big mug.

'Well, that would be incredibly kind.'

Was that a catch in Lewis's voice? I'd never heard him sound so deflated.

'I'll be there before you know it,' I said, and started whisking.

Lewis was sitting outside the Intensive Care Unit, one long leg crossed over the other to form a makeshift desk for his notebook, while he attended to his emails on his phone. He was frowning, worrying, obviously trying to keep the plates spinning at Rosemount even in the middle of this disaster.

He was back in his suit, for appearance's sake, but the red Lycra of his cycling top peeked out from underneath his shirt, and the flash of his white sports sock, just visible under his trouser leg, was a sudden reminder of being behind him on the tandem, close enough to hear his quick, athletic breaths, so different from the controlled professional man who ran Rosemount like a well-oiled machine.

I stopped to study him for a second, before he saw me. Who *was* Lewis, when he wasn't at work? Who looked after him, the way he looked after everyone else?

But the corridor was too quiet for the sound of my footsteps to go unnoticed. I'd only paused for a second before he looked up, quickly, and when he saw it was me, he smiled. Not the usual Lewis smile, much lower wattage and more careworn, but still a smile.

'I can't believe you've come in,' he said. 'This is so kind of you.'

'What? No, I'm just round the corner, it's no bother.'

He shifted some papers off the chair next to him. 'Sorry, I'm snowed under with paperwork. I have to file an incident report, and senior management are already requesting quite a lot of additional feedback for legal reasons . . .' He stopped, as if he'd said too much.

'I admire a man who keeps on top of his admin.' I started to unpack my cool bag, putting the flask and two cups down on the chair between us. 'I've brought you some coffee. And some fruit. And this.' I opened the Tupperware box and offered him the contents.

Lewis peered inside, then looked up with a grin. 'A mug cake!'

'It's still a bit hot, be careful.' I passed him the little pot of cream to pour on top. Somewhat belatedly, I wondered if this was a weird thing to do. Too late now. 'I find them comforting in stressful situations.'

He sniffed it appreciatively, like someone savouring a fine wine. 'Is it the warmth, do you think? The chocolate?'

'Yes, but . . .' I hesitated, then decided Lewis deserved more detail. The extra cream. 'My mum used to make them for me when I was upset about something. She'd get out the ingredients and line them up, pretending we were on a cooking programme. We'd make it together. The silliness of it used to take my mind off whatever was upsetting me.' I didn't add, 'Which was usually Dad,' although it was. 'Sift this, whisk in that . . .' I mimed the mixing. 'She never used to measure anything, she just had that knack of knowing when it was right.'

'And she's never given you the recipe? She made you work it out for yourself?'

'Mum died when I was twenty-two,' I said. 'And she probably wouldn't have known herself even if I'd asked.'

'Oh.' Lewis looked mortified. 'I'm sorry, I didn't mean to pry.'

I handed him a teaspoon. My best teaspoon, a silver spoon I'd found in a charity shop. 'It was complicated. She wasn't well.'

'Didn't you make one for yourself?'

I reached into the bag and took out a teacup. I hadn't felt like eating when I made it – I just did it to be companionable – but now I dug in with my other good spoon, and we sat in companionable silence, eating hot mocha pudding together.

The antiseptic smell of the corridor, and the night ward sounds brought back some sharp memories: of Mum, and the last night in the ICU, when she'd looked at me and begged me to tell the nurses she'd had enough, my heart physically cracking inside me. I hadn't felt old enough for us to swap places like that, me being briefed by doctors, her lying there with her head turned towards the corner, blank eyes, lank hair.

Dad hadn't returned my call until the next day. When I'd decided I didn't need his help anyway, and never would again.

I stared into my half-empty cup, and wished I'd heard the real story of Mum's life. Even though now I was old enough to understand there wasn't one definitive story that told the whole truth. Just our stories, collected together, to make a rough approximation. The best I could do now was keep our own stories alive, in myself.

I dug my spoon into the cup and scooped out the molten heart of the cake, the best bit.

'This has really hit the spot,' said Lewis. 'You're a life-saver.'

That was exactly what I was not. 'So tell me about Linda and Hugh.'

'Linda's broken her hip, but she's still managing to tell the nurses what to do. That might be the painkillers, though. Hugh . . .' Lewis pressed his lips together. 'Hugh's not so good. His son's on the way from London. Jonathan.'

'Oh.'

'Pam brought Kay in to see Hugh earlier, but took her home. There's no point Kay sitting here all night, especially when she's not—' He stopped himself.

'Not what?'

Lewis debated with himself, then decided he might as well just tell me. 'Kay is, between you and me, living with a cancer diagnosis. It's not confidential but she's a very private person. Please forget I told you that.'

'Of course.' I wouldn't have guessed, I thought. But then who knew what people were living with, medical or otherwise.

'I said I'd stay until Jonathan arrives, just in case Hugh comes round. I'll pop down to see Linda, of course, but I suspect she's having a nap.'

'She and Bill don't have children, do they? They told me that,' I added, 'I'm not snooping.'

Linda (and Bill, I suppose, in his own way) had been very open about their disappointment at not having a family, but 'it was what it was', and 'it gave us more freedom to travel'. 'And we've got each other,' Linda had added, 'which is more of a blessing than most.'

'That's why I don't mind doing my paperwork here tonight,' said Lewis. 'I don't want Linda to feel we've left her on her own.'

I watched him scraping out the last of his mug cake with the tip of his spoon, meticulously enjoying every last trace, then his email alert pinged again, and he put down the mug, knitted his brows in thought, then rattled off a swift reply. Then he went back to his mug. There was an old-fashioned capability about Lewis that you'd normally associate with pre-war matrons, or benevolent gods. Velvet-covered steel, or steel-encased velvet, I wasn't sure which.

'Lewis, can I ask you something?' I said. 'How did you end up running residential homes?'

'I'm a *huge* fan of bingo.'

'No, really,' I said. 'I'm interested.'

He shrugged. 'Are you sure? It's a long story.'

I glanced at the clock. 'I don't see us going anywhere in a hurry.'

'I was brought up by my grandparents.' He ran a hand through his hair. 'My mum died when I was seven, and my dad was in the RAF and couldn't cope with me on his own, so he sent me to his old boarding school. We'd already moved around a lot on postings; he thought it would be best for me to have some stability. I used to spend my holidays between Dad's parents, who lived in Edinburgh, and Mum's family, who had a smallholding in Herefordshire. Not too far from here, actually.'

He stared down the corridor towards the swing doors that led to Hugh and the ICU, but I didn't think that's what he was seeing.

'All four of them were such interesting human beings. Grandpa Levison took me fishing, Grandad Pugh let me drive a tractor. Grandma Levison was a secret shopper, and Grandma Pugh had been a typist at GCHQ and she taught me shorthand so we could write each other letters in code from school. They did everything they could to salvage some happiness for me, to give me a childhood, and I loved them exactly as much as I missed my mum.'

'A lot, I'm guessing. In both directions.'

He nodded. 'They were a bit older than my friends' grandparents, and they used to tease me about spending the holidays with 'old people' – but I never thought of them as being old. They were *people*. Young people like me who'd just been around longer. And as I got older myself, I tried to look after them the way they'd looked after me.'

I thought of the courteous way Lewis treated every resident, anticipating their requirements, making sure they were comfortable, respecting their dignity.

'I bet you did.'

His face clouded. 'Not as well as I wanted to, unfortunately. I wasn't there often enough. I started my career in a different field, property, in London. I missed some important moments. And then I . . . Then I decided to move into the care sector, and made a promise to myself that no one in any home I ran would ever have to be on their own at the end, or feel scared, or be afraid to ask for decent treatment, no matter how many hours that took.'

At what cost to himself, I wondered. He was sitting in a hospital corridor with his paperwork, no supper, no one waiting for him at home.

'And you've done that,' I reminded him. 'You've transformed Rosemount.'

Lewis shook his head. 'Two residents in hospital and everyone talking about us on social media again? That's my fault. No one else's.'

'It's not. It's not your fault, Lewis.' Without thinking, I reached out and took his hand, squeezing it.

His hand was warm, but he carried on staring at the double doors without squeezing back, and to my surprise I felt a hollowness in my chest. The absence of a response made me realise I'd expected one, and that I'd really wanted one.

Disappointment bloomed inside me like a rock dropping into water.

I'd barely begun to process that thought when the double doors swung open, and a doctor appeared, followed by a nurse.

'Mr Levison?' Her sombre expression was enough to know that the update from Hugh's bedside wasn't going to be good.

Lewis gave my hand a brief squeeze back, a friendly squeeze of thanks, then he stood up, adjusted his cuffs, and said, 'What news, doctor?' The little boy had gone, and Rosemount's manager, capable of dealing with anything, was back.

Chapter twenty-three

After Eddie's update in the office, I'd emailed Allen to see how he was, and he'd invited me to drop in the following week for a cup of tea 'and a debrief'.

Devora showed me through to the conservatory, where Allen was using his recuperative 'down time' to record short instructional reels for his new social media account.

If anyone was a model for the power of Making a Change, it was Allen.

He asked me how things were going at work, and I told him: the email with my new job description had come through the previous night, but I'd made my decision before I even opened the attachment. It boiled down to old job, worse boss, or worse job, lower pay. But it wouldn't have mattered if Christian had offered me his job, at treble pay: it was time to find something new.

'I think you're making the right decision,' said Allen when I'd got to the end of the whole sorry saga. He was wearing a polo shirt with the logo of his new business on the breast pocket, and a pair of trousers that had been adjusted to accommodate the huge medical boot on his foot. 'Write your resignation letter, get on the interweb, and look for another job. And for God's sake, Beth, book a holiday.'

He said it so sincerely I didn't correct the 'interweb'. 'You don't think I'm overreacting?'

'What? No! Sod 'em. If there's one thing I've learned in the last month it's that there's no time to waste. You'll have no trouble finding another job with your ability and experience. The important thing is to find one you *enjoy*.'

I couldn't disagree with that. When it came to Jacobs', I could see now that I'd got stuck in the same kind of wishful thinking spiral I'd been in with Fraser, hoping that I'd wake up one morning and work would be inspiring and challenging again. But what did I think would change, if I didn't make some changes myself?

That was the theory, anyway. The reality was that the thought of interviews and networking and having to find smart outside clothes to wear to meet strangers gave me instant pit sweat.

Allen sensed my wobble. 'Or don't be an accountant! Do something else! Retrain as a pastry chef if you want!' He waved a biscuit at me; I'd persuaded Pam to give me her gingersnap recipe and had baked him a tinful. 'You're not indentured to Jacobs' for life. You don't have to wait for Christian to give you a sock so you can leave. What other things would you like to do?'

'That's the problem,' I said. 'I'm not sure.'

I'd been scrolling through career change websites, trying to find something that fitted my transferable skills, and though I had more options than I'd initially thought (including retraining as a dog groomer; keeping Tomsk's odour at a low hum had really honed my shampooing skills) so far nothing was leaping out at me.

'You could always retrain as a BSL signer?' Allen suggested, with a few careful hand gestures which I assumed translated to the same words. 'I'd give you a job any day of the week.'

'That's very kind,' I said, and to show him I'd read the links he'd sent me, I put my fingertips on my chin, and made a 'thank you' sign.

Allen beamed and made the same gesture back. And some more that I didn't understand but hoped were positive.

I checked my phone throughout the day in case of an update from Lewis, but there'd been nothing since I'd left him at the hospital with the doctor delivering the sad news: Hugh had died, without regaining consciousness.

All afternoon I lay on my sofa with Tomsk, failing to make a new job visualisation collage and instead willing the universe to make Linda's operation go smoothly. And for Hugh and Kay's son Jonathan to be there, looking after Kay. And for someone to be taking care of poor Bill, alone and silent without his Linda. Most of all, I hoped Lewis wasn't blaming himself for what had happened.

No text came. There was no reason for Lewis to update me. I couldn't stop thinking about the weight of the world on his shoulders outside the ICU. I couldn't concentrate on anything. I jumped when Martine rang me at ten o'clock to tell me five facts about Bath, and I realised that (a) it was ten o'clock, and (b) I hadn't thought about Fraser and his brand-new family all day.

Needless to say, that was something I didn't feel able to discuss with Martine, which made our conversation shorter than normal, and I resented Fraser for that too.

The next morning, I decided I had to do *something* to help, and loaded Tomsk in the car straight after our morning walk.

'Come on, Tomsk, we're going to see if we can comfort an old man,' I said, and he gave me a look through his fringe that said, 'I know what you're up to, but whatever.'

I could feel the sadness in Rosemount the moment we stepped through the door. Instead of the lounge-music strings that had been floating in the corridors on my last visit there was mournful classical music instead. Pam was stationed on the reception desk instead of Wendy, and she was braced like someone manning the last machine gun.

When she saw it was me, she relaxed, but only slightly. Her eyes, red-rimmed and without their usual mascara, kept darting to the front doors, or to the stairs, as if she was expecting residents to escape, or some officials to arrive.

'It's been so stressful,' she confessed. 'Lewis has been in meetings since eight this morning. Norris Schofield's family arrived to remove him at lunchtime, we've had total strangers phoning up asking how many residents died, and are we ashamed of ourselves . . .' She blinked fast. 'I didn't know people could be so cruel!'

'What do you mean?'

She got her phone out of her cardigan pocket, winced, and handed it to me.

Ellie, appointed social media strategist by Lewis, had created an account to 'showcase Rosemount's happy community' – table gardening, Story of My Life vignettes, teatime, etc – but someone called @LonghamptonDad had posted, *Happy to PLAY GAMES while your residents are LITERALLY DYING! DISCUSTING! U should be ASHAMED!* and others had agreed and liked and added more weird accusations about old people being run over by bicycles ridden by laughing staff.

I handed the phone back, feeling hot and cold. No one had mentioned a fat woman on the tandem with the manager but if they'd noticed Lewis on a bike they could hardly have missed me. 'It was so sad what happened to Hugh, and Linda, but what else could Lewis have done? If he'd been in the house he could hardly have reacted much faster than he did.'

Pam looked ashen.

'Pam?'

Her eyes darted to the door and back again. 'I'm so worried, Beth. We're going to get closed down, aren't we? I've had people calling saying they're from the BBC, wanting a statement. Lewis says I've to refer them to him, but like I said, he's been in meetings with *his* boss, and then obviously Hugh's family arrived, so he's been dealing with them, and because Linda doesn't have any family, he's been advocating for her with the hospital, as well as trying to make sure Bill's OK, and . . .'

I seized the opportunity. 'That's what I've come for. I thought maybe I could sit with Bill, for some company?' I indicated my hairy companion. 'He seems to relax with Tomsk.'

'Oh, would you? We're so worried about the poor man.' Pam seemed relieved. 'You know what Bill's like, bless him – it's hard to tell if it's sunk in. We've explained that Linda's in hospital but it didn't seem right to make any promises about when she'd be back.' She covered her mouth with her hand and squeezed tears away.

Tomsk shifted next to me, as if bracing for the next hour or so.

'Come on,' I said. 'This dog's had intensive training in therapeutic silences.'

I could tell straight away that Bill was upset, not because he said anything to that effect, but because he barely noticed us come in.

'Beth's here to keep you company for a little while,' said Pam, putting a tea tray down on the teak G-Plan side table with the fancy tiled top ('A wedding present from my Auntie Win, you thought she had a look of Joan Crawford, didn't you, Bill?') It was eerie, not having Linda's constant narration, and her voice played in my head anyway.

Bill turned towards me; I wondered if he expected to see Linda too, since I only appeared to hear her reminiscing, but seeing I was alone, his eyes dropped to the carpet again with such a despondency that I could almost feel the pity ricocheting between me and Pam.

'I'll pop back in half an hour,' she whispered to me. 'That OK?'

I nodded. Half an hour would be a long time without Linda's monologues about the *Billy Cotton Band Show* and party telephone lines, but if it would make Bill feel less alone it was the least I could do.

Tomsk let out a sigh and lay down next to Bill's slippers.

I listened to Pam's quick feet retreating down the corridor, and the silence in the room reasserted itself.

I swallowed, and racked my brains. This was hard, but I was here now.

'I was so sorry to hear about Linda's accident,' I said, to get it out of the way. 'She's in good hands, though. They're taking good care of her.'

According to Pam, the operation on her hip had gone 'as well as they hoped' but the doctors were monitoring her for a few days.

Bill carried on staring out of the window, touching his arthritic first finger to his thumb, then his second, then his first again, over and over.

I looked around the room, searching for inspiration, then gave up. This frightened old man didn't want some stranger wittering on about the weather, or the football; he just wanted to hear about his wife, and that she'd be OK. That she was coming home.

I couldn't promise that, though. I wanted to, but I couldn't.

He turned and met my gaze and I could see fear in his watery eyes. It scared me. How did the nurses deal with the weight of residents' emotions, as well as their physical well-being? Bill's unhappiness was almost enough to drive me out of the room, but I couldn't bear the thought of him sitting here alone, so I made myself stay.

What could I do? I didn't want to recap the stories Linda had told me, in case I got them wrong. Then I had an idea.

'You know, I've been meaning to thank you, Bill,' I said, as lightly as I could. 'You and Linda have introduced me to some great new music. I wrote down your favourites so I could listen to them in the car. Shall I play that now?'

Bill's anxious finger tapping stopped for a moment.

'OK.' I found the playlist on my phone, put it on the tray next to the French fancies and pressed shuffle. 'I'll put it on shuffle. If you don't like a song, just let me know and I'll skip on. Like that jukebox Linda used to love in the pub, eh?'

The first tinkling piano notes of 'Bonnie and Clyde' by Georgie Fame rang out and I reached to change it to something more appropriate, less murderous.

But a tap from Bill's chair stopped me in my tracks.

'This.' It was barely a word, more a breath. Then more definitely, 'This.' The ghost of a smile crossed his wrinkled face.

For a second, Bill's eyes brightened, and the handsome young fruit wholesaler was here, again. My heart gave an almighty ache because, really, he'd never gone.

If I thought about that too much I knew I'd end up in tears, so I turned up my phone, and we sat back and listened to the Animals and Manfred Mann and Dave Dee, Dozy, Beaky, Mick and Titch, which conjured up stock footage of *Ready, Steady, Go!* for me, but, I hoped, full colour, real-life memories of sociable Saturday nights and Butlin's holidays for Bill.

After a while, he seemed to settle in his chair, while Tomsk snored, and I started to relax.

If Lewis hadn't started the Story of My Life project, I thought, watching the way Bill was slowly slipping into sleep, none of this would be possible. Lewis and his positive energy had brought something precious to Rosemount. He'd listened, and he'd helped people talk. He'd healed Rosemount's soul, the same way he'd mown the lawn and cleaned every window, not just the ones within easy reach.

As I thought about Lewis, a protective feeling bloomed in my chest, and when I was sure Bill had dropped off, I quietly retrieved my phone and looked again at what people were saying about Rosemount online.

My jaw dropped, and I could feel my blood pressure rising as I read – accusations of negligence, shocking claims about old people left to die in rooms . . . it was libellous, surely? Could he sue? Could Rosemount's management sue? It was typical anonymous keyboard-warrior bollocks, but exactly the kind of 'no smoke without fire' allegations that made people rush in to take their elderly relatives away.

This wasn't Lewis's fault, I fumed. He was a decent man, a *lovely* man. None of this should be laid at his door. I wanted to help him, because I could tell this was going to get worse, not better. And the fact that he'd been late to the drama because of me only added a nasty, shameful edge to my outrage.

Sadly, the good ideas refused to come, and I too let my brain drift away to a Waterloo Sunset, where it was paradise.

Pam knocked softly on the door a few songs later, with a nurse called Dawn.

'Dawn's going to give Bill his meds and sit with him for a bit,' she whispered.

'Pam mentioned Bill was in the fruit trade,' murmured Dawn. 'My grandad was too, so we can have a wee chat about Covent Garden market.'

I gave her a thumbs-up.

'Lewis made a chart for the staff room,' Pam whispered as we left. 'We had a look at the stories to see if we could link up the staff with the residents when it came to birth places and grandparents' jobs and whatnot.'

'What a good idea,' I whispered back.

'Speaking of which, Gayle's in reception, and I'm not sure what to do. She had a meeting scheduled with Lewis to discuss rolling out the story project in the other homes in the group, but obviously he's not available now. She's come all the way from Malvern.'

I still hadn't made my appointment to talk to Gayle about my manuscript but any thought I had of swerving the conversation vanished when she spotted me and Pam approaching.

'You!' She pointed at me. 'We are overdue a chat.'

'This isn't the best time . . .'

'There's never a best time.' Gayle turned to Pam. 'Beth and I will be in the library if Lewis manages to get out of his meeting. Can you let him know where we are?'

'No problem.' Pam had taken up her station at the reception desk with grim determination again, and I was being swept down the library by my creative writing coach.

Gayle sat down on the chairs that Kay and Hugh Lloyd usually sat in to do their crosswords, and launched straight into her critique of *The Road to Love is Long* (a title I'd pulled out of the air when I had to call it *something* to email it to her).

'I like what you've written so far,' she said. 'But I know exactly why you can't get it over that hump. It's obvious, once you see it.'

'Is it?' I'd been working on this story on and off for about ten years, so I was hoping the problem might be a little more complicated than that.

'Beth, who is this story about? Who is the central character driving the action?'

'Isabella.' Once I'd made the spontaneous decision to give my heroine a more normal name, she'd turned into a real person in my head: the blond hair, blue eyes description I'd put in my spreadsheet had solidified into a real face, with thick hair that went frizzy in the rain and dark eyebrows that could look unintentionally stern.

'So tell me Isabella's story.'

'Isabella is in love with Arthur, the youngest son of the landowner next door,' I recited. I knew the set-up off by heart. 'But she's poor, and Arthur needs to marry into money, so when their fathers find out, Arthur is forced to seek his fortune in the gold fields of the Yukon for a year, and Isabella is sent north to look after her aunt.'

Gayle tipped her head. 'Go on.'

To be honest, it was hard to raise much enthusiasm for my manuscript, what with the events of the last twenty-four hours. It all felt stale. But I might never get the chance of an editorial critique like this again, so I did my best.

'And then, well, I know how it *finishes*,' I said. 'Arthur returns from America or wherever he's been, having spent months and months trying to track Isabella down, and they're reunited. It's in the middle of a rainstorm, and he tells her he made a terrible mistake in not standing up to his father, and that he wants to marry her immediately.' I frowned. 'I just can't get past the bit in the middle.'

To be fair, it was quite a big bit.

'OK, so let's brainstorm this.'

I didn't really want to, but Gayle was being more enthusiastic about my story that I was, and I was hoping Lewis might emerge from his office before I left.

'What does Isabella do in between? She doesn't just sit there waiting for Arthur to come back, right?'

'No, of course not.'

'So what does she do?'

Truthfully, I had no idea. The bit between the parting and reunion was unspecific beyond 'they miss each other and Isabella writes him letters' – the possibilities were too vast to pin down, and I ended up floundering in the infinity of it.

'Um . . .' I cast my eye around the library for inspiration and saw a pencil sketch of a horse. 'She becomes an artist,' I said. 'She's always been good at drawing so she starts sketching the neighbours' horses. And children. She's observant. People relax with her.'

'Maybe she's a little too realistic in some of her drawings,' Gayle mused. 'That could be funny!'

'Yes!' I said. 'A bit of controversy about someone's big ears, or someone's child who looks more like their godfather than their dad?'

'Exactly! I like the symbolism of Isabella being a portraitist, it's clever.'

'Thank you!' I angled my head subtly to see if I could spot Lewis in the corridor.

'So what does she learn about people through doing it?'

'How to read people's faces? How to see beneath the surface and paint someone's soul?' I don't know where that came from, it just popped into my head. 'And maybe she could do a self-portrait which helps her to look at herself more honestly . . . so I guess she learns about herself, while she's observing other people.'

Gayle pointed at me as if I'd just said something brilliant.

'And she meets various neighbours, gets commissions from them, maybe the rugged local landowner with a mysterious past who could fall in love with her. Then when Arthur comes back from his travels,' I went on, surprising myself with my own powers of invention, 'she goes into her sketching room expecting to see the landowner, ready for his sitting, only to find Arthur sitting there! What?'

'Why not the mysterious landowner? He sounds interesting.'

'Because the whole point of the story is that Arthur comes back. He's journeyed across the world for Isabella.'

'So you're setting half the book in the Gold Rush?'

God, no. That sounded like a *lot* of research. 'No, but . . .'

'So why should we care about Arthur's journey?'

'Because he has to go away to come back for Isabella.'

Gayle shrugged, as if I'd answered my own question. 'That's why you're stuck. Isabella's the hero, give *her* the journey. Even if she stays in a tiny village the whole time.'

I could see the logic of this, but it felt very at odds with the book in my head. Even though the book in my head had huge gaps in it.

'Everything you need is already there. You just have to ask yourself what happens now? Ask it aloud, if it helps.'

I screwed up my nose. 'What if Isabella doesn't immediately recognise Arthur, after the travails of his journey, but as she carries on sketching and he talks, she realises that though his features are familiar, she doesn't recognise his personality, because she hadn't had time in their whirlwind romance to get to know the real him.'

'Every heroine needs a blind spot, an Achilles heel,' said Gayle. 'Maybe Isabella's is Arthur? She can see everything clearly apart from what a bore he is. Sorry.'

'But that's not going to fit in with the end,' I insisted. 'Isabella and Arthur get married.'

'Why? The end of the book is often the least interesting part. Stop thinking about the end of your story, think about the middle. You might find it ends somewhere completely different. You've intrigued me with this mysterious neighbour.'

Despite my attempts to keep Arthur and Isabella front and centre in my mind's eye, new images were pushing their way forward. Suddenly I could see Douglas, the neighbour, his old coat thrown over a chair, leaning on a fireplace pretending to stare out at the fields but covertly stealing glances at Isabella at her easel; I could see her frown of concentration as she filled in the detail of his face, her pencil hesitating over Douglas's crooked front teeth, the smear of coffee above her lip that he'd been too polite to tell her about.

I could see them trying not to look at each other; I could even see the polished brass oil lamps and the patterned tiles on the fireplace in a room that I'd never imagined before in my life.

And actually, Douglas wasn't a rich landowner, he was a farmer who bred shire horses and took in the ageing foxhounds when they couldn't keep up with the pack, letting them sleep in his kitchen.

I stared at Gayle, stupefied. I'd never had such a rush of ideas.

She seemed pleased. 'Go away and write whatever you've just seen in your head,' she said. 'I want the whole thing by the end of the month.'

That brought me back to earth with a bump. 'What? No, that's impossible.'

'Beth, you've been working on this for how long now? Too much thinking time. Just write it.' Her eyes twinkled. 'Let Isabella tell her own story.'

I got up, feeling a bit dazed but also twitchy. I needed to get these ideas down before the inspiration faded.

'Don't forget, Isabella's the hero of this story,' she called, as I left. 'Not Arthur.'

I thought about nothing else for the entire drive home, as Isabella and Douglas chatted in my head, as real as old friends, but when I pulled up outside Coleridge Drive, and wondered if I should tell Martine about Hugh and Linda, I was suddenly struck by a very different thought.

Life was so short, and so unpredictable. Martine ought to know someone up at Rosemount had memories of her that still filled them with happy nostalgia; what she decided to do with that information was up to her. We need never speak of it, but it wasn't for me to come down in judgement about something that happened over sixty years ago.

Before I could change my mind, I went inside, put all the Nessy memories in an envelope with a brief note, and posted them through Martine's door.

Chapter twenty-four

Lewis took a moment to absorb what Eric Alexander had just said to him. It was so completely out of the blue, so *wrong*, that he struggled to make it fit with the reality he was currently inhabiting.

Lewis had thought his week – no, his year, maybe even his career – had reached its low point four days earlier, when Pam had phoned him to tell him that a fourth resident that week was being withdrawn by their families, citing loss of confidence in the facilities. It had taken considerable reserves to keep strong in the face of that, and he'd only managed it for the sake of his staff.

'You've frozen, Lewis,' said Eric. 'Have we got a bad connection?'

'No, I heard what you had to say, but I don't feel it's the right decision.'

'I appreciate it's disappointing, and I don't want you to take it personally.' He paused. 'But I'm afraid there was always the likelihood that this would be the outcome. We've had several evidenced complaints over the last few days which I was going to bring to your attention in our next meeting – over and above the current investigation. Add to that, the final quotes for the upgrades required for the CQC reinspection, which are well over the budget we'd allocated, and well . . . I called a crisis meeting this morning, and the general consensus was that the Rosemount tanker is simply now impossible to turn around. As we've discussed previously, it was haemorrhaging money even before these unfortunate events, and since you've just lost another four residents . . .'

'Poor choice of words,' said Lewis pointedly.

Eric coughed. 'Yes, of course. Apologies. But the bottom line is that it's just not feasible to throw good money after bad at this point. It makes more sense to sell Rosemount and use what cash becomes available to shore up more profitable homes for the future.'

Lewis stared at the painting of the Duchess of Longhampton, sitting on an armchair with four of her favourite ferrets. They all had beady eyes, and they all urged him to put up a fight.

'Eric, what we do isn't just about money.'

'But it *is*,' Eric reminded him. 'In this case, it absolutely is. Rosemount was a headache long before you arrived. The negative publicity is already impacting our other properties, and this latest incident is getting national attention.'

'Our social media manager is working flat out to contain that.' By which he meant Ellie was deleting every vicious comment she saw popping up; frankly she'd done little else since the first ambulance arrived. The comments had started immediately, which was so concerning Lewis had allocated it a separate slot in his head to worry about.

Eric was bringing the conversation to a close. 'You've given it your best shot, but we need to draw the line somewhere. The group accountants have been briefed to prepare Rosemount for sale. They'll be in touch. And I've got to be honest, I doubt if anyone's got pockets deep enough to take it on in its current format. We're anticipating offers from developers. You'll need to update the staff, and also the residents – of course we'll do everything we can to support them in finding alternative accommodation. But hold fire on that until I've spoken to our legal team about a timetable.'

Lewis didn't know what to say. He was numb with anger and guilt and disbelief and disappointment, so much that he barely dared open his mouth. But he was also exhausted.

'Lewis? Are you there?'

For a moment, he came very close to hanging up on his boss without even speaking, under the pretext of losing signal, but Lewis was a professional, and a man who'd been brought up by four people very hot on manners, and he just couldn't do it.

'Please keep me in the loop,' he said, and then he ended the call.

It took Lewis a moment to gather his shattered thoughts. He usually resisted overemotional descriptions, but that was exactly how he felt: broken into tiny pieces, as if everything he'd tried to do, every plan he'd devised for Rosemount, everything he'd believed about the supposedly people-focused company he worked for, and above all, everything he believed about himself, had been unexpectedly smashed into insignificance with one punch.

Well, one punch, preceded by a lot of sneaky little kicks to the shins.

On autopilot, he began walking to a small productive task, anything that could be completed without much active thought, and found himself outside. The lawn needed mowing – a simple job that always gave him headspace to ruminate efficiently on other, bigger projects – but once he was up on the ride-on mower, Lewis's brain flooded with more questions, and he came to a halt.

He'd known that something was wrong in the house; his dream had told him that quite clearly. So why hadn't he been more rigorous in rooting it out?

And what was it that had been malfunctioning – the call bells, or Hugh's heart . . . or Lewis himself?

'Lewis?'

A finger was jabbing him in the back.

'Lewis! Are you all right, man?'

Robotically, he turned to see Nigel Callaghan standing in the middle of the lawn, staring at him, his hands on his hips. What on earth was Nigel doing out here?

It dawned on Lewis that Nigel was in the middle of the lawn because he was in the middle of the lawn, on a stationary lawnmower.

'Have you run out of petrol?' Nigel inquired. 'Or are you doing some fancy new pattern?'

'Neither,' said Lewis. 'I'm just very disappointed.'

'In what?'

It probably wasn't the discreet thing to do, but Lewis told him. Nigel, he sensed, would understand the bigger reasons for his disarray; he was a man of the world, who'd looked at the best and the worst human beings could do to each other, and prepared a balanced report on it for *Newsnight.*

'But what cuts me to the quick,' Lewis finished, 'apart from not being given a fair chance to fulfil my brief, is the anonymous complaints.'

Nigel stared at him. 'More than the implications that you've been criminally negligent?'

'Well, yes. At least there'll be a report that I'm confident will exonerate me.' Lewis really did hope it would exonerate him. 'I've been open about tackling any issues here since the day I arrived, and I've asked people to be open with me in return. So why didn't they come to me? I don't think I'm intimidating, am I?'

'Quite the opposite.'

'And yet there's someone here at Rosemount who doesn't trust me to solve their problems. And of course,' he added, 'I hate the thought that there *are* problems. I thought we were getting on top of things.'

Lewis rarely used the word 'hate'. Similarly, 'nice', 'tasty' or 'pardon', all vetoed by the grandmother who'd worked at GCHQ.

Nigel didn't answer. He was staring up at the blank windows of the garden rooms.

'Why would someone want to complain anonymously?' Lewis didn't mean to be whiny, but he was struggling to superimpose his professional persona over the hurt personal one.

'Indeed,' said Nigel, and narrowed his eyes at the windows. 'Leave it with me.'

Lewis gave himself exactly one minute to sit in his shallow puddle of unmanly emotions, then he pulled himself together and finished mowing the lawn. The lines weren't as straight as he'd have liked, and he imagined himself mowing out swearwords into the now-lush green of the grass, but it was done.

If Lewis had hoped that Eric would have reflected on his conversation over lunch and changed his mind, he was disappointed.

Just after two o'clock, an email arrived with official guidance on how he should start informing key staff of the proposed sale, and, reluctantly, he began with Pam.

She entered his office with red eyes, and began crying before she'd sat down.

'I know what you're going to say and I'm sorry, so sorry,' she wept, offering him an envelope. 'I've already written my resignation letter.'

'What?'

'The call bells! I should have checked with the electrician, he must have disconnected the wiring when he came in that day. I don't think any of them were working! I went up to check and that corridor was all off!'

'What are you talking about?'

'When the electrician came the other week, you asked me to show him round? I should have checked what he was doing but Dawn and Rosie needed me to help turn Marjorie, so I just left him to it.' It was hard to make out what she was saying through the hiccups. 'It's *my* fault Hugh and Linda were on their own for so long. I won't let you take the blame for it. You've been so good to me, I've learned more about managing people in the last few weeks than in my whole career, and the one time you trust me to—'

'Pam, stop right there.' Lewis pushed the box of tissues across the desk. 'It's not your fault. The buck stops here, for everything.'

And he was to blame, he thought, guiltily. He'd stayed chatting to Stan rather than supervising the electrician, because he'd wanted advice on how to approach Beth.

'That electrician was called in to look at the wiring in the whole house – none of it's up to standard.' Another David Rigg botched contract. 'Besides, the nurses reacted with remarkable efficiency. I should be commending you for keeping their skills up to date – the paramedics were particularly complimentary about Kemi's chest compressions.'

Pam snuffled into her tissue. It sounded like thanks.

Lewis sighed. 'I have some sad news to share, Pam, but it's not down to one single event.' He gave her an edited version of Eric's call, and noted the visible collapse in her expression as the news sank in. When he told her they'd have to help the residents find new accommodation as soon as possible, concern – and fresh tears – filled Pam's eyes.

'Oh, Lewis, no! Some of them have been here for years! They don't have family to help them. What about the Memory Ward residents? It'll be so distressing for them!'

'Believe me, no one is more devastated about this situation than me,' he finished. 'In an ideal world, I'd fix the problems and we'd all stay here forever. Me included.'

'They ought to come and see it, instead of sitting in their offices, looking at their calculators. You've turned this place around.' Pam blew her nose loudly. 'It's never been better, in all the years I've worked here. Cleaner, happier, safer, more *fun*. None of this makes any sense to me.'

Or me, thought Lewis. But it was what it was.

He knew he was putting off talking to the rest of the staff, but he went up to the hospital for visiting hour to check up on Linda Horrobin, and then spent half an hour with Kay Lloyd.

She was subdued but 'bearing up'. Already there was a crop of sympathy cards covering the sideboard and tables like roosting birds, tucked between the framed photographs and Staffordshire pottery ornaments that filled the Lloyds' stylish display units. Any word of medical troubles went through the home faster than a summer breeze through net curtains, and the residents were of the generation that liked to keep a stock of suitable cards in a bureau, just in case.

Their son Jonathan, a grey-haired man a few years older than Lewis, had arrived just after his father had passed away, and then stayed in Rosemount's guest room, overnight. He had then had to fly back to London for work; he was something senior in a bank, he couldn't easily take time off. But he'd be coming back, Kay said, to finalise the funeral arrangements.

'It means a lot to us both that you were there with Hugh, at the end,' she said, taking Lewis's hand. 'He thought you were a good chap. His words. He used to say, I'd have Lewis crewing for us, wouldn't you? That was his highest praise.'

It should have made Lewis feel better, but it didn't. He decided not to share the news with Kay that she too would soon have to find a new berth. Not today.

Lewis was heading back to his office, ready to pull up stumps on one of his worst days ever, when Ellie ambushed him by the open door of the library.

She looked flushed and her hair, usually neatly swept into two plaits, was in a rough ponytail.

'Isn't it your day off, Ellie?'

'It is, but Pam phoned me. I had to come in – is it true? That Rosemount's going to close?'

Lewis cast a cautious glance over her shoulder; there were a couple of people in the library – Nigel was talking to Eunice, by the window, and Stan was deep in conversation with a striking widow called Belinda.

He frowned. This was supposed to be done according to guidelines, but it was a bit late to be berating Pam for breaking a professional confidence. If anything, it had saved him a job he hadn't been looking forward to.

Had it come to this, Lewis thought, disappointed in himself. Have my standards slipped so much already?

'Do you want to come into my office?' he said and she set off at a trot.

Once inside, Ellie didn't waste any time.

'First off, you need to know that no one blames you for anything that's going to happen to Rosemount,' she said. 'We can see you've done everything you can to try to save this place.'

Who was 'we'?

'That's very kind of you, but I . . .'

'We think you've been hung out to dry,' said Ellie fiercely. 'It wouldn't surprise me if David Rigg was behind this.'

Always David Rigg, thought Lewis. Even now.

'And if I sent head office an anonymous email about the mould it was only to draw attention to his bad management, and that was *ages* before you arrived,' she said in one hurried breath. '*Anyway*, I've been doing some research.' She brandished a sheaf of papers. 'About what we could do to save this place. It's like you say, there's always something you can do.'

Lewis nodded warily.

'So, go with me on this,' she said. 'I'm in a WhatsApp group for care-home nurses, and one of them works in a community care home – one like this, that was bought out when the owners wanted to sell up. It's like a community pub but a residential home.'

'Safeguarding adults is a bit more complicated than pulling pints and running a darts competition once a week.'

'The community don't do the nursing, they just organise it. And fundraise for it. I'm not saying it's easy, I'm just saying it's a thing. I also found some charities that own independent care homes. I've printed out the details, here, have a look. Could we do that? If we got some funding from somewhere? I mean, are there grants available to set up a community care home? Does the council have any historic bequests we could access? Can we do a crowdfunder?' Ellie paused, indicating she'd reached her main question, the big hurdle. 'How much do you think we'd need to raise?'

Lewis had to hand it to Ellie, she'd covered a lot of ground in a very short amount of time. Maybe there *was* a career in detective work in her future.

'I don't know exactly,' he said honestly. 'I could take an educated guess based on similar properties, but there's the issue of the CQC inspection hanging over it, and reputational damage. That can affect price considerably.'

He didn't say as much to Ellie but the speed with which Eric had moved from 'there are problems' to 'it's for sale' made Lewis wonder if he had, perhaps, had an approach on the quiet from someone who wouldn't have the overheads of staffing and renovations to consider. A property developer, in other words. Someone who could put the rooms with existing plumbing and original Georgian windows to a very profitable new purpose.

But Ellie was still talking, and she deserved his full concentration.

'Roughly how much, though?'

He guesstimated a figure that, he could tell from Ellie's flinch, was more a lot than she'd anticipated.

'Maybe less. But that's what it would cost to buy,' he said gently. 'You'd still need to find additional funds on top for renovation and staffing. It's not a cheap business to run.'

Ellie set her chin. 'But it's possible?'

'It's possible,' Lewis agreed because it was, he supposed, *possible.*

What was wrong with him? Negativity had struck him down like a bad cold. It wasn't just that Eric's reaction had disappointed Lewis, it had undermined his core faith, somehow. People, positivity, that good would out, despite everything.

'We'd need some proper legal and financial advice,' Ellie continued. 'Which I get will be expensive, but I was looking at the life stories file – sorry, I know it's not what it's for – and Vincent Greville and Esther Hope were both solicitors, and they've got relatives who are too – could they advise? And Beth Cherry's an accountant. Could she help? She sorted out my mortgage for me.'

'We could ask,' said Pam, who had let herself in, mid-presentation. Lewis's open-door policy in action. 'I'm sure she'd want to help. She popped by with her dog the other day to see Bill. She's such a thoughtful young woman.'

'Yes, maybe I should call Beth?' suggested Ellie.

The way Pam and Ellie tried not to exchange glances confirmed that this had been pre-discussed.

Lewis pinched his forehead. They kept saying 'we', as if the crew of HMS *Rosemount* could somehow plug the big hole in her side, and carry on steaming, despite the icebergs still blocking her path. A crew with Captain Lewis in charge, even though Captain Lewis worked for Eric Alexander, and would probably be deployed to any other care home in the group in a matter of weeks.

If he wasn't sacked, pending the reports.

Lady Longhampton arched her eyebrows at Lewis from her gilt frame by the fireplace. What was it Stan had said? You only regretted the things you didn't do. Because they showed up your own cowardice, as much as the lost opportunity.

'I'll phone her,' said Lewis, and felt a flicker of his usual get-up-and-go in response.

Beth was gratifyingly quick to agree to drop by for a quick chat.

'I wanted to see you anyway,' she said, which made him feel happy and worried at the same time.

He explained the situation and she listened with the same concentration that he'd seen her show to the residents while they told their stories; always the same, whether they were about gold medals or scout badges. Lewis had to remind himself that Beth did this to everyone, or else he'd have lost track entirely.

The only time she seemed to pull back was when Lewis moved on to the practicalities of Ellie's suggestions, and asked whether Beth would advise them on the accounting requirements.

'God, no,' she said, sitting back in her chair as if pushed. 'It's a specialist field, charity finance. We had someone at work who did nothing but that – it's one of those areas that you don't want to get wrong. Most people who set up charities get into all sorts of pickles.'

'But do you know anyone who specialises in it?' He paused. How much would a consultation with a specialist cost? 'Could you speak to them off the record, maybe? As a favour?'

Beth's brow creased. 'I could. But it might be a bit awkward. I've just handed in my notice. My line manager has said I don't have to come in again – not that I've done anything, I've accrued a lot of holiday.' She added that, as if he might think she'd been committing some murky accountancy crime that made her unsafe to be around.

'Should I be commiserating or congratulating?' he asked.

'Congratulating. It's time for a change. Pastures new.' She said it firmly, as if she was still trying to convince herself. 'But if Rosemount is sold . . .' She bit her lip, then burst out with, 'It's so unfair. Where will *you* go? What will you do?'

'I don't know, to be honest. I'm more concerned about the residents.' Until now, Lewis hadn't really thought about himself; he knew that would sound pious if he said it aloud, but his brain had genuinely stacked the immediate problems ahead of his own. He'd never considered the possibility that he wouldn't turn Rosemount around, but he wasn't so sure now what his options were. There was the very real possibility that Eric might sack him for the public failings here, and, in any case, Lewis wasn't sure he had the energy to launch into another recovery mission. Rosemount had taken more out of him than any other project.

He forced out a positive smile. 'I'm sure something will turn up. If anyone will have me – I hear I've been running over residents like skittles!'

Beth looked aghast, which hadn't been his intention. 'It's outrageous, it really is. I've never met anyone who puts as much effort into improving other people's lives than you. Her cheeks flushed a deeper pink. 'And I include myself in that. I wish I'd taken you up on that tandem ride sooner – I can't put my finger on it, but I've felt so invigorated ever since. I feel more . . .' She struggled for the word, then made a punching motion with her fist. 'Motivated.'

'Good,' said Lewis. 'That's the magic of cycling.'

'No,' said Beth. 'I think it's the magic of you. You and your positive energy.'

Their eyes met, and he knew this was his chance, but it felt wrong to take it. What had followed that transcendent moment had been awful, the exact opposite of the joy he'd felt flying through the air with her. How could he turn Hugh Lloyd's tragedy into a moment for himself? It was wrong on every level.

But Beth was still gazing at him, now with the beginnings of a smile on her lips, as if she too wanted to say more than she thought was strictly appropriate in the circumstances.

I can't, thought Lewis, agonised. A man has *died.*

But that man was Hugh Lloyd, said a voice reminded him. A man who celebrated life with every cheesy Disney song in his body.

The moment stretched between them, until eventually Beth said haltingly, 'I do feel terrible, though, that I might have delayed you getting help to Hugh and Linda.'

It punctured the moment as precisely as a pin in a balloon. Quite rightly, of course.

They looked unhappily at one another. Lewis recovered first.

'Please don't think that. Any responsibility is mine. I've nearly finished the incident report form and I'm sorry, but I'll have to get a statement from you.'

'I'm happy to provide a statement,' said Beth. 'I'm happy to tell anyone who wants to know that you have moved heaven and earth to make Rosemount as good as it can possibly be, and that you've only ever had the interests of the residents and their families at heart. You are a manager in a million, Lewis. You don't deserve to be made a scapegoat for someone else's negligence.'

Lewis didn't think he'd ever seen her look so beautiful and grim at the same time. There was a determination to her expression that he hadn't seen before, and it was oddly exciting that he was causing it.

Beth picked up her bag. 'I'll make some calls. I'll find the right accountant to advise you. It would be an absolute outrage if this home is sold for flats. We owe it to everyone here to maintain continuity for them. Let me see what I can do.'

And she left in a rush, moving across his office in that silky undulating way that made every step look like sculpture in motion, and Lewis's miserable week took an unexpected leap towards something better.

Chapter twenty-five

It was only on my drive home from Rosemount that the implications of what I'd just rashly promised Lewis began to sink in.

I did know a specialist accountant who dealt with charity set-ups and specialist funding brokers, but – just my luck – they were located four floors above Jacobs', in the same building.

Even though I'd resigned, the thought of going anywhere near the office still filled me with a kind of dull, sick feeling, on top of the anxiety I felt at the thought of any face-to-face meeting outside the comfort of my own laptop. There was every chance I'd have to be in the lift with someone from Jacobs, and thanks to Natasha, I wasn't sure what sort of reception I'd get.

I hadn't mentioned it to Allen – or Lewis – but appended to the official job offer email that had triggered my resignation was an official warning for workplace bullying (in other words, telling Natasha to fuck off) which the management apparently took 'extremely seriously'. I'd never told anyone to fuck off in my life before, but I could imagine how Natasha had probably rushed straight to HR, 'so worried' about my 'unprovoked verbal assault' – more concerned for my sake than hers, naturally – and then rushed to the kitchen to make sure everyone else knew too.

I *hated* the idea that anyone might think I was a bully.

The second stress factor was that this was the first external meeting I'd had in years, and I didn't have a thing to wear that didn't look as though Tomsk had been sleeping on it in his basket.

I knew it was time to face facts, so I dragged out the mirrors I'd hidden, then examined myself in the least worst outfit.

It wasn't a pretty sight.

I'd pinned my grey suit trousers back together, and they fitted better than a month ago, more thanks to stress than the steps and the intermittent fasting, but when I stared at my reflection, wondering where I could get them repaired, I had a moment of clarity: why was I allowing a ten-year-old trouser suit to dictate my life?

Who was in charge here: the trousers, or the woman inside them?

I flinched but forced myself to see the bigger, softer, but still recognisable version of me. This was who I was now. I couldn't keep putting my life on hold until I was a different shape. Maybe I would never *be* a different shape. Time wouldn't reverse if this zip went up. They weren't magic trousers. I had to let that version of me – and her increasingly dated wardrobe – go, and focus on the here and now.

Of course, that was easier said than done. The thought of trying on new clothes made my stomach churn almost as much as the meeting I needed them for. So I called the one person who knew where to find reliable makeover help, but more importantly, knew exactly how hard it was for me to ask for it.

'Do you want me to come with you?' Ashley offered, after she'd shared the contact for the personal shopper her mum and sister had booked for her. 'I've got to be honest, Tia's great but she did talk me into buying a pleather mini-skirt. And that's me. You know how hard it is to talk me into anything. God knows what you might walk out with, unsupervised.'

I think this was Ashley's idea of an olive branch, so I took it.

We met up outside John Lewis on Saturday morning; I'd brought her favourite takeaway coffee, which was my own idea of an olive branch. It was a double soya latte with caramel syrup: stupidly expensive, in my opinion.

'Don't tell me,' she said when she saw it in my hand. 'If I gave up a takeaway coffee every day for fifty-eight years, I could buy . . . a house?'

I grinned. 'You're welcome.'

We looked each other up and down. It was only a few months since Ash had moved on to a new life with Leo, but there was something different about her, that confident bounce that you only get when your life's moving forward in a direction you like. I envied it. Could I ask the personal shopper to bring me a few rails of that?

'Deep breath,' she said, reading my thoughts. 'It's not as bad as you think, I promise. If Tia brings out the pleather miniskirts, I've got your back.'

I left three hours later with a pair of miraculous trousers, a couple of shirts, a crazy print dress, two pairs of shoes, and, don't ask me how, a pleather midiskirt. I'd never have picked them off the rail myself and the personal shopper refused to let me look at the size labels, but somehow, when she spun the mirror round, I looked like a different woman. Not the old Beth, but a new Beth I actually liked. Tia kept going on about my amazing hair, my gorgeous eyes and my 'peachy bum', to the point where I forgot to look at all the bits of me I hated.

In between the shopping, Ashley and I picked our way carefully through our updates; it was easier to confess the whole Fraser debacle between outfit changes than if we'd had dinner, and by the time I was handing over my credit card we were back on familiar ground and discussing where to go for a drink.

'We need to get together and wear our pleather skirts,' said Ash in the bar later. 'We can start the Pleather Ladies' drinking society.'

'We can probably spot other Pleather Ladies round town. We can't be the only ladies Tia's pleathered.'

Ash snorted, and clinked her glass with mine. I'd forgotten how nice it was to have running jokes.

She tilted her head. 'You know, you're looking different. Did you get your hair cut?'

'I've lost a bit of weight?' I suggested self-consciously.

'Tshuh. No, not that.' She peered at me. 'Have you met someone?'

'Definitely not.'

'Hmm. You sure?' Ash gave me a side look.

'Maybe it's just the magic of a fresh start.'

'Maybe,' said Ash.

I'd arranged to collect Lewis from Rosemount before our meeting with the broker, because I had a strong suspicion that, left to his own devices, he'd cycle there, and I wasn't sure I could project a confident business persona while Lewis was talking about CQC reports in head-to-toe Lycra. I was nervous enough about this as it was, despite my new outfit.

'You look very smart,' he said, as soon as he got into the car.

'Almost as smart as you.'

Why had I worried about Lewis presenting a professional front? He always looked comfortable in his suit and tie, but this morning he'd stepped it up into a different league. His hair and moustache were freshly washed, his white shirt spotless, and his polished shoes gleamed in the messy footwell of my car. I kicked myself for not hoovering it out last night. I'd have to offer him the emergency roll of Sellotape.

Lewis also smelled gorgeous, which I tried not to notice. I'd found the cologne he wore while Ashley and I were browsing in John Lewis: it was Eau Sauvage, a classic.

'So,' he said, fidgeting with his leather portfolio, 'do we need to talk strategy before we get there?'

'Just so we're absolutely clear, I'm happy to be here as moral support, but specialist business funding isn't my field of expertise,' I said, but he stopped me.

'It's not mine either. I can run a care home, but I've never tried to buy one.'

I turned to look at him properly, and realised he wasn't joking; Lewis was nervous.

'Has something else happened?' I asked, wondering if there'd been another departure, or an outbreak of locusts in the library.

'No.'

'Then what?' I paused. 'What's said in the car, stays in the car. Come on, you can tell me. Is it Linda? Is someone else ill?'

'No.' Lewis squeezed his forehead. 'I'm just not sure this is going to work. I'm flattered that Pam and Ellie think I can snap my fingers and save Rosemount, but it's not as easy as they think to set up a deal like this. I'm a manager, not a business owner. It's a completely different skill set.'

'Well, that's what this meeting is for. Finding out whether it's financially viable or not – if it's not, we won't get the money, simple as that.'

Lewis looked at me, and I realised I'd said 'we'.

I'd never said 'we' when discussing clients before. That was the trouble with Rosemount; it got under your skin.

I acknowledged that with a wry grimace. 'Let's not get overemotional. It's a meeting to clarify options. We're not signing over our houses.' I paused. 'Not that I have a house to sign over, you understand.'

He managed a weak smile out of politeness more than anything else.

This didn't fit with the confident, unflappable Lewis who'd gone through Rosemount like a dose of cleansing salts. This was Lewis with his batteries taken out.

'What is it?' I said, more gently. 'Really?'

Lewis turned to stare out of the window towards Rosemount's impressive facade. 'I don't want to let anyone down.'

I turned off the ignition. He sounded so anguished, it felt wrong to drive away now.

'I should have been able to turn Rosemount around. And I haven't. Eric hasn't given it enough time, but still, there's nothing that isn't fixable. I *should* be able to do it. But taking it on on my own, with total responsibility for the business, as well as people's lives . . .' He paused. 'It just feels like something's not quite right. I don't know if that's Rosemount, or me.'

I wondered if Lewis had failed before, whether he'd always managed to move mountains with that superhuman energy and nuclear-strength positive thinking. The events of the last few days seemed to have knocked him off track. A little train upside down, with its wheels slowly spinning to a halt.

'No one expects you to work miracles,' I said. 'You're the only one who expects that. All you can do is get the facts, then decide.'

'I'll be honest, part of me thinks, why jeopardise what I've got – a solid career with Acorn, regular income . . .' He paused, and looked up at me. 'But another part of me thinks, this is a once-in-a-lifetime opportunity. The chance to be the one making the decisions, applying everything I've learned – and with a team of people I really believe in. Motivated, honest people I trust.'

'If there's one thing I've learned from Rosemount,' I said, thinking of the stories I'd heard of failed businesses, emigrations, immigrations, lost houses, career changes, all recounted with the same 'ah, well' attitude by people who'd lived to tell the tale, 'it's that some things work out, some don't, but you have to try.'

I'd even managed to take that advice myself lately. I'd applied for a couple of accounting jobs, and signed up for a short course in therapeutic dog massage. I'd also Blu-Tacked the phrase *Action cures fear* to my desk. I told Lewis about the dog-massage course, and it raised a flicker of a smile.

'Right,' he said. 'You're right, of course.'

'For what it's worth,' I said, 'I think you're the man for the job.' I held his gaze. The familiar determination was slowly coming back. I realised how much he must trust me to show any sort of wobble. Poor Lewis. Who did he have to share this burden with?

'I can't think of anyone better,' I said firmly. 'Let's go and find out how you buy a care home. No one's going to make us sign anything. You can do this, Lewis. You just haven't done it *yet*.'

I plugged my phone in; the first song that came up on my Rosemount playlist was 'Walking Back to Happiness', one of Eunice Stafford's favourites.

It felt like a strong start.

Kevin Allison, a specialist business finance broker, did not know that Lewis and I were care-home-buying novices, and even if he sussed us, he barely stopped talking long enough for us to reveal our ignorance.

Once we were installed in his uncomfortable chairs, he embarked on a detailed spiel about financing plans, sweeping us through the legal requirements, the CQC inspection burden (Lewis maintained a dignified silence), staff qualifications. I found it fascinating, so much that I forgot to be nervous, and instead asked a lot of questions. Maybe too many questions. I sensed Lewis wasn't quite as intrigued by asset vs share purchase nuance as I was.

'Your main challenge,' Kevin told us, 'will be securing finance. Lenders require substantial deposits, much more so than for residential properties. Particularly if you don't have previous ownership experience. Did you have a particular property in mind?'

'No,' I said, not wanting to commit to anything. Unfortunately I spoke at the same time as Lewis said, 'Yes.'

Kevin raised his eyebrows. 'Do you have a business plan?'

'That's underway,' said Lewis, at the same time as I said, 'Yes.'

We looked at each other, and I was relieved to see some of the confidence back in Lewis's eyes. He raised his eyebrows at me, which made his moustache lift too. I had to stifle a laugh.

'You've given us a lot to think about,' I said. 'But it's sounding positive.'

'I hope so! It's a tricky sector, but a rewarding one.' Kevin got up to escort us out. 'We supply more and more finance for care homes – we're currently looking for experienced accountants to join our team to meet the demand, if that's something that you might be interested in?'

A move into care-home brokering? Hmm. But it was the first time in ages that I'd left a meeting without worrying if I'd made a fool of myself – that was surely the magic of trousers that swished in exactly the right point on your ankle.

It was only when we'd got back to the car that Lewis told me a woman had been staring at me as we'd swept through reception.

'Short hair, pink top? She was waving at you,' he said. 'Didn't you see?'

I shook my head. I'd been too distracted by calming Lewis' nerves to notice Natasha. What a win.

Once safely back at Rosemount, Lewis and I sat down in his office, and – in a rare violation of his 'always open' door policy – he closed his office door.

'Don't want to be interrupted,' he said. 'Not until we've got a solid update to offer.'

We went through my notes and, together, drafted the business plan. Most of it was easier than Lewis expected; he'd already got a good idea of what due diligence would turn up, and he knew the staff, and the turnover, and the CQC situation. Running the place wasn't an issue; finding a deposit for the mortgage was.

'It's going to be at least a couple of hundred thousand,' he concluded. 'And we don't know the asking price yet.'

'I'm guessing you don't have that stashed under your mattress?'

'I have some savings,' he said cagily.

I flipped through Ellie's notes. 'Ellie's found local council grants that we can apply for? Plus funding from charities.'

'But how long would it take for the money to come through?' He ran a hand through his thick hair. 'When Eric makes a decision, he actions it. If he says it's going on the market, he means next week.'

'Is there no way you can persuade him to wait until—' I started, then stopped abruptly at the sound of knocking on the door.

Before Lewis could say, 'Come in!' Nigel Callaghan flung it open, and Eunice Stafford entered at pace, with Nigel two steps behind her.

'Eunice has something she wants to tell you,' said Nigel, without preamble, then turned to her. 'Eunice?'

He folded his arms, and sat down in the chair by the door, daring her to leave.

'Do take a seat, Eunice,' said Lewis, in such a relaxed tone you'd imagine he and I had just been discussing holiday plans.

Eunice scowled between Lewis and me, but didn't speak.

'Fine,' said Nigel, 'then I'll tell them. Lewis, with regard to our conversation the other day, you'll be very interested to hear what Eunice has been—'

'No!' It was almost a squeak. Eunice turned to Lewis, and said, 'I just want you to know, before I say anything else, that I appreciate everything you've done for me, Lewis. The bike rides and getting my tea right, and just . . . asking me what I think about things. You're a gent.'

'Eunice?' snapped Nigel.

She glared over her shoulder. 'I'm not scared of you, Nigel Callaghan. I've spent my whole life being told what to do by men, it's water off a duck's back.'

'What's going on?' I asked.

'My inquiries have concluded,' Nigel said to Lewis, as if that should mean something to him. 'And the person you need to speak to about the ghost stories, and the missing lightbulbs, and the issues with wiring . . .'

'Is me!' Eunice lifted her chin. 'Me!'

'What?' I looked between Eunice, Lewis and Nigel, baffled.

'I won't beat about the bush, my son Michael's made an offer for Rosemount. Cash. He's gone in with a friend of his, they're planning to turn it into an HMO, whatever that is. Flats, I assume.'

'How much?' asked Lewis.

'Not as much as you'd think,' said Nigel. 'Because, Eunice?'

Eunice's face twisted.

'Because . . . ?'

'Because Michael got me to tell him things he could complain about. For a discount. He made the initial complaints to the inspectors, said it was dangerous. Which it was,' she added, quickly, 'you *know* David Rigg was up to all sorts. Michael said I was a whistleblower, a heroine! But then he made up some of his own, for good measure. Went overboard, if you ask me. I did tell him to stop.'

'So those stories that were being leaked to the local paper – tell me that wasn't you?' Lewis sounded astonished.

Eunice nodded, and now she seemed less confident. 'Not intentionally, mind. Michael kept asking me, was I warm enough? Did I get decent food? And I suppose I might have been a little bit, well, dramatic.'

Lewis spluttered.

'I didn't know what he was up to!' she protested. 'It was the first time our Michael had ever taken much of an interest in whether I was comfortable or not. He kept asking about hygiene, and safety, this and that and the other. I thought he was just being caring, looking after his old mum for the first time in his life.'

'He brought in the mice,' Nigel added. 'From Pets at Home. And he messed about with the electrics.'

My eyes widened. 'The *electrics*?'

'He did an apprenticeship,' muttered Eunice. 'Years ago.'

Lewis and I exchanged looks. So poor Pam and Ellie were blaming themselves for something that hadn't been their fault. Or the electrician's.

'To cut a long story short, Michael told me that if I played my cards right, and he played his, this place'd be shut and he could end up making a lot of money.'

'Sawing off the branch while you were still sitting on it,' said Nigel. 'You must be so proud.'

'Did he tell you what would happen to you, when the home was sold?' Lewis asked.

'If the house got sold, he said he'd buy me my own place, by the seaside. I asked him again this week, but he'd changed his mind, said I'd be moving in with him and Mandy.' Eunice leaned forward, for emphasis. 'I don't want to go and live with Michael and Mandy. They've got this penthouse flat in the middle of Jesmond with no garden and five cats and everything *grey*. I can't stand Mandy and she can't stand me. I reckon they're going to shove me in the nearest, cheapest home, as soon as this place is shut down and he's got his money, and that'll be that.'

'Goodness me,' said Lewis, which seemed quite a generous reaction in the circumstances.

'So, Eunice, you plan to rectify this by . . . ?' Nigel prompted her.

Eunice glared at him. 'Did anyone ever tell you you were a bossy bastard?'

'All the time.'

She turned back to Lewis. 'Ellie says you're trying to come up with a plan to stop the home being sold. I can tell you exactly how much Michael and his business partner have offered, if it helps.'

'That would help,' said Lewis.

'And if you need another investor, I've got some money of my own.' Eunice's chin hoisted again. 'I had a little win on the Premium Bonds that I never told anyone about, back in the eighties. It's been sitting in a bank account ever since, ticking over nicely. I'd rather chuck it in the canal than let Michael get his paws on it now. The sneaky sod.'

'I've got a nest egg I can throw in too,' said Nigel. 'If it would help. At my time of life it hardly seems worth making sensible financial choices.'

I looked at Lewis, who seemed stunned.

'Really?' he said. 'You'd really do that?'

I was reminded of the last scenes in *It's a Wonderful Life* when the whole town turns up with nickels and dimes to save the Building and Loan. (I'd had to extend my frame of cultural reference into Classic Cinema lately.) Of course they'd do this for Lewis. He was the James Stewart of care-home managers.

'Christ, yes,' said Nigel. 'I'm done with moving. And I don't have any family to live with. Most of us here are in a similar situation. I've spoken to a few people, on the quiet, and they'd rather invest a few bob to see the place stay as it is, under different management. You seem like you'd make a decent fist of things, why not?'

'You've done your best for us from the start, Lewis,' said Eunice. 'For *us*. You've cared more about whether I'm happy than my own family has. I'm sorry I've been part of this trouble you're in, I was misled. If I can do anything to put that right, I will.'

I thought Lewis was going to cry. Oh, wait. He was. He got a perfect white handkerchief out of his pocket and blew his nose noisily.

'Pull yourself together, man,' said Nigel.

'It's a wonderful gesture of confidence,' I said. 'And it's warranted, Lewis.'

Lewis looked at me, as if the doubts he'd shared with me in the car had been answered.

I smiled, encouragingly, and he nodded.

Nigel cleared his throat. 'And I'm afraid the ghost story was my fault. A misinterpreted comment to that journalist. Thought it might generate interest, not drama. Apologies.'

Lewis made a choking noise.

'Right.' Nigel slapped his thighs to indicate that the matter was now closed. 'Let us leave you to it. Eunice? I believe you're interested in joining a poker circle.'

She gave me and Lewis a shifty glance. 'Maybe.'

He made a gallant 'after you' gesture at the door and the pair of them departed, leaving me and Lewis to stare in shock at each other.

Had Eunice and Nigel just saved Rosemount?

'It might not be enough,' he said.

'But Nigel says others feel the same. What if we put it to the residents as a proposal? Fees up front? Or something?'

My mind was shuffling figures around, trying to create a framework. 'At least let's *try*.'

'Is it ethical, though?'

'Is it ethical to sell a care home to a fraudster?' I prodded the desk. 'Call your boss right now. Ask him to delay the sale till the end of the month, so you can put together an alternative proposal, for the sake of the residents.'

'But . . .'

'Tell him,' I said, thinking of the impromptu movie screening in Iris's room, and Eunice shrieking with joy on the tandem, and Minnie Little pottering in the garden she'd always wanted and never had, 'tell him that if he really cares about the reputational damage Rosemount is supposedly inflicting on his other homes, the optics of selling off a care home for flats to a man who abuses pet-shop mice will be much, much worse. And, *and*, hint strongly that one of our residents is well known in television documentary circles. That's before you get on to the CQC to tell them about potential sabotage.'

Lewis picked up the phone, then hesitated. A slow smile spread across his face, reaching his eyes.

I was on a roll. 'And you can tell him that the residents feel that . . . what?'

He was gazing at me with an admiration that made me feel deeply, but not unpleasantly, self-conscious.

Lewis had beautiful eyes. Kind, and emotional. *The eyes of a farmer who let arthritic hounds sleep in his kitchen instead of in a stone-flagged kennel.*

'I couldn't have done this without you,' he said simply.

'Oh, you would,' I said.

But Lewis shook his head. 'I've got to make a call. Can you hang around for ten minutes?'

I lingered outside the door, and from the first words Lewis spoke to Eric, I could tell he'd switched into his business mode. His tone was confident, assured. 'Eric, glad I've caught you. There's something I need to speak to you about as a matter of urgency.'

I loved it when Lewis talked like that. Although I'd never have told him.

Chapter twenty-six

I went home so filled with energy that I sat down with my giant plotting notepad and scribbled on Post-it notes for hours, barely noticing the sun setting and the dusk falling softly across the garden as I sketched out every scene I'd need to bring Isabella and Douglas together, then apart, then finally together again. It felt as if my heart and my brain and my imagination were turning like perfectly aligned cogs, and it filled me with utter euphoria.

Now I'd seen Isabella and Douglas in my mind's eye, there was no stopping them as they met, and flirted, and edged their way towards each other all over the Northumbrian market town where I'd decided they lived; sometimes in the woodsmoke-scented studio where Isabella did her sketching, sometimes in the assembly rooms of the town's coaching inn where Douglas presided wearily over the bickering town council. Even Arthur suddenly sprang into focus, albeit in the form of very dull letters from America, full of nothing. Instead of Arthur's return being the big finish, I decided to move it forward and get it out of the way: I had a much better big finish in mind for Isabella now, one that wasn't decided by someone else's actions.

Whenever I hit a blank spot, and panicked that I'd run out of ideas, I asked myself aloud, 'So, Beth, tell me what happens now?' and miraculously, it turned out I always knew.

At ten o'clock, the phone rang as usual and I was surprised to see how late it was.

'Hello, Beth,' said Martine. 'Are you still up?'

'I am. It's been a busy day!'

'How are things at Rosemount? Any news?'

I knew Martine would ask, and I hadn't been looking forward to telling her. 'Linda's stable and responding well to treatment but Hugh . . . I'm afraid Hugh died, Martine. Not long after he was brought in. The doctors said he had a heart attack.'

'Oh!' She sounded as if the breath had been knocked out of her.

'Lewis and the staff did everything they could,' I went on. 'His son was with him.'

'His son?'

'Yes, Jonathan. He came from London as fast as he could.'

There was a long silence at the other end.

'Martine? Are you still there?'

It sounded as if she was blowing her nose. 'Yes, I am. Do you have a moment, darling? There's something I'd like to talk to you about.'

'Give me a minute, I'll come up.' I was in my pyjamas, but I could easily change. It was dark now, and if Martine fell over something in the garden we'd never hear the end of it from Jackie.

'No, I'll come to you. Why don't you put the kettle on?'

Martine looked small in the saggy armchair that Tomsk normally curled up in. She perched on the edge with her knees neatly together, and her hands clasped in her lap.

A lifetime of Pilates, I thought, would never give me posture like that.

I made a pot of tea (there were two teapots, left over from unsuccessful attempts to teach the au pairs proper British beverage preparation) and put it on a tray with some of the gingersnaps left over from Allen's tin.

Martine sat, holding the cup in her hands, and didn't speak immediately. I didn't hurry her. I sensed this was going to be one of those conversations where my job was to listen, not contribute much. Fortunately, I'd had a lot of practice lately.

'Beth,' she said eventually, 'have you ever had a soulmate? Someone who really understands you. Better than you understand yourself?'

Had I? No. Not even Fraser; even at our best, there were things I hadn't told him, things I didn't want him to know about me. And clearly there'd been more of an understanding gap than I'd wanted to see. Mali had been a good friend at university, when life was straightforward, and I supposed Ashley and I had weathered some pretty bad times together. But to have a proper soulmate you needed to open up that secret hatch to your vulnerabilities, and I'd always kept mine firmly sealed. Adolescence was the time for making forever friends; like horse-riding or skiing, you never quite threw yourself into it in later life, for fear of injury. I didn't want anyone, least of all cruel teenagers, to see the chaos, emotional and literal, that Mum and I lived in. It was preferable to be thought weird at school, rather than *known* to be the child of a woman who sometimes didn't wash for a week.

'No,' I said. *Not yet.* 'Have you?'

I already knew the answer to this. She knew I knew.

I was expecting her to start explaining about the blackcurrant-picking but she didn't; she crossed her legs, and changed tack again, as if she couldn't get comfortable in her own story. 'Did Fraser ever tell you anything about my family?'

'Just that you were born here, you and Ray were childhood sweethearts. And that you two bought this house when you were first married, and Jackie was born in—'

'Not our family. *My* family. Fraser's grandparents.'

'Not really. I guess he felt it was insensitive to talk too much about his family, when he knew I didn't really have one.' I thought that was pretty gracious of me, to be honest.

Martine considered this, as if surprised Fraser would be so sensitive.

'Well. The first thing you need to know about my family is that business was everything to them. *Everything*,' she said. 'They came over from Ireland without a penny and they built a little empire from nothing. My father was completely consumed by it, as were his father and uncles, and their father, and so on. But unfortunately for Dad, he was an only child, and even more unfortunately, he only had me. No male heir. He made absolutely no secret of what a disaster that was. I mean, that sounds nonsensical now, doesn't it? It was ridiculous *then*, but some people still thought like that. And yet the top champagne houses were run by women – Bollinger, Pommery, Clicquot. How hard could it be to run a high-street wine merchant's?'

'Stop a minute,' I said, processing this new information. 'Longhampton Cellars is *your* family business?'

'Of course.' She seemed surprised that I didn't know. 'That's why the house label has the lions and the castle on it – it's the O'Shaughnessy crest. A total affectation, but that was my grandfather's idea. He was the one who hustled and hustled for the royal warrant.'

Why had I always assumed it had been Ray's family business? He'd always spoken as if it was – talking proudly about '*our* place on the high-street tradition' and '*our* long connection with the Board of Trade'.

'Anyway, we weren't all armchair psychologists back then, so I didn't know I was growing up in a "toxic environment" of "repressive misogyny",' Martine added helpful air hooks, 'I just sensed from a young age that I wasn't what anyone had hoped for.' She shook her head. 'I did my best to make my father happy. I worked as hard as I could at school, I played the piano, I grew my hair long because Daddy thought girls should have long hair, I did everything I possibly could to get any tiny crumb of approval from him. I didn't realise until I was about fifteen that I was wasting my time, and that there was no way I could make him happy, because I *wasn't a boy*, but by then my whole personality was based around pleasing other people. School, orchestra, pony club. I tried my hardest at everything, and everyone made fun of me because of it.' She paused. 'I didn't like myself much either. I always felt out of place.'

I felt so sorry for her. Even now, Martine's shoulders were hunching. I'd never seen her like this.

'But then I met someone who made me feel like there might be a different Martine. I found a soulmate.'

A small smile touched her face, remembering, and her whole demeanour changed. I nodded, not wanting to say the wrong thing.

'Kathleen and I came from very different backgrounds, but inside we were like two peas in a pod. I'd never had a friend like her – well,' she corrected herself, 'I'd never had friends, not real friends. I knew lots of *people* because my parents were part of that 'black-tie dinner with the mayor' set, always having awful sherry parties to collect people like Happy Families cards, but no one I could really *talk* to. Be completely honest with. That was the big thing Kathleen and I had in common: both of us secretly wanted to be someone else.'

'Who did Kathleen want to be?'

'*Someone.* She didn't want to settle down at seventeen with the boy down the road. She didn't want a job in the factory, or a baby. She didn't know what she could do though, because no one in her family had ever been further than the next town. I don't want to sound dismissive; people didn't have many options then. When I met her, she'd left school but she had such a hungry brain, always asking questions. Why this, why not that? But she never thought of anything like that for herself. Whereas I had all those advantages, and I never thought to ask, *why not*?'

Martine took a sip of her tea, gathering up the threads for the next part of her story. 'So. I'd persuaded my parents that I should go to university and they'd agreed because I think my father thought it made him look modern, having a daughter studying for a degree, even if I wasn't going to do anything with it. And I didn't see why Kathleen shouldn't have the same opportunity, since she was so much cleverer than I was, so I helped her apply for a course at a poly nearby.'

'How did her family feel about that?'

'Not keen. Didn't want her getting ideas. But we went, and it was . . .' Martine paused, suddenly lost for words. Or maybe overcome with too many words. 'It was the most wonderful time of my life. Everywhere was exciting in the sixties, everything was new and different and *changing*, but to be in a city – you can't imagine how exhilarating that was for country girls like us. We loved pop music, soul music, and it felt like there was music everywhere, all the time. Kathleen and I had digs in an absolute madhouse, sharing with actors and gay couples and runaways – oh, it was such fun. The boys would make us put on plays, and my God, how we *laughed*. We laughed all the time. I didn't have to please anyone, or disappoint anyone – I was free to make mistakes. We got up to some crazy antics. No one remembered a thing in the morning, and if people did remember, they never held it against you. They certainly never took pictures, the way they do now.'

'Martine!' I said, pretending to be shocked. 'What are you *saying*?'

She gave me an arch look; I could tell she was delighted to have shocked me. 'Oh, everyone was very live and let live in those days. Not like now. It wasn't quite Woodstock but . . . We had such adventures, me and Kathleen. Two peas in a pod. Two halves of a whole.' She smiled sadly. 'Soulmates. I adored her. I absolutely adored her.'

There was something about the way she said that, that made me want to ask if they'd been more than just best friends. I didn't want to ask, and if she didn't want to say, I wasn't going to press her, but there was a softness, a dreaminess, in the way she spoke that made me yearn for something I'd never felt myself, and that made me think it must have been love.

'So what happened?' I asked, even though I knew. Would Martine's version be different? Was that what she wanted to tell me, to set the record straight?

'Dad didn't mind me reading books for a year or two, but he didn't see it as something that should distract a woman from her real vocation in life, which was to get married – and, in my case, produce a son. I think he'd have forgiven me for being a girl if I could have popped out a grandson quickly enough. And I realise now, my mother probably wanted that even more than I did.' Martine sighed, and looked more sympathetic. 'Looking back, my mother was "ill" quite a lot. As I got older I realised . . . well, Dad was determined to get that heir. The closer I got to graduating the more they kept dropping hints about friends' sons, and where did I want my twenty-first birthday party? I didn't want a twenty-first birthday party! It was the sixties, I was going to sit-ins and raves and whatnot. But they went on and on, and eventually I said yes, just to shut them up, and that's where I met Ray.'

'Did your parents invite him?'

'Of course. His parents knew mine through some society or other – the Hendersons had connections across the county.

They knew the businessmen, the farmers, the sportsmen, the drinkers, everyone. That was important to Dad. He loved the social side of the business most, I think, guild dinners with the mayor, golf-club dinner-dances. To be fair,' she conceded, 'Ray was ambitious and likeable and good at his job.'

Martine frowned. 'Anyway, my parents kept throwing us together, and I kept trying to make it clear – politely – that I wasn't interested. To put them off a bit longer, I persuaded them to let me do a teacher-training course. Kathleen was working by then, for a radio station, terribly hip, and we were having so much *fun*. Why would I want to be with some boring man who'd want me to stay at home, and ask permission to breathe, when I could be having the time of my life, with someone who made me feel anything was possible?'

'And did you . . .' I didn't know how to ask this. It was impossibly delicate but I sort of felt she wanted me to. 'Did you want to marry *anyone*?'

Martine looked me in the eye. 'I didn't want to live any other way than the way I was right then. With Kathleen.'

They were lovers. They had to be.

She was rushing through the painful part. 'I'll cut to the chase, because this isn't nice. And I never ever want you to repeat this to Fraser or Jackie, but you need to know to make sense of what happened next. Ray proposed at my parents' Boxing Day sherry party. He went down on one knee in front of the Christmas tree, in front of everyone. I had to say yes. What else could I do?'

I winced. 'Public proposals are creepy. I don't know why they're supposed to be romantic. More like coercive control.'

'I know. I *know*. Dad obviously knew it was going to happen – he was pouring champagne for everyone and being congratulated as if I was some prize heifer he'd just auctioned off.' She looked furious, even now. 'When everyone had gone home I told Ray that I wasn't going to give up my course, that I wanted to get a job. It was something Kathleen had made me realise – I needed to *do* something. I needed to make a difference. I thought that might put him off, make him think he could find a more amenable wife somewhere else.' Martine bit her lip. 'That didn't go down well. My mother came into my room that night, demanding to know why I wanted to put my father in an early grave? Dad was more subtle – he said he'd only ever wanted the best for me, and that marrying Ray would not only ensure the family business stayed in safe hands, but would make him happy. Didn't I want to make him happy? Wasn't that the biggest difference I could make?'

'Of course you wanted to make him happy.'

'Right.' Martine exhaled, and stared up at the ceiling. 'But I'd promised Kathleen I'd move to London with her when I graduated. She'd already been offered work there, and she'd turned it down because she wanted to wait for me. She wanted us to go together. And you know, we were *feminists* – we weren't going be some man's little lady. We were going to live together in London, have a house of our own, the way we wanted it. We even talked about having the acting boys live with us, as lodgers. We had it all worked out.'

'So what did you do?'

'I tried to please everybody. I went home as little as I could, I kept Ray's ring – which was actually my grandmother's – in a bag and only wore it once I was on the train. And then I'd reapply my lashes and black liner on the train back to Kathleen, and go to protests and drink beer, and argue about books, and sing, and just . . .' She ran out of words. '*Live*.'

'But didn't she guess something was going on?'

'Maybe. Maybe she didn't want to see it. I thought if I said nothing, I wasn't lying. But that's not how it works, is it? If you say nothing, the only person you're hurting is yourself.' Martine looked miserable. 'Because it means you're not worth telling the truth to.'

'So what happened?' I was fully invested now. I didn't want the final explosion to be anything less than cataclysmic but I felt guilty for thinking that. This wasn't a story, it was Martine's life.

Her head dropped. 'You've read it. That's what happened. I can't argue with a word of it. I should have made a decision, but in the end, Dad staged a kidnapping and that was that. I was so ashamed of how badly I'd behaved that I had what you'd now call a breakdown, but I convinced myself I didn't have a choice. Then my mother genuinely did fall ill, so I had to look after her, and then I suppose I just resigned myself to the mess I'd made. Ray and I got married. I had four wonderful children, three clever, talented girls and eventually the son that Ray wanted as much as my dad had. The son who didn't want to take on the family business, after all that!' She laughed, a quick and humourless bark. 'Can you imagine? The irony! All that, just to sell it off anyway! Some might say that was my punishment.'

'For what?'

'For hurting the one person who truly cared about me. Who just wanted me to be me.' Martine blinked, startled by the sound of her own words. I wondered if this was the first time she'd ever spoken that thought aloud.

'But couldn't you just have said no to your dad? It sounds so Victorian, forcing daughters to marry for the sake of the family business.'

'It sounds ridiculous now, but that was still the "what Dad says, goes" era, just about. I was brought up to believe that family, and the family business, was who I was. *All* I was. And deep down, I just wasn't as strong as Kathleen. I loved my parents, I didn't want to let them down.' She leaned forward, making sure I didn't misunderstand. 'Don't get me wrong, I'm not saying I've lived a miserable life. Ray was a decent man, kind. I . . .' She looked askance. 'I didn't mind that side of things. As my mother said, one has to take the rough with the smooth.'

'But he wasn't Kathleen.'

'No one could have been. I remember thinking, the night before I got married, I'd just have to keep looking forwards, like the old drayhorse. Dabinett, she was called. Darling old thing. She had embroidered blinkers for special occasions, navy velvet with gold hops. Couldn't go backwards. Dad said she was too stupid to go any direction but forwards, but I'm not so sure. Poor Dabinett.'

Martine stared down at the floor and the pain in her eyes was unbearable.

'And Kathleen never contacted you? Or you her?'

She shook her head. 'I didn't want to. I knew she'd be successful. I knew she'd achieve big things. I wanted *everything* for her, more than I wanted for myself, but I didn't want to see in case it made me resent what I had. I missed her so much it burned a hole in me. I tried to carve a role for myself where I could, and I found tremendous fulfilment in being a good mother. If I was a bit pushy on occasion – and I know what Fraser will have said to you! – it was only to make sure the girls were never limited the way I was. Not that I'd ever want them to know that, so please don't tell them.'

Fraser's tales of his mother's relentless tiger parenting, before it was even a thing, made a sad kind of sense now. 'I won't repeat any of this,' I said quickly.

'I just wish—' she started, and stopped. 'I just wish I'd had the chance to *do* something for myself.'

'It's not too late,' I said. 'Write another book. Go travelling. Spend some of that money your family made.'

'Ah! That's the other thing. I can't! I probably shouldn't tell you this, but why not, it's the cherry on the cake – when Fraser told us he didn't want to carry on the business, Ray sold it, as you know, to a chain. Didn't consult me, of course. Anyway, he struck a very good deal, largely because of wine my father had laid down, bought himself a Jaguar. But unbeknownst to any of us, he put the bulk of the money in a trust, one that can only be spent on charitable works in the community, and it's called, wait for it, the Raymond Henderson Foundation.'

'What? But it's your family money! Shouldn't it be the O'Shaughnessy Foundation?' I was amazed at the casual arrogance of Ray Henderson. Although not totally surprised. I could see Fraser doing similar.

'Quite! I only found out recently, when the solicitor went through the financial arrangements with me. And now Jacqueline's asking me which park bench we should order for Dad, when I think what he had in mind was something more in line with the Albert Memorial. I'm afraid it's made me rather furious. Too furious to know what to do.'

'I think you should tell Jackie some of this,' I said. Not the Kathleen parts, obviously. 'She's worried about you. If she knew why . . .'

'No.' Martine's eyes were adamant. 'The last thing I want to do is diminish their memories, Beth. Ray adored them, and he was a good father. You saw last weekend how they feel about our marriage – it's what holds our family together.'

But at what cost to you, even now, I wanted to say? At what cost to them? But this wasn't my business.

Martine got up to go, and I walked down the stairs with her. She paused at the door, took my hands in hers, and said, 'Thank you, Beth.'

'What on earth for?'

'For listening. And for keeping an eye on me. I know that's what you've been doing – you're more discreet than Jacqueline.'

'You're welcome,' I said, and she squeezed my hands.

'I've always been very fond of you, you know,' she said. 'You reminded me a lot of myself, constantly worrying what people thought. If I pushed you too, when you and

Fraser were together, I'm sorry. I just wanted you to believe in yourself.'

'You didn't,' I said.

I mean, she *had*, but now I saw why. It was quite touching.

Martine's face was sad, and serious. 'You deserve more, Beth. Much more than I suspect Fraser could ever give you.' Then she turned to go, and I realised there was one major question I hadn't asked.

'Martine!' I called. 'Wait! I wanted to ask who . . .'

She turned, and said clearly into the night air, 'Kay.'

Then she smiled again, more sadly, and went back to her empty, beautiful house.

Chapter twenty-seven

At his own request, Hugh Lloyd's funeral was a quiet affair – family-only cremation followed by a scattering of his ashes at sea – but Lewis arranged a celebration of Hugh's life at Rosemount a few days after, to which I was invited.

Kay, via Pam, asked if I would read one of his Story of My Life stories, and invited me round to discuss which would be most appropriate from the dozens that I had in my notebook. I wasn't sure whether Kay really wanted me to read something, or whether she just wanted a chance to talk to me on my own. It was a strange conversation to start, given my unusual God-like insight into her past lives.

The night after Martine and I spoke, she had written a letter which she'd asked me to take to Kay at Rosemount the next day. I duly did, and then, later that afternoon, at her request, I'd dropped Martine off at Rosemount in person. She looked nervous but immaculately dressed, and she was carrying something in a gift bag. I don't know how long she stayed; she said she'd call a taxi to collect her. In a funny role reversal, I hovered anxiously by the kitchen window, checking to make sure she'd got home safely, and finally, at eleven, her light went on and Martine called me, briefly, to let me know she was back.

I don't know what was said, and I thought it diplomatic to wait to be told. The following day, I got an update of sorts when I returned from Tomsk's afternoon walk to find a bottle of blackcurrant cordial and a bottle of champagne on my doorstep.

When I drove over to Rosemount to talk to Kay, I found her sitting at the table in her room, furiously writing on a laptop. Her fingers were flying – almost as percussive as her piano playing – and she was frowning in concentration. I envied her touch-typing speed.

'Beth! Come in!' She gestured at one of the mid-century armchairs that made her and Hugh's apartment look unusually *Mad Men*; every other apartment I'd been in was styled in the comfortable tradition of 'generic British soap opera'. 'I'm collating some notes for Lewis, he wanted some stories to tell about Hugh. I asked Susan if she had any good ones and she's sent me some corkers that even I haven't heard.' She paused, and frowned at the screen. 'I'm not sure they're entirely suitable, but that's so Hugh.'

'Susan?'

'Hugh's second wife, Jonathan's mum. He married her in . . .' Kay glanced down at the laptop again, 'Seventy-two? His first wife, Theresa, died in seventy-one. Better get that right! I don't think there was an overlap.'

'Hugh never mentioned he'd been married before.' Hugh and Kay had that comfortable companionship that I'd assumed had been formed over decades of marriage. I thought of all the stories Hugh had recounted; not once had he mentioned any woman other than Kay. Although, thinking about it, most of them had been about his professional experiences, or his later life. There was a sort of gallantry about that, I thought. I wondered if that was why Kay had felt she had to keep her own memories so private.

She read my expression. 'Hugh wasn't the sort to dwell on things that didn't work out. He loved Jonathan, and that's what mattered, as far he was concerned.'

I told Kay how very sorry I was for her loss, and how much I'd enjoyed the entertaining afternoons with her and Hugh, feeling part of that exciting world. I'd have loved to have worked with Hugh, although probably not as his accountant. 'You both made that time come alive for me. I'll never see any of those adverts the same way again!'

'Well, it was lovely for us too.' She put her laptop to one side. 'There's something comforting about sharing your memories with a new generation. I mean, not the "feeling like a history project" part, that's quite sobering when you still feel thirty inside, but feeling as if there was some significance to what you did with your youth. It reminded us what fun we had. Although as Hugh said after you'd gone, we should tell these youngsters about the bloody dull parts too. Can't have them thinking it was all expense accounts and speed boats, as he put it.' She paused. 'Although in his case, it *was* mainly expense accounts and speed boats.'

Kay was wearing a black silk shirt and black trousers, so simple they had to be expensive. The monochrome was broken up with a pair of leopard-print loafers that reminded me of Martine's gold lamé slippers, the ones Jackie forbade her to wear in case she fell down the stairs. Pam had told me she was 'bearing up well'; she looked tired, but philosophical.

'Did you enjoy the story project too?' I wasn't quite brave enough to ask directly, but Kay knew what I was getting at.

'I did. I think Hugh wanted to get his best stories down before he forgot them, but your questions kept me awake at night. They made me think about what my life would look like, from the perspective of someone who hadn't lived through the things I had. What the big turning points actually were – not the job changes, or the awards, but the moments when *I* changed, as a person. Your perspective on what's important shifts, you know, as you get older and you start to understand yourself, warts and all. You can't always see the turning points at the time.' She gave me a knowing look. 'Sometimes you just need to push on. Onwards and upwards, you know? I hadn't allowed myself to think about some things for years, but once those memories were bouncing around again, in my mind's eye, I had to write them down. To stop them bouncing around.'

'What did you want me to do with them?'

Again, the amused half-smile. 'Nothing, to begin with. Just *have* them, so I knew that those happy days were alive in another memory. Like uploading them to the Cloud. I wasn't sure if she . . .' For a moment, Kay's composure cracked, but she carried on. 'But it was important to me to write them down, and acknowledge that those moments changed my life. If you were creating a big picture of human history at Rosemount, so you could understand my generation better, and have a record of who we were, and *why*, then I wanted those moments to be a part of it.'

I wanted to ask if Hugh had known about Martine but I hesitated. Even when Kay had pulled back the curtain on her most private, precious memories, I knew she hadn't been talking to me. They'd always been for Martine.

Kay tilted her head, as if she could read my mind. 'I was nearly fifty when I met Hugh. We'd both lived what you'd call interesting lives, but we were the sort of people who looked forward, not back. Broad brushstrokes, as he put it. There were things we didn't talk about, but it didn't matter because – well, you met Hugh, we had more than enough to talk about. It used to make us laugh, you know, when we first moved in here, and everyone treated us the same way they treated Bill and Linda, as if we were a venerable old married couple. People do assume, when you're older, that you've been together since the year dot. We kept our own flats for years, because he was such a fusspot, and I'm a night owl – we only got married because he'd booked a holiday somewhere you needed a wedding ring, or else. We were sixty-eight. It was quite a joke, being the oldest couple at the registry office. It made us happy, being unconventional, kept us in touch with our groovy selves, he used to say.' Kay suddenly looked sad, properly bereft. 'We mightn't have been joined at the hip like Linda and Bill, but I can't tell you how much I'll miss Hugh. He was the greatest company you could imagine. He could make any room feel like a party.'

'We'll all miss him,' I said. Which was the truth.

We discussed which of Hugh's stories I would read at the celebration; Kay decided on a touching memory Hugh had shared about seal-watching in Pembrokeshire after his father died, rather than one of his more 'of its time' racy anecdotes, which we agreed only he could do justice to. I asked her if she wanted to continue with the Story of My Life project, because I genuinely wanted to hear more of her stories about elbowing her way through the boys'-club atmosphere of PR in the seventies and eighties, and she seemed genuinely pleased that I wanted to know.

'And I suppose I could carry on playing the piano for the singalongs.' Kay arched an eyebrow. 'Hugh hated Andrew Lloyd Webber, so the first time we sing *Cats*, it'll be for him.' I didn't like to tell her there might not be many more, if Eric Alexander had his way.

We didn't mention Martine again, but as I was leaving I noticed one small but significant change to Kay's room: in amongst the condolence cards, the solitary black Staffordshire dog that I'd never really noticed before had now moved on the main shelf – where it was united with its partner.

'Beth?' Lewis called me as I was almost out of the front door. 'Have you got a moment?'

I followed him into his office, where he left the door just ajar so it was technically open, as per his 'open door' promise, but not invitingly so.

'I just wanted to update you on the plans.' Even though we were alone, he mouthed the word 'plans' in the same way I mouthed the word 'walk' in front of Tomsk. 'We're at eighty per cent of the estimated deposit target!'

'Really?' Kevin Allison, the broker, was exploring the financing options for Lewis; it was going to be tough, Kevin had warned him, but he 'never liked to say impossible'.

(I liked to say impossible a lot with clients. Managing expectations, then occasionally exceeding them, had been a big part of my strategy.)

Lewis nodded. 'Ellie's been hunting out funding from the most extraordinary places. I've had residents walk in here with family members, saying how heartbroken they'd be to see Rosemount close, and offering investment then and there. Actual cheques. It's incredible. *Incredible.*'

It was perfectly credible to me that some people would put a cash price on not having their father-in-law and his banjolele installed in their spare room indefinitely, I thought, but didn't say anything.

'I'm waiting for an update from Kevin.' He gestured at the phone on his desk. 'He said he'd call before close of play today.'

'And you have to let Eric know about your business plan when? Friday?' Two days away.

He nodded, and raised double crossed fingers.

'It's a strong business plan.' I'd double-checked the figures and Lewis had sprinkled the copy with some top-quality management-speak that even Christian would love. But it was also realistic, reinforced with proposals for community outreach, history projects with local schools, gardening schemes and so on. Lewis had poured his heart into it, as well as his business experience. It couldn't have been more Lewis Levison if he'd attached a moustache comb to the front cover.

'I couldn't have done it without you,' he said sincerely.

'Don't be daft.' He'd said that before, and I didn't know why – all I'd done was make some suggestions. It probably hadn't needed the three sessions we'd spent with our heads together in the library; we could have finished it in one afternoon, if Lewis hadn't kept having ideas about memorial gardens and therapeutic choirs, and we hadn't kept going down conversational rabbit holes about mug cakes and tandems. And just . . . sharing some long looks.

I'd been having some thoughts about Lewis. They crept up on me, and were all the more disorientating for their surprise quality. Our last session on the business plan had taken place on a warm afternoon, and Lewis had rolled up his shirtsleeves, as if jokily indicating the seriousness of the task in hand. Something about the way he did it, the brisk folding action, and his strong, tanned forearms, gave me a giddy lurch in the pit of my stomach. His forearms! Had *I* started to think like Isabella the Victorian portrait painter now?

I changed the subject, unable to look at Lewis and feel what I was feeling about his forearms at the same time. 'Any news on Linda?' I asked. 'And how's Bill?'

'Oh, Linda's—' Lewis started, and then the phone rang.

'Might be Kevin,' I said. 'Better answer it.'

Seeing me about to leave, Lewis made a 'wait!' sign as he picked up. 'Lewis Levison! Ah, *Kevin*, hello!'

I didn't want to put him off by staring, so I checked my phone for work emails. Christian had accepted my resignation, and I had so much outstanding holiday that I could have stopped then and there, but I wanted to make sure I wasn't leaving clients high and dry. Quite a few of my clients had been gratifyingly distraught at my news, and if I'd wanted to go freelance, I could probably have set up a decent roster of private individuals, but after deploying my new strategy – asking myself aloud, 'Beth, what do *you* want to happen next?' instead of immediately asking someone else – I'd decided a clean break was what I needed.

I was faintly aware that Lewis hadn't spoken for a while, so I looked up to see him standing at his desk, staring out over my head, stricken.

My heart flipped over. What had happened? What had Kevin said?

'What?' I mouthed.

He shook his head. 'Yes, I appreciate that. Yes, but we are about to be reinspected and I'm very hopeful that . . . No, well, of course I can't guarantee it, but I'm confident that . . . No, OK, I see.' A long pause. A frown. A rub of the face.

God, this was awful! What was Kevin *saying*?

'OK. Well, I appreciate the time you've taken to explore every avenue, and if anything changes then I'd . . . Fair enough. No. OK. Well, thanks again for your time, Kevin!' he finished on a note of positivity that was evidence of his manners, if not his acting skills.

Lewis hung up the phone and we stared at each other across his desk.

'It's a no,' he said, somewhat redundantly.

Before I knew what I was doing, I was across the room and wrapping my arms around him in a hug. It seemed the only possible response to the desolation on Lewis's face.

'You gave it your best shot,' I insisted, into the shoulder of his suit.

Lewis's arms wrapped around me, one sudden, eloquent squeeze, pulling me very close: I breathed in the warm, clean smell of his skin under that disarmingly attractive aftershave and was suddenly, acutely, aware of the sensation of my skin touching his, my forehead against his neck.

His neck was smooth, and warm, and I could feel the pulse in his throat.

Stop it, I told myself, as the tingles spread through me. This was absolutely the worst time to have thoughts like this. The poor man. This was the end of his job, maybe his career. Stop it, Beth.

I pulled away, just as he did too.

'Sorry,' said Lewis, rather thickly, 'I was just . . . I'm disappointed. Not just for me, for everyone.'

'Me too.' I fussed with my hair to break up the tension, and it was a good job I did, because at that moment, Pam knocked on the door once – a very cursory knock that might lead a cynical mind to think she'd been listening behind the door for the end of the phone call – and burst straight in.

'So? Have you heard from the mortgage broker yet?' Her eyes were bright with hope, and I knew this was the cruellest part of all for Lewis. He'd let his team believe he could do it, he'd basked in their confidence, and now he had to let them down. They weren't going to get their *Wonderful Life* ending after all.

Lewis glanced across at me, and I knew he didn't want me to see this painful conversation.

But I was here for him. I was going to stay, no matter what.

I gave him an imperceptible nod of support, and he turned back to her.

'Pam,' he said calmly. 'It's not great news. Sit down.'

On my way home, I got a call from Zara, the world's most lackadaisical estate agent, to inform me I finally had a moving-in date for my new flat.

'The tenants' sale has completed,' she trilled, 'so they're moving out this week, and it'll be ready for you as soon as it's been signed off our end.'

What? My head spun. 'When did that happen? It's very short notice.'

'I left messages,' Zara insisted unconvincingly. 'I mean, I *think* they were on your phone . . .'

I had had no messages. Whatever, the deep-cleaners would be going in at the end of the week, the same day as Lewis's deadline, and I could move the following Monday.

I should have been thrilled, but I wasn't. Even if I wasn't drained from that meeting with Lewis, the thought of moving thirty miles away from the Wild Dog Café and its lemon tarts, from the municipal gardens, from the shops on the high street, from Rosemount, Lewis and Martine – it gave me that dank 'end of the holiday' sadness. Not only were Tomsk and I on nodding terms with nearly every dog on our routes, but I'd lined up meetings with a local nursery chain and a farming co-operative, both looking for an accountant. My therapeutic massage course was starting the following week, and Rachel at the rescue had grabbed me for some volunteer sessions; the post-walk bacon sandwiches, she assured me, were worth it alone. Longhampton was starting to feel like home.

But, I reminded myself, turning into Coleridge Drive, this wasn't my home, was it? It was Fraser's home. He was the reason I'd come here, and he'd always be part of the story if I stayed. If I was going to take control of my own narrative, I needed to strike out on my own.

I parked outside number thirteen and sat for a moment, taking a long look at the house I was going to miss so much.

The funny thing was, Fraser wasn't even the first thing I thought of now when I saw this house: I thought of Martine's chatty late-night calls, the blackbirds singing in the garden, the way the roses smelled sweeter last thing at night.

I'd come here hoping to bump into Fraser, but it had been bumping into Martine that had changed everything. It was Martine I'd miss the most.

I wondered how I should tell her about my impending move. It maybe wasn't a great time for her to be on her own; hopefully she and Kay would find their own way back to one another, and their memories and their special connection, but maybe that road would be rocky. Maybe it wouldn't lead anywhere at all. I was the only other person who knew – if there were tears or accusations, or doubts and distress, how would Jackie interpret that?

I thought of Martine sharing her life story with me surrounded with her family's boxes of junk, how her face had lit up, then darkened, as she talked. She still wanted to do something, to be important in her own right. And she still could, but not if she was trapped in the lies she'd told her family.

I felt cold. Was I abandoning Martine at the worst time?

'Beth,' I said aloud, 'what do you want to happen now?'

I want to stay. I want Martine to fulfil her dreams. I want Lewis to save Rosemount.

And then it came into my head, fully formed.

'Oh!' I said, again aloud. Then, as the idea started to take solid shape, and I began to panic that this wasn't any of my business, and it might not work, and argh, how do you even suggest it, I made myself leave the car, knock on the door, and tell Martine straight away.

She didn't seem surprised to see me at the door, and ushered me into the sitting room, where the tea tray was out, and her laptop was open.

It was amazing to think that only a matter of weeks ago, I'd brought a panicking, frail old woman home, a woman who'd nearly fallen over the coffee table. The present Martine was in full technicolour, hair freshly blown out in that flattering bob, red lipstick in place, glasses on a chain around her neck. She'd returned to life. Her natural bustling bossiness had reasserted itself, in a good way.

'I know what you're going to say,' she said. 'It's about Rosemount, isn't it? The owners are putting it up for sale.'

'How did you know that?'

She looked momentarily self-conscious. 'Kathleen told me. No one's told her officially, I think they're trying to be kind to her after Hugh, but someone called Eunice Stafford's been holding meetings. It's such a shame. What's Lewis doing about it?'

'Between us, he's trying to form a company to buy it. But he's struggling to get funding because of the inspection failure.'

'Oh dear.'

I took a deep breath. My heart was racing, and there were parts of my brain yelling at me for doing something that might backfire, but I had to do it.

What if Fraser goes mad at you? What if Jackie accuses you of robbing them of their inheritance?

'Martine,' I said, 'you told me the other night that you wished you could do something that would change the world a little bit. Well, it might not be the whole world, but you could change everything for the residents at Rosemount.' I felt as if I were at the top of a diving board, looking down. A long way down. 'That money Ray put in trust for charitable projects – why don't you set up a charity and buy Rosemount, then run it as a not-for-profit operation?'

She looked at me, and said nothing.

Had I offended her? Had I gone too far? Was I being as bad as everyone else in her life, telling her what to do?

I thought of Lewis and pushed on, my heart hammering.

'Lewis won't be able to raise the money on his own. But his team believe in him, and the residents believe in him. And backed by someone like you, who really understands the area, he could make Rosemount a centre of excellence. You've got the ideal committee experience, you could direct the charity exactly as you wanted it. It would be your legacy.'

She put her glasses on, and regarded me through them. The stare went on for a minute, then more.

Oh God, I thought, I've overstepped.

Finally, she spoke. 'Is that possible?'

'Absolutely.' Ellie had investigated not-for-profit care homes; I'd read her printouts.

'And . . .' Martine hesitated. 'Do you think I could do it?'

I nearly laughed. 'Yes. I do. But you don't need me to tell you that.'

'I wouldn't want to be a figurehead,' Martine went on, as the idea slowly became a reality in the room. 'I'd have to be personally involved with strategy. I might end up there myself, after all, so I want to be sure Rosemount is somewhere I'd want to live.'

'You'd consider moving? Leaving Coleridge Drive?'

Martine made a 'yes/no' head movement, as if it was still an idea she was considering. 'I always hated the idea of being moved into one of those institutions, where I didn't know anyone, but everyone has to eat soup together and pretend to be interested in handbell ringing. But now I have a friend there . . .' A tiny twinkle. 'After all, I remember living in a shared house with a lot of strangers and it was wonderful.'

I was reminded of Martine's expression, when she talked about 'the cherry on the cake' of Ray's betrayal, corralling her inheritance and making a trust in his own name. Well, that topped it. That she could use that trust to spend the rest of her life living with the woman she'd had to give up – perfect.

'I have one condition, though,' she said. 'I'd like you to be a trustee. I need someone I can, well, *trust.* Someone who understands the numbers, but also . . .' She hesitated. 'Also the people involved. Could I persuade you to do that?'

It was my turn to consider, but only for a second.

'Yes, Martine,' I said. 'I'd love to.'

Chapter twenty-eight

The Martine Henderson who called me at five past nine the following morning, to inform me that my presence was required at her solicitor's 'at two on the dot, and, Beth, please don't be late – he's squeezing us in as a special favour because we do *not* have a lot of time to get this arranged', was the Martine I remembered from my early days with Fraser: a strong, politely fierce, Arpège-scented wind that blew your clothes straight and hustled you along the pavement at pace.

Somehow, in the hours between deciding she was going to set up her own charity to save Rosemount for Longhampton's golden-age community, and my opening the car door for her, she'd amassed and processed the detailed information required to instruct her solicitor to put things in motion, most of which she relayed to me as I drove to the meeting. Her lipstick was immaculate, her suede shoes were pointy, her attitude was so confidently propulsive Christian would have offered her a job on the spot. My job, probably.

But, to be fair, this Martine did at least say please, and thank you so much for making time to do this, and complimented me on my hastily assembled 'agreeing to be a trustee for a charity' outfit – reassurance I gratefully accepted, because I don't mind admitting that I was somewhat daunted by the scale of what we were about to undertake, even if it had been my idea to begin with.

Martine, however, was not daunted in the slightest.

'I've also asked Jacqueline to act as trustee,' she told me, checking through her paperwork, paperclipped and presorted. 'She's got masses of committee experience, so she'll be able to tell me what to do for once, which I suspect she'll enjoy. She got terribly emotional on the phone, talking about Ray's legacy and how proud he'd be, the two of us working together in his memory and so on.' Her expression remained neutral. 'She agrees that this'll be little more memorable than a park bench.'

'Did you explain about the funding? And why it's important for *you* to be in charge of this?' That was a diplomatic way of putting it, I thought. Quite the tip of a conversational iceberg. But it was a conversation that needed to be had.

'I said her father had tied up the money from the business sale in trust for charity. Not quite *all* the ins and outs, though – let's get this out of the way first.' Martine shuffled some papers. 'However, you'll be pleased to hear it's not going to be the Ray Henderson Foundation. Or the O'Shaughnessy Foundation. I've decided to rename it the Cellars Trust. I thought that was fair.'

'And very appropriate,' I said, trying to lighten the mood, 'given that the residents are ageing like fine wines.'

'But I will speak to her. And the other three.' Martine glanced across the car. 'You know, it's never easy to see one's family through someone else's eyes, Beth, especially when you're forced to confront behaviours you'd rather ignore – including one's own. You've made me realise how much we've been held back by things that shouldn't matter anymore.'

'Please don't pin this on me!' I said, only half-joking.

'But none of this would have happened without you. No, don't try to shrug it off – if you hadn't bumped into me in town, I wouldn't have invited you to stay, and if you hadn't been staying, I wouldn't have known about the story project at Rosemount, and if I hadn't . . . Well, it's quite a sequence of events, but I believe we've ended up in a good place.'

She patted my knee. 'And you were the inciting incident! The call to action!'

I smiled, but I didn't say what I was thinking, which was: I wasn't the inciting incident. Fraser was.

I won't lie: I had moments when I thought about Fraser and went hot and cold, then hot and queasy. Sometimes cold and sad. It had only been a matter of days, after all. What's that they say about the five stages of grief? There must be at least five stages of relationship break-up; I'd done denial, anger, and bargaining ages ago, but now I was ploughing through disorientation (so many of my future assumptions collapsed overnight, leaving me facing weird gaps), as well as self-recrimination (what was wrong with me that I'd allowed myself to think like that?). Even if I was finally crawling into the healing phase, after five long years, it still felt exhausting, recognising how much I'd have to rebuild from scratch. In my darker moments, the craven thought crept across my mind that it'd be so much easier if Fraser admitted he'd made a big mistake.

I hadn't heard from him since I'd left him at the Wild Dog Café. He hadn't returned to Martine's, and I didn't know what, if anything, he'd told his family about his new life. It was unsatisfactory. I didn't like loose ends – Fraser had remained front and centre in my life for five years simply *by being* a loose end – but I was too scared to pull on this thread yet.

I sidled up to the issue slyly. 'Are you asking all the siblings to act as trustees?'

'Of course, but as usual, it's only Jacqueline who's come up trumps.' Martine was checking her make-up in the mirror. 'Cara says she's happy to do it remotely, Heather says she's not sure if she's eligible, goodness knows why, and I haven't even had a reply from Fraser. I know he's busy but even so.' I could see she was struggling to find an excuse for him.

'He must realise how significant it is to you.' I paused then added, 'I think that's quite rude, actually.'

'It is, isn't it?' It burst out of Martine with startling force. 'I thought this was a good resolution to that unpleasantness about the Cellars, but no, he can't even be bothered to respond. I suppose he could be on holiday, or thinking about it, or . . .'

'No, it's rude. Not replying to you is rude. It's OK, Martine. You're allowed to be pissed off.'

I caught a tiny twitch at the corner of Martine's mouth; she pretended to look out of the window at a new cake shop, but – I saw it.

'I suppose it'll just have to be the women sorting things out,' she said. 'As per usual.'

Jackie was waiting for us at the solicitors' office, wearing shades and looking uncharacteristically shifty. 'No, no! Don't fuss! If anyone from school spots me, I'm in serious trouble,' she hissed, when Martine asked if she was expecting paparazzi.

'Darling!' Martine looked amused. 'Are you bunking off?'

'Yes, I am! I'm supposed to be in an English-language curriculum meeting right now. I told them I had an urgent legal matter to deal with. Which I suppose I do.' She peered at me over the sunglasses. 'Hello, Beth. Did you imagine you'd be signing up as a trustee to a charitable trust at the start of this week?'

I shook my head. I had worried Jackie might feel I'd overstepped. Crashing in your ex's mother's spare room was one thing; elbowing yourself into a place on the family charity board was another. 'I'm very honoured to be asked. I hope my financial background might be useful, but if you need to replace these initial trustees with more qualified people at a later date . . .'

'Certainly not,' said Martine. 'Think of your CV, Beth.'

Jackie regarded me for a moment, then rolled her eyes conspiratorially: a 'WTF? we'll have to discuss this later over a coffee' kind of look. She shouldered her bag. 'Come on, then, let's get this show on the road before Mum decides to buy a school too.'

Once we'd cleared the paperwork, the next step was the meeting with Eric Alexander to persuade him that selling Rosemount to a charitable trust looked better than selling it to property developers to be turned into luxury flats.

The strategy for this came from a seasoned PR expert. 'Lean on the optics. Pitch it as an organic marketing opportunity,' said Kay, when I found her in the library, doodling on the piano. 'Say you've found a tame journalist to write it up as positive exposure – "leading national care provider going above and beyond to help a grassroots charity launch a small-scale social enterprise", blah blah, "handing over the baton of tailored care to the community", and so on. They get to gloss over the fact that they were hanging their existing residents out to dry, they look like social pioneers, but still get their money.'

She paused. 'And if he's got any sense, Eric Alexander will realise that the same journalist placing a news feature about a charity being outbid by a property developer so old people are turfed out on to the street won't look great either.'

'Isn't that blackmail?'

Kay winked. 'I prefer to call it strategic manipulation.' She played a few dramatic Abba chords. 'I hear you're leading the sales pitch next week?'

Were there no secrets in this place? 'Who told you that?'

'A little bird. Good choice. I think you're the perfect person to do it.'

I wasn't sure about perfect, but I *was* the person leading the presentation to Eric Alexander. Lewis had immediately ruled himself out ('I do still technically work for Acorn Care Homes, you know . . .') and Martine refused ('I'm the same age as the people *in* here, I can't make it look as if I'm trying to buy a house for myself!'). In any case, I could tell she had that familiar bit between her teeth about pushing me to push myself, but this time though, she was pushing on an open door.

I wanted to do it. It had been my idea, born out of a genuine desire to protect something I cared about, and the harder everyone else worked to put the framework in place underneath, the more I wanted to do it justice.

That said, between my paranoid preparation and the general heightened atmosphere around the place, when the morning of the meeting finally dawned, my stomach was churning so badly I was convinced I'd got IBS.

Although I'd put on a confident front for Pam and Lewis, the niggling insecurities I'd been collecting for years silently gathered like swallows on phone wires, preparing for mass flight, sometimes dropping into my head as individual worries (What if I blanked on key figures? What if someone else had an accident while Eric was there?), sometimes flocking together in one smothering blanket of stress (What if Eric was just humouring me, a small-business accountant with zero experience of care homes, and told us he'd already done a deal?) I'd been having dreams about my mum, for the first time in ages. Dreams in which I asked her questions and she just smiled at me, and I knew I'd only ever hear my side of her story, and I woke up, dark and lost with aching.

I arrived far too early, having got up at five to bath and brush a bemused Tomsk – he'd been pressed into duty to demonstrate Rosemount's 'pets as therapy' programme. Pam was already up and about, looking dynamic in a navy-blue jumpsuit that was probably giving certain male residents flashbacks to their time in the RAF.

'I'm so nervous I've gone beyond nervous,' she said, offering me a bottle of homeopathic stress tablets, which I declined. I'd seen what mixing herbal medicine with espresso could do and I didn't want to tell Eric Alexander to fuck off by accident.

'You've no need to be nervous,' I told Pam. 'I mean, look at this place! It's spotless. It speaks for itself.'

Everything was gleaming. The cleaners had been working double shifts. Volunteers had raided their gardens (and Tesco) to create flower arrangements, and every corridor smelled light and bright. The whole place hummed with happy energy: Ellie's 'Do You Remember . . . ?' memory boards had been replenished with fresh photos of soap stars and discontinued chocolate bars, and there was something going on in every public room – but casually, as if every day was filled with optional enrichment activities. As we'd established in our strategy brainstormer – me, Lewis, Pam, Martine, Ellie, Nigel and Eunice, as the residents' reps – we wanted to convey a powerful impression of what might be lost if the home was sold for flats.

Lewis had agonised over how much he should be involved in the meeting with Eric. 'I don't want him to think I couldn't make this place work for Acorn, and yet I could suddenly make it work for an outside interest,' he explained. 'Best if we take the line that you want to carry on the sterling work Acorn has done, but sadly can longer continue to sustain in the current difficult climate. And I'm here to advise you on that.'

'But you'll stay if Martine buys it?'

'I'll have to wait to see if I'm offered a job.' He kept his face straight, but above his moustache, his eyes twinkled.

Lewis had been waiting with a strong coffee for me when I arrived – so God knows what time he'd got to work, or how much coffee he'd consumed himself – and nobly offered to take charge of Tomsk while I delivered Martine's pitch.

I thought this was brave, given both his nervousness around dogs, and his newly cleaned suit, and I told him so.

'Whatever I can do to help. I'm right behind you, Beth.' He'd gone into maximum efficiency mode, I could sense, but now I knew Lewis better, the nerves were there underneath. 'You're going to do a great job.'

'You're sure?'

Lewis nodded. 'You don't need me to tell you that. Do you want to run through some figures again?'

He'd only tested me on a few when Ellie skidded round the corner. 'Beth! Beth! I think he's here!'

I handed my coffee to her, parked Tomsk temporarily in Lewis's office, and brushed myself down as my heartbeat sped up.

You can do this, I told myself, as Lewis and I went to the front door to welcome Eric Alexander.

Lewis's boss was smaller than I'd expected, but apart from that, exactly as I'd anticipated from the sheaf of meticulously prepared research Nigel Callaghan had slipped me. ('Sure you're on top of this, but just in case. Old habits, and all that.')

Lewis introduced me – as Martine's head trustee and business advisor, no less – and we shook hands and exchanged pleasantries.

'I appreciate you're a busy man,' I said, my heart hammering, 'but before we start the meeting, I wonder if I can show you – very quickly! – some of the projects that have become such a vital part of the residents' experience here.'

That was Lewis's cue to excuse himself for a social care meeting, and, with one last secret squeeze of my arm, he left me to steer the ship.

Eric allowed me to escort him to the library, which was occupied by Kay and the ukulele orchestra, then to the dining room, currently playing host to a 1950s pop-up Italian coffee bar, complete with table jukeboxes, to the refurbished beauty salon which Pam's cousin Lesley, a hairdressing tutor at the further education college, had offered to staff, twice weekly, with volunteer students. Perms were, it turned out, back in.

As we passed through the various areas, I noted a general upswing in the standard of dress amongst the residents. Stan Walkingshaw was wearing his medallion but over a polo shirt. There was also an unusually high attendance rate in the morning activities, including the classical music hour, which usually only had two people, both asleep.

My phone vibrated in my pocket. While Pam was telling Eric about the magic of group singing, I checked it sneakily, in case Lewis was warning me of impending disaster, but it wasn't Lewis.

The floor fell away from under my feet.

It was Fraser. The first line of the message read **Hey Beth. *Really need to discuss*** but then it was cropped.

I stared at the screen in disbelief. Just seeing his name triggered an involuntary reaction: I'd willed him to text me for so long and now, there it was. Dark hysteria swirled in my chest. No no no. I didn't want to think about Fraser right now.

He's reaching out to you. He needs your help. This is all you dreamed of for years. Aren't you going to answer him?

'Beth?'

Pam was looking at me. 'Sorry!' I dragged on a smile and shoved the phone in my pocket. 'Shall we head back to the office, Eric? Are you ready for a cup of tea?'

Eric asked me whether the famous Rosemount ghost had made another reappearance, and I wasn't sure if he was joking or not. My balance had been thrown by Fraser's text; half of my brain was now focused on that – what it meant, whether I should reply – and I couldn't concentrate. Fraser's text had hurled a stone into the lovely clear pond of my preparation, stirring up old feelings of confusion and helplessness, despite my attempts to stay in control.

My phone vibrated again, as we approached the family conference room set up for our meeting, and again, I checked it, in case it was Lewis, but again, it was Fraser.

Beth, I really need your

'Oh God,' I said under my breath.

'Sorry?' Eric turned.

'Nothing!' I gestured towards the room, where Martine was waiting at the table. She gave me a quizzical look, which made me wonder if my confusion was so evident. As I was introducing them, my phone buzzed again – seriously? – and I bit my lip.

What happens next, Beth?

I felt the phone vibrate again. My armpits were damp with sweat. 'Sorry,' I said, as Eric took a seat. 'Before we begin, would you excuse me for one moment?'

He nodded, but checked his watch, and I felt a momentary panic.

Martine's quizzical look intensified. I tried to give her a reassuring smile, and slipped into the corridor, out of earshot.

I stared at my phone. Three messages now from Fraser. My finger hesitated over the screen.

Whatever it was must be urgent. Had he found out about the trust? Had something happened with Iwona? Did he want my advice about—

'It doesn't matter.'

I looked round quickly. The thought was so loud and clear I wasn't sure if I'd spoken it aloud. Had I?

I gripped the phone, as my brain held the thought in front of me like a huge placard.

It really didn't matter what Fraser wanted. Or what he wanted me to do. What anyone wanted me to do. This wasn't even really about Fraser, it was about letting other people push in front of me, in my own head.

I'd had the idea for this project. I'd set the wheels in motion. I was leading the meeting. I could make this happen. Was I going to let someone else derail it?

Yes, I'd had help from people who wanted this as much as I did, and yes, I'd asked for advice where I needed guidance, but ultimately this was down to me. *Me.*

I felt a sudden elation in my chest, as if all the swallows of stress gathered on the wires had simultaneously launched themselves skyward, lifting me with them.

Carefully I turned my phone off, placed it inside a brass plant holder where it could wait till later, and went back into the meeting room.

It was too quiet. A little frosty, even. The refreshment tray had been delivered but was sitting there, untouched.

'Tea, Eric?' I asked, picking up the teapot with a warm smile. 'I can't wait to talk to you about what a difference Rosemount's been making to the people of this town, and all the ideas we've got to pick up the baton and take it to another level, if you're willing to work with the Cellars Trust.'

'I'm all ears,' said Eric, and sat back with a custard cream.

And with that, I got my slide show started.

An hour later, we waved Eric off as his Bentley disappeared down the drive, and I let the adrenalin slowly dissipate.

I had done it. With some appropriate contributions from Martine, and subtle use of Nigel's briefing notes to push Eric's hot buttons (community, dignity, Newcastle FC), the meeting had gone from formal to, as Martine put it, 'positively chummy' by the end.

Once Eric had left, I retrieved my phone, turned it back on, and checked Fraser's messages. They were all, as I'd suspected, panicky questions about 'what Mum wants to talk about', asking me if I could 'test the waters'. He thought she'd found out about Iwona, not that she was trying to involve him in her new project, and I found myself thinking, God, how *old* is this man?

I told Martine that I thought Fraser had been trying to get in touch with her and left it at that.

Lewis reappeared from his office, covered in dog hair. Tomsk hadn't even been called upon to do his PAT thing, so he'd spent the morning on Lewis's sofa instead. 'How did it go?'

'I think it went well?' I lifted my crossed fingers, then thought, *no, own it*. 'Actually, no. It went *great*.'

Lewis grinned. 'Come outside, I want to talk to you about something.'

We walked out into the gardens, admiring the last flush of roses Lewis had coaxed out of the neglected beds, deep orange shading up through apricot to pale champagne.

(I asked him what his secret was. 'Chicken manure,' Lewis explained. 'And lots of it.')

When we got to the bench, dedicated to Hugh Lloyd 'and all who sail with him', he sat down, and patted the space next to him.

I sat down. Lewis seemed too serious. Was he going to tell me he'd been offered a job somewhere else, and couldn't stay? I felt woozy with dread. This project wouldn't work without Lewis. I tried to keep my voice light. 'So what is it? Is there something you didn't tell me about that meeting?'

'Beth, I wasn't completely honest with you when we did that first Story of my Life session.'

'No?' I braced myself. What was he going to admit?

'You asked me what the most significant moment of my life was, and I said passing my Cycling Proficiency Test.' He glanced downwards. 'That wasn't strictly accurate.'

'I can't say I'm not relieved to hear that, Lewis.'

'I should have been honest: it was Mum dying. It changed everything. For me, for Dad, for everyone. I used to wonder what my life would have been like if she hadn't died, whether I'd have been happier, or different, whether I'd have found relationships easier . . .' He shrugged. 'Who knows.'

'Me too,' I said. 'What if my mum had married someone she loved, what if she'd been allergic to vodka instead of addicted to it? What if she'd left Dad sooner? But then I wouldn't be the person I am now. Being me is my job, not someone else's.'

'True.'

'And you know, broadly speaking, I'm happy with the person I am now.' I'd said it to make Lewis feel better, but as the words left my mouth, I realised I meant it. I was happy with this Beth. Wobbly stomach, wobbly self-esteem, wobbly plans – but the sun was starting to rise again.

'Me too. I mean, I'm happy with me.' He looked flustered. 'And you. No, stop, you're putting me off. I had this rehearsed.'

'Sorry.'

Lewis reset, with a frown. 'I didn't want the first thing you knew about me to be something so sad. You'd have felt sorry for me, and that wasn't what I wanted.'

I sensed this was Lewis's attempt to sheepdog the conversation somewhere specific, and tried to help. 'What *did* you want?'

Lewis met my gaze, honest and open. 'I wanted you to like me. As much as I liked you.'

I smiled, he smiled back, and I had to look down now, to break the huge grin that threatened to swallow my face. I didn't want Lewis to think I was laughing at him. I just couldn't help smiling. My whole body wanted to smile.

'I wasn't quite truthful either,' I said, to my feet. If Lewis could make himself vulnerable like this, I could open my heart to meet his. 'When I said my accountancy exams were more significant than my mug cake recipe.'

'No?'

'No, I was being a snob. Anyone can cram for exams.' I tilted my face back up to squint at him against the summer sun. 'My mug cakes are perfect. And when I make them, I feel as if my mum's with me. The best version of my mum, the mum who looked after me as best she could. And when I give them to people who need a hug . . .'

'. . . you're looking after them too.' He nodded slowly. 'I know.'

'Plus, I wanted you to be impressed with my job, and not just think I was some fat woman obsessed with cakes.'

Lewis frowned. 'Why would I think that?'

'Because—' I started, but Lewis interrupted.

'Because you are the most beautiful woman I have ever met,' he said, slowly and clearly. 'That is just a fact.'

We sat for a moment, in that warm glow of anticipation, just savouring each tiny baby step towards what the spiralling butterflies in my stomach told me was coming.

My hand inched along the bench, and found Lewis's hand inching towards mine. Silently, our fingers touched and interlinked. My breath quickened in my throat. I'd never felt quite so excited by someone touching my hand. The 1950s teens up there in Rosemount knew what I was feeling now, my whole body alive and tingling. All of it. Even the bits I didn't like.

'I think what I'm trying to get round to saying,' said Lewis, turning towards me on the bench, 'is that if you were going to ask me a similar question again, at a future date, *Tell me about a significant moment in your life*, I would have to say: When a hospital transport rota was accidentally messed up.'

'And why's that?' I knew the answer, I just wanted him to say it.

'Because that's when you walked into my office and I understood every cheesy pop song that's ever been written.'

Lewis's eyes locked with mine and I felt myself melting into the intensity of his gaze. A faint smile played at the edges of his mouth, as if he couldn't quite believe this was happening, then slowly, very slowly, he leaned forward, and I leaned forward, until our mouths were only a breath apart, and then, finally and gently – and then surprisingly passionately – he kissed me.

I was so lost in the moment I didn't even really notice his moustache, which was much softer than I expected.

This was where our story started, I thought, as Lewis's arm pulled me closer, and my fingers sank into the thick hair at the nape of his neck. It didn't matter what the previous chapters had been, beyond bringing us to this point, or how many there'd been. From now on this was us. And I had never felt happier about not knowing how it would turn out.

We sat there for a long while, kissing. I could hear the birds singing, and I could feel Lewis's heart beating, and I could feel my own soul lifting as his fingers slowly traced the line of my jaw. I could have stayed there forever.

'There's one more thing I want to do, while it's still light.' He got up and reached for my hand to pull me to my feet.

'What? Lewis, what?'

He kept hold of my hand as he led me to the garden sheds where, I realised, he'd parked his tandem.

'Ah, no . . .' This wasn't the time. I was wearing my good interview trousers and he was in a *suit*.

But Lewis was unlocking the door with a smile on his face, humming happily, and unexpectedly I felt that gaudy lava lamp bubbling away inside me again. My heart started to beat faster and my pulse quickened, and I needed to let out this surge of joyful energy and *fly*.

'Lewis,' I said, as he wheeled the tandem out, 'I'd like to go in front. I want to be the driver.'

'Go for it.' I saw complete confidence and trust in his face. I don't know if I'd ever seen it directed at me before, not like that. I felt as if Lewis was seeing a whole new Beth. 'I'm right behind you. Literally.'

I looked at the tarmac drive in front of us; there was soft grass on each side. If the worst came to the worst, we could crash-land somewhere soft. But we weren't going to crash, I told myself. I was going to steer this thing. I gripped the handlebars, as Lewis steadied it for me, then felt him swing his leg over.

'One, two, three, *go*,' I shouted, and we were off.

Momentum carried us down the slope of the drive, then we were flying, legs pumping in unison, perfectly balanced. I felt my heart beating faster and faster but my body had never seemed more my own, more connected to my heart and my brain and my soul.

I heard a noise behind me: it was Lewis laughing.

And then he pointed, up towards the windows of Rosemount which seemed full of fluttering doves.

The windows were full of people waving white handkerchiefs, paper napkins, face flannels. Old people who were still young people inside, who remembered falling in love, or who were in love. People who had broken hearts, or had theirs broken, but had got up and tried again. People whose life stories were delivering surprises, right up until the final page.

I raised my hand to wave back, and then I blew them all a kiss.

Epilogue

Eric agreed to sell Rosemount to the Cellars Trust two days before the end of the week deadline, and as soon as the contract came through, Martine offered me a new job: financial director for the charity, with specific responsibility for Rosemount.

It was the quickest yes I've ever said.

Lewis, obviously, agreed to stay as the manager, and the rest of the staff barely noticed the change. Pam became the deputy manager but with more fundraising responsibilities, something she seized upon with real enthusiasm. Eunice agreed to represent the residents on a special panel set up to prevent any of what Lewis discreetly called the 'communication issues' that had plagued Rosemount before. And Nigel engaged his formidable brain on writing a formal history of the building; much to our consternation, he actually uncovered two genuine Rosemount ghosts, neither of which anyone has yet seen.

I *loved* my new job. I loved the variety that every day offered, the relationships I built with the residents and their families, the big sweep of forward planning and the nitty-gritty of the daily accounts. I loved working as part of a team that genuinely liked one another, and I loved seeing that I was making a difference to Minnie, and Stan, and Linda, but also to the people from the town who came to learn how to garden with our new groundskeepers, and the children who brought their school history projects into the library for personal insights.

(Although I will admit to being freaked out the first time they brought a Millennium 'history' project in for *me* to advise on.)

I loved Martine's projects, and she was bursting with new ideas. She'd meant it when she'd said she didn't want to be a figurehead: every week she met with me, Pam and Lewis, and always had a notebook of suggestions. Projects, improvements, enrichments, decoration.

Her latest idea was very close to my heart.

'When I was at university,' she told the team, 'the actors in our house would bring home a play to learn and everyone would have to take parts. Just for fun, with a glass of wine, on beanbags. It was a hoot. Can we do that here?'

I said we could. Without the beanbags. There was no way I'd get the occupational therapist to clear beanbags *and* wine.

'Do you have a play in mind?' I asked.

'Yes,' said Martine, with a twinkle. 'I do.'

And that is how we came to be performing a readthrough of *Isabella on the Moors*, my novel-screenplay-drama, in the library with a tea urn and a selection platter of Pam's cakes on the table in front of us.

Kay and Martine were seated together, as always, on one sofa, with Eunice and Nigel opposite. Linda Horrobin, in her wheelchair, was sitting with Bill (not joining in, but happy to be there), with Stan Walkingshaw and Minnie Little and several new residents attending with printed-out scripts for everyone to read along. Stan had a pair of coconut shells, and was enthusiastically playing the part of several horses. Tomsk was playing the part of Douglas's faithful wolfhound, Baskerville, and was snoring gently through his role.

I'd had to write in more parts – a lot more parts – to give everyone a chance to be part of the story, but the main roles were still Isabella, Arthur and Douglas, the broad-shouldered farmer who let the old dogs sleep in his kitchen. The need for more characters meant I'd written in a lot more of Isabella's mishaps and intrigues as a portraitist to the local community, and that had meant dispensing with quite a lot of the letters from the boring and self-obsessed Arthur – which was all to the good, I think.

Martine had been the second person to read my script after Gayle and said she *adored* it. She adored a lot more things lately; the only time hard-to-please Martine reappeared was when she came into the office with a new idea for something borderline impossible, which Lewis generally made happen. We'd even discussed the possibility of a collaboration on the sequel.

I looked over at Lewis, who had taken half an hour out of his day to read Douglas's part. Jackie had donated a box of unused props from her school's drama department, and he was wearing a hat and tweed jacket which kind of suited him, although I wasn't going to tell him, in case he started wearing it all the time. Nigel was Arthur, whose lines he was droning with some relish, decked out in a cape and a slightly self-important attitude that made me wonder if he'd perhaps met Fraser.

I was Isabella, of course. A woman in charge of her own destiny now, not waiting for anyone else to tell her what to do, who to be, what to look like. The heroine of her own story; the author, not a bit player.

'Are you ready for me now?' Lewis tipped his hat and winked.

I winked back.

Maybe I'd tell him about the hat. It actually looked quite hot, in combination with the moustache. A sort of brooding period-drama hotness.

'Quiet at the back. Ready!' Martine had appointed herself director. No one had dared argue. 'And action!'

Lewis reached for my hands, and I took his, gazing into his eyes with a smile that I couldn't help.

'My life has had many interesting chapters,' he said solemnly, 'but my dear Isabella, this new development is without question, the most unexpected of them all. I had not anticipated such bliss could exist here in Calderbridge.'

He bent forward as if to kiss me, but was interrupted by a sudden flurry of clip-clops, and a wild '*Neeeeiiiiiigggghhhh*' from Stan.

'Oh, sorry, turned two pages at once. Sorry, sorry! Carry on!'

And if I wrote myself the best lines, I thought, so what, as the room dissolved into hysterics and, in Tomsk's case, confused barking. That was the whole point from now on.

My life, my story.

My own happy ending.

Acknowledgements

I'm so lucky to be surrounded by people who love stories: telling them, tinkering with them, sharing them with others and celebrating their weird powers to do more than just entertain (although, obviously, that's a pretty vital element).

I'm so grateful to my inspirational editor, Jo Dickinson; and my extraordinary agent, Lizzy Kremer, and her extraordinary assistant, Orli Vogt-Vincent, for the invaluable creative insights which made such a difference to the final version of Beth's story. And also for their patience. Thanks too, to Kate Norman, Alainna Hadjigeorgiou, Olivia French and everyone at Hodder for their enthusiasm and support; and to Rachael Sharples and the translation rights team at David Higham for taking Longhampton to places I can only dream of visiting.

Thank you, Chris and Alex, for the wise advice and the supportive PJ4FC meets; to my step-daughter Katie, for the thoughtful, endless listening; to Monty and Aurora, ditto, albeit with fewer helpful editorial suggestions. Thank you, Janine Giovanni, for giving me some fantastic ideas (and notes to stick on my laptop).

The biggest thanks are to you, the reader, for being part of the magical daisy chain that is storytelling – it's a privilege to share time in your imagination! I hope if you take one thing away from this book, it's to ask a friend or an older relative for their memories: not just the familiar ones they love sharing (although there's always a place for those), but the tucked-away details they don't even see as particularly interesting – their favourite outfit as a teenager, the funny things their grandparents said. Open up the photograph album, go for a drive around an old haunt, see what surprises emerge . . .

Stories, after all, are what connects us as human beings, to our family, our friends, our communities, the wider world – and to ourselves. I hope we never stop telling them.